TUG

OF

LAW

Bernadette Mackenna Cases

Book Four

D.R. BAILEY

Tug Of Law Copyright © 2021 by D.R. Bailey

This book is a work of fiction. Names, characters, places, and incidents either are products of the author's imagination or are used fictitiously. Any resemblance to actual persons, living or dead, events, or locales is entirely coincidental.

Please note the spelling throughout is British English.

Cover Design by Sarah Bailey
Photographer: LVAB
Cover Model: Lily V Brazier

Published by Twisted Tree Publications
www.twistedtreepublications.com
info@twistedtreepublications.com

Paperback ISBN: 978-1-913217-32-7

I want to dedicate this book to our good friend Giulia. She has always been true to herself and her sexuality. She's a lovely person who was kind and generous to us, she gave us the gift of staying in her apartment in Florence for our honeymoon. We will always be grateful for that. Giulia speaks several languages, is an explorer, has lived in many countries and she loves dogs. She is loyal to her friends and family. We have enjoyed some nice meals together in Brighton many moons ago. Her dog Tequila is the love of her life. But I hope she will one day also receive the happiness of finding a beautiful and loving partner to spend her days with. That is my wish for her. Thank you, Giulia, for being the person you are and being yourself without compromise.

CHAPTER ONE

*J*ustice Fin Campbell regarded Bernadette with interest. He was around forty-years-old and wore thick, black-rimmed glasses which made him look somewhat forbidding. Coupled with a clean-shaven square jaw and unsmiling temperament, he wasn't a judge to be trifled with. His piercing blue eyes took in Bernadette's brown ones with a cool stare. She waited patiently for him to speak.

"So, Ms Mackenna, if I hear you rightly, you are asking me for some leniency with your client in spite of the fact he has pled guilty to a crime, which I understand is not his first offence. It's also not the first time I've had your client in front of me either."

"Yes, Judge, I am," she replied content to simply confirm rather than explain.

"I see. I assume you are going to give me some or even, several, good reasons why I should do this?"

"Yes, Judge, I certainly intend to." She smiled at him in a disarming way, which wasn't reciprocated.

"Fine, you can do so after a short recess as I'm in dire need of a cup of tea, not to put a too finer point on it. And

I'm sure your client can wait at the court's pleasure for a half an hour."

"Yes, Judge, I'm sure he can."

"Very well."

The Tipster entered quickly and called the court to rise. Without further ado, Justice Campbell swept from the room.

Bernadette looked down at her junior counsel, Imogen, who had come along today for the ride. Imogen's full lips smiled back at her with a hint of laughter playing behind her green eyes. Her red hair framed her face as a counterpoint to the freckles which were now appearing since it was now early summer. In Bernadette's view, they only served to make her prettier.

"Coffee?" said Imogen brightly.

"Why not."

The two of them left the courtroom with alacrity but as they exited the doors, Bernadette's hand was possessed by a shapely blonde with sky blue eyes.

"Eve!" said Bernadette, "You nearly made me jump out of my skin."

Eve laughed and said to Imogen, "Can I borrow my fiancée? I've just got to talk to her about something."

"Sure," Imogen replied, "I'll get the coffees in and meet you in the meeting room over there."

"Great." Eve then pulled Bernadette urgently by the hand. "Come on, no time to waste."

"What? Where are we going? And what is it that's so urgent?"

Without another word, Eve dragged her into a nearby disabled toilet and locked the door.

"What are you—" Bernadette began, but she got no further as Eve had pushed her up against the wall and planted her lips on Bernadette's.

"Mmm," muttered Bernadette as her senses exploded. Eve always had this effect upon her, she was immediately inflamed as if a small furnace had just been ignited inside her.

"God, I want you, I want you so much, I couldn't wait, honey, I couldn't," Eve whispered her lips just touching pulling out of the kiss.

"I know but..." Bernadette managed to say, however, Eve's hand was already pulling up her skirt and snaking its way into the waistband of her knickers. "Oh God, Jesus," Bernadette gasped as Eve's fingers found their mark.

"I wish I was at home," Eve said softly, "Fucking you..."

"What are you doing now then? Oh... oh... Shit... don't stop... Eve... oh, my darling... oh God... I love you... so... much... so... mu..." Bernadette was fighting for coherence as the wave began to crest. She was lost in the sensations and the suddenness of it made her all more aroused.

"Is this what you like?" said Eve, increasing the intensity with her fingers.

"Oh... yes... darling... I just want... I... ohh... ohh... ohh..." What Bernadette wanted was lost in the climax which engulfed her. She bit down on her hand so as not to cry out too loud, although truth be told she wanted to scream the house down.

Her body tensed and untensed, and her toes curled in the strappy black sandals she was wearing. She gasped a few times, as her orgasm eased just a little and she waited for the light-headedness to dissipate. Eve held her gently now planting light and gentle kisses on her lips.

"Oh, Eve, oh God," said Bernadette once she was able to breathe a little normally, "Oh, you little witch."

"I know, but you love it, don't you?" Eve cocked an eyebrow at her.

"I should..." Bernadette began moving her hand to the button on Eve's jeans.

"There isn't time, you can do it later, my darling." Eve smiled.

"I will, oh I will." Bernadette was defenceless against her fiancée's desire. Eve aroused her so much, completed her in so many ways.

"I know you will, darling, but let's get that coffee now." Eve planted one more kiss on her lips and let Bernadette straighten up, and smooth down her skirt.

"Now I know why you insisted on a skirt today," said Bernadette in admonishing tones.

"Oh, but you look so sexy in your outfit."

It was true, Bernadette was wearing an above the knee pleated skirt which she had complained made her look like a schoolgirl. Eve demurred and said she was eye candy. Bernadette had laughed and twirled around. The black skirt was coupled with a lilac blouse and a blue blazer style jacket. Eve had insisted such skirts were all the rage and not to complain. So, Bernadette did not. Eve had become her dresser and laid out her clothes every workday before doing Bernadette's hair. Bernadette luxuriated in the pampering she felt from her partner.

"Well, it obviously got you going!"

"Oh, yes, all morning." Eve looked at her watch. "Only ten minutes, see, I'm getting so good at this. Let's go and join Imogen."

Bernadette chuckled in a satisfied way and checked her hair, then the two of them left the toilet. As they were walking to the meeting room Bernadette said, "Did you come up just to do that?"

"Not just to do that, no, although it was worth it even if I had. I am going to the gallery to see Valentino, discuss some more of my controversial work," Eve laughed.

"You didn't tell me!"

"Because I wanted to surprise you, silly."

"You certainly did so!"

They reached the meeting room and Imogen was already sitting at the table sipping her coffee.

"You're looking a bit flushed," she said to Bernadette furnishing her with a knowing smile.

"Oh yes, well, as to that…" Bernadette began.

"It's my magic fingers," Eve chuckled.

"Oh, Eve!" Bernadette said pretending to be shocked. In reality, there were no secrets with Imogen. The three of them were like sisters, and Imogen was well aware of the ins and outs of their love life, as they were of hers.

"Bernadette always says you are a witch," Imogen observed drily.

"She is!" said Bernadette taking a seat and picking up her coffee, "Though a very beautiful one."

"For sure, I mean I'd do her… if she wasn't marrying you."

They all laughed at this and then the three of them sat for a moment enjoying their drinks.

"Are you coming to watch the rest of the hearing?" Imogen asked Eve.

"No, I'm seeing my gallery owner, he wants me to do some more pictures," said Eve.

Eve was an accomplished artist, and now very successful. Her opening show had made very good traction to launch her new career. In fact, all of her paintings and drawings had been sold and she had made a significant sum of money which she and Bernadette were now sinking into the conversion of their outbuilding into a small gym and creating a conservatory at the back of their house.

"Are those the flagellation pictures?"

"Of course, you *would* be interested," said Bernadette dryly.

She and Eve were both were fully aware of Imogen's sexual proclivities, which now included disciplining her girlfriend D'Arcy Brown as part of their relationship with various implements including a paddle and a riding crop.

"Yes, I am."

"Oh. It's kind of a metaphorical way of releasing my demons about my sister," said Eve.

"Is it though? Purely metaphorical?" Imogen shot back.

"Of course," said Eve lowering her eyes.

Bernadette did not miss this and filed it away for future reference. Eve's sister had caused her much grief regarding Eve's sexual orientation. Her sister was heavily religious and felt Eve was a mortal sinner and had not hesitated to tell her so. Her sister lived in New Zealand and they had parted ways recently when she had upset Eve yet again. With Bernadette's encouragement, Eve had written a letter severing all ties. However, Bernadette suspected the scars ran deeper than she knew, and that Eve had not told her everything. Fear, however, held Bernadette back from asking. The fear of losing Eve. No matter how much they loved each other, there was still a nagging doubt in Bernadette's mind Eve might go. Eve had done nothing to indicate this would happen, it was irrational, and she knew it, but she was prey to the dreadful fear all the same. The fear came from the past, Bernadette knew it but every time she felt perhaps she had dealt with it, it rose up again.

"So, you're not staying to see Bernadette triumph in court?" Imogen changed the subject, not missing Eve's hidden thoughts either.

"No, Valentino wants more of the risqué paintings and drawings, and he loved that one I did of you in the corset and heels, with the whip. He says he can sell some more."

"Really? I'm flattered."

"I should pay you some of what I get."

"No. Just do the one you promised for me and D'Arcy without my face being hidden."

"Yes, I will, I'll get onto it, sorry things got a bit hectic as you know."

"Sure, whenever you are ready, it's OK."

"We'll have to get back," Bernadette said draining her cup, "I'm sorry, darling."

"I'm sorry too, but I'm looking forward to seeing you later," Eve told her.

Although Bernadette came home every night and Eve was always there, Eve missed her and was happiest when Bernadette was at home. Bernadette missed her too, but her work was a calling which she also could not deny. Eve would never deny it to her either.

They all stood up to go, and Eve enveloped Bernadette in a lingering kiss.

"I love you, darling."

"I love you too," said Bernadette.

With the flash of her radiant smile, Eve was gone.

"So, what were you doing in the disabled toilet?" Imogen said slyly as they walked back.

"How did you..."

"Oh, I don't miss a thing, darling," Imogen giggled.

"Eve ambushed me if you must know and then before I could do anything, her fingers were down the front of my knickers."

"Sounds delicious."

"It was, oh yes, it was, it was all I could do to stop myself from shrieking at the top of my voice."

"That would have been one for the gossips," Imogen laughed.

They entered the courtroom and became serious at once, walking up to their lawyer station to get ready for the fray.

Over on the prosecution bench, one of her old adversaries Riona Robinson nodded in her direction. She was dressed as usual in very high stilettoes and a black skirt suit. Her pristine white shirt and ponytail made her look quite severe. Imogen had remarked on it before and they both wondered if Riona was gay or perhaps had a little bit of the dominatrix in her. However, neither of them was disposed to find out, so it was perhaps destined to remain a mystery.

The Tipster announced the judge, who arrived looking slightly less fierce than when he'd left. Bernadette hoped he had, perhaps, mellowed out with his cup of tea. He sat down and when the court was settled to his satisfaction, he addressed himself to Bernadette.

"Now then, Ms Mackenna, let's see what you can do to persuade me not to exact the maximum penalty the law allows on your client."

Bernadette sighed inwardly, obviously, the tea had had not made Justice Campbell any more congenial.

"Judge," she began, "My client, Mr Arthur Dooley, is an old man."

"I can see *that*, Ms Mackenna and believe me it's not going to sway my judgement one iota," he shot back irascibly.

"Yes, Judge," said Bernadette, rapidly revising her speech in her head.

"Good, so let's make some progress, shall we?"

"Judge, I know Mr Dooley has been before this court a number of times."

"More times than I've had hot dinners, Ms Mackenna," said the judge interrupting again. There were amused chuckles from the public benches.

Bernadette furnished him with a hard stare. It was one thing to make amusing remarks, but she didn't take kindly to the judge's attitude. He caught her look and subsided a little. "Very well, Ms Mackenna, continue, continue." He waved her on and gave an exaggerated sigh and it seemed as if his mind was certainly already made up.

Arthur Dooley shifted uncomfortably in the dock. Bernadette glanced over at him. He was nothing more than an old man with the gift of the gab. He wore a suit which had seen better days, and which he claimed was his wedding attire for the time he married his much-lamented deceased wife. Arthur plied his trade by picking up what he assumed to be junk, repairing it in a half-assed fashion and selling it on. He left a string of dissatisfied customers including one who had, this time, reported him to the Garda. He had apparently taken some boxes from outside a local white goods store which contained brand new cookers. Unable to believe his luck, he had sold them long before the retailer discovered his loss. However, when arrested, Mr Dooley claimed he had thought they were being thrown away, as usually anything on the pavement was fair game. However, the law took a different view and he was now up before the judge on a charge of theft.

The case was being tried in a summary hearing before the judge in the District court. As a rule, Bernadette did not take such cases, but she knew Arthur Dooley of old when she was a junior counsel and she took it *pro bono* for old times' sake.

"Judge, Mr Dooley, in his defence, and as he has stated under oath, took the goods in question in good faith..."

The judge appeared as if he was going to say something and then seeing Bernadette's expression subsided. Bernadette could be quite intimidating at times regardless of whether one was a judge or not.

"He testified it's his mode of *Operandi* to take away things people have discarded and recycle them. In that respect, I submit he is offering a helpful service. However, in this case, he admits his wrongdoing and has pled guilty. He was overcome by the discovery these were new cookers,

Judge. Imagine a man in his position, it would be the equivalent of the holy grail. The temptation was far too great."

She stole another glance at her client who had composed his features into something suitably remorseful. Arthur Dooley was a man of around sixty or so years, with a shock of grey hair and prone to wear a flat cap. He possessed a silver tongue which had enabled him to sweet talk many a person into buying something they did not want. Apparently, in his youth, he had also talked his way into the beds of many a young lady too.

"My client did not resist arrest, and he didn't attempt to deny it per his statement which this court has heard. Whilst I agree he has committed several offences in the past, surely the circumstances and his remorseful attitude must go some way towards mitigating your intended sentence. Mr Dooley also has an ageing feline to which he is extremely attached, and who would no doubt suffer were he to be placed in detention for this offence. I am sure, Judge, you can't wish an animal to be put in such distress."

She was clutching at straws and she knew it. He was apparently very fond of his cat, but Arthur had already told her it could be taken care of very well if he had to go 'inside' as he put it.

"Judge, in closing I ask you, for leniency in Mr Dooley's case, if it may please the court."

She ended off her speech bestowing the judge with what she hoped was a winning smile. She knew she did not have a winning argument. In fact, she had informed Arthur of this from the outset, but he had begged her to try. She had a soft spot for the old man and wanted to help him if she could.

"Have you finished, Ms Mackenna?" said the judge politely but not in a manner which boded well for her client or his cat.

"Yes, Judge," she replied taking a seat.

"Alright, let me take a moment to consider your arguments," he said putting his fingers together and bringing them up to his nose, as if he was lost in thought.

Bernadette grimaced at Imogen who shrugged sympathetically. At least he did her the courtesy of thinking about it which was more than she expected.

The deliberations lasted around five long minutes before Justice Campbell reached a decision.

"Mr Dooley, if you could please stand up."

Arthur Dooley got to his feet exhibiting some stiffness in his joints judging by the way he pulled himself up using the rail in front of him. He stood impassively awaiting his fate.

"Mr Dooley. Your counsel has attempted, at least, to put forward some persuasive argument as to why I should not issue a custodial sentence in your case. A case which, in spite of your protestations to the contrary, does not persuade me that you were unaware you were committing an offence from the outset."

Arthur hung his head. It did not sound as if it was going to go well at all. Bernadette slipped her hand into Imogen's for comfort. She found herself feeling for the old man no matter what he had done. Imogen squeezed it and Bernadette shot her a grateful smile.

"I take into account the fact you did plead guilty, although I can't imagine how you could have done otherwise," Justice Campbell continued acerbically, "Even if it had been as you say, a grievous mistake, and I use the word grievous advisedly, you still continued to capitalise on your good fortune by selling what were stolen goods. You could have returned them to the owners having discovered your error, but you did not."

He paused for effect and frowned direfully at Arthur Dooley who appeared to quail just a little under his scrutiny.

"No, you did not, and instead sold the goods and pocketed the money. Your counsel asserts the temptation was too great. Was it indeed? So great you just felt compelled to commit a crime, and if you cannot withstand such compulsions then I'm persuaded you should perhaps not be allowed at large in the community any longer."

Arthur Dooley's face fell on hearing this. Bernadette squeezed Imogen's hand tighter, hoping there might be some redemption in spite of all appearances to the contrary.

"In addition, you appear to have a string of convictions which are as long as my arm, much as I hesitate to use the vernacular," said the judge with a great deal of acidity, "Of which this is, unfortunately, just one more."

Justice Campbell paused to allow the full weight of this to sink in.

"Therefore, I sentence you to two years in prison."

There were gasps in the courtroom as this was pronounced, and Arthur went white as a sheet. Even he had not expected such a harsh outcome. The judge though, it seemed, had not finished.

"But... I am not unsympathetic, to your age nor to the fact you have a cat at home who is dependent upon you," he said in kindlier tones, "It so happens I have a cat myself and

I understand the attachment these can bring. With this in mind, I recommend the sentence be converted to one year and carried out under home detention with the very, very strict caveat that if you break the conditions even once then you shall spend the rest of it in jail, and you will have to make arrangements for your cat. Now, do you understand, Mr Dooley?"

Arthur looked as if Jesus himself had appeared from heaven to save him. "Yes, sir, Judge, yes I do."

"You understand home detention means just that, no going to the pub, the shops or anywhere else. You must remain at home with your cat."

"Yes, I do, Judge, I do indeed, I do."

"Good, see you abide by it, and be certain if I ever see you up in front of me again, I will send you to prison for a very long time!" The tone was mild, but the judge still looked severe as if to reinforce his strictures on Arthur.

"Yes, Judge, thank you, Judge," said Arthur much relieved.

"What's the name of your cat?"

"My cat?" Arthur looked surprised.

"Yes, it has a name I presume?"

"Yes, Judge, indeed, she... her name is Molly, Judge."

"Ah, Molly, sweet Molly Malone, a very nice name for a cat, ah yes. Well, see you look after it properly and I'm sure Molly will be more than happy to have you home."

"Yes, Judge, she will, that she will."

"Very well, then unless anyone has anything further to say?" The judge looked around the room daring anybody to attempt it.

Nobody dared speak, particularly in case, Justice Campbell took it all back.

"Excellent. Well, I'll be off then, this court is adjourned."

The Tipster hurried in, everybody stood up and the judge left the room. As soon as he had gone there was pandemonium on the public benches. This was going to be a great story for the daily papers. "Cat saves man from prison," would be the tenor the headlines the following day.

Imogen beamed at Bernadette. Neither of them could believe their luck or Arthur's.

Bernadette hurried over to the dock to speak to him before they took him away.

"I'm sorry, Arthur, we did our best," she began contritely.

"Ach, don't you fret about it, Bernadette, now, it's probably the best outcome." He smiled.

"I hope so, for your sake, at least you're not going to prison."

"I thought I was a goner, and no mistake. The cat was a stroke of genius."

"Arthur," she said suspiciously, "You do have a cat, don't you?"

"A cat? Oh yes, yes." He reached into his pocket and pulled out a dogeared photograph of brindled tortoiseshell moggie.

"Very handsome," said Bernadette handing back the photo after she had looked at it.

"She's my pride and joy, now, now my wife..." His eyes misted over just for a moment.

"Time to go, Arthur," said the court official beside him.

"Ah well, thanks again, thanks again," said Arthur smiling and shaking her hand.

"Bye, Arthur," said Bernadette, she watched him go.

She returned to her bench where Imogen was waiting. Imogen had packed up their papers into a briefcase and was ready to go. However, before they could leave, Riona came over to them.

"Good result," she said amiably.

"For sure, I'm glad for him, he didn't deserve to go to prison."

"No indeed, we live in modern times now, not the old days. I'm happy at the sentence he received."

"Really? Though you were pushing for a custodial sentence," Imogen pointed out.

"What the prosecution service wants and what I want are not always the same," said Riona confidingly.

"That's a refreshing attitude." Bernadette smiled.

"Yes, indeed, I mean obviously some offenders do deserve their sentences or perhaps more," Riona mused.

"More?" Imogen picked up on this.

"Yes, like in the old days," said Riona with a smile.

"And what would happen in the old days?" Imogen enquired with interest.

"Oh well, they'd get a damn good whipping..." With that, Riona winked at Imogen, returned smartly to her desk, picked up her briefcase and left.

"Did she just say what I thought she said?" Imogen asked Bernadette.

"Not only did she say it, but I would say *that* was an invitation, if ever I heard one," Bernadette chuckled.

"Stop it! Anyway, how did she..."

They looked at each other and both said it at once, "Shane!"

Shane Wilson was a prosecution barrister who was a colleague of Riona Robinson. Imogen had had a brief fling with him which resulted in an initiation by Shane into the world of Fifty Shades. Imogen developed a taste for it afterwards but now preferred to dish it out rather than take it.

"Fucking Shane," Imogen muttered darkly.

"Do you think that he? They?" Bernadette wondered meaningfully.

"I don't want to know," said Imogen firmly picking up their briefcase. The two of them left the courtroom and wended their way to the car.

"Mind you," said Imogen, "Riona's pretty hot, and if I wasn't so besotted with D'Arcy..."

"Now *you* stop it!" Bernadette chided.

The two of them burst out laughing.

✳ ✳ ✳

They returned in Bernadette's red Audi R3 Quattro. Not that Bernadette was a car buff, nor was she 'car proud' but for some reason, she liked this particular car and its colour. It also intimidated the hell out of the male lawyer fraternity which she found excessively amusing, as did Imogen. She parked in Mount Street finding a lucky parking space and the two of them entered the stone fronted building through the familiar black door set in an arched portico.

A long narrow corridor stretched out in front of them with its familiar soft green walls and cream ceiling with its ornate mouldings. The floor was tiled in polished light stone. An L shaped counter stood not far from the entrance behind which Juanita Fernandez, PA and receptionist, was sitting reading *Hello* magazine, as was her wont. Juanita was a raven-haired Spanish beauty to whom the term buxom was a perfect fit. She did far less work than she should and regarded the office as part of her leisure time. Since she was well protected by her boss Andrew, everyone tolerated her ways with varying degrees of irritation or amusement.

"Imogen, your girlfriend is in the magazine again," she said holding up a page for Imogen to see.

There indeed was D'Arcy Brown who had lately completed shooting of a movie in the US and was currently at home much to Imogen's pleasure. The picture was of D'Arcy, however, walking out in town with her co-star's arm around her waist. The catchline said, "D'Arcy's new beau?"

On seeing this, Imogen pursed her lips. Juanita regarded her from under her lashes, which had excessively long extensions.

"She was very friendly with him, no?"

"Yes, he's just a friend. It's just her way," Imogen snapped back crossly.

"Juanita don't forget to move my car," said Bernadette dropping the keys on the counter and observing Imogen with some dismay.

"Of course, I move, I always move, all the time, I don't forget," said Juanita dismissively. She turned back to her magazine satisfied with her mendacious behaviour.

Juanita was, perhaps, jealous of Imogen's good fortune in some small way. She was also a big fan of D'Arcy Brown and friendly with D'Arcy's housekeeper, Constantina, who was also Spanish. On the other hand, Bernadette did not think Juanita was deliberately malicious either but perhaps just liked to stir the pot.

Bernadette reflected there was nothing to the photograph really but media stirring, however, her friend was excessively jealous and still a little insecure even though D'Arcy loved her to pieces. Unfortunately, being with a celebrity meant one would be subjected to much of the conjecture and the lies in the press. Imogen knew this and had been on the receiving end but was still perhaps not used to it.

At that moment, Andrew Bond, who was in charge of the finances of the firm chose to come out of his office. He was a good-looking man with short grey cropped hair and a kindly face. He was wearing a suit with a blue shirt and red tie. Bernadette thought he was looking quite dapper.

"Ah, Bernadette, I was hoping to see you," he said in affable tones.

"Is that right?" she replied, at once suspicious. Usually, this approach preceded a complaint about her not charging fees or her expense account or some such.

"I'm going upstairs," said Imogen.

One glance at her told Bernadette that Imogen's eyes were glistening and brimming with tears. She felt for her but at the same time, her finance manager probably needed placating.

"I'll bring you a coffee, darling," she told her, "Just as soon as I've seen Andrew."

"Sure," Imogen replied in a choked voice and swiftly walked away.

"Is she alright?" Andrew enquired solicitously.

"She was," Bernadette said stealing a dark look at Juanita's back, "I'm sure she will be OK in a while, I'll go and check on her when we are done. In the meantime, how can I help?"

"Just step into my office," Andrew said holding the door open.

Bernadette did so taking in the familiar green walls and filing cabinets with files piled on top of them, and the desk also piled high with papers. She didn't approve of this untidiness, but it was how Andrew worked, so she forbore to comment. He was a lynchpin of the firm and additionally earned quite a bit of revenue on the side by doing accounts for various clients.

"How's your charming wife?" said Bernadette immediately disarming him as she took a seat opposite him at his meeting table.

"She's fine, fine, of course," he said with a smile, "But that's not what I want to discuss."

"And what do you want to discuss?" Bernadette replied looking at him a little coolly.

"Well, now... the thing is, I mean," he coughed and she at once divined he was going to find this difficult. This informed her that her first supposition was correct.

"Come on, Andrew, spit it out, there's a dear." She smiled.

"Oh, stop, that's exactly what Jessica says to me almost word for word."

Bernadette laid her head back and laughed. Jessica was a flame haired Irish lass who was almost a perfect foil to his British reserve. She was as volatile as the red haired suggested and subjected him to the sharp end of her tongue when she was annoyed. However, apparently, the making up part was just as passionate according to what Jessica had alluded to when she and Bernadette got into girl talk. This was not often since she mainly saw Jessica at work get-togethers and so on.

"Honestly, you females are all the same, and I'm surrounded by them in this office," he complained.

"I suppose it can be intimidating," she acknowledged with a chuckle.

"Yes well, never mind that, Bernadette, am I right in thinking you just did a *pro bono* case?" He had obviously worked up the courage to finally come out with it.

"Yes, you are, Andrew, for an old friend."

"We've talked about this. Your *pro bono* and Legal Aid cases are costing the firm money."

"I don't see how. This is the first one I've done for a while *pro bono* and it was a favour for old times' sake, and you still get the Legal Aid when I do those, so I don't see the problem."

In truth, there really wasn't an issue, and they both knew it, but Andrew liked to see what he felt were *bona fide* clients coming in who could afford to pay. Bernadette was about justice and not always the bottom line. The truth was, her attitude brought more paying clients in as a result, however, Andrew liked to argue the point. It was a particular bee in his bonnet.

"The problem is, surely it's taking your time away from cases where we could be earning, don't you see that? Time is money, Bernadette, to the firm at least, if not to you."

He looked so concerned about it that she almost felt sorry for him.

"Really, Andrew? I think I know how to manage my time after all these years, to make sure the firm doesn't suffer."

"Yes, but... you know... it's just..."

"You worry too much, Andrew, that's your problem."

"The finances of this firm rest on my shoulders," he said assuming a long-suffering air she knew well, "It's a big responsibility."

"And I love you for it, darling, you're absolutely the very best."

"Yes, well, flattery... you and Jessica are just the same," he said but was looking decidedly mollified, as she knew he would. She was usually an expert at handling him, as was his wife.

"Andrew, you know I would never do anything to jeopardise this firm, after all, I started it way back when and all these people depend on me, and you too."

"I know, Bernadette, I know... I just... you don't understand."

"I understand completely that you worry for all of us, and I'm eternally grateful, now if there's nothing else I must go and see to Imogen, she needs me." She had done her duty for the moment, she felt, to soothe his ruffled feathers.

"Sure, of course, but can you at least try not to do any more."

"I will do my very best, darling." She smiled and stood up, leaning down to plant a kiss lightly on his forehead.

He blushed a little at this show of affection. They had known each other a long time and it meant nothing more than friendship, but Andrew was not a demonstrative man.

He was British to the core of his being and as such very understated in manner. This was sometimes a great cause of frustration to his wife, but since he worshipped the ground she walked on, she forgave him his foibles.

"OK, if you could, I would be very grateful," he said watching her go with a sigh. He had never won an argument with her yet, but it did not prevent him from trying.

* * *

Armed with two cups of coffee, Bernadette entered Imogen's office. She had only lately been given her own office and it was spacious enough with an outlook onto the back gardens of theirs and other offices. They sometimes used the back garden in the summer for impromptu lunches and team gatherings. The office was decorated in the same soft dark green with a cream ceiling, and apart from the desk and filing cabinets, there was a sofa on one side and a coffee table. Imogen's eyes were red, and she had obviously been crying.

"Oh, my darling," said Bernadette at once putting the cups down. She hurried over, knelt down and embraced her friend, who immediately engaged in another bout of bitter tears.

"There, there," Bernadette said softly stroking her hair. She had been on the receiving end of Imogen's comfort many times, so it was apt for her to reciprocate.

After a few moments the sobs subsided, and Bernadette took Imogen's hands.

"Come on, come and have a coffee, you'll feel better."

Imogen followed her to the sofa and gratefully accepted the cup, she took a long drink and sighed.

"Oh, fuck!" she said, "I'm so silly."

"No, no you're not."

"I am, D'Arcy's bound to get a bit friendly with her co-stars and I have to accept it." It was evidently a bitter pill to swallow by her tone.

"OK," said Bernadette, somewhat pleased to hear a little bit of rationality on the topic.

"I just don't want to see it, fucking Juanita, why did she have to show it to me?"

"I'm sure she didn't mean to upset you..." Bernadette began.

"Didn't she? I wonder."

"Are you going to talk to D'Arcy about it?" Bernadette wondered trying to divert her attention from the hapless PA.

"Yes, oh yes, I will be talking to her about it alright."

"That's good, I'm glad to hear it. Talking is the right way to go about it."

"Then I'm going to give her such a spanking."

"Right." This was more the tone Bernadette had been expecting her to take. Imogen had assumed the dominant role in her relationship, and one which, to be fair D'Arcy seemed to wholeheartedly embrace by all accounts. Chastisement was part and parcel of it now, and it seemed to work for them. Bernadette was still not wholly on board with it but she and Eve also had their games, so she didn't feel able to be censorious.

"She deserves it, not because of what she did but because she didn't tell me," Imogen continued.

"But maybe she didn't tell you *because* of the consequences?"

"That's worse! We are supposed to be honest with each other. I know she's going to get friendly with her fellow actors..."

"Then what's the issue?"

"I don't know, really," Imogen sighed.

"Is it that you are insanely jealous?" Bernadette said mildly sipping her coffee.

"Oh! Why do you have to be so perceptive and right!"

"It's just a knack I have, and I know you only too well."

"Bugger! I am a fucking jealous bitch and I don't know how to curb it. I love her so much, Bernadette, so fucking much it hurts."

"I've given you the answer," Bernadette said gently, "Before..."

"What was it? I can't remember."

"You're a lost cause, my sweetheart, ask her to marry you for God's sake. Then you will at least feel more secure." Bernadette shook her head.

"Oh, oh yes."

"And?"

"I'm scared."

"Of?"

"That she will say no." Imogen shrugged.

"I'll put money on her saying yes, she is probably dying for you to say it, darling, trust me."

Imogen thought this over for a moment while she finished her coffee.

"OK, but you have to help me choose a ring, and you and Eve need to be there for support. If you're there, then she's less likely to refuse me."

"Oh, you are silly, but OK, if that's what it takes," Bernadette chuckled.

"Don't laugh at me, the struggle is real!"

"I know, believe me, I know."

"Anyway, when are you two getting married?"

"Oh, I don't know, soon I hope but it seems so daunting arranging the wedding and all that."

"Why does it have to be a big deal? You and Eve can have a small one you know. Anyway, the good thing is that you've got the license as it takes so long. All you have to do is decide about the wedding and do it."

Imogen had a point and Bernadette knew it. She wanted to get married very badly and finish the job she'd started. They both had rings, so her procrastination wasn't from lack of desire. She didn't know why, other than the exhausting thought of arranging a wedding and keeping all her friends happy in the process. Something she felt was incumbent on her, but she couldn't really explain why. In fact, she and Eve spent nearly all their time together, and her circle of friends was very small. It seemed so silly.

"Yes, I guess so, I've got to get my head around it. Eve *made* me get the license," Bernadette chuckled.

"What's that telling you then? Just remember, if you don't do it then the universe will find a way to force you to do it." This piece of pithy wisdom had been imparted by Imogen before and Bernadette had certainly found it to be true.

"It could equally apply to you."

"Yes, it could, and I should take my own advice."

"When did you ever?"

They both laughed at this.

"Are you feeling better now, my heart?" Bernadette asked her.

"Yes, I suppose."

"Then I'll go and do some work before Andrew complains."

"What? Was he complaining?"

"Oh, just the usual..." Bernadette favoured her with a pithy rendition of her exchange with Andrew just before.

"Ach, that's just Andrew being Andrew," said Imogen dismissively.

"I know, he's a sweet soul underneath it all," Bernadette said moderating the disparagements she had just made on their finance manager.

"Yes, he is, that's true."

"Anyway, I'll go and do some work, we can catch up later, maybe have lunch?"

"Sure, why not, on my expenses, that'll give Andrew something else to moan about," said Imogen with a wicked expression on her face.

"Yes, good idea, let's, we'll go to the usual?"

"We will."

Bernadette got up to go.

"I'm still going to give D'Arcy a spanking, you know that don't you," Imogen told her in resolute tones. Some part of her picked up on the mild disapproval Bernadette felt for her extracurricular activities.

"I didn't doubt it for a moment," Bernadette replied before slipping quietly out of the office smiling to herself. Imogen was incorrigible and that was all there was to it.

* * *

An hour or so passed during which Bernadette sat at her computer dealing with emails, and various ongoing queries to do with cases which were slow in coming to court. Her PA, Alison, who was also Imogen's now she was a junior partner, ably dealt with so much she had become indispensable. In truth, it was getting to a point where Imogen probably would need her own PA too. As she continued her progress towards senior counsel, she was taking on some of the less tricky cases herself. This was as it should be. She and Bernadette would, however, work together on important ones as Imogen still had more to learn. Bernadette was an astute teacher and as Imogen always said, she was learning from the best. Many junior barristers would love to be in Imogen's coveted position as Bernadette was highly respected in legal circles, and also feared by her opponents. She won more cases than she lost, and in the courtroom she was formidable.

The door opened, and Imogen entered. The two of them seldom knocked so close was their working relationship, and friendship to boot.

"Guess what?" said Imogen.

"What? You've bought a new spanking implement?" said Bernadette wryly.

"Not that no," Imogen chuckled, "Though to be fair I have been thinking about it. But anyway, no, we've got a new prospective client."

"Oh?"

"And I don't think about *that*... all the time... I'll have you know..." Imogen protested.

"But you do, darling... a lot of the time."

"OK, fine, guilty as charged, I can't help it. It's part of my make-up and well, I don't want to change it." Imogen shrugged.

"I'm not asking you to, and I love you for it, because you're so honest with yourself and that's a good thing."

"It is?"

"Yes," said Bernadette firmly, "Now, about this client."

"He's in the meeting room."

"Any clues?"

"Um, not yet, he runs a haulage company, but I was waiting for you, to find out more."

"Then we'd better meet him," said Bernadette getting up.

The meeting room was quite large and painted in the same shade of green as the rest of the office. Bernadette liked the colour because it was restful and calming. There was a meeting table and also two sofas with a coffee table. The sofas had been introduced for less formality with clients and it seemed to work well.

Sitting on one of the sofas was a man in his fifties, he had short grey hair, stubble on his chin and brown eyes. His face was round and the features a little rugged. He stood around average height and was wearing a grey suit with a white shirt and blue tie. Bernadette thought he looked a little uncomfortable as if suits were not his normal attire.

"Hello," she said offering her hand, "I'm Bernadette Mackenna, senior partner and this is Imogen Stewart, my junior partner."

The man stood up and said, "Hello, I'm Rhys Jenkins, it's pleasure to meet you.

He shook hands with Bernadette and then Imogen in turn. His accent wasn't exactly Irish but more Welsh with a hint of Ireland in it.

"Nice to meet you too, Mr Jenkins," said Bernadette.

"Oh, don't stand on ceremony with me, call me Rhys, please."

Noting they were still standing, Bernadette said, "Please, take a seat, would you like a coffee or tea?"

"Oh well, I won't say no." Rhys smiled.

As if on cue, Alison arrived to enquire about beverages and disappeared again to make them.

"My goodness it's as if you run this place by magic," Rhys laughed.

"I wish we did. It would make our job a lot easier," said Bernadette laughing too.

He was an easy man to talk to from the off, and he had a twinkle in his eye which many women no doubt found attractive, Bernadette mused.

"How can we help?" Imogen put in.

"Ah well, I'm not here about myself, it's my son you see," Rhys began.

"Your son?" said Bernadette.

"Yes, I probably should give you some background." He stroked his chin meditatively. "I run Jenkins Hauliers, you've probably seen our trucks around, we're quite big as it goes, in Ireland."

"Yes?" Now he came to mention it Bernadette had certainly noticed trucks with that name on quite often.

"We haul everything and anything, from frozen goods to wind turbines, we've done it all. We go all over Europe but particularly across to the UK. We do regular business there with another firm, and sometimes we swap trucks for jobs and then they bring them back, see."

"OK, I get the picture, so far."

"And your son?" Imogen asked.

"He's one of my drivers, as well as being my pride and joy, see. And he…" Without warning Rhys became all misty eyed and it looked as if he was going to burst into tears.

At this moment, Alison arrived and broke the mood a little. She distributed the drinks and departed with a smile.

Rhys gratefully took a sip of his drink and then somewhat more composed, he continued, "My son, his name is, Callum. He's all I've got. My wife, she died years ago, God rest her soul. I never married again and so it was just me and him, all through those years. He wanted to join the firm and I let him, though I wanted him to go to university and now I wish I had insisted…" he broke off again choking up a little more.

"You wish you had insisted because?" said Bernadette gently. Sometimes it took people a while to get to the point and Rhys seemed to be struggling quite a bit with it.

"Because he's been arrested and they want to extradite him to the UK, that's why, and he's not guilty, he's not done anything, he…" Rhys shook his head and put his hand up to dash away the wetness forming in his eyes.

"What's he accused of doing, Rhys?"

"He's... well... human trafficking that's what... human bloody trafficking and him who would never hurt a fly... never... he's never... he's not a criminal, he's not..."

The emotion was too much for him and he put his face into both his hands. His shoulders began to shake. Imogen got up and fetched a box of tissues from the shelf of one of the bookcases in the room. They kept the tissues exactly for such a purpose. Although it grieved Bernadette to see her prospective client overcome in this fashion, she did not move to comfort him. Some people did not want that, and he seemed to be a proud man. The two of them waited silently and patiently for him to work through it, which he did eventually. He accepted the tissues gratefully, wiped his eyes, and blew his nose. Then he drank the rest of his tea while they sipped their coffee.

"I'm sorry..." he began.

"Don't be," said Bernadette, "I can tell this is very distressing for you and court proceedings usually are. You would not be the first by any means."

"Thank you," he said gratefully.

"Perhaps you could talk us through it from the beginning, it might help us to understand," said Imogen furnishing him with a smile.

"Yes, you're right, here I am jumping in and you've no idea about any of it."

"No, but just tell us in simple terms."

"OK. My son was to drive a truck, which contained large drums of flour or some such. I don't know exactly. The truck was sealed as it was packed by a shipping company in Europe, it came in via Cherbourg. Once it's sealed for customs, which it was, we have nothing to do with the contents. We've just got an inventory. He picked it up from a depot and drove it on the ferry over to Holyhead, and then to London. He dropped it off and returned to Ireland."

"And then?"

"Then the next thing we knew was they had discovered a load of Vietnamese illegals in the truck. About twenty of them I think, hidden in the barrels. God knows how they survived it."

"So, if he knew nothing about it, then surely he's in the clear?" said Bernadette.

"He would be," said Rhys patiently, "If the person they had arrested for the crime had not implicated him in it and has made a sworn statement Callum knew about it."

"Oh, I see."

"Anyway, the British Police have filed for extradition and my son was arrested two days ago, he's in Mountjoy prison."

"Right, and when's the hearing?"

"Not for a while, I'm not sure, I don't really understand the legal stuff. I'm a trucker, not a lawyer."

"OK, so I'm going to have to ask you a serious question. Apart from him being your son and your natural inclination to protect him, how do you know he's not guilty and not involved?" Bernadette said her voice now a little soberer in tone.

It was an important question. She wasn't prepared to defend a guilty man, it was not her style. Unless it happened to be an old friend like Arthur Dooley.

"I sat him down, I looked him in the eyes and I asked him straight," said Rhys without hesitation, "I said 'Callum tell me now if you had anything to do with this, the truth mind', and he said 'Dad, I never had any idea, I didn't know.' I knew it was the truth because Callum has never been able to lie to me, not from a child, never once. So, I know, and I would swear on anything you like he's innocent."

"OK, fair enough. So why did you come to me?"

This was a question she always asked. She wasn't the only defence lawyer in town and there were others equally good in her opinion. The motivation for seeking her help was important.

"I wouldn't have anyone else," he replied at once.

"And why is that?" It wasn't a sufficient answer for her.

"Because everybody knows you are the best, ask any lawyer you like, and I've rung up few. My own solicitors, I use all the time. They don't want to touch it, but they all said your name, and now that's the truth!" He regarded her a little defiantly.

"I admire your honesty, though you could have just come to me first."

"I would have, but..."

"But what?" She wondered what to expect. He didn't like lesbians or women, something of that nature?

"I was afraid you wouldn't take it."

"What?" She was a little taken aback.

"You're a highflier, you know, I mean I've followed some of the cases you've taken. Looked them up on the internet. Who am I? I'm just a haulier with a son who's in trouble. Not famous or anything, not a big deal, I mean why would you even look at me?"

"You've got the wrong impression, if you think that." She smiled. "Yours is exactly the kind of case I take. You know what interests me most? It's not fame or notoriety or any of those things. I've defended famous people, yes, but not because they were famous. No, it's stopping injustice. It's protecting the innocent from a system which will otherwise fail them."

"Oh well, that's what other people told me too."

"There you are then."

"Will you..." He left the rest of it unsaid.

"Take the case?" she supplied, "Provisionally, though I would like to talk to your son first. We also need to get him out of jail and on bail."

"That's good enough for me."

"I'm just going to say this, and it's not I don't believe you, but if I find he is guilty then I won't represent him, is that fair?"

"It's more than fair, much more, because if he was really guilty, I would not ask you to," he said almost fiercely.

"Great, so we are almost done, apart from the financial aspects—"

"Oh, it's not an issue, I can pay, don't you worry," he said interrupting.

She gave him a slight nod in acknowledgement, Andrew would be happy.

"And also, I will need all the papers you have been served, and some more details, which Imogen will take from you. First, however, let's take you to meet our finance manager, Andrew Bond, and he'll arrange the fees and so forth."

"Thank you, yes, whatever you need, I'll do it," he said gratefully.

"You are welcome. We will do our very best, but obviously, we can't guarantee the result," she replied, feeling the caveat was needed.

"Yes, I know you can't do that, I understand completely."

"Great, let's go and see Andrew."

* * *

The meeting with Andrew was successful, as she knew it would be. He was nothing if not transparent and when a paying customer appeared, he became incredibly amenable. However, he was also financially astute, and he made sure the firm got its money's worth. A retainer was usually required. Rhys agreed to all the terms and rates without demur. Andrew had factored in Imogen's time too, as he felt justified in having a junior barrister for such a case.

Imogen took some details from Rhys, and he promised to send over all of the papers by courier as soon as he got back to his office.

As they bade him goodbye, Bernadette suddenly said, "I'm curious, your accent, you are... Welsh?"

"Oh, yes," Rhys laughed, "For my sins, born and bred in Aberystwyth, ach. I spent a good part of my life in Wales but when my parents passed, I wanted to make something of myself. I came to Ireland and started up my business with one truck, driving it all myself. The rest is history."

"A self-made man."

"Yes, and I've never lost my accent. Callum is different, he grew up here. I married an Irish lass and she was the apple of my eye. It's partly why I moved here I suppose, so she could be at home. It's shame she was taken so soon," he said in a voice tinged with sadness.

"I'm sorry." Bernadette did not like to ask what his wife had died of. No doubt it may come up at some point, but now was not the time.

"No matter, anyway, I'll get off, thank you again."

They shook hands and watched him leave. He was obviously a proud man who felt things deeply.

Bernadette looked at Imogen. "It's nearly lunchtime... shall we?"

"Yes, why not."

"We're out to lunch, Juanita," said Bernadette over her shoulder as they opened the front door. What Juanita had to say about it was lost on them as Bernadette closed the door behind them.

They walked from the office to their favourite haunt, Mamma Mia. This was a small restaurant nearby where the tables sported red chequered tablecloths and was a bright friendly establishment with great food. The menu was Italian. Since Bernadette was no longer on a strict diet, she was able to choose more widely and without consulting her fiancée.

As a result, they both chose the Bruschetta and the *Panino Salame* which was a mutual favourite. This was topped off with sparkling water.

"Quite a case to get stuck into," said Imogen after consuming a mouthful of her panini.

"Yes, very much so."

"Have you dealt with an extradition case before?"

"I haven't, to be honest, well, not directly. I have been peripherally involved in one or two whilst learning the job. This would be the first defence I've led," Bernadette said toying a little with her sandwich before eating it.

"A learning curve for us both," Imogen mused.

They ate in silence for a few moments, enjoying the food.

"God that was scrumptious," said Bernadette as she finished the last mouthful.

"Mmm, bet you are glad you are not on the diet."

"I'm on a maintenance diet so I have to watch what I eat, and I'm answerable to Eve if I start to put on weight." Bernadette smiled.

"Oh? Answerable in what way?" Imogen was always interested in the details of their relationship and pounced on this at once.

"You know." Bernadette's eyes twinkled. "Hands on the wall for thirty minutes, that sort of thing."

"Oh yes, naked and wearing stilettoes," Imogen laughed, "I remember now."

"That's right, though the lovemaking afterwards is always so intense. My God, I screamed the house down last time."

"Yes, it's the same with D'Arcy after the paddle," Imogen replied with a sly grin, "I have tried Eve's methods too, but only *after* D'Arcy gets a spanking, I guess Eve omitted *that* part."

"Yes, she did, and I don't want her to include it, either," said Bernadette firmly.

"Back to sex again, what are we like?" Imogen laughed.

"Terrible."

"I'll order coffee and we'll focus on the case," said Imogen calling the waiter over.

"Yes, please do," Bernadette said with mock severity, but she didn't mean it in the least. They both enjoyed their girly chats.

"So, the first thing?" said Imogen as the coffee arrived.

"We need to get the papers, lodge our representation and get all of the evidence which is being presented as part of the proceedings."

"OK." Imogen took a sip of her coffee.

"We also need to see Callum, and set up an urgent bail hearing, there's no way he should be in jail."

"Yes."

"Would you take the lead at the hearing?"

"Sure, I'll do it, no problem." Imogen smiled.

"That's a change of tune," Bernadette replied, pleased.

The first time Bernadette had asked her to do this, Imogen had been shit scared of failing. The hearing had, however, gone well and since that time Imogen had taken on more minor cases albeit under Bernadette's supervision.

"Ah well, I'm a bit more battle hardened since then." Imogen winked at her.

"Yes, and that's good, you are gaining in confidence and rightly so."

Imogen had a few wins under her belt at least, getting people of minor criminal charges or reducing their sentences. She had done well.

"Assuming we get him out of jail, what then?" Imogen wondered.

"We will have to see what witnesses they have or don't have. But one of the places we should try is the depot where Callum picked the truck up from, maybe we can interview someone from there, perhaps."

"And what if they are somehow involved?" Imogen replied with concern.

"We will find out very quickly I'm sure."

"And then?"

"We revise our approach."

"OK."

They sipped their coffee both thinking through any other strategies but at this point, there wasn't much they really knew. More would be revealed as they got hold of the documents.

"I guess the Irish prosecution service will be representing the British prosecution service," said Imogen at length.

"Yes, yes they will. It's their job and after all, the lawyers from the UK won't be able to represent themselves in Ireland. Logically it would be our prosecution service," Bernadette agreed.

"What if it's Shane?" Shane was still a sore point with Imogen, Bernadette could tell.

"Then we simply whip his arse in the courtroom once again," Bernadette laughed.

"I'd like to whip his arse for sure, but not so much in the courtroom," Imogen said crossly recalling her issues with him once more.

"You'll have to content yourself with D'Arcy's arse," said her friend mildly.

"I know, I have to keep Shane out of my thoughts when I'm doing that... otherwise..."

"Poor D'Arcy."

"I've never gone too far with her, I'll have you know," said Imogen indignantly, "And if she really didn't want me to, then I wouldn't, you know that!"

"I do know, darling, and I'm just winding you up."

"Oh don't. I do feel guilty sometimes about it as it is... well, not too much, but a little."

The two of them burst out laughing. Imogen indicated to the waiter that she wanted the bill and got out her credit card to pay.

* * *

Later that afternoon, Imogen came into Bernadette's office with a sheaf of papers.

"We've received the documents from Rhys," she said.

"OK, what have we got?"

Bernadette moved over to her sofa and Imogen sat down beside her. She shuffled through the papers.

"We've got the pleadings for the extradition, and additional papers. It names their chief witness as Kevin Clinton who has been charged with trafficking people for sexual exploitation, which is the main charge, and carries a maximum sentence of fourteen years in jail."

"I see, and this Kevin Clinton has provided a statement?"

"We will have to obtain all the evidence from the court, but Alison is preparing a notification of representation to be sent to all parties, it should go today once you've signed it. However, it's noted in the pleading that affidavits are to be filed containing the evidence against Callum."

"OK, so, apart from that?"

"There are actually nineteen Vietnamese women aged from fifteen upwards who were intended for sexual exploitation. Obviously, they did not know it. They have filed for asylum and their claims are being processed. They are currently in temporary housing," said Imogen reading further.

"What is the basis of their claim?" Bernadette wondered.

"If they are returned, they will be killed by the gang who they paid to smuggle them out here."

"I wonder why they wanted to come here?"

From what Bernadette knew of Vietnam it wasn't such a bad place although many lived in poverty. It was a place she had always wanted to visit and now she had Eve, she would love to take her. A fleeting thought of a honeymoon there crossed her mind, although with work commitments this seemed it might prove difficult.

"I don't know, we should find out."

"Perhaps we may be able to interview one of them or more, it might provide some useful insights into what happened to them," Bernadette mused.

"Would they make potential witnesses?"

"I don't know, it depends on what they do or don't know, I suppose," said Bernadette.

"I'll make enquiries as to whether or how we could interview them," Imogen said making some notes.

"It would, of course, mean a trip to the UK on expenses," said Bernadette, smiling.

"With or without partners?" Imogen wanted to know.

"Oh, I imagine we might squeeze in a partner or two." Bernadette gave her a wink.

"Won't Andrew object?" Imogen said looking worried.

"He'll cross charge it to the client, so we'll have to be good, not go overboard."

"Oh, D'Arcy will cover any overspill," Imogen laughed.

"If you say so." Bernadette shrugged diplomatically.

D'Arcy was worth several million Euro by now and so most things to her were small change. However, Imogen was very circumspect about this subject and she did not want D'Arcy, who was very open-handed, to way feel in any she was being taken advantage of. Bernadette didn't want to be thought of as taking advantage either.

"If I tell her to, she will," said Imogen firmly, "And anyway she would want to, she'll want to come."

"OK but not to any interviews, or stuff like that. Apart from anything else I don't want to put either D'Arcy or Eve into any danger or compromising situations."

"No, of course not, if I know her, she will take Eve shopping down Knightsbridge or something."

Bernadette laughed. "Tea at Harrods?"

"Exactly, that would be her style."

"Then see if we need to go and, if we do, ask Alison to figure out places to stay. I don't want anywhere naff, but not the Ritz or Savoy either, that would not be fair on the client."

"I'll figure something out," Imogen assured her, "I'm not staying in any sort of hovel."

"Anyway, back to our case..." said Bernadette gently.

"If we are going to the UK then perhaps, we should talk to the UK police involved, if they will talk to us. I mean, we are the defence team after all..." Imogen suggested after some thought.

"It's not a bad idea, if they would. It's a shame we can't talk to their main witness, but that will have to wait until we get him on the stand."

"So that's all I can really glean from this, not much, we need to full evidence."

"OK, so in the meantime let's see Callum tomorrow and get the bail hearing in progress."

"Already getting Alison onto Mountjoy and we've got a provisional date for Friday for the bail hearing."

"Wow, fast work, but I hope Alison isn't overloaded with all this," said Bernadette anxiously.

"She's a little stretched, but you said we couldn't get more help."

"No, however, I may have to bite the bullet and tackle Andrew on it," Bernadette sighed.

"Shall I come with you, when you do it?" said Imogen with a smile.

"Yes, why not, we'll form up a posse and take him on."

The two of them chuckled over the ludicrous idea of Andrew in cowboy gear.

* * *

Bernadette pulled her car into the driveway and the automatic gate closed behind her. Her house was in a nice area of Dublin in Sandymount. It had a mock Georgian style portico, and windows with wooden shutters. It had three bedrooms upstairs, and downstairs, a kitchen, dining and living room. Now it was not just her home but also Eve's and she loved that part the most. She opened the door with the keycode, hung up her jacket and kicked off her shoes.

The familiar smell of delicious food wafted through from the kitchen. Eve cooked for them and in the main looked after the house, as well pursuing her newfound art career. Bernadette was content with their domestic arrangements, as was Eve. She was a far better cook than Bernadette for starters.

Bernadette padded barefoot into the living room. Eve was sitting on the sofa wearing a pink shoestring strap short summery dress with a white flower pattern and sketching. She had crossed her legs and was dangling a leather flipflop sandal from one foot. This aroused Bernadette at once. She had a penchant for feet, and also shoes, it was one of her vices which Eve knew only too well. She was certain Eve played it her advantage, since she began to slap the sandal against the bottom of her foot with her toe. She would have heard Bernadette arrive and once her fiancée was standing in front of her, she laid the sketchbook aside and stood up to greet her.

"Hi, my beautiful witch," said Bernadette playfully.

"Hi, baby, I'm so pleased to see you." Eve snaked her arms around Bernadette's neck and planted a kiss on her lips. It turned into something more passionate almost at once.

"Mmm, God you smell delicious," Bernadette whispered.

"It's my new perfume, it's called Intense. Do you like it?"

"Like it, I love it and I love you."

Unable to help herself, Bernadette ran her hands under Eve's dress while her fiancée hissed in a breath at her touch.

"Fuck, I love it when you do *that*," she breathed.

"Do, you? And how about this?"

Bernadette's hands roamed gently across Eve's skin, caressing, softly, and around her breasts. Eve's nipples hardened at her touch, and Eve laid her head back. Bernadette planted kisses on her neck.

"Oh, God, baby... oh my God," Eve said squirming with delight.

"And... do you like it when I do this?" Bernadette enquired, her fingers moving down between Eve's legs, finding to her satisfaction that Eve was wet as anything.

"Oh... God... yes... I want... you to....do... that... so much..." Eve gasped, "Oh... oh God... baby... don't stop... please don't... stop... ohh."

Bernadette had no intention of stopping and her fingers continued relentlessly as she felt Eve's body begin to tense before Eve finally screamed, "Ohh... oh my God... oh... ohh... ohh... ohh," as her climax washed through her.

Bernadette smiled, holding her tight, pulling her closer. Eve's body shuddered as she felt the sensations intensify and then subside slowly. Then she smiled.

"I've been wanting you to do that all day," she whispered.

"I know, and I've been wanting to do it to you," Bernadette said kissing her again.

"Shall we have dinner?" said Eve straightening up after a few moments.

"Yes, let's, I'm starved."

"And then after dinner, we will have... dessert." Eve smiled lasciviously.

"Yes please," said Bernadette catching the allusion to further bedroom activity.

Eve led Bernadette into the dining room, and Bernadette sat at the table to wait. Eve had laid the places as usual and she shortly brought in dishes of rice, salad and Thai green chicken curry.

"Oh God, my favourite," said Bernadette, "Or one of them."

"Enjoy." Eve ladled a portion onto Bernadette's plate.

"Oh... mmm," said Bernadette taking a mouthful and savouring it with great appreciation.

Eve poured her a glass of Merlot and then one for herself. Although Bernadette was a big wine buff, her wine intake had been severely curtailed during her diet. Now they had perhaps one or two glasses of an evening and no more, and sometimes just sparkling water.

"You like?" Eve smiled taking her place at the table and serving herself some food.

"I love it, it's... orgasmic."

"That's how I like my food," Eve giggled, "And my woman too."

"I do my best," Bernadette said enjoying another forkful of rice and curry.

"You do better than your best, my darling."

"Thank you." Bernadette blew her a kiss.

"How was your day? Anything interesting happen?" Eve said between mouthfuls of food.

"Well, I was in court and this blonde dynamo, sexy as fuck, took me into the toilet and fucked me."

"Wow, really? How very bad of her. I should have a talk to her about that," said Eve keeping a straight face.

"So bad, so very bad but I loved it."

"I'm so glad, my sweetheart. But apart from the sexual encounter?"

"Oh well, Arthur Dooley got a year's home detention, which was lucky because I thought he was getting two years in jail to start with."

"Oh, my goodness, well done you," said Eve impressed.

"I was lucky I think, and also because Arthur has a cat and so does the judge."

"What?" Eve paused with a fork halfway up to her mouth.

"Arthur said he couldn't leave his cat and the judge agreed," Bernadette explained.

"Oh, I see... how funny."

"Yes, and we've got a new client."

"Do tell."

Bernadette spent a few minutes explaining the new case and what it involved. Eve was always fascinated by her work and loved to hear about it. She had taken an active role in a couple of them at least, particularly the one with D'Arcy Brown where D'Arcy had insisted on her being there at the hearing for support and paid her handsomely for doing so.

"Well," said Eve once she had finished, "It sounds like quite a challenge."

"Yes, it is, and I think it will be, but you know me, I'm up for it."

She paused for a few minutes to catch up on her food and then laid down her cutlery.

"So, how did it go with Valentino?" She wanted to know about the gallery meeting.

Eve had made Bernadette her manager, as regards her Art, and she had initially funded the framing and expenses for Eve's first show. The revenue for the show had been well in excess of anything they had spent, so those were easily covered.

"So, apparently there's a market for, shall we say my more risqué pictures like the ones of Imogen, and the others

I made, and perhaps a bit of BDSM, you know, that sort of thing."

"OK, if it's making you money and you want to do it."

"If it's making *us* money, for *both* of us," Eve corrected her.

"Sorry, I do mean that."

"Good, because you're always saying what you earn is our money and not just yours. So, it's the same for me."

"Yes, true, you are right, I'm sorry," said Bernadette smiling.

"You can make it up to me later." Eve ran her bare foot up Bernadette's leg.

"Oh, I will."

"I know you will."

"Witch!"

"And you love it."

* * *

As she sometimes did, Bernadette lay thinking in the early hours of the morning. They had gone to bed soon after dinner and made love until they both fell asleep. But as often happened with difficult cases, they would penetrate her consciousness and she started to go through them in their mind. Eve was awake almost at once. It was as if she had a sixth sense and could always tell when Bernadette was troubled.

"What's wrong, darling?" she asked Bernadette.

"Oh, nothing, just the case," Bernadette sighed, "It's nothing... really."

"Don't fret, my honey. It will work out, it always does."

"I know. Sorry."

"Don't be sorry," Eve told her pulling Bernadette around to face her. She kissed her lightly. "Just try to think of something different."

"Well," said Bernadette recalling something she had forgotten earlier, "I meant to tell you about Imogen."

"Oh?"

"She wasn't happy today..." Bernadette recounted the article in Hello magazine and the consequences for D'Arcy.

"So, D'Arcy was going to get a spanking?" said Eve with sudden interest.

"Yes, so I gather."

"Mmm, tell me more..." Eve said her hands starting to rove over Bernadette's skin.

"I don't know the actual details." Bernadette's fingers reciprocated and strayed lower to between Eve's thighs.

"Then... make it up... just tell... me... a story... I want you to... please... oh... oh God..."

Bernadette smiled indulgently. It wasn't the first time Eve wanted a dirty story like this.

"Well... Imogen gets home and then after discussing her misbehaviour... she sends D'Arcy to the bedroom I expect..."

"Oh... God... and then..."

"She goes upstairs... and tells her to strip..." Bernadette's fingers continued doing what they did best.

"Oh... oh God... oh and then..."

"She tells her she's going to be getting a spanking with the paddle..."

"Oh my God... oh yes... yes... don't stop... ooh... oh... ohh... tell me more..."

The story did not last much longer before she brought Eve to a shuddering climax. After Eve had reciprocated, Bernadette spooned up to her fiancée and fell into a satisfied sleep. Her last musings were about Eve, and how she seemed to enjoy getting off on these kinds of stories, and then there were the pictures she was drawing. Bernadette hadn't thought much about it before but perhaps there was more to it than Eve was letting on. One of these days Bernadette was going to have to have a more in depth conversation about it with Eve.

CHAPTER TWO

When morning stole under the blinds with small shafts of light. Bernadette awoke to see Eve gazing into her eyes and smiling.

"Hello, beautiful," said Bernadette.

"I love you, darling, so much," Eve replied. She was misty eyed, and Bernadette felt her emotion almost as if emanated from her like a wave. Bernadette often felt the same way, as if her heart was full.

"I love you too." Bernadette drew her into a kiss. They lay like that, kissing gently without doing anything more, just enjoying the intimacy of being with each other.

At length, Eve pulled away slightly and said, "Go and have your shower, I'll put out your clothes."

Bernadette obediently slid out of bed and went to the bathroom. By the time she had washed her hair, and soaked in the steaming hot water, she felt refreshed. When she returned to the bedroom, Eve had laid out a pink blouse, grey skirt and jacket, and pink heeled thong sandals. Bernadette sat patiently while Eve deftly wove her hair into one long plait which would dry nicely. Eve quickly did Bernadette's makeup and then went downstairs to make breakfast, leaving Bernadette to apply any finishing touches and get dressed.

When Bernadette arrived downstairs, the usual tantalising smell of scrambled eggs, bacon and coffee assailed her nostrils. Eve believed in a good breakfast setting you up for the day. Bernadette had been subjected to this regime since Eve arrived in her life, and she could only agree.

Eve put a plate in front of Bernadette containing scrambled eggs on wholemeal buttered toast, with a side of bacon and mushrooms. She slid a cup of coffee over to Bernadette and sat down next to her at the breakfast bar with her own plate of food. Bernadette took a moment to admire the way the red satin robe hugged Eve's naked curves and lightly slid her hand down Eve's body.

"Eat your food, darling," said Eve with a smile.

"Thank you, but you are so fucking gorgeous, I can't help it." Bernadette smiled back.

"I'll still be here later."

"I know."

Bernadette addressed herself to her repast enjoying the creamy eggs and the crispy bacon just the way she liked it. When she finished, she sat back on her stool drinking her coffee.

"So, what's today?" Eve asked her.

"We're going to see Callum Jenkins to find out more about what actually happened, and more about him, I hope. We are seeing him in Mountjoy, so that's not really conducive to a congenial atmosphere. However, our next job is to get him out on bail."

"Do think you can?"

"We've a damn good chance, Imogen is leading it because I asked her to, she did well at the last bail hearing." Bernadette took another sip of her coffee.

"Yes, I'm sure she will."

"I've got to go," said Bernadette draining her cup and standing up.

"I wish you didn't, but I always say that." Eve smiled.

"I do, and it will be the weekend soon."

"Hmm, yes..."

"What are you thinking? I know *that* look," said Bernadette suspiciously.

"Oh, nothing," said Eve running one fingernail down Bernadette's arm, "It's just it's been a while, since you know..."

Bernadette knew very well, Eve wanted a Shibari session. This was Eve's enduring fetish, and if she didn't get one every so often she would begin to crave it. It had become their game. Eve would do things to misbehave and Bernadette would give her a session as 'consequences.'

"Yes, I know, perhaps I need to start compiling a list."

"Maybe you do," said Eve smiling saucily.

"Anyway," said Bernadette heading for the door with Eve in tow.

Eve tilted her head up for her goodbye kiss, this was their ritual. Eve insisted on it and Bernadette never left without it. The kiss was explosive as usual, sending tingles up Bernadette's spine and making her dizzy. She pulled apart after a few moments with fireworks still going off in her head.

"How do you do that?" she asked Eve, a little breathless.

"I'm a witch, remember." Eve's eyes twinkled.

5

"Yes, you are, by God you are," Bernadette replied with a laugh.

"I feel the fireworks too you know."

"Good, I'm glad, now behave yourself while I'm gone." Bernadette kissed her lightly.

"I won't," said Eve with mock defiance.

"Then you know what will happen."

"Oh, yes."

"Bye then, my darling." Bernadette picked up her bag and walked out the door.

As she drove away, Eve was standing in the doorway watching her and waving, clad only in her robe.

"Fuck," said Bernadette glancing at her in the rear-view mirror, "God she's such a sexy bitch."

She turned on the radio and began to hum to the latest tunes, as she pulled out into the main road heading for the office.

* * *

Bernadette had not long dropped her keys at Juanita's desk, and procured herself a coffee, before Imogen nudged open the door. They always had a morning chat together, which more often than not ranged over many topics which were not exclusively work related.

"Hi, darling," said Bernadette transferring herself to the sofa.

"Hi," said Imogen who had brought her own drink and put it on the coffee table to cool.

"So, how was your evening?"

"Well, it was very good, of course." Imogen smiled a secret smile.

"And how is D'Arcy?" Bernadette wondered how the evening had actually played out, and whether the mooted chastisement had eventuated. The two of them were very frank with each other about their private lives, and so naturally they would tell each other everything.

"Oh well, she's fine. We discussed the whole thing from *Hello* magazine, and she explained it all. I mean, she and this guy have been long-time friends, and it didn't mean anything. It was just typical of the papers. I suppose I have to get used to it. I've got to try and curb my jealousy too," Imogen sighed.

"Yes, yes you do, and did you..."

"No, I didn't spank her after all, I mean, she was so contrite and so nice about it. She kissed me so softly and gently, made me go so weak at the knees... I just couldn't. We made love instead, and that was just so nice."

"Really, that's very restrained of you, well done." Bernadette looked approvingly at her.

"Yes, I surprised myself, really. Mind you, I'm planning to make up for it at the weekend, I'm sure the paddle with come into play then."

"I see," Bernadette said with a crack of laughter at this candid disclosure. She shook her head as if to say this was no more than to be expected.

"What? What? I'm not *that* bad!"

"Oh, you are, darling, you really are..."

"Oh you! And I suppose you're not planning another Shibari session!"

"Eve wants one actually, at the weekend too."

"There you are then!" said Imogen triumphantly, "It's no different. I'm just doing what D'Arcy wants."

"Does she?" said Bernadette wondering if it was true.

"Yes, she does, I mean, she wanted me to last night, but I didn't."

"Well, in that case..."

"She said, 'I suppose you'll be needing this' you know, handing me the paddle, and I said, 'no, I won't, and I kissed her instead."

"You surprise me, but in a good way."

"I have to try a little harder to curb my natural impulses," said Imogen assuming a saint like expression which made Bernadette laugh.

"Anyway, have you thought any more about... wedding rings?"

"Yes, and I should, and we should go and buy one, maybe from the shop where you got one before."

"OK, this week?"

"Definitely!"

"So, what about Callum?"

"We've got a meeting this morning and so we should get going soon, I cleared it with the prison yesterday."

"Right, let's talk about what we want to find out from him, and also what you need for the hearing."

✳ ✳ ✳

Within an hour Bernadette and Imogen were en-route to Mountjoy prison. This was the main prison for men in Dublin and sat adjacent to the Dòchas Centre which was the prison for women. The prison complex was shielded from the main road by an extremely high brick wall. The wall had inset mouldings to make it a little less forbidding and turrets at intervals, like a castle.

There are major differences, however, between the women's and the men's prisons. Dòchas has courtyards and resembles something more like a set of halls of residence. The aim of Dòchas is to rehabilitate and prepare inmates for the outside. The rooms are not so much like cells, and they have wooden doors to make them less intimidating. By contrast, Mountjoy has corridors, bars and metal cell doors, just like most traditional prisons. The cells are a little more spartan, although many are painted in a yellow colour which perhaps reminds people of sunshine and can be stimulating or soothing. Perhaps the authorities felt it was better than a uniform and drab grey. Many improvements had been made over the years when previously the prison had been heavily criticised for the conditions in which inmates were forced to live.

Bernadette and Imogen were escorted to an interview room, which was carpeted and decorated in half yellow and half cream walls. There was a table, and some chairs. The window had bars on it. They waited patiently while Callum Jenkins was brought to them.

The door swung open eventually and Callum was let into the room. He had been allowed to wear his own clothing, which was at the governor's discretion, but since he was on remand, it tended to be the rule. Callum was quite thickset with a shaved head. He was wearing a t-shirt and jeans with trainers. He was well built, and well-muscled too. Bernadette noted he evidently worked out. Standing at around one point eight metres in height, he was tall. He had a slightly round face with blue eyes, and full lips, there was a carefully crafted line of stubble around his chin.

The door shut behind him, Bernadette and Imogen stood up.

"Hi, I'm Bernadette Mackenna Senior Defence Counsel, and this is Imogen Stewart my Junior Defence Counsel."

She held out her hand and he shook it in a firm grip, and then did likewise with Imogen.

"Take a seat," Bernadette told him, indicating a chair opposite. He did so regarding them with interest, and perhaps a little bit of hope in his eyes. "I'm sorry about the surroundings. We are going to try our best to get you out of here if we can."

"Oh, it's not too bad," he demurred, "I mean, not so far anyway."

"Callum, we are here to talk to you about the extradition hearing, as I'm sure you will have guessed, and also getting you out on bail."

"Yes, I spoke to my father yesterday, I'm allowed phone calls to sort things out. He told me he'd engaged your services."

"Good." She smiled. "I'm sure I don't have to tell you this certainly doesn't look like an easy case. We have applied to the prosecution service for their evidence, and it will give us a clearer picture. In the meantime, we want to ask you what happened, from your perspective."

"Sure, I'll answer whatever questions you have."

"I need you to answer honestly, truthfully."

"I will, I really will," he said earnestly.

"OK."

In spite of his looks, he was deceptively mild in manner and tone. His voice which one might expect to be deep was much lighter. Bernadette noticed, unlike his father, his accent was Irish and put this down to being brought up here. Sometimes the parent's accents overrode the local ones but not in Callum's case.

"What happened with the truck?" said Imogen taking over the questions. It was best to cut to the chase, she felt and did so.

"The truck was driven to a depot, here in Dublin, on the outskirts, by another driver. It came from Spain, in the south. A long drive up to Cherbourg and then across on the ferry to Dublin. It was dropped off there for the handover, and then I drove it across to Holyhead and left it at another depot, and drove a different truck back, that's all there was to it." He shrugged.

"So, the goods were sealed, you never looked inside the trailer?"

"No, it had a customs seal on it when it came over and as far as I know the seal was not broken. Well, not until they found those illegals in it."

"What's your take on that? The illegals, has anything like this ever happened before?" Bernadette asked him with interest.

He shook his head emphatically.

"I don't know, not to me at least. They were being trafficked, it's what they said isn't it? I was arrested for that."

"Yes, they were, but how did you feel about it when you found out?"

Bernadette and Imogen watched him narrowly, to gauge his reaction.

"I felt sorry for them, of course. I mean, I don't know how they managed to survive all that time. I'm against any kind of human trafficking, I find it abhorrent. I would never be involved in anything like that," was all he said.

"How *do* you think they survived, or could they have been put into the truck at the depot here?"

"I don't know because I have no details. I don't know how you could manage to live in a barrel for several days and would probably be hot. But they probably had been through much worse for all I know. I just know what I'm accused of, I told you, not any details. I don't think they could have been put in the barrels here, because of the seal, I mean, you would have to break it and only customs can provide a new one. This one was from the Spanish authorities."

"Interesting," mused Bernadette, "We'll leave it for now."

"OK."

Callum shifted in his seat. Bernadette could sense somehow there was something he wasn't saying or was not willing to say. It was a feeling as much as anything else. How to find out what it was, would be a different matter.

"Before we go any further, there is something I need to ask you," she said without warning.

"OK."

"Are you telling the truth? Is it really true you know nothing about those poor women who were smuggled in? I need you to be honest with me now." She fixed him with a penetrating stare, and he looked a little uneasy.

"Yes, it's true. I didn't know, I had no idea. I will swear on whatever you like, bible, my mother's grave, anything. I had no clue about it until I was hit with this warrant."

His denial was emphatic, forthright. There was no prevarication or caveat. So, whatever he wasn't telling them, it wasn't that.

"There's a witness," she said trying again.

"Yes." His eyes shifted away at the mention of this. He would no doubt have known about this part.

"A witness who says you were involved, and you knew all about it."

"Yes, I know, the detectives told me." His eyes slid from her gaze once more.

Bernadette glanced at Imogen and she had noticed it too. They were on the right track here, for certain.

"His name is Kevin Clinton," put in Imogen, "Do you know Kevin Clinton?"

"Yes." Callum seemed to become even more agitated at the mention of his name.

"So, how do you come to know Mr Clinton?"

"I worked with him, I mean, he was a driver too, he…" he trailed off. They were both looking sceptical at his answer.

"No, Callum, no, you didn't just work with him, did you?" Bernadette said perceiving this was possibly pay dirt as regards the secret.

"What is this, the Spanish Inquisition?" he shot back, but his expression was so guilty, Bernadette wondered what on earth they had stumbled into.

"No, it's not but we told you at the outset we wanted total honesty. Callum, we are trying to keep you out of jail and it's only going to happen if you tell us the absolute unvarnished truth," said Imogen severely.

"I... I can't..." he said suddenly emotional.

"Why can't you?"

"Because you won't want to represent me, you'll be disgusted in me and..." He wasn't looking at her now, he was looking down at the floor very unhappily.

"Of course, we won't be," Imogen insisted, "But you *have* to tell us."

Something occurred to Bernadette and it came to her in a flash. There was something blindingly obvious which she should not have missed.

"Are you gay?" she asked without warning.

"Fuck!" said Callum, "Fuck, fuck, fuck, fuck."

He looked dismayed, as if the worst secret in the world had just been revealed.

"You are gay, aren't you." It was a statement and his reaction had confirmed it. It also settled the issue as to whether Bernadette's gaydar was working or not.

"Yes, yes I am," Callum sniffed, and tears welled up into his eyes. He put his head into his hands.

"Your Dad doesn't know about it, does he?" Imogen added. She could also see which way things were going and why Callum had been so reluctant to speak.

"No." Callum let out a big sob and his shoulders heaved in a sigh. He had evidently not come out.

"Well, for the record, I'm gay, and so is Imogen here or, at least, she is bisexual," Bernadette told him in matter of fact tones.

"I'm most probably gay to be fair," said Imogen agreeing.

For a few moments, Callum said nothing, and then as if what they said had only just penetrated his consciousness, he said, "Pardon?"

"I said I'm gay and so is she," Bernadette repeated.

He looked at her as if she was speaking Greek.

"Oh? What? You're gay? Both of you?" He seemed unable to credit this.

"Yes, is it so strange?" Bernadette smiled disarmingly.

"But you're... lawyers," he protested, as if this noble profession would, perforce, preclude anyone who was not strictly heterosexual.

A crack of surprised laughter came from Bernadette. "You think lawyers can't be gay?"

"I... no... of course... that's silly, I'm sorry, I didn't mean. I'm just not used to talking about it and... it's just *I* can't be... and the problem is, I am." He looked crestfallen.

"Why can't you? And why is it a problem?" Imogen wanted to know. She asked it a little more gently, as it was obviously a very difficult issue for him.

He hesitated, thinking about it, before speaking.

"My Dad, I mean, he would hate it... he... I mean, he just doesn't like gays, he—"

"Employed us, and it's well known I'm gay," said Bernadette cutting in. Since her father had consulted several other lawyers there is no way it would not have come up.

"What makes you think he doesn't like gays?" Imogen asked him.

"Things, he said, when I was young, and well... he's always wanted grandkids, and looked to me to provide them..."

"Being gay doesn't mean you can't do that."

"Yes, I know but..."

"Has he ever said anything homophobic? Ever been anti-gay?" Imogen continued.

"No... he hasn't but..."

"Callum, your father loves you, obviously. He was distressed when he came to ask for our help," Bernadette told him.

"He cried," said Imogen.

"He did?" Callum looked surprised.

"Yes, so let's not worry about it now, anyway, you will have to tell him though. Trust me when I say it is the least of his problems right now. His bigger issue is keeping you out of a British jail."

"I guess." Callum didn't look convinced. Bernadette was sure Rhys would not be unhappy to find out his son was gay. In the end, he obviously cared for his son beyond anything.

"So, let's go back to Kevin Clinton," said Bernadette a little remorselessly, "Was he your lover?"

There was silence for a moment and then Callum nodded. "Yes."

It was clear from his demeanour he didn't really want to discuss it, however not discussing it wasn't an option.

"OK, so how long have you two been seeing each other?"

"I don't know, about six months, more, it was just a casual thing. When I went to London or he came over here, we'd meet up, you know, and..." He left the rest of it unsaid.

"Right, and did you have any idea he was involved with a criminal smuggling gang?"

"I didn't know anything about that, no."

He seemed to be telling the truth and had relaxed a lot since his secret was out in the open. They needed to understand the real extent of their relationship, however.

"What did you two talk about?" Imogen enquired.

Callum sniggered. "Not so much talking, not really *that* much."

"So basically, you were fucking," she said bluntly.

"If you want to put it that way, then, yes."

"Where did you do it?"

He shrugged. "In a hotel sometimes, or the cab of the truck, you know there's a bed in there behind the driving seat."

"So, it was a very physical relationship?"

"Yes, yes it was, essentially."

In a way, this was good. The less they had talked the better. The less he knew about the other party the better.

"Were there feelings involved from either of you?" This was important and could potentially be used on the witness stand.

"I wasn't in love with him, or he with me, not really."

"OK, so he wouldn't feel any loyalty towards you?"

"Obviously not if he's written a statement against me."

"You'd be surprised what criminals will stoop to once they are under pressure," Imogen said wryly.

"Why would he implicate me though?" He sounded annoyed suddenly, even affronted by this.

"He might be offered a deal, if he dobs someone else in. He might get a lighter sentence by pleading guilty and giving up some other members of the gang to take the rap."

"Yes, but why me? For fuck's sake, I never did anything to him. Surely there are others in the gang he could implicate?"

"I have no idea, and we won't know until we get him on the witness stand," said Bernadette, "It could be too dangerous for him to betray the real criminals, you are an easy target."

"But they can't prove I did anything!"

"They don't care about *that*. They just need to get you into the UK where you can be charged and prosecuted. In the process, the British Police will work you over to try and extract a confession, and then you are stuck in their justice system."

"Fuck! Fucking bastards!" said Callum upset now he saw what he was facing.

"Fuck indeed, that's what we are here for, to stop it." Bernadette smiled at him sweetly.

"What else do you need from me?"

"We need some assurances, if we get bail then you'll stay put where you're meant to be, surrender your passport, and not try to do a runner," said Imogen.

"You've got it, I'll stay with my Dad, he'll see me right."

"OK, that's good to know. You may be asked by the judge to give those same assurances to the court."

"I will agree to whatever they want."

"Good," said Bernadette, "That's what we want to hear."

"Can you? Get them to stop it?"

"We'll give it our best shot."

"And her best shot, is better than anyone else's best shot, believe me," Imogen added.

Bernadette shrugged and smiled, modestly. She found it hard to take praise, even when it was merited.

"She is the absolute best," Imogen continued, noting Bernadette had slightly coloured up, "If anyone can get you off it's Bernadette."

"Now, you've bigged me up, it's probably time to go," said Bernadette laughing.

"Will I see you again?" Callum asked.

"We will see you at the bail hearing, brief you beforehand, and once that's over we can get down to business."

"Can you get me out of here, really?" he said with a worried expression.

"We've got a good chance of it, yes."

"Relax," said Imogen, "We've got this."

"OK."

They said goodbye, then called the guard to take Callum back to his wing.

"We've got this?" said Bernadette chuckling as they walked back to the car.

"Of course, we have, I'm running it, so yes," Imogen said with a mock pout.

"I admire your confidence, a lot different to last time." Bernadette was still chuckling.

"I learned from the best, I keep telling you, and plus I'm a Domme now, well, partly, so I'm feeling much more assertive these days," Imogen laughed.

"Ha! So! You finally admit your inner dominatrix, I knew it!" said Bernadette triumphantly, pressing the key to open the car doors.

"Yes." Imogen sighed sitting in the passenger seat and doing up her seatbelt. "I've struggled with this for a while, but really I'm going to have to admit that I'm the Domme and D'Arcy is the sub, in our relationship."

"Sounds like you've been doing some reading." Bernadette raised an eyebrow, backed the car up and pulled out into the main road.

"Yes, I have, so I've got all the terminology now, and some more techniques."

"So, I gather, and how does D'Arcy feel about this?"

"Oh well, I've still got to broach it with her," Imogen admitted her confidence deflating.

"What are you like?"

"I know, I'm all talk, no walk, except when it comes to the paddle," said Imogen sadly.

"Get the ring, ask her to marry you, worry about the other stuff later."

"Yes, you're right, but..."

"What?"

"Are you going to tell Eve?"

"Yes, but neither of us is going to tell D'Arcy if that's what's worrying you."

"Oh, phew, that's OK then."

"As if."

The two of them went off into peals of laughter.

* * *

During the drive back, they stopped off to buy a sandwich to take back to the office for lunch.

"We could go to Mamma Mia's," Imogen had suggested, but Bernadette said they should probably not go every day on expenses, particularly if they wanted to tackle Andrew about another PA.

"Shall we talk to Andrew this afternoon?" Imogen asked her.

"We could, I mean it wouldn't hurt to broach it."

"Hopefully we'll get those papers..." Imogen tailed off. Bernadette had been looking in the mirror rather more than usual as they were driving. "What's up?"

"I don't know. It just feels like we are being followed," said Bernadette.

"What?"

"Look around carefully, a black Merc, it's been on our tail for a while. I tried a few turns which were not heading for the office and it was still there."

"Maybe they are just going the same way we are," said Imogen subtly trying to crane her head around. She spent some time looking surreptitiously out of the back window. "Maybe you are right."

"You think?" Bernadette asked her anxiously.

"I get a feeling about it, is all."

"I do too."

"OK." Imogen began to sound worried. "What should we do?"

"I don't know, we could just act as if we don't know and go back to the office."

"We could but I'm not totally down with that as a plan."

They both remembered how D'Arcy had been followed by her ex-lover who had turned out to be a psychopath plotting to kill her.

"Get their number," said Bernadette.

Imogen looked again and wrote it down.

"Got it."

"Great." Bernadette reached for the button which activated her phone which was connected to the car controls. "Dial Olivia Thompson," she said out loud.

Imogen gave her a strange look but said nothing. DS Olivia Thompson was a detective who had been unwittingly involved in a couple of their court cases. Olivia was also sweet on Imogen which made Imogen feel awkward. However, Olivia was well aware of Imogen's attachment to D'Arcy and in addition, Bernadette had set Olivia up with Carole Cooperson, a prosecution junior counsel. Hopefully, that was still going well.

After two or three rings, Olivia answered, "If it isn't Ms Mackenna."

"Hi," said Bernadette.

"Hello, and to what do I owe the pleasure?" came what sounded like a smiling response.

"I need your help," Bernadette said not in the frame of mind to engage in banter.

"Oh?"

"I'm driving back to the office from seeing my new client in Mountjoy and I think I'm being followed by a black Mercedes. We've got the registration."

"We?"

"Imogen has it."

There was an audible chuckle. "Oh, Imogen too, well, a full house."

"Yes, but I don't mind telling you, Olivia, I'm a bit scared, and so is Imogen," said Bernadette who had started to feel quite anxious.

"OK, well, tell me where you are and also the number of the Merc," came the calm response.

Imogen told Olivia, who said, "Just a moment."

The line went quiet and then it came on again.

"Just keep driving, I've sent someone out to perform a routine traffic stop, you'll see the car being pulled over, once it has been stopped, then go back to the office and meet me there. I'll see what I can discover, OK?"

"Yes, thank you," said Bernadette relieved.

"That's OK, I'll make sure you are safe."

The line disconnected. Bernadette kept driving, and Imogen looked round to check on the car which was still there. Suddenly on a wide stretch of road, a Garda vehicle pulled out past the Merc with lights flashing and siren going. It slowed to a stop in front of the car and as soon as this happened Bernadette picked up speed and left it behind. In the rear-view mirror, she could see the Gardai getting out with a view to talking to the occupants of the car.

"Phew," said Imogen as they finally crossed the river and headed for the office.

"See, Olivia does have her uses," said Bernadette.

"I know." Imogen smiled. "I don't mind so much now she's stopped trying to hit on me."

Bernadette laughed. "She never really hit on you, darling, but I know she was sweet on you."

"You weren't the one being hit on!"

"Let's hope she and Carole are all good then."

"Yes, I bloody well hope so, indeed."

* * *

They reached the office without incident and managed to park the car outside in the road.

"That was lucky," said Bernadette as she locked it. There was a paucity of empty spaces in their road and they often had to park further away.

"Very," Imogen agreed.

They walked up the steps, Bernadette swiped her security card and they entered into what she always felt was a haven of sorts. The green walls had been her choice when first moving into the offices, and she liked the slightly old world feel they gave to the environment, as well as being soothing. It was also in keeping with the period in which the offices had been originally built, although they would, at one time, have been houses of well to do gentry.

Juanita was sitting at her desk as usual, and as Bernadette dropped the keys on the counter, Juanita wordlessly placed a woman's magazine beside them opened at a double spread about D'Arcy Brown. Imogen, who was just behind Bernadette, snatched it up at once. There was a still photo from her new movie Blades of Thunder, where she was seen was kissing her co-star. The headline seemed to be asking if there was more this than her on screen romance.

"You can take it," said Juanita airily, without looking, "I finished reading it."

"Thanks," said Imogen who had suddenly become very tight lipped and walked swiftly upstairs with it clutched in her hand.

Bernadette rolled her eyes, this seemed to be Imogen's lot, to read stories about her girlfriend and she was not taking them very well.

"Must you?" she asked Juanita.

"Ay, I just thought she would be interest, that's all, it's nothing, just the gossips, it's means nothing. Constantina tells me, I know, I know. D'Arcy loves Imogen so much, it's true."

Bernadette said nothing but stood looking at her dumbfounded.

Juanita turned and for once seemed quite earnest. "I swear, Bernadette, on my life. D'Arcy will die for her, I swear it."

"OK, that's good to know," said Bernadette mollified, "But try not to keep showing her the gossip, you can see how it upsets her."

"Ay, OK, OK... I will not show..." said Juanita, now evidently feeling she had exceeded the maximum effort she could expend on the issue.

"There is a detective coming soon, Olivia, to see us, just send her to the meeting room, OK?"

"Ay, this one, she likes Imogen too, ay."

Bernadette shook her head at this and said instead, "Don't forget to move my car."

"I don't forget, I never forget..." Juanita was already reading another magazine.

Bernadette went upstairs and seeing Imogen's door was shut, opened it quietly and slipped inside. Imogen was talking on the phone which was on loudspeaker. Bernadette was about to make a quick exit when Imogen pointed for her to sit on the sofa and listen. She did so, albeit with reluctant fascination.

"It's nothing, darling, please, believe me, I swear, it's just a stupid article," D'Arcy was saying to Imogen.

"OK, but the article said you were spending a lot of time together," Imogen shot back.

"Going over the script! We had to read it over together, honey. There wasn't anything more than that. I told you about the times I went out to lunch or dinner with him when I was there, don't you remember? Please, darling, it's not what you think." There was a certain pleading note in D'Arcy's voice.

"Fine," said Imogen, looking a little happier.

"So, do you believe me?"

"Yes, yes I do."

"Promise?"

"Yes, of course, I promise I believe you, sweetheart, I do," said Imogen her voice softening.

"I suppose you're going to spank me later though." The tone of this remark did not suggest the thought was unwelcome.

"I... I haven't decided."

"But... I've been bad, and don't you think you should?" The pleading note was back.

"I will tell you when I get home, I'll have to see how I feel."

"Do you... still love me?" This was the sotto little girl voice Bernadette recognised.

"Yes, of course, I do, I love you more than I can tell you, darling." Imogen's voice had gone quite gooey to Bernadette's interest.

"Promise?"

"Yes, I promise, I love you, D'Arcy, I really do."

"I love you too, and I'd never do anything, anything ever to hurt you, my darling. I love you so much, Imogen, I do!" D'Arcy sounded so impassioned. Imogen smiled with pleasure as if the cat had got the cream.

She started to retract from what must have been her earlier position, "I know, and I'm sorry for being such a bitch sometimes."

"No, don't be, I deserve it sometimes," said D'Arcy earnestly, "I'm a little brat, I know I am."

"Yes, you can be *that*," Imogen laughed.

"I'll... leave the paddle out... just in case.... you might want it," said D'Arcy who was obviously still angling for chastisement.

"OK, and listen I've got to go, I'll see you very soon, OK."

"I miss you," said D'Arcy making kissing noises.

"I miss you too."

"I love you."

"I love you too."

Imogen disconnected the phone and looked at her friend. Bernadette was acutely aware she had been a privileged party to something very private. Not that she hadn't seen Imogen and D'Arcy in a much more intimate liaison, she had as an unintentional voyeur at D'Arcy's house. But this was different. This was the secret language of two people who were very much in love.

"You know," said Bernadette frankly, "You really do need to curb your jealousy."

"I know." Imogen was contrite.

"What did you say to her at first?"

"I said, 'What the fuck is this article in Women's Way, D'Arcy?'"

"Now you see, *that* is exactly what I'm talking about."

"Yes, I realise I was over the top."

"And I'm going to suggest it's because you feel insecure."

"Yes." Imogen fell silent for a few moments, and then said, "We are getting that ring tomorrow, and I'm going to propose this weekend. You and Eve must come to dinner on Saturday night, stay over, and I'm going to do the deed."

"OK. How exciting!"

"Yes, maybe her publicist can announce it to the press or something. Let the world know she's mine," said Imogen firmly.

"Very good plan, I'm sure it will help both of you. Have you thought maybe D'Arcy wants you to propose? Perhaps this seemingly wayward behaviour is part of it?"

"I never thought of *that*, but maybe."

"Anyway, do you feel better now?"

"Yes, I do."

"OK, well, Olivia should be here soon. If I leave you alone, you're not going to do anything silly?" Bernadette said grinning.

"No, I won't. I'll see D'Arcy when I get home."

"Are you going to fulfil her wishes?"

"No, I'm going to beg for her forgiveness, instead."

"Wow, well, that's a turnaround, and very good, very good indeed."

"I'm trying, see, really I am."

"I can see, darling and I'm very proud of you." Bernadette got up and gave Imogen a fleeting kiss. "Now behave yourself."

"Yes, mother," Imogen laughed.

* * *

DS Olivia Thompson sat in the meeting room on one of the sofas opposite Bernadette and Imogen. She silently methodically stirred her tea almost as if it was an act of meditation.

Bernadette and Imogen both knew there was no interrupting or rushing Olivia over her tea. She seemed to relish coming to their office for a cuppa. It was apparently one of the highlights for her. Once she had finished stirring in an almost maddening fashion, she lifted her cup and took a sip. She closed her eyes in satisfaction at the hot liquid.

"This really is the best tea in Dublin," she said at length.

"Is it?" said Bernadette taking a sip of her coffee.

"Oh yes, absolutely the best. I can assure you of that."

"I'm glad, and of course you're welcome anytime."

"So," said Olivia taking a few more sips, "This car which was following you..."

"Yes?" said Imogen eagerly.

"And it was, yes, most definitely following you."

"Oh?"

"Yes, most definitely."

In her typical exasperating fashion, Olivia sipped her tea once more and took a bourbon cream from the plate on the table and consumed it with relish.

Bernadette glanced at Imogen who was exhibiting signs of impatience but trying to curb it.

"Yes, following you they were," said Olivia licking the tips of her fingers.

"Who, who was following us?" said Imogen slightly annoyed now.

"I was coming to that." Olivia smiled. "Erm, it was a couple of detectives from the Met."

"What?" said Bernadette astounded.

"Yep, operating right out of their area they were, and so we told them."

"You told them?" Imogen put in.

"Yes, once the patrol found out who they were, these chaps flashed their warrants, they were escorted to the station and I had a chat with them, so did our super. He wasn't happy as it goes to find British cops on his turf, not at all."

"Why the fuck were they following *us*?" Bernadette exclaimed.

"Now that's a good question, as it goes, they didn't know you were lawyers. Thought you were associates of young Callum Jenkins in there," said Olivia taking another biscuit.

"What the fuck?" said Imogen.

"The super said much the same." Olivia's eyes twinkled.

"So, he ought to," said Bernadette pardonably annoyed.

"I can see you're upset about all this," Olivia continued, sipping her tea once more.

"That's one way of fucking well putting it." Bernadette made a face.

"I can assure you the super is, if you'll pardon the pun, super upset. This has gone much higher. The DCS, the AC and the Commissioner himself have been involved. People have been shouted at on both sides. It has been, to put it mildly, a shit show in the making."

Olivia put down her empty cup and regarded it regretfully.

"Would you like another cup?" Imogen asked helpfully, realising there was more to be said.

"That would be most welcome, indeed." Olivia smiled.

Fresh cups were procured and once the stirring ritual had been completed, Olivia continued with her tale.

"So, what are they doing in the country?" Bernadette ventured.

"Apparently they were sent here, to make investigations, albeit unauthorised nor sanctioned from our end, into the affairs of Mr Jenkins," Olivia replied.

"For the extradition proceedings?"

"Precisely but apparently beyond that even for their own ongoing investigation." Olivia shrugged and sipped her tea.

"But that's preposterous!" Bernadette said, infuriated by these revelations.

"Again, that is pretty much the view of the Garda top brass who don't take kindly to UK police spying on our citizens, innocent until proven guilty and all that."

"So, what's the upshot?" Imogen wanted to know.

"Ah, the upshot, indeed. They have been asked to go home or otherwise cease and desist from all further investigations. If there is any investigating to be done, we will do it, that is, if we want to do it." Olivia took yet another biscuit and consumed it with great relish.

"And do you want to do it?" Bernadette asked her.

"Let me ask you something. Why don't you tell me about this case of yours? I'm not really *au fait* with the whole extradition thing, so enlighten me."

"On or off the record?" said Imogen at once.

"Off the record if you wish, naturally."

"OK," said Bernadette, she could see no harm in bringing Olivia into the fold. In fact, it might serve them well if they needed help with the case. Olivia had, so far, proved herself extremely useful on previous occasions. "This is what we know..."

Olivia listened patiently sipping her tea, while Bernadette gave her the lowdown on the case.

"I see," Olivia said when Bernadette was finished, "It seems a fairly flimsy case on first hearing, of course, you haven't received all the evidence as yet."

"What do you think, then, as a detective?" Imogen asked her.

"What do I think. Hmm, well... the illegals could have been put on in Spain, but they also could have been put on in Dublin."

"What about the customs seal?" Bernadette wondered.

"Customs seal?" Olivia laughed, "You think that can't be faked? Or these gangs can't get hold of copies of the seal makers? They have access to huge resources, millions of Euros are made from this trafficking, replacing a seal would not be hard."

"Really? That's very interesting, though hard to prove."

"Do you know anything about trafficking here? Are there any ongoing investigations?" Imogen added.

"I don't, but I can find out, I'm sort of involved at least on the periphery," Olivia replied eyeing the biscuits in a way which indicated she was considering eating another. Apparently, she had quite a sweet tooth, something Bernadette filed away for future reference should more persuasion ever be needed.

"Couldn't you get involved more?" Bernadette asked her hopefully.

"Let me see," said Olivia, "I see what you're doing, you're wanting me and maybe the Garda to bolster your case, if I'm correct?"

"Well..." Bernadette shrugged.

Olivia chuckled at her expression. "I'm not against it, after all, you think this chap isn't guilty, but I'm going to need a reason to get involved, if you catch my drift."

"And how can we do that?"

"It's something you need to figure out." Olivia smiled. "I can't do everything for you, let's just say if you found some interesting information linking the smuggling to here, then it could very well suddenly become a Garda matter. Also, since you brought it to my attention, I'm in pole position as it were. Added to which, thanks to you and the matter of Emily O'Neil's case, the super thinks the sun shines out of my arsehole at the moment."

"I see, that is fortunate."

"Oh, it is, believe me. A lesbian bitch detective like me? I wasn't having an easy time of it but then Burnsy fucked it right up, he got well slammed by the inquiry and has been reassigned. He was the super's blue-eyed boy, now turned pariah. So, guess who took the number one spot? Ms Lesbian herself." Olivia's eyes twinkled and she laughed.

She had been referring to her colleague Finian Burns who had originally brought the case against Emily O'Neil allegedly for killing her father. Bernadette had proved otherwise in spectacular fashion in the courtroom, and Olivia had arrested the real culprit who was now serving time.

"I'm glad things turned out well for you."

"Oh, they did, very much so thanks to you, well, both of you, I'm sitting pretty. I might even be able to make Inspector soon," Olivia said in confidential tones.

"OK, so if we can find a way to generate your interest, then you might be on board, is that what you are saying?"

"Oh, yes, we're not keen on human trafficking in this country and if I can catch a few smugglers or even the big fish then I'm certainly going to go up in the popularity stakes."

"Is that what it's all about, popularity?" Imogen asked, a trifle acidic.

Olivia regarded her but did not appear at all put out by the question. "No, no, of course not. I care about my job and I care about people being trafficked. But at the same time, I'm doing this for pay and if I'm going to be paid then I might as well get the best out of it if I can. I've risen through the ranks the hard way, rode the jibes, the bullying, the teasing. I've knocked some sense into one or two Gardai around the back of the station, who overstepped the line. Nothing was said but I got left alone afterwards."

"I'm sorry," said Imogen contrite, "I didn't mean..."

"Of course, you didn't, and I'll forgive you anything," Olivia said pointedly.

"How's Carole?" Bernadette asked aware they were straying into territory which Imogen would not be comfortable with.

"She's definitely a nice girl, and we are still going out. Is it love? I don't know. Is it going the distance? I don't know. Coming to think of it, we should go *all* out, you two, me and Carole, make a foursome."

"What about our partners?" Imogen asked.

"They can come too, we'll make a sixsome," Olivia laughed.

"Sounds like an idea," said Bernadette being non-committal.

"It's OK, you don't have to." Olivia shrugged. "It was just an idea."

"I didn't say *that*," Bernadette demurred seeing her slightly disappointed face, "We could maybe have dinner, you two could come over, perhaps?"

"Sure, we'd like that too," said Olivia smiling at the suggestion.

"Right, so where do we stand? Are these British cops going to follow us around anymore?"

"No, definitely not and if you do see anybody doing so, ring me right away no matter when," said Olivia seriously.

"OK, thank you, it's very reassuring."

"My pleasure," Olivia replied, draining her cup. She looked at her watch and sighed. "I'm going to have to love you and leave you, duty calls and all that. Got other cases to crack, not just rogue police officers doing things they're not supposed to."

"You don't want another cup?" Bernadette cocked an eyebrow.

"Much as it pains me to say no, I won't, not today, but save it for another day." Olivia got up from her chair. "I'll see myself out, stand easy."

With a smile and flick of her hair which seemed a little longer these days, she was gone.

"Well!" said Imogen once they had heard her going down the stairs.

"Productive meeting, I would say. I mean, at least we haven't got people following us trying to murder us in our beds," Bernadette joked.

"Don't," said Imogen seriously, "I have nightmares about stuff like that."

"Do you? Do you really?" Bernadette looked concerned.

"I do. I have terrible dreams sometimes, and then D'Arcy comes and saves me," Imogen laughed.

"Sounds like an analogy for your life." Bernadette smiled.

"Oh... you mean D'Arcy has saved me?" Imogen thought about this for a while. "Well, you're right I guess, she has in a way."

"There you go."

"Anyway, what are we to do next?"

"On the case?" Bernadette pursed her lips. "Maybe we should visit that depot, see what we can find, ask questions."

"Stir things up you mean? Is it wise? What if they really are criminals?"

"In which case, we will soon find out."

"I see where you going with this... you want to get Olivia involved."

"Yes, because maybe they will uncover something to help us with the case."

"And what if they incriminate Callum after all?"

"Then he's been a very good liar." Bernadette shrugged. "It's worth the risk."

"Good plan, I concur."

"Should we take Micky with us? For protection?"

"Micky?"

"Well, he has been doing martial arts."

Micky was their lead investigator. He was young and eager and had proven himself useful on some very important cases. Micky viewed Bernadette somewhat in the light of Wonder Woman, and she could do no wrong in his eyes. He would also do virtually anything she asked and follow her to the ends of the earth, such was his loyalty. He had come a cropper on a case not long ago and earned a black eye for his trouble. Bernadette was concerned and paid for him to do martial arts training, which apparently, he had taken to like a duck to water.

"I guess, but wouldn't it be better if we looked more like vulnerable women?" Imogen suggested, "They might let something slip."

"You think they *are* involved," Bernadette said perceptively.

"I have a hunch."

"I've a better idea. We can take Eve, she's a martial arts expert too, they would never suspect."

"OK, sounds fun."

"Yes, I'll tell her tonight and we can have lunch afterwards."

"Good idea. Maybe I can get D'Arcy to buy us lunch at her favourite and very expensive restaurant," Imogen giggled.

"You are bad, but OK, deal."

"Great, I'd better get on with the prep work for the bail hearing."

"Yes, and I hope you are still going to do what you said tonight?"

Bernadette fervently hoped Imogen would keep her word, as she privately felt Imogen did sometimes go too far with her girlfriend. She did not want Imogen to lose D'Arcy, who was the best thing in Imogen's life as far as Bernadette was concerned. D'Arcy had brought stability and certainty and above all love. She didn't want her friend to learn the other side of the coin, the pain of breaking up, ever.

"I will, I promise, I'm planning to ask her to come to the bedroom and then I'm going down on my knees, probably naked, to ask her to forgive me for being such a jealous cow," Imogen said earnestly.

"Then I don't see how she can resist," Bernadette laughed.

"Me neither."

Satisfied all would be well in that department at least, Bernadette returned to her desk until it was time to go home.

* * *

Bernadette was in the act of hanging up her jacket when Eve came bowling into the hallway and flung herself into her arms.

"Oh, my goodness, what's brought this on?" Bernadette said laughing after a lengthy and smouldering kiss.

"I just love having you around, and I'm happy you are home," said Eve smiling.

"You're wearing a bikini," said Bernadette only just noticing this interesting fact.

"Yes, and that's because we are having a little barbecue, outside, I mean, it's quite warm and then we're going to have a hot tub."

"Are we?" Bernadette's eyes lit up.

"Yes, we are, now go and get changed, I've left something upstairs for you, while I start cooking."

"Sounds like fun," said Bernadette starting off for the stairs.

"Don't be long," said Eve smacking her bottom playfully as she passed.

"Oh, you cheeky bitch," Bernadette laughed.

Eve skipped off into the kitchen, while Bernadette went up to change. Eve had laid out a black bikini top and bottom which when put on left little to the imagination. Bernadette slid her feet into a pair of black flip-flop sandals and picked up the gaily coloured towel which was also on the bed.

"Fuck, you look so deliciously hot," said Eve admiringly, when Bernadette ventured out onto the patio. Eve was cooking an assortment of pork loin, sausages, and various vegetables such as aubergine and peppers. There was a salad sitting in a bowl, and two glasses of sparkling rosé.

"Thank you, and so do you." Bernadette smiled and ran her fingers lightly down her fiancée's back.

"Don't, I won't be able to finish cooking if you do," Eve laughed.

Bernadette picked up her glass and sat down at their outdoor table to watch her. Eve was barefoot and wearing a white leatherette bikini with gold fittings.

"Have you been shopping?" Bernadette enquired, taking a sip of her wine.

"Maybe, why do you ask?" Eve shot her a sly glance.

"I've never seen that before and nor have I seen this before," Bernadette said meaning her own.

"You're always telling me to spend money, and well, I was saving these as a surprise..." Eve sounded suddenly guilty.

"Oh, don't... I love it that you've got them, I love them, I was just teasing you, darling."

"Do you really? Like them?" Eve asked her shyly, turning over the food on the grill.

"Yes, I do, of course, I do."

"But it was a bit naughty don't you think?" Eve said with a meaningful look.

"Was it?" Bernadette replied at once and then realised Eve's intention, "Oh well, yes perhaps it was."

"So, shouldn't it go on the list?"

"If you feel it ought to then..."

"I do," said Eve firmly. She was pushing Bernadette most definitely in the direction of a Shibari session and Bernadette knew it.

"Then it will."

"On the fridge, where I can see it?"

"Yes, of course, most definitely, I don't want you forgetting your misbehaviour," said Bernadette with a smile.

It was amusing to her, how in a way Eve orchestrated the whole thing. Bernadette played the game, but Eve was really the mistress of the game. When she wanted something, she made sure she got it. Bernadette could only admire her for it.

"OK." Eve returned to her cooking and shortly served it up. She ladled out some salad to go with the barbecued food and put it down on the table. There were various sauces also available. Bernadette put some sweet chilli sauce and mayonnaise on her plate. She took a bite of her food.

"Delicious, I love it," she said.

"I'm glad," said Eve sitting next to her and picking up her food to eat with her fingers.

"Oh, are we doing it this way?" Bernadette asked with a grin.

"Yes, of course, apart from the salad, how else should you eat it? So much better when you do things with your fingers, don't you think?" Eve shot her a saucy smile.

"Witch!" Bernadette picked up her pork chop and proceeded to copy her fiancée.

"Tell me about your day," said Eve.

"We saw Callum..." Bernadette proceeded to relate the events including the worrying incident when they were followed, in between bites of her food.

"I'm glad it wasn't anyone bad," said Eve when she'd heard the whole.

"So am I, we were both very worried at first."

"Well, just anyone dare to lay a hand on you, or Imogen, they will have me to deal with!" said Eve darkly.

"Thank you, darling, and with that in mind, I've a proposition for you tomorrow."

"Oh?"

"Will you come and be our bodyguard?"

"What?" Eve laughed a little nervously.

Bernadette explained the intended visit to the transport depot and how it might be prudent to have her with them.

"I mean you did such a great job in the court that time, so I thought..."

Eve pushed away her empty plate and took a sip of her wine.

"Of course, I will, my sweetheart. I'd like nothing better. I get to spend the day with you or some of it, and I get to protect you."

"Good, it's settled, come with me to work tomorrow."

"Oh, now I'm really looking forward to it." Eve smiled.

"Bring your art stuff, you can do some work in my office, and then you don't have to go home. Apparently, Imogen is to persuade D'Arcy to take us all to lunch."

"Ooh, nice."

"Yes."

"Anyway, working in your office gives me plenty of chances to misbehave," Eve said with a pout.

"What are you like? A one-track mind!"

"You love it though."

"I do, and I love you, now what about that hot tub?" said Bernadette having finished off her salad for which she used cutlery. She drew the line at eating it with her fingers, and Eve had not done so either.

"Yes, let's jump in, I've had it going for an hour or so, it should be nice and hot."

They moved over to the hot tub which they had installed some time ago. Now the weather was better, Bernadette was happy they could use it more often. It was also strategically placed in a secluded position and more recently they had put screening around it to hide it from prying eyes.

This had another benefit as both women once behind the screens shed their bikinis and stepped into the water buck naked. Bernadette put their glasses on the side of the tub and lay back relaxing in the steaming water.

"Oh God, that's lovely, so warm and nice," she said closing her eyes.

"Isn't it just," Eve murmured moving up close.

After a few moments, Bernadette felt Eve's lips on hers which were wet from Eve having ducked her head under the water. She kept her eyes closed and enjoyed the sensations of the kiss. Eve's arms enveloped her body and she felt her hands caressing her under the water. It felt nice, tingly. She lay back her head as Eve kissed her neck and cheeks, content to let her take lead. Eve's fingers were circling her nipples hardening them nicely and then one hand strayed down between Bernadette's legs.

"Oh God," Bernadette breathed softly, "That's so good, it's so good... mmm..."

Eve was kissing her all the while, her finger at work sending shivers through Bernadette.

"Oh... fuck... oh God... don't stop... don't... mmm... yes..." Bernadette whispered.

"Sit up, darling, on the edge," Eve whispered back.

"What?"

"Sit up."

Bernadette opened her eyes, and saw Eve looking into them with urgent desire. Bernadette slid up onto the side of the hot tub and Eve buried her head between Bernadette's legs.

"Oh my God!" Bernadette gasped at the insistent flicking of her tongue, "Fuck... oh... Eve... oh... oh..."

The slick wetness of her skin and the whole situation of doing this out of doors made it seem so horny and somehow daring. It ramped up her arousal rate by as many degrees as the hot tub was warm.

"Fuck... oh... fuck... fuck... fuck... my God... oh my God..." Eve's tongue was relentless, pushing the crest of the wave closer and closer, until finally, it broke. The climax washed through Bernadette's body and she tensed with pleasure. "Oh... my... God... my God... oh... oh... oh... Eve... ohh," she cried, it was almost a full throated scream but she managed to control mindful of the neighbours who even if they could not see her, might well have heard her. Her toes curled, then uncurled and she went limp, slipping back into the inviting water into her fiancée's embrace.

"I love you." Eve was kissing her. "I love you so much."

"I love you too..." Bernadette whispered, "Let me..."

She was anxious to reciprocate, but Eve stopped her. "Soon, let's have a little spa first." She smiled and turned on the bubbles while still holding fast to Bernadette. In these times after they had made love, everything seemed right with the world, and their bond seemed completely unbreakable. Bernadette closed her eyes once more and let the soothing bubbles lull her into a soporific state, with Eve's head next to hers, and a smile on her face.

CHAPTER THREE

The alarm woke up Bernadette, bars of sunlight were sliding through the gaps in the blinds.

"Time to get up, darling," she said reaching across to Eve. They often slept holding each other but Eve had turned away in the night. Eve sleepily turned over and slid into her arms.

"Mmm, do we have to?" she murmured.

"Yes, my love, we do, and you're being my bodyguard today, remember?"

Eve's eyes flew open. "Oh! Oh, yes."

"Come on then sleepyhead, come and shower with me."

The shower took a little longer than anticipated because Eve, predictably, became frisky. Bernadette ended up pressed against the glass while Eve's fingers went to work. Bernadette screamed loudly as she climaxed much to Eve's satisfaction.

"Get yourself dry, honey, I'll get our clothes ready," Eve told her.

"But I didn't do you," Bernadette complained.

"It'll keep, I promise, you don't always have to, I'm happy I made you scream." Eve smiled.

"God, did I ever."

"You did, indeed," Eve laughed.

By the time Bernadette came out of the bathroom, Eve had laid out a black suit with trousers and a very light pink shirt for Bernadette. She was already dressed in a similar outfit with pink canvas trainers. For Bernadette, she had laid out thong sandals with heel straps which would stay on if she had to run. Bernadette preferred sandals, strappy and high, but sometimes she had to wear court style shoes as it was more appropriate. She tied Bernadette's hair into a French plait and did her makeup. Once this was completed, Eve took her fiancée's hand and led her downstairs to the kitchen.

"I'm looking forward to today," said Eve busying herself about the stove, making scrambled eggs, mushrooms, tomatoes and bacon. She popped a couple of slices of wholemeal bread into the toaster.

"I am too, but I'm not sure what we might be walking into," Bernadette said doubtfully.

"I am ready," Eve said assuming a defensive stance.

"Impressive."

"I should teach you some moves," Eve replied getting back to her cooking, "It might come in handy. We could do some when we're training."

They did not train every day, unlike when Bernadette was dieting. Eve insisted they did physical training three times a week. Hopefully, they would soon be converting the outbuilding at the end of the garden, and this would become a mini gymnasium. Eve was looking forward to it. Bernadette wasn't sure but she went along with it for her fiancée. Bernadette enjoyed the physical exercise although she complained quite vociferously when doing it, to Eve's amusement.

"Sure, if you want to."

"I do," said Eve putting a plate of scrambled eggs on toast, mushrooms, bacon and tomatoes across the counter, followed by Bernadette's cup of coffee.

"Thank you, darling. Where would I be without you?" said Bernadette gratefully digging into the food. "Delicious as always."

"My pleasure, and you would be up the creek without a paddle, and nobody to have sex with in the shower," said Eve with a giggle, sitting down next to her.

They ate their food chatting amiably about the prospects for the day. While Eve was putting the plates away in the dishwasher, Bernadette walked very deliberately up to the fridge. She knew Eve was watching her as she wrote something on a magnetic pad which was attached to the front. The top of the list was headed "Miss Behaviour".

Eve came and looked over her shoulder, there was one item on the list, "Frivolous spending".

"I shouldn't be putting this on here," said Bernadette, "I don't want you to stop doing that."

"Oh, you should, but I won't... I've got a taste for it now."

"That's good, there's not enough on the list right now, though," Bernadette told her with a cheeky smile.

"Oh? How many do I have to have?"

"At least five, I would say."

"Shouldn't be too much of a problem," Eve said with a playful grin.

"Come on, get your things, we have to go," Bernadette laughed.

"OK, my sweetheart."

Eve almost skipped out of the room, and Bernadette mused at the pleasure it afforded her to watch her fiancée's enjoyment at even the smallest things. Eve was so wise in many ways, and so youthful in others. Eve was younger than Bernadette which had initially worried her, like many other things had in the beginning, but now she barely gave it a thought. She felt secure in their relationship. This was new, it took some getting used to. Her previous love, Rebecca had betrayed her over and over again, and then cut her to the quick by leaving her. She was still healing under Eve's ministrations.

Bernadette went into the hallway to find Eve waiting with a large portfolio case containing a sketch pad and materials.

"Come on then, shall we go?" Bernadette said.

"I still want my goodbye kiss," Eve said tilting up her head.

"But I'm not leaving, you're coming with me."

"I don't care, now kiss me!" Eve commanded.

"OK." Bernadette took her in her arms and let Eve's lips gently form against hers. They were soft pliable, and they felt as if they were on fire. The sparks were going off in her head, and for those few moments, she was lost, utterly. Eve had woven a spell which she renewed every day, particularly with the goodbye kiss.

✳ ✳ ✳

They arrived at the office in a short space of time having both sung lustily to the songs on the radio. Their house was a very short distance away from the office. This was a bone of contention between Bernadette and Andrew who complained about her having such a large car, and also driving such a short distance to the office. Bernadette laughed it off and it had become just another piece of banter.

Juanita looked up and saw Eve. She smiled at her. Eve seemed to bring out the best in people, Bernadette mused. She had a calming effect, almost like an aura. Of course, by now Bernadette had also seen the other side of Eve. The angry bitch she could become. In a way, Bernadette was glad, she was nowhere near perfect herself, and Eve had appeared so at first. In reality, Eve was as human as anyone, and certainly had her triggers.

"Hi, Eve, how are you?" said Juanita standing up.

"Oh, I'm fine, honey." Eve leaned over the counter and did air kisses.

"Good, good, so nice to see you two. Such a lovely couple."

Bernadette couldn't tell if this was meant sincerely or with a tinge of sarcasm. However, Juanita didn't seem to have a sarcastic bone in her body, and if she did it was so subtle it would be hard to recognise it. Bernadette let it pass and took it at face value.

"Thank you, Juanita. You are looking lovely yourself."

"Do you think so?" said Juanita turning this way and that, fluttering her eyelashes, "I have this new outfit, is it OK?"

The outfit in question was a skin-tight faux leather dress and along with the push-up bra she was wearing it emphasised all of her assets. Juanita also often wore what

Imogen insisted on designating "Stripper Shoes" which were platformed and very high heeled sandals or mules. This was in spite of the fact that Imogen possessed several pairs like it herself at D'Arcy's and wore them in the bedroom, along with several other ensembles which could put Juanita's one to shame.

"Oh, for sure, if I wasn't married, I'd be asking you out myself," said Eve with a wink.

"Oh, you are funny, Eve... so funny," said Juanita laughing. She sat back down and picked up her magazine.

"Don't forget my car, darling," said Bernadette putting the keys on the counter, "We are going out soon though."

"Sure, sure," said Juanita in dismissive tones without looking round. Bernadette was left feeling she wasn't quite in the same league as her fiancée as far as Juanita was concerned.

In the kitchen and small dining area, Bernadette made them both a coffee from the machine. The kitchen was long and thin leading out to the back terrace. It had green scallop fronted lacquered units and a couple of tables by a large window opposite where people could sit if they wanted.

"You've got a fan there," said Bernadette with a sardonic smile, "None of us get *that* sort of treatment."

"Maybe she just fancies me," Eve giggled.

"Stop it, she's not even gay!" said Bernadette with mock disapproval, "It's probably because you are nice to her and you don't work here so you're not going to ask her to do anything."

Work and Juanita were mutually exclusive things. However, Andrew would not hear of her removal on account of her having a sick mother to support in Spain. Bernadette wondered if the sick mother was a real thing, but Andrew insisted it was and that he had seen pictures. Bernadette let it rest, it gave her an extra bargaining chip when she wanted something.

They went upstairs and had only just settled down with Bernadette at her desk and Eve on the sofa, when Imogen walked in.

"Oh! Eve! I had forgotten you were coming, how lovely to see you."

Eve jumped up at once and embraced her with great affection. They kissed lightly on the lips.

"Oh my God, I can see why D'Arcy loves your lips," said Eve with a saucy smile.

"Put her down, honey," said Bernadette her eyes twinkling.

"Or what!" Eve shot back.

"You know what..."

"Oh ho!" Imogen chuckled, "Playing that game are we." She was very quick to pick up on these nuances.

"I might be," Eve admitted.

"She is and that's going on the list," said Bernadette firmly.

"Shibari?" Imogen wanted to know.

"If she carries on like this, yes!"

Imogen just laughed.

"And how was your evening?" said Eve with great interest. Bernadette had filled her in on Imogen's intentions, as she always did.

"Oh well." Imogen led Eve to the sofa and the two of them sat down. Imogen took a sip of her coffee.

"Did you do what you said you'd do?" Bernadette enquired.

"I did," said Imogen.

"Come on, I want all the details!" Eve said at once.

"Oh you!" Bernadette laughed.

"What? I do, spill the beans, darling."

"OK, so I apologised to D'Arcy like I said I would..." Imogen began.

"I said details," Eve cut in.

Imogen flicked a glance at Bernadette.

"What can I say, she likes things spelt out." Bernadette shrugged.

"Fine." Imogen knew what she was like, and there really were no secrets between the three of them. "I got home, and we had dinner, it was lovely Beef Stroganoff..."

"Oh, don't..." Bernadette said, her mouth starting to water, "My favourite."

"Yes, her chef made it but anyway, afterwards I asked her to come to the bedroom. Now when I got there, the paddle was sitting on the bed, where I normally leave it as a signal to D'Arcy..."

"Oh God," Eve exclaimed, she had an expression of bright-eyed anticipation at this, Bernadette noticed.

"I wasn't planning to use it though. So, I just ignored it and I stripped off. She said, 'what are you doing?' and I said, 'This', I got down on my knees in front of her. Then I told her how much of a jealous bitch I am, and how sorry I am for being like that. Then I bent right forward in supplication almost... can you imagine me doing that? But I did... and I literally begged her to please forgive me."

"Wow," said Bernadette.

"I know someone who did something similar to me once," said Eve looking at her fiancée.

"Yes, Bernadette told me," said Imogen.

"Sure, I might have guessed," Eve said wryly.

"What did D'Arcy do?" Bernadette wanted to know.

"She burst into tears, knelt down and held me, kissing me and saying I was the best thing that had ever happened to her. She said nobody had ever done such a wonderful and kind thing before. Then we kissed, and well, you can imagine what happened then."

"So, no paddling?" Eve said sounding disappointed.

"Not this time no, she was very loving and giving, caring. I just couldn't, it would not have been right, even if she wanted it," said Imogen.

"I'm proud of you, really I am, you did well," Bernadette told her.

"I get a gold star?" Imogen's eyes twinkle.

"Oh at least five for that," Bernadette laughed.

"I don't get gold stars," Eve said with a mock pout.

"That's because your gold star card is already full," her fiancée shot back.

"Good answer," Eve chuckled.

"Is D'Arcy coming out today?" Bernadette asked Imogen.

"Oh, yes. She wanted to come to this depot, but I said no, absolutely not. Afterwards, though, she's taking us to Chapter One."

"Oh, I love that!" said Eve excitedly.

Chapter One was an exclusive restaurant in a basement in Parnell Square. D'Arcy ate there quite often because the staff knew her well and they were very discreet. It was also extremely expensive, but Bernadette had long since dropped any scruples since D'Arcy would do what she wanted, and she could certainly afford it.

"Wow, look at you, who's all material girl now? You used to be quite the hippy," said Bernadette with an indulgent smile.

"You've taught me different, and *now* I'm an artist!" Eve replied.

"Aren't they bohemian though?" Imogen put in.

"Not this one, not anymore," Bernadette laughed.

"You told me to go shopping, buy nice things." Eve pouted.

"I did and I love you for it, I'm just teasing."

"Right, well," said Imogen finishing her coffee looking from one to the other, "I'll get on with my preps for Friday, and we can go to the depot in about an hour if that's OK?"

"Sure, go for it, Eve is going to draw," Bernadette replied.

"Just draw?" Eve enquired as Imogen left the room.

"For the moment, yes, I've got work to do," Bernadette said firmly.

"But there's a whole hour..."

"For you to draw!"

"OK," said Eve meekly, "But I might misbehave later."

"I'm sure you will and that's OK." Bernadette smiled and turned to her computer.

* * *

Balik Transport was situated in the docklands of Dublin. The yard seemed vast to Bernadette as they drove in through the gates. It was surrounded by a low metal fence with spike tops turned outwards. A rather understated sign declared the premise to be those of the company. On the right-hand side, there were parking spaces and a prefab building which appeared to be the company offices. In the yard were many trucks, cabs and trailers. At the back of the yard was another much larger prefabricated warehouse where no doubt the trucks were loaded and unloaded. There were bays and dark openings into the building. A few people wandered around the yard, but it appeared not to be very busy. She parked her Audi outside the front of the offices next to several other cars.

"This is it," said Bernadette as she turned off the ignition.

"What are we going to say?" Imogen wondered.

"We can be straight up front, no need to prevaricate, let's see where it gets us."

"OK, you're the boss," said Imogen.

"She certainly is." Eve gave a light laugh.

"Enough from both of you," said Bernadette with mock severity, "Let's go."

"So assertive," Imogen laughed.

"God, she is, you have no idea," Eve giggled.

"You two, honestly!"

They left the car and Bernadette locked it. There were steps up onto a deck and then inside there was what appeared to be a reception counter. As they walked in, a woman behind the counter eyed them suspiciously. She was of average height, blue eyes, short black hair, wearing a hoodie.

"Hello, can I help?" she asked them as they approached the counter. Bernadette could not imagine anyone looking less like a person who wanted to assist.

"Hi, erm, we're lawyers, is there someone we could talk to? We are seeking information, to do with a case," said Bernadette.

"Oh? Well, I dunno. Who are you exactly?"

"Lawyers," Bernadette repeated.

"Have you some form of identification, a card?"

Bernadette was about to fish into her jacket pocket for a card, albeit reluctantly, when a man appeared behind the counter. He was wearing what appeared to be an expensive suit, coupled with a blue polo neck jumper. He had black hair, and from his complexion looked as if he was a mixture of European and Middle Eastern origin.

"Cherry, who are these people?" he asked the girl. She turned around and regarded him with slightly wary eyes. His accent sounded a little like Turkish or Greek.

"They said they are lawyers." She shrugged.

He turned to Bernadette. "Who are you? What are you doing here?"

The tone was aggressive, and a little intimidating. Bernadette was glad she had Eve at her back.

"I'm a lawyer and these are my associates. I'm working on a case and I wondered if you could help."

He regarded her steadily for a moment. Then broke out into what seemed quite fake looking smile which did not reach his eyes. "Ah, I know you, you are that lady lawyer, huh, you defended that actress, I think, yes?"

"Yes, I did, you're right."

"Mack... Mackenna is it?" he said smiling which reminded Bernadette slightly of a crocodile.

"That's right, Bernadette Mackenna, and you are?" she replied, as there was no point in hiding it now.

"Yes, yes, I thought so," he said coming out from behind the counter, "Come this way, we can talk in here. I'm Omer Dermici, I am the owner."

He indicated a windowed room with a table and chairs to their left, it was devoid of furniture otherwise.

"OK."

The three of them went and sat around the table He took a seat himself. Bernadette deliberately did not introduce the others. He didn't ask, knowing her name was enough if he wanted to find out more. Eve sat next to her, pressing her knee against Bernadette's, which was comforting, and Imogen sat at her other side.

"What is this all about?"

Bernadette had been thinking quickly while all this was happening, as to what her line of questioning should be. She would have to wing it and see where it went.

"You do business with Jenkins Hauliers? Your depot takes their trucks, am I right?" said Bernadette.

"I deal with many companies," he said offhandedly. He waved a well-manicured tanned hand which had a heavy gold signet ring, and flashy gold bracelet on his wrist.

"Yes, but specifically, Jenkins Hauliers is what I am asking about," she batted it back.

"So?" He smiled sardonically almost goading her to try and get him to answer anything.

"A truck was picked up from here containing illegal aliens, which were discovered in the UK." There seemed no point in beating about the bush.

"Really?" He looked blank.

"It's been on the news, surely you couldn't have missed it?" She smiled.

57

"I don't watch the news really." He shrugged.

"The client we represent is the subject of extradition proceedings, he picked up the truck from here," she continued.

"Trucks come and they go. They use our depot to keep them while they change drivers, we are a handover place mainly. We don't know anything about what is in the trucks."

His answers were bland and certainly not believable.

"So, you don't load anything on here?"

"No, not at all." His eyes belied his words, he was looking defensive, guarded even.

"You've a got a big place here though," she said conversationally, "A large building over there, I mean like some sort of warehouse is it?"

"It's just for maintenance, stuff like that, we don't keep goods there," he shot back picking up her implications.

"OK, so what you're saying is that the trucks come here, sealed by customs? Then you don't touch them at all, until they are taken away again."

"Yes, that's right."

"Amazing business you have then, I mean, it must make you a lot of money for not very much work." It was slightly acidic and risky, but she was pushing him just a little.

"We fix trucks, stuff like this, we offer space. In case you hadn't noticed space is at a premium in Dublin, so people are willing to pay for it." The answer was a little pat and too smooth.

"So, you wouldn't mind showing us where the truck might be parked while it was waiting?" she said innocently.

"Why? You can see the yard from here, there's nothing to it."

"Yes, but if we knew the approximate position we could tell if maybe someone could have opened the truck at night, from outside, perhaps, put the illegals in?" she offered by way of explanation.

"Pah, it would never happen. We have CCTV, at night there are dogs, security, nobody can get in here without us finding out."

"And what would you do if you found out?"

He just laughed, but it wasn't a nice laugh. Bernadette guessed he wasn't calling the Garda.

"OK, but even so, couldn't you show us where it might have been positioned?" she persisted.

"No, I can't, for one thing, I've no idea, we have hundreds of trucks coming in and out, how the fuck should I know where one of them was parked." His voice was a little sharper as if he was rattled.

Imogen smiled to herself. Bernadette could have that effect on people. Even without seeming to do so, she was capable of getting to them.

"OK, well, it was just a question." She smiled.

"Yes, well, unless you have something else, you will have to search for answers for Callum Jenkins somewhere else," he said sounding annoyed.

Imogen, Eve and Bernadette exchanged glances. This was a slip up on his part.

"I didn't tell you my client's name. How did you know?"

The question hung there while he registered his fuck up.

"I... saw it on the news," he said without thinking.

"The news you never watch..."

59

Her tone had moved a little more into one she used when pinning a witness down on the stand, it was perhaps a little rash, but she couldn't help it.

His expression became dark. "It's time for you to go. There's nothing for you here."

"Oh? Are you sure you don't know Callum Jenkins after all?" It was a goad and Eve nudged her. The man looked very much on edge.

As if by magic two more men appeared in the room. They weren't looking friendly. One was a wiry individual with curly hair, and a nasty scowl. The other was built something like a brick shithouse, Bernadette mused, and had the classic bald head tattoos look just like the old clichés in the movies.

"Like I said, it's time for you to go," he said with a hint of steel in his voice, "I don't know anyone called Callum Jenkins and I've told you everything I can."

"OK." Bernadette held out her hands in mock surrender. "Thank you, we won't take any more of your valuable time."

She stood up, along with Eve and Imogen. Omer watched them start towards the door without moving.

The wiry thug suddenly made a lunge towards Bernadette, he took hold of her arm. "Like the boss said, get out and don't come back or..."

This was a mistake. Without warning, Eve had grabbed his arm, twisted it and swept his legs from under him. She slammed him down onto the floor, put her foot on his neck and twisted his forearm. He was completely unable to move.

"Get your fucking hands off her, you fucking pig," she said in ice cold tones.

"Oww, fuck. Get off me, get her off me!" shouted the wiry one.

The bald-headed thug started forward, but Omer held up his hand to stop him.

"Shut the fuck up, or I'll fucking break it," Eve told him not moving at all.

"Would you, erm... would you mind letting up my associate?" said Omer mildly, "I apologise for his bad manners."

Eve looked at Bernadette who nodded for her to release him. She did so and the wiry man stood up glaring at her and rubbing his forearm.

"Thanks for your time." Bernadette nodded, and the three of them walked casually out of the office.

Behind them, they could hear Omer berating the other man in Turkish.

Once out of the office, they hurried to the car. Bernadette gunned the motor and rapidly drove away.

"Oh my fucking God," said Imogen, "Eve you're amazing!"

"Just a trick or two I learned over the years," said Eve modestly.

"I am very grateful you did that, it showed him we were not to be messed with!"

"You *have* to teach me some of those moves."

"Why don't I teach you all some at the weekend when we come over?" Eve suggested.

"Marvellous idea, yes, let's, D'Arcy would love it."

"Great plan but what about our friend back there, what do you think?" Bernadette asked them.

"He knows more than he's letting on and he's hiding something," said Imogen.

"I agree," said Eve.

"Have we got enough for Olivia to start an investigation?" Bernadette wondered.

"We could run this by her," said Imogen, "Or what about getting Micky to do a bit of surveillance?"

"I don't want to put him at risk, those people don't look like they fuck around."

"You are probably right."

"What now?" Eve asked Bernadette.

"Well, we've got some time to kill, so why don't you two come and help me chose a ring!" Imogen put in.

"Oooh... yes... let's." Eve was excited.

"Calm down children," Bernadette laughed.

* * *

Bernadette drove them to Jervis shopping mall. It was a sprawling mall with a brick-faced exterior and interior of large white columns holding up a large circular central atrium. The floors were paved with large white tiles. She picked the mall because it had Fields, the jewellers, where she had obtained the engagement ring for Eve.

The three of them went excitedly up to the store and as they entered, Bernadette noticed the assistant was the same one who had served them last time. She was blonde with slightly longer hair still in a bob, with a white shirt and black suit. She looked them up and down, sizing them up and her manner informed them she recognised them too.

"Ah," she said, "How can I help?"

"An engagement ring, we want an engagement ring," said Imogen.

"Really?" The woman raised an eyebrow. "And who might this one be for?"

"This one?" Eve looked questioningly at Bernadette.

"We bought your ring here," Bernadette admitted.

"Oh! How lovely!" Eve exclaimed.

"It's for me," said Imogen, "Well, for my girlfriend."

"I see," said the assistant plainly not seeing at all.

"This is my fiancée, Eve," said Bernadette feeling she was owed an explanation, "I bought her engagement ring here."

"Yes, it's sooo beautiful," said Eve beaming and showing the assistant.

"I remember, and yes it's a beautiful ring." The assistant smiled.

"We're getting married, but Imogen here is also going to propose and getting a ring, you see," Bernadette continued.

"Ah well, right then, over here are the engagement rings," said the assistant showing them an array of rings through the glass.

"Oh Christ, there's so many," said Imogen helplessly.

"What colour is her hair?" the assistant asked. She had asked Bernadette last time, as apparently, this had helped her to recommend the right ring for Eve.

"It's blonde."

"What about these?" said the assistant bringing out a tray of white gold.

"Hmm, yes, very nice but even so."

Imogen looked over the rings once more and then something caught her eye in the display.

"What about those?" she asked pointing at another tray.

"Ah, these are platinum," said the assistant bringing them out with a smile, "They are much dearer naturally."

"Oh, I don't care about *that*," said Imogen picking up a diamond solitaire.

"Oh, that's very beautiful," said Bernadette.

Indeed, it was. The ring consisted of a six clawed one carat diamond set in platinum. It was beautifully and classically crafted.

"It's lovely," Eve agreed.

"How much?" Imogen enquired.

"Six thousand nine hundred and fifty Euro," said the assistant without batting an eye.

Eve gave a low appreciative whistle at this.

"Are you sure you want to spend so much? You don't have to just because it's D'Arcy, she won't expect it from you," said Bernadette quietly.

"I like it, and D'Arcy will love it," said Imogen, "And I love her."

"D'Arcy? Did you say, D'Arcy?" asked the assistant looking at them strangely.

"Yes, why?" Imogen replied.

"I thought I recognised you, you're... you're going out with D'Arcy Brown, oh my God, I'm such a fan!" The whole demeanour of the assistant changed in that moment.

"What? How did you?" Imogen said non-plussed.

"Oh, I read it in a magazine not long ago, I should have known at once."

"Right, yes, a magazine, of course," Imogen sighed.

"She's been a client of this very store," the assistant continued, "So beautiful, you are so lucky."

"Yes, yes I am."

The other two stared in amazement at this conversation.

"Anyway, sorry, anyway, look, I'm sure we can do something, just a moment," said the assistant and disappeared into the back of the store.

"What the fuck is going on?" whispered Imogen.

"You are going to marry someone famous, that's what is going on," Bernadette laughed.

"Fuck! Is this how it's going to be?"

"I am afraid so, and also now you are going to have to bring forward the proposal because the cat is out of the bag!"

"Oh, shit, oh fuck, yes, but can't I just ask her to be quiet?"

"Forget it, she's probably going to tell everyone she knows."

"Fuck!"

"Look do it at lunch, it's the perfect time," said Eve.

"But I wanted to set the scene and all that, and you were coming for the weekend," Imogen complained pursing her lips.

"We can still come, darling," said Bernadette.

"Oh fine, lunchtime it is," said Imogen in resigned tones.

"She will love it, and be so happy, so focus on that."

The assistant returned with a big smile on her face.

"Now, I've had a chat with my area manager and well, we can offer you a considerable discount for this ring. If you take it, we can let you have it for one thousand euros less than the list price!"

"Wow, really?" Imogen exclaimed, "OK, then I'll take it."

She reached into her purse for her credit card.

"Can I ask you something?" said Bernadette to the assistant, "How many people have you told, about this, so far?"

The assistant flushed a little at the question. "Only my area manager, I swear," she replied.

"Hmm, can you do us a big favour, please, when we've gone just call him back and ask him to keep this quiet at least until maybe say three pm, and if you could do the same, we'd really be grateful. You know, because we want it to be a surprise. After that, well, you can tell anyone you like."

"Oh! Oh! Yes, sure of course I will, for sure, I promise you *that*, I will." The assistant realised she was being let in on a very big secret and suddenly no doubt felt extremely important.

"She is proposing at lunchtime today, you see," said Eve.

"Oh goodness, wow, good luck, yes."

"Thank you." Imogen smiled, and handed over her credit card.

The assistant took it and the ring. She returned it in a beautiful box which she assured Imogen was the very best box they had in the shop for rings.

Imogen was suitably grateful, put the box away in her bag, along with her card and receipt. They said goodbye to the very grateful and excited shop assistant.

"Well, fuck," said Imogen as they returned to the car, "If I can get a discount like *that* just for dropping D'Arcy's name..."

"Oh God, here we go," Bernadette laughed.

"What? What? If you've got an advantage, then I say use it."

"Well, let's hope she keeps her mouth shut until after lunch at least."

"Oh, she will, I'm sure she will," Imogen said happily.

* * *

They were due to meet D'Arcy at Chapter One in Parnell Square. The restaurant was accessed via external stairs to a basement. It had a stone arched foyer and apparently, Imogen was recognised at once. They were ushered to D'Arcy's usual secluded spot which was a cubby hole with an Elmwood table surrounded by plush upholstered benches. The lighting was subdued and added to the mood of the dark green walls and dark floor tiles.

D'Arcy was sitting with a glass of wine when they walked in. She was very beautiful, all of them would acknowledge. Her hair was coloured blonde, and she had beguiling green eyes, and perfect lips. Imogen had waxed lyrical about her lips in the past. She was very slim and wearing a pink woollen top which hung seductively off one shoulder, coupled with a very short gym style skirt and sparkly flip flops. As always, she had beautifully manicured nails and on this day, she was wearing pink nail polish.

When she saw them, she let out a squeal of delight and quickly eased out of her seat to give them a hug in turn. There was air kissing but no lips kissing as this had resulted in some difficult discussions between her and Imogen in the past. This was ironic since Imogen always kissed both Bernadette and Eve lightly on the lips.

"Oh God, it's so nice to see you, darlings," she gushed as they all took their seats.

"Lovely to see you too, D'Arcy," said Bernadette.

She had had in the past a bit of a love-hate relationship with D'Arcy, as D'Arcy had done many things to wind both her and Eve up. However, now she had represented D'Arcy in court, and D'Arcy was destined to become a permanent part of Imogen's life, Bernadette found she loved her foibles after all.

"You are looking gorgeous as usual," Eve put in.

"Oh, thank you, Eve," D'Arcy said happily. She flicked a quick glance at Imogen to check if Imogen was OK with her accepting the compliment, but Imogen just smiled at her benignly. Bernadette looked on with approval hoping that Imogen was indeed curbing her jealousy.

"Let's eat, I'm famished," D'Arcy announced.

Bernadette reflected she always was hungry, and yet D'Arcy never seemed to put on any weight at all. She did, of course, have her own gym and followed a strict regime but even so, it was galling to the mere mortals who did have to watch what they ate.

D'Arcy had gone ahead and ordered for all of them, which Bernadette was more than happy about since it made things easier. The restaurant was expensive, and it took any agonising about spending D'Arcy's money out of the equation. The first course was brought in consisting of *Irish Sweetcorn Soup* with smoked haddock and accompanied by small bread rolls.

"So, tell me how it went today?" said D'Arcy buttering a roll.

"Well, Eve was magnificent..." Imogen began and related what had passed at the transport depot. In the meantime, Bernadette and Eve concentrated on the delicious soup.

They listened to Imogen's animated recounting with some amusement.

"Oh, Eve, I could kiss you..." said D'Arcy spontaneously when the story was finished, and then glanced again at Imogen, "But I won't though... of course."

"D'Arcy," said Imogen at this second reference to the disastrous kiss of yore, "You can kiss Eve and Bernadette on the lips... but no tongues, OK!"

They all laughed, and it eased the tension.

"Ooh, that's lovely, thank you, darling," said D'Arcy in delight, giving her girlfriend a kiss.

"I'm trying to change, I told you," Imogen said softly.

"Don't change... too much," D'Arcy whispered, though they all heard it, "I still want you to, you know."

"I won't, don't worry about *that*," Imogen whispered back.

Bernadette and Eve exchanged glances, they wondered when Imogen was planning to pop the question. Bernadette took another sip of her mineral water, since she was driving. Imogen got chauffeured into work and back again now she was pretty much living at D'Arcy's house full time.

"Has everyone finished?" said D'Arcy brightly, spying the waiter hovering at the entrance to their cubbyhole.

The main was brought of *Braised Short Rib of Beef*, with accoutrements. Bernadette was delighted at this, beef being a favourite of hers. General chit chat and banter ensued with some talk about the impending trip to London. Compliments were made on the food to D'Arcy's delight, they knew she enjoyed treating them.

"I'm taking Eve to Harrods, and shopping in Knightsbridge," D'Arcy announced at once.

"I told you!" said Imogen.

"Also, don't worry about the hotel, I will arrange it all. I know a wonderful little bijou place, an exclusive boutique hotel. I will sort out the flights as well."

"That's lovely, although we are supposed to charging the client for expenses," Bernadette mused.

"I am sure we can work something out with Andrew," Imogen said sensibly.

"Yes, of course, and thank you D'Arcy for being so generous."

"Don't, you are practically family to me, at least the only real family I've got," D'Arcy replied and then became quite tearful and had to be comforted by Imogen.

D'Arcy was a handful, Bernadette mused. She tended to take over in her inimitable style and she also was prone to huge emotional swings. In some ways, Bernadette could understand why Imogen had become a little dominant towards her, and reflected if she was with D'Arcy, she'd probably be tempted to give her a good spanking too. In fact, she had felt like it on more than one occasion once she had made D'Arcy's acquaintance. Bernadette thanked her lucky stars for finding Eve.

The mains passed off without further incident, and a light dessert of *Hot Chocolate Mousse* was brought along with coffee. They all refused a cheese board on account of being full, even D'Arcy said she could not eat anything else, to Bernadette's surprise.

Both Bernadette and Eve were looking expectantly at Imogen. It was now or never in their minds. Imogen caught the look and the conversation had suddenly died. D'Arcy who was ladling the last of her mousse into her mouth, suddenly realised and looked up. "What?" she said sensing something afoot, "What?"

"Darling," said Imogen, "I want you to come here, just come out and stand here with me for a moment."

"What? But why?" D'Arcy said puzzled.

"No, listen, darling, just, please... do this for me, D'Arcy, please." Imogen took her hand and pulled her gently out into the space just in front of the table.

"Well, I don't know what you are doing but—"

"Shhh, darling, just... shhh," said Imogen placing a finger on D'Arcy's lips.

"OK... I—"

"Hush, my pet... please."

D'Arcy saw something in Imogen's eyes which for once made her zip it, and this was also coupled with the fact Imogen had used one of her private little endearments.

Imogen took D'Arcy's hands in hers and looked into her eyes, much in the way she had seen Bernadette do when she had proposed to Eve.

"D'Arcy. You know I love you. I mean, I love you so much, my darling, and I know how I've been such a bitch, and I want to be a better person and..."

"You said all this, yesterday..." D'Arcy said softly, "You don't need to..."

"D'Arcy, please, you're not making this... any easier." There were tears in Imogen's eyes now, and her voice was becoming choked with emotion.

"OK, OK. I'm shutting up now," D'Arcy said gently realising something quite significant was occurring though she was still not sure what.

"Oh you!" Imogen laughed through her tears. "This is more than I said to you yesterday, much bigger than that, so much more. I love you, D'Arcy. I love you so much, I can't imagine living without you, ever... you are everything to me, my whole... everything.... and... and I just.... I just... I just want to be... with you for always... and I don't know... I really don't know... if you feel the same, but I'm... I'm going to do this anyway."

D'Arcy's eyes were round as saucers, as she listened to this halting tear-filled speech. Imogen fumbled in her bag and in the next moment she was down on one knee.

"D'Arcy," she said, "D'Arcy, please will you... will you please... marry me..." At which point she opened up the box containing the ring.

D'Arcy gasped and stared at it almost as if she had been struck dumb. What seemed like a very long minute went by with this frozen tableau. Bernadette and Eve were holding their breath, wondering what the hell was taking her so long. Was she going to refuse Imogen now? The consequences were something Bernadette could not even imagine. Imogen would be broken beyond measure.

"Please, D'Arcy, say something!" said Imogen at last the tears flowing unheeded now down her cheeks.

After an almost eternal second, D'Arcy erupted into a loud squeal, "Oh my God, yes, yes, yes, yes, yes!"

"You will? You really will?" said Imogen almost unable to believe it.

"Yes, of course, I will, this is my absolute dream come true, oh get up, get up, come here, my precious angel."

Without further ado, Imogen was enfolded in a kiss which seemed like it was going to continue for some time.

Bernadette looked at Eve, and they slipped past the happy couple and headed for the ladies' room. The restaurant actually had individual unisex cubicles and they picked one.

"That went well," said Bernadette as they took turns on the loo.

Eve was adjusting her makeup, in the mirror. "Yes, after a heart stopping minute."

Bernadette laughed. "Did you think D'Arcy was going to say no?"

"I was beginning to wonder when she didn't say anything!"

"I think she was just overcome."

Bernadette finished her business and washed her hands.

"Shall we stay here a while?" Eve said eyeing her speculatively.

"Oh no, not like you did last time," said Bernadette fully recalling how Eve had her pinned against the wall and used her fingers in this very same cubicle.

"You're no fun." Eve pouted.

"On the contrary, I'm lots and lots of fun. I also think that counts as intent to misbehave and should go on the list."

"Ooh, goody!" Eve giggled.

"My God you've turned into such a girly girl these days, you are beginning to sound like D'Arcy," Bernadette observed.

"Is it such a bad thing? I mean, I've got the blonde hair..."

"No, darling, no it's not. I love you, whichever way you are."

"Even when I'm a fucking moody bitch?"

"Even then."

"That's alright then."

Bernadette kissed her and they held each other closely.

"I remembered how you proposed to me, that time, made me cry so much with happiness," Eve whispered.

"I'll never forget it. I was scared shitless."

"Of what?"

"You would say no," Bernadette replied seriously.

"I wouldn't have, of course not."

"Thank you, for saying, yes."

"Thank you, for asking me."

"Should we go back? I think they should be settled down by now," said Bernadette.

"If you aren't going to let me do anything then…"

"Come on, you little witch."

As they approached the cubby hole once more, Bernadette suddenly motioned Eve to stop. There was a distinctly recognisable noise coming from within. Muffled gasps and little moans. Bernadette ventured a small glance around through the opening.

D'Arcy was sitting on the bench at one side of the room out of immediate sight, with her legs apart and her skirt rucked up. Her head was laid back, her eyes were closed, and she was biting down on one hand. Imogen was kneeling in front of her with her head between D'Arcy's legs. There was no mistaking what was occurring. Bernadette whipped her head back.

"Oh my fucking God," she whispered to Eve.

"What?"

"Look."

Eve peered around for a moment and then back. She put her hand to her mouth.

"Fuck!"

"Exactly!"

"What should we do?" Eve wondered.

"We'll stay here and make sure the waiter doesn't come down," Bernadette said still whispering.

"OK, but maybe I could take another look."

"Don't you dare!"

Eve looked at her speculatively and then thought better of it, but she smiled a secret smile. It was true Bernadette had seen D'Arcy and Imogen having sex at D'Arcy's house, but she felt boundaries which D'Arcy seemed to entice them to cross with ease, perhaps were better for being preserved.

As it was, several minutes passed while they stood silently listening to the performance going on just the other side of the wall. Visuals were completely unnecessary. All of sudden D'Arcy let out a long gasp and a squeak which was probably a suppressed scream. They soon heard normal whispered conversation coming from within and judged perhaps the happy couple had had time to sort themselves out.

Bernadette started talking loudly to Eve and they strolled in just as if nothing had happened. They wouldn't let on to D'Arcy, but Bernadette was certainly determined to bring it up with Imogen at the next opportunity. Reckless seemed to be her friend's middle name.

"So," said Bernadette as they walked into the cubby hole.

Imogen and D'Arcy were sitting very close together. Imogen looked like the cat who had got the cream. D'Arcy was starry eyed.

"Oh, darlings, just look how this ring suits me," she said showing them her left hand. It most certainly complemented her pale complexion.

"It's beautiful," said Bernadette.

"So lovely," said Eve.

"She's so naughty, spending so much money on me," said D'Arcy a little disingenuously.

"You're worth so much more than I could ever spend, my darling," Imogen murmured.

"You are so sweet."

"Shall we have another coffee?" said Bernadette, "You seem a little flushed, D'Arcy."

"It's just hot in here and I was very emotional with such a beautiful proposal in front of my best friends." Her eyes told them a different story, but Bernadette didn't let on about what they knew.

"I'm sure." Bernadette smiled.

"Imogen was going to propose at the weekend, but events overtook her," said Eve.

"Oh!"

"The assistant heard your name and that was that, I didn't want the press finding out before you did," said Imogen, "I *was* going to tell you, I'm sorry."

"Don't be, this was perfect, more than perfect," D'Arcy assured her, "But, does this mean you two are not coming this weekend after all?"

She looked absolutely crestfallen and Bernadette immediately said, "Of course we are coming, we want to, don't we, Eve?"

"Of course, we do," said Eve at once.

"Oh goody!" D'Arcy clapped her hands.

Bernadette shot a look at Eve who had used exactly that expression and mannerism not long since. Eve suppressed a smile and looked innocently back at her. It seemed as if the association with D'Arcy was somehow rubbing off on her. The Eve Bernadette knew was changing, becoming more sophisticated somehow. Bernadette realised this was part of Eve maturing. It worried her only in that she sometimes thought Eve might outgrow her and she didn't want that. But Eve seemed to have found her wings and Bernadette had to let her fly wherever it took her. She just hoped Eve's feet would always be planted firmly with her.

"Eve is going to teach us some martial arts moves for self-defence," said Imogen.

"Ooh, I would love that!" D'Arcy squealed.

"I knew you would," said Eve smiling.

After coffee and having admired D'Arcy's ring for the umpteenth time. They decided to leave. D'Arcy called up Carragh her driver and bodyguard to come and pick her up. He would have been waiting a short distance away in case of need.

"What?" she said on the phone, "How many? Oh fuck! Oh well. We're coming out now."

"What's the matter, honey?" Imogen said at once.

"It seems there's a lot of press outside on the pavement," D'Arcy sighed.

"Is there a back way?" Bernadette said practically.

"Not really no, this is a basement," D'Arcy said sadly.

"Well, so much for being discreet, I'm going to have words with that assistant!" said Imogen grimly.

"You don't know it was her, it might have been her area manager," Bernadette said.

"True but even so."

"I guess we will have to face the music," said D'Arcy ever practical about such things, "It would have been better to do a press release, but no matter, I can still get one arranged, but we might as well announce it."

"OK, but I'm not really dressed," said Imogen.

"You look lovely," her fiancée reassured her.

"Shall we?" Bernadette suggested.

"I'll take you in my car to wherever your car is parked, and I'll bring Imogen back to the office," said D'Arcy.

"Why don't you just take her home, we can deal with things tomorrow."

"OK."

"Thanks, darling," said Imogen smiling.

"You'll want to celebrate," Bernadette replied.

The press was waiting en-masse. D'Arcy was most gracious introducing Imogen as her fiancée and told them Imogen had just proposed. Pictures were demanded including of the ring, and Imogen down on one knee on the pavement repeating her performance. After they'd had their fill of pictures, Carragh got them into the car and drove them away. He circled around and dropped Bernadette and Eve at their car. They said goodbye to D'Arcy and Imogen, then watched her black Hyundai Santa Fe 4WD Premium Plus seven seater drive away.

* * *

"It will be all over the world by tomorrow," Bernadette observed once they arrived back at her office, "D'Arcy Brown engaged, who would have thought it."

"Nobody, I guess." Eve smiled. She shut the door behind her and locked it.

"What are you doing?" Bernadette asked her, although she had a pretty good idea.

"What I've been wanting to do all day and you wouldn't let me," said Eve advancing on her.

"But I've got wo—"

Eve's lips closed over hers and Bernadette was lost in the magic of her kiss. There was no coming back from the sensations which were running through her body, Eve was busily snaking her hands under Bernadette's blouse. With deft hands, she snapped open Bernadette's bra and circled her fingers over her taut nipples.

"Oh... God... Eve... what are you doing to me," Bernadette murmured.

"Come on, over here," said Eve as she guided Bernadette gently to the sofa and sat her down pulling off her sandals, trousers and knickers.

"I should have made you wear a skirt," said Eve softly, running her tongue up the inside of Bernadette's thigh.

"Oh fuck... oh... shit... Eve... my God... fuck... ahh." Eve's tongue found her sweet spot and began to flick.

"My God... Eve... fucking hell... oh... oh... oh my God... fuck... oh... God..." Bernadette was trying to keep her voice down, but the wave was building in her head making her want to scream at the top of her lungs. Her hands dug hard into the sofa.

Eve didn't stop, she carried on relentlessly, and Bernadette began to grind herself into Eve's mouth, as her orgasm started to break.

"Ah... oh... God... God... fuck... Eve... my God... fuck...ohh," Bernadette cried out as her body tensed and untensed, and wave after wave went through her.

Finally, it subsided, and she opened her eyes looking at Eve. "You witch, what are you doing to me?"

"Just my magic," Eve giggled.

Bernadette slid to the floor and pulled Eve down with her, her hand slid down frantically undoing Eve's trousers. Her fingers found their destination and Eve gasped.

"Now, then my beautiful witch, I'll show you some magic," Bernadette whispered as her fingers began to move.

"Oh... oh God... oh my darling... oh... oh... oh... oh... oh... oh... ah... darling... darling... oh my darling... oh... oh... ohh." Eve was bucking and writhing as she was quickly brought to a climax. "Fuck... oh... fuck... oh... fuck... ohh."

Afterwards, they lay on the floor together in each other's arms.

"I'm supposed to be working you know." Bernadette smiled kissing her softly.

"I know but this was necessary."

"Was it?"

"Yes, because I said so."

"Well, who can argue with that," Bernadette chuckled.

"Exactly."

"I love you, darling, I love you so much."

"I love you too."

They kissed again, long and lovingly. In a while, their lips parted.

"This is still going on the list," said Bernadette.

"Have I got five things yet?"

"Most probably, yes," Bernadette told her.

"Oh..." Eve lay back with a satisfied sigh.

"You'll be facing some consequences at the end of the week, my girl," Bernadette murmured.

"Thank fuck for that."
"You're incorrigible."
"I know."
"And a witch."
"I know that too."

CHAPTER FOUR

Thursday had been taken up with preparations for the bail hearing, and now the morning of the hearing had arrived. Bernadette came out of the shower to find Eve waiting as usual. She brushed Bernadette's hair into a ponytail, and then did her makeup. She chose red for the lipstick and nails, as a power colour, even though Imogen would be leading their case.

Once she had finished, Bernadette put on her clothes. A light pink blouse, black jacket and skirt. There was a pair of high heeled black strappy sandals. Bernadette put them on and went downstairs. Eve was preparing breakfast. As Bernadette took a seat, Eve put a plate of eggs on toast and a side of bacon in front of her. Bernadette gratefully took the cup of coffee and sipped it with evident satisfaction.

"So, is it the hearing today?" Eve asked her.

"Yes, it is."

Bernadette cut into her eggs, and Eve followed suit. After consuming a mouthful, Eve said, "Is Imogen up to it?"

"For sure, she'll be great."

"What if it's Shane again?"

"Then, she'll slaughter him a second time." Bernadette laughed taking another mouthful. "Lovely bacon, darling."

"It's from a local butcher I found down the road."

Eve didn't want a car for herself as she didn't go too far. She liked to walk or take the bus. Bernadette had also bought her a bike, particularly as the weather was more clement.

"Well, it's very nice."

"So, after your bail hearing?"

"Then we'll probably try to persuade Olivia to investigate that transport firm."

"Will she?"

"I hope so, I mean, they seemed very dodgy to me."

"They did, for sure."

"I'm certainly not going back there, at any rate."

"I won't let you put yourself in danger," Eve replied firmly.

"Thank you."

They kissed and returned to eating their food. Once finished. Bernadette sipped her coffee.

"And after that?"

"Well, I'll come home," Bernadette said in non-committal tones.

"And then?" Eve flicked a glance to the fridge, where her list was now filled in.

"That's for me to know and for you to find out," Bernadette told her, picking up on the signals.

"OK." It seemed Eve was happy with this answer.

She wanted her craving fulfilled, Bernadette knew it, and she fully intended to do so later on that night. On Saturday they would go over the D'Arcy's and return on Sunday night. So, it had to be tonight.

Eve ran her bare foot up and down Bernadette's leg. Bernadette put down her coffee cup, stood up and pulled her in close. She kissed her and Eve tasted of coffee and bacon. She liked the combination.

"You're so beautiful," she said stroking her hair.

"No, you are."

"Come on, I've got to go."

Eve followed her out for a goodbye kiss.

"Are you going to behave?" Bernadette asked.

"No," said Eve with a smirk.

"Witch."

It was their game. They kissed then and the firework show began. It was uncanny, almost as if Eve turned on a magic spell. Eve told Bernadette that she wanted to make sure Bernadette didn't forget her when she went to work. Bernadette's lips were certainly tingling as she drove away watching Eve wave goodbye in the rear-view mirror.

The thing about misbehaving was a joke between them, but Bernadette sometimes wondered what Eve really did do at home all day, apart from drawing, and keeping house. Eve had pretty much stopped being a personal trainer as her income from her art started to roll in steadily. Valentino had some international buyers now for it, and there was talk of an exhibition further afield. Nothing had come of this yet.

Upstairs in the bedroom, they had a drawer full of toys, rabbits and many other things acquired between them. Bernadette was no fool, she was sure these got some use while she was away. Did Eve watch porn? Did she care if she did? In truth no. Bernadette never enquired, it was an unbroken trust. They had an agreement of no secrets but truthfully there were still parts of Eve she did not know and had yet to discover. Eve knew almost everything there was about her, but it wasn't the same the other way around. There were hints of things from Eve's past which had gone unsaid. Her attitude to certain things, her interest in certain things sexual and otherwise. Was it wise to know or would it be opening Pandora's box? Bernadette knew one day she would need to ask for her own better understanding of the woman she was to marry. However, that day was not today. Happy to let things lie, Bernadette turned on the radio.

✳ ✳ ✳

Once she got to work, Bernadette dropped her keys at the counter for Juanita. She went upstairs with two coffees and into Imogen's office.

"Hi," said Imogen as she entered. Imogen was gathering up the papers for the hearing and putting them into a small wheely suitcase.

"Coffee before we go?" said Bernadette brightly.

"Yes, for sure." Imogen accepted it gratefully and sat down on the sofa next to Bernadette.

"We've got time, don't fret," said Bernadette detecting a hint of nervousness in her junior's demeanour.

"I'm not fretting," Imogen protested, "OK, I am, but I've got this!"

"Yes, you have, now don't worry."

"I've been over and over it in my mind, I've got the notes, I've spoken to Rhys, he's coming to the hearing, I might call him to the stand as needed."

"Then it's all under control, so take a breather for a few minutes and tell me how D'Arcy is," Bernadette said sipping her drink.

"Oh, she's over the moon. I never thought it would go so well. She was so happy, really happy. We... well, you know."

"Yes, I do know, Imogen, both Eve and I know."

"Oh!" Imogen coloured up.

"It's not for me to say but, darling, is it wise to go down on your fiancée in a restaurant."

"Oh fuck, you saw?" There was a momentary flash of embarrassment in Imogen's eyes.

"I heard and then I popped my head around," said Bernadette with a smile.

"Oh my God!"

"Don't sweat it, I didn't stay to watch."

"Not like last time!"

"No, not like last time."

"So now you've seen me having sex with D'Arcy... twice," Imogen began.

"Don't even go there," Bernadette warned her knowing Imogen's hints that she'd never seen Bernadette and Eve in a compromising position, it was the source of banter between them. "Anyway, you chose to do it there, so it was hardly my fault."

"I know," Imogen sighed, "We just got carried away..."

"Yes, so I gathered."

"Besides, the restaurant knows D'Arcy of old. She told me that bastard Christophe full on fucked her in the very same room... so..."

"No!" Bernadette looked shocked, but then knowing Christophe it was hard to be surprised at anything he had done.

"Oh yes!"

"You weren't?"

"Jealous? Oh, fuck yes I was when I heard it, but I couldn't be angry and you'll be proud of me, I just said, 'oh really' and we moved on."

Bernadette reached out to her and squeezed her hand affectionately. "Good girl, you are learning."

"I'm trying, I really am," Imogen said with great sincerity.

"Keep it up."

"So, you see, what I did wasn't really so bad... was it?" Imogen said in hopeful tones.

"Oh, it was, very bad," Bernadette laughed, "But... hey, heat of passion and all that, and luckily we were there to stop the waiters coming in."

"You won't tell."

"D'Arcy? No, not a word."

"Thank God, thank you." Imogen looked relieved but Bernadette knew there were some things better kept between friends. She wasn't quite on those terms with D'Arcy yet, in any case. Although perhaps she might be one day considering Imogen was to marry her.

"Don't thank me, it's what friends do."

"You're the best."

"So apart from that?" Bernadette was expecting more torrid tales.

Instead, however, Imogen said, "She loves me and wants to get me a ring. I told her nothing more expensive than what I paid."

"Really?"

This wasn't that much of a revelation to Bernadette really. Imogen was very modest about her spending habits particularly when it wasn't her own money. She didn't like D'Arcy to feel she was taking advantage, although D'Arcy, conversely, wanted to shower her with gifts. Imogen insisted she was more restrained, much to D'Arcy's annoyance sometimes.

"Yes, and we probably are going back to that shop, it'll give that assistant a heart attack."

"It probably will. D'Arcy can pay for her medical treatment."

The two of them chuckled at the thought.

"Anyway, I'm so glad for you, and do you feel better, more secure now?"

"I do and you were right."

"Of course, I was, well, I am sometimes, at least about *that* at any rate," Bernadette laughed.

"I wouldn't have done it if you hadn't pushed me, and D'Arcy admitted she had been wishing very much I would ask her."

"There you are."

"How did you know?"

"Women's intuition, so much better about other people than about myself."

"And you?" Imogen continued sensing perhaps a little bit of a troubled tone in her friend's voice.

Bernadette hesitated but then decided to confide what was bothering her. "I... oh it's probably nothing, but Eve seems incredibly interested in anything related to corporal punishment lately. There's those drawings she's doing and then she wanted details from you."

"Well, surely it's not so bad? I mean, look at me..." Imogen grinned.

"Yes, I know but the Shibari is one thing, and I enjoy that. I don't want to become a dominatrix at home," Bernadette said in a way which her friend could tell she felt it deeply.

"But you don't have to, not that you wouldn't make a very good one, I'm sure. I've heard your assertive tone and it makes me go weak at the knees," Imogen giggled.

"Oh stop! I just want to understand her better that's all. I mean, I always try to accommodate her needs. I don't want her looking elsewhere for it. I feel as if she's keeping something of herself from me that's all."

"Why don't you just ask her?" Imogen said frankly.

"I will, I want to but..."

Imogen's tone softened. "You're afraid, is that it?"

"Yes, I am shit scared of her leaving me."

"Oh darling, you shouldn't be," said Imogen moving closer and giving her a hug.

"I can't help it, I'm damaged, I'm fucked up, I'm a mess..."

"You are not!" said Imogen firmly, she looked at Bernadette and saw her eyes were wet, "Oh, darling, is it Rebecca?"

"Yes," Bernadette whispered.

"I thought Eve was healing you, my sweet."

"She is slowly but I have my demons, and they come to haunt me."

"We all do, stop worrying. She won't leave you, ever, I am sure of it."

"I know and part of me wants to believe it, then there's this other part."

"Oh!" said Imogen crossly, "I could put you over my knee right now, stop it!"

"You're funny," said Bernadette smiling weakly as a tear tracked down her cheek.

"Don't think I won't..." Imogen began, and then seeing the tears, "Oh don't, darling, don't..."

She held Bernadette tightly for a few moments while she suddenly cried into Imogen's shoulder.

"Hush now, it's OK... it's OK," said Imogen stroking her hair as if Bernadette was a frightened child. Imogen was quite often a comforter to many, especially Bernadette.

After a little while, Bernadette pulled away.

"Better?" Imogen asked with concern.

"Yes, you always make me feel better, you do the best hugs."

"Better than Eve?"

"As good as," Bernadette amended not wanting to be disloyal.

"You'll have to fix your makeup."

"Shit, and I've made your jacket wet."

"It won't be the first time, it will dry," Imogen laughed. It was true, Bernadette had cried on her shoulder many times before.

"I'm a stupid maudlin cow," said Bernadette crossly.

"No, you're not, don't say so. You are human like the rest of us. But if you'll take my advice, just finish the job you started and get married for fuck's sake."

"I know, I should."

"Then stop procrastinating, set a date and get on with it. That or see a counsellor."

Bernadette nodded. "I know, I will, I will..."

"I don't quite believe you but anyway, I'll keep nagging you until you do!"

"Thank you, you're a good friend and I love you so much," said Bernadette filled with emotion.

"I love you too, now go and fix yourself up so we can get going, I don't want to be late."

"So assertive," Bernadette laughed.

"You better believe it."

"I thought I was the senior..."

"Go!" Imogen ordered in her best commanding tone and pointed to the door.

The two of them burst out laughing. Bernadette hugged her gratefully before going to sort out her mascara.

Bernadette parked the car not far from the Criminal Courts of Justice. They walked up to the building and mounted the long sweeping steps. The courthouse was quite awe inspiring, Bernadette mused, it had a vast curved fascia of windows on the exterior of the property. This was the main court building where justice was administered in Dublin. Every lawyer aspired at one time or another to defend or prosecute cases here. Justice was Bernadette's passion and now it was Imogen's too, so to her, this felt a little like home.

They located a meeting room and Bernadette went to procure them a coffee. Normally Imogen would do this, but Imogen was running the defence for the hearing. Bernadette felt it was only fair. Shortly Bernadette returned, and passed a cup to Imogen. The two of them sipped their drinks while Imogen went over the main points again to be sure she had it all down cold.

"Stop worrying," said Bernadette, "You've prepared yourself to the nth degree, it will all be fine."

"Yes, I know but I always worry, don't you?"

"Yes, darling, yes I do but I'm here to give *you* advice, not take my own," Bernadette laughed.

"Oh you!" Imogen laughed too.

They finished their drinks and made their way to the court. Imogen had spoken by phone to Callum and so there wasn't any need to see him for final words after all. He would be in a holding cell downstairs in any case awaiting the time for the hearing.

They entered the courtroom which like many others was panelled with wooden wainscoting. The Judges' bench was higher than the rest of the courtroom in order for the judge to be able to see the entire proceedings. On one side were the jury's benches and the other the dock where Callum was already waiting accompanied by a court officer.

They made their way to their lawyers' station past the public benches. Rhys was also there sitting on one of the benches, he jumped up as they walked past.

"Hi, Rhys," said Bernadette, "How are you?"

"I'm fine, yes, fine," he said smiling anxiously.

"So, you may get called during the proceedings, just answer the questions, as I went over them with you before," Imogen told him.

"Sure, of course, what are our chances?"

"Good I'd say," said Bernadette.

"I'll keep my fingers crossed."

They made their way to their own bench and Imogen got the papers out from the suitcase and laid them on the table. As the prosecution counsel was not yet in evidence, Imogen went over to speak to Callum and make sure he was alright. As she returned, Shane Wilson swept into the room. Beside him was another man Bernadette did not recognise also wearing lawyer's robes.

Shane nodded to Bernadette and went to set up his own station. Bernadette looked at Imogen with concern. Last time Imogen had gone up against Shane, she had gone to pieces. Bernadette had been obliged to talk to her very severely before she would return to the court and face him. Today, however, Imogen pursed her lips and looked even more determined.

Shane wandered over. "Ah, Ms Stewart and soon to be Ms Brown, if the newspapers are correct?" he said sardonically.

"Yes, yes, they are," she replied her eyes shooting metaphorical daggers.

"Back for round two then." He smiled in a supercilious way which merely served to enrage her further.

"Yes, yes indeed."

"Well, good luck, may the best lawyer win." He held out his hand.

She took it albeit reluctantly, he continued smiling and returned to his seat.

"Calm yourself," Bernadette whispered to Imogen noting the effect it had had on her junior.

"I'd like to whip his backside until he can't sit down for a week," Imogen hissed.

"Well, I doubt you will ever get the chance now, so do it in the courtroom."

"Oh, I intend to. That smug bastard, I hate him."

"You need to focus, Imogen, he's trying to psyche you out and it's working."

Imogen let out a big sigh. "Yes you are right. OK."

"Deep breaths, darling, deep breaths, and relax, please. I need you to focus on the job in hand."

"Yes, yes, sorry," said Imogen contrite.

At that moment the Tipster entered the courtroom and announced the judge.

"All rise for Justice Nolan," he said.

Bernadette recognised her at once, she had presided over the last bail hearing which Imogen had fronted. Justice Fiona Nolan was a slim woman of around forty-five years old. She was blonde and sported kindly green eyes. She was wearing makeup and red lipstick. Bernadette thought she was good-looking, if not extremely attractive. Bernadette wasn't above admiring other members of either sex who were handsome.

Justice Nolan sat down at her bench and took a look around her courtroom. She examined Callum thoroughly before giving the paperwork her attention. After what felt like an age, she addressed the barristers.

"So, what we have here is a bail application for the release of one Callum Jenkins on bail, who is awaiting extradition proceedings, am I right?" she said seeking confirmation.

"Yes, Judge," said Imogen standing up.

"Ah." Justice Nolan looked her up and down. "Now I recognise you."

"Imogen Stewart, Judge, representing our client, Callum Jenkins. And with me my senior counsel, Bernadette Mackenna."

"Yes, indeed, Ms Stewart. You came before me with another bail application if I recall correctly."

"Yes, Judge."

"Very good, very good." She turned to Shane Wilson. "I recognise you as well."

"Shane Wilson, Judge, and I was at the same hearing you mentioned, earlier."

"Yes, I remember," said Justice Parker not looking quite as benignly on him, "Now who is this beside you?"

"This is Mr Mason Beamish QC, erm, purely here in an observation capacity, Judge," said Shane smoothly.

"Observation capacity? What do you mean observation capacity?" said the judge irascibly.

"Mr Beamish is representing the Crown Prosecution Service from the United Kingdom, he's a Queen's Counsel, Judge," Shane said by way of explanation.

"I know he's a Queen's Counsel, Mr Wilson, I'm not a fool, but what is he doing here in my courtroom?" Justice Nolan wasn't happy, and Bernadette could tell Shane wasn't doing a great job of explaining himself.

"Judge, what I meant when I said he was an observer is, Mr Beamish is pursuing the extradition proceedings from London and effectively he is my client. I take, erm, my instructions from him," said Shane, taking out his handkerchief and wiping his brow.

"I see, so he is your client and yet he's sitting on your bench."

It seemed Justice Nolan did not approve of this at all.

"Well, the thing is, Judge, if he's not on my bench I can't consult him very easily," said Shane reasonably.

"There is that I suppose, however, the proper thing to do is to ask the court's permission first, and of course it depends on if the counsel for the defence has any objection."

Justice Nolan glanced over at Imogen.

"Judge," she said standing up, "We have no objection to the presence of Mr Beamish."

"Very well," said Justice Nolan, "I take it, Mr Wilson, you are requesting the court's permission to have Mr Beamish on your bench?" She raised a quizzical eyebrow at him.

"Yes, Judge," said Shane with a sigh, "If it may please the court, I would request Mr Beamish to sit on my bench."

The judge let the sigh pass, having made her point.

"Yes, he may but only as your client and is not allowed to address the court directly."

"Understood, Judge, and thank you," said Shane sitting down.

"Right, now we've got that out of the way, we can get on with the main event," said Justice Nolan cheerfully, "Ms Stewart, whilst I have your written submission here, please explain why I should grant bail to your client Mr Jenkins."

"Judge." Imogen began standing. "Our client is accused of trafficking for sexual exploitation, a charge which he stringently denies."

"No doubt," said Justice Nolan dryly.

"Judge, to date, though we have requested it from the prosecution service, we have not received any of the evidential submissions with regard to this charge. As far as we know the reliance on the charge is on the say so of one witness which we would submit is tenuous." Imogen was determined to sink Shane any way she could, so she was happy to put the knife in.

Justice Nolan received this intelligence with a frown. "Mr Wilson, have you anything to say as to why the evidence has not been forthcoming?"

"Judge," said Shane, "I can't answer that I'm sorry. If a request was, indeed, made then we would have serviced it promptly."

"So, you're saying a request wasn't made?" Justice Nolan said allowing a hint of scepticism to creep into her voice.

"No, Judge, I'm not saying that...."

"Well, they are saying it was made. Are you calling the defence counsel a liar?"

This was blunt and to the point. It was very possible the judge had now recalled Shane's earlier performance in court where she had not been enamoured of him either.

"No, I'm definitely not, but it's just that I..."

"You don't know, am I right?" said Justice Nolan with an air of finality.

"Yes, I will have to look into it."

"See that you do, Mr Wilson, see that you do," she said sounding annoyed.

"Yes, Judge, I will."

"Good, then let's turn back to you, Ms Stewart." She furnished Imogen with a smile of approval. It seemed perhaps for the moment, Imogen was at least winning hearts and minds.

"Judge, I will come back to the charges if I may, but if I can take the first point. Whether the defendant is likely to flee or not. We don't believe so and he is prepared to surrender his passport and reside at his father's residence in Dublin. His father will post bail. We have every intention of mounting a vigorous defence of his innocence and he is definitely committed to that."

"I see. And who is the father, what does he do?"

"His name is Rhys Jenkins and he owns Jenkins Haulage. His son Callum is a driver. Mr Jenkins is in court today."

Imogen turned and pointed Rhys out to the judge.

"Right, well, we might want to hear from him shortly, if we need to, but carry on."

"Is Callum Jenkins likely to commit a serious offence whilst on bail? I submit not. He is denying the charge and has no other offences against him. Considering the nature of the charge and he will be committed to remaining at home, I would say the likelihood of him doing so is nil," said Imogen firmly.

"Alright, hmm, I get your drift so far." She glanced over to Callum. "Mr Jenkins, if you were to be extradited and prosecuted in the United Kingdom, would you intend to plead not guilty?"

"Yes, Judge," he said on being nudged to stand by the official beside him.

"Good, thank you. What else have you got, Ms Stewart?" said the judge with interest.

"We do not believe Mr Jenkins will attempt to contact or interfere with witnesses. In any case, the witness is in custody in the United Kingdom, as far as we know."

Imogen forbore to mention the main witness was a fuckbuddy of Callum's. The prosecution might not know this either, or at least they had not given any indication they did.

"Right, anything else?"

"In conclusion, Judge, we submit there is no reason for Mr Jenkins to be detained in prison pending his trial. We have no date for the extradition hearing as yet, and it seems unreasonable to keep him there until then. Given he denies any involvement in the offence, we request the court to order his release subject to any bail conditions you may set."

Imogen sat down and Bernadette gave her an approving smile. Her submission had been short and to the point. Hopefully, it was good enough to convince the judge.

Justice Nolan directed her attention to Shane. "Mr Wilson, are you still opposing bail?"

"Yes, Judge, we are."

"On what grounds?"

"On the grounds, Judge, that this is a serious charge with serious consequences. Mr Jenkins has committed a very serious offence for which he should face justice in the United Kingdom," said Shane somewhat pompously.

"I see," said Justice Nolan in a tone which indicated she did not see at all, "Let me remind you that in this country we operate on the principle of presumption of innocence, as it is in the UK. So, when you say he has committed then I think you mean you allege he has committed, do you not?"

Shane looked slightly discomposed by this, but he was the one who had slipped up. "Yes, of course, that's exactly what I meant, I apologise for the slip of the tongue."

"Slip of the tongue, is that what you call it?" said the judge with no small amount of acidity. It was clear she was going to pick up on anything and everything which was not done or said correctly. "So, he is accused of a serious offence, I get that, but other than the extradition which in itself is by no means a verdict of guilt against Mr Jenkins were it to be allowed, what objection can you have to the arguments put forward by the defence?"

Shane bent down to speak to Mason, in a hurried whispered conversation. The judge waited patiently for this to finish.

"Judge, we would move this hearing is postponed so that further evidence of the seriousness of the offence can be brought to the court, to illustrate... erm..."

This was clutching at straws and the judge knew it.

"No, absolutely not. If you had the evidence you should have brought it here today, and since you can't even supply the defence with the evidence they requested then I can see no reason to keep Mr Jenkins in custody while you dig up some more evidence, as you put it. Furthermore, it's not this court's business to hear the evidence other than to hear something which might jeopardise the conditions of bail," she said firmly.

"Right," said Shane not looking happy, "If I may..."

The judge nodded and he sat down to have a further conversation with his counsel. At length, he stood up.

"Even based upon the arguments put forward we still consider Mr Jenkins is a flight risk."

"And that is because?"

"Well... he.... We feel he may abscond in spite of his assurances," Shane shot back.

"Abscond where?"

"I... well..."

"Without his passport..." The judge added giving him a very hard stare.

"Ah yes, well, he could cross the border to Northern Ireland."

"Which is UK territory and where he can be arrested by the UK police thus negating any necessity to extradite him, it's hardly likely, don't you think?" said Justice Nolan smiling at him sweetly.

"When you put it like that, then no, I imagine not."

"And by the same token he couldn't go to the UK, could he? So, his only option is Europe or further abroad and he won't get very far without his passport." Once more the fateful eyebrow was raised. Bernadette mused he was probably hating it by now.

"I suppose," said Shane in a tone which very much signalled resignation.

"So, do you have any further cogent objections to bail?" the judge asked. She was trying now to give him an out, otherwise, he would just appear completely stubborn in the face of reasonable argument.

Shane once more consulted with his colleague and stood up again.

"Judge, we register our continued position opposing bail."

"Right, I see," said Justice Nolan unimpressed, "Well, since the prosecution has failed to convince me of any reason why your client should not be granted bail, then I am minded to allow it on the condition he remains at home, he surrenders his passport, he reports to the Garda once a week, and a bond of ten thousand Euro is lodged with the court."

"Thank you, Judge," said Imogen smiling.

"Any questions?" The judge smiled back.

"No, Judge," said Imogen.

"No, Judge," said Shane looking deflated, as well he might.

"Once the order is issued, which I will do directly, and the bond is lodged, Mr Jenkins can be released."

She stood up with an air of finality and the Tipster, caught slightly off guard, hurried in and adjourned the court.

Rhys rushed over to see his son before they took him away. Bernadette squeezed Imogen's hand.

"Well done."

"So, Ms Stewart two, Mr Wilson nil, a clean sheet so far, well played," said Shane walking up to offer his hand once more.

"Thanks." Imogen gave him a tight smile.

"I shall come about, just you wait, and I forgot to say congratulations on your impending nuptials."

"Thanks."

"I'll be expecting an invitation," he teased.

Imogen said nothing to this, she knew he was trying to goad her.

"Anyway," said Shane, "See you around, no doubt."

With that, he re-joined his colleague and left the courtroom. Imogen's eyes were flashing but she had no chance to say anything as Rhys came up to thank her.

"That was great, so good. Thank you again," he said.

"This is just the start," Imogen replied, "We've got to get through the hearing next, but in the meantime, we will be examining and gathering evidence."

"Yes, I know, but at least I've got him home until then."

"We are going to do our best to keep him home," said Bernadette, "In this country, where he belongs."

"Yes, thanks," said Rhys again.

"You are welcome, we are going to need to talk to you again, I'm sure, and probably Callum," said Bernadette.

"Sure, just call me, you can come round anytime, and I promise you Callum will keep to his bail conditions."

"He better had." Bernadette smiled.

"He will, I'll go and sort out the bail money."

"Yes, do that, we'll get the order shortly and then it should be all systems go, we'll have it sent around to your office," Imogen told him.

"OK, thanks. See you later then."

"Bye."

"Bye, Rhys," said Bernadette.

They watched him go.

"So, what now?" said Imogen.

"Firstly, let me give you a hug," Bernadette giggled.

She did so and then Imogen put away the papers, after which they left the court.

"We'll get onto Olivia next," said Bernadette, as they made their way to the car. "Why don't we invite her to lunch?"

"Are you joking?" Imogen said looking at her alarmed.

"No, we've got to sweeten her up, if we want her cooperation."

"OK, sure, sorry, I shouldn't be so jumpy, after all, she's going with Carole now. As far as I can tell she hasn't got any more designs on me."

"You shouldn't, you are right. I am sure she would never try to come between you and D'Arcy."

"She better had not."

"What are you like? Come on, let's go, we'll ring her from the car," said Bernadette laughing.

✳ ✳ ✳

Bernadette, Imogen and Olivia sat around a table at Mamma Mia's. She had had no hesitation in accepting their invitation.

"Mmm," said Olivia perusing the menu at length.

Both Bernadette and Imogen were used to her by now and so refrained from ordering until she was ready.

"I think I'd like the *Pizza Piccante*," she said finally. This was a pizza with spicy salami.

"Good choice," said Imogen and called the waiter over, she ordered *Pasta Boscaiola* for both her and Bernadette, and mineral water for all of them.

"Are you twins?" Olivia said amused.

"What?" Bernadette looked puzzled.

"Just that you both ordered the same thing."

"Oh," Bernadette laughed, "We've been here a lot, I suppose we both know what we like."

"Hmm, I'm definitely in the wrong job. Detectives don't get an expense account."

"It is my firm. So I can sort of do what I want, but I do have a finance manager to reign me in."

"So, do we, we've got a finance unit, strict guidelines, etcetera." Olivia rolled her eyes.

"Is this better than our tea?" Imogen enquired.

"Hmm, now that's quite a question, I love your tea, and of course the ambience of your offices. But I do very much appreciate being asked to lunch."

"It's our pleasure," said Bernadette.

"The least we could do," Imogen added.

"OK, now I'm suspicious," said Olivia looking from one to the other, "What are you two after?"

"I would say just your company," Bernadette laughed, "But you wouldn't believe me, although to be fair, your company is nice too."

"Kind of you to say so," said Olivia smiling, "As it goes you two are very good company."

"Really?" Imogen said in disbelieving tones. She could not imagine Olivia kept very good company at work, if that was the case.

"You are gay for a start, so there's that," said Olivia lightly, "And so you get me. Plus, I like you, both. So..."

"That's nice to know," Bernadette replied, and thinking it was enough platitudes decided to cut to the chase, "The thing is we do want something or rather to tell you something."

"Let me guess, it's about the transport depot, am I right?"

"Yes, we went there, and well..."

"Dodgy?" Olivia raised an eyebrow.

"Very."

"I expected this."

"You did," said Bernadette surprised.

"Yes, indeed, I did a little digging myself..."

Just then the food arrived, and so a few minutes were taken up with eating before she resumed where she left off.

"I think they are dodgy too, delicious pizza by the way. I never figured this place would be that good. Driven past a few times."

"One of the best," Bernadette said taking another bite of her panini.

"What did you find out, anyway?" Olivia asked them.

"So, we went there, slightly mob handed," Imogen said.

"Yes, we took Eve as our bodyguard," Bernadette put in.

"Good choice," Olivia replied, having witnessed at first-hand what Eve was capable of before.

"Anyway, we didn't get a very good reception," Imogen continued. She related the events at Balik Transport, and what had happened with Omer Dermici and his thugs. Olivia laughed when she heard about what Eve had done and voiced her approval. "He also made a slip up and mentioned Callum when we hadn't said anything about Callum to him."

After Imogen had finished, Olivia addressed herself to her food. Consuming each piece with great relish and seemingly lost in thought. Knowing this was her way, the other two finished their own food, and waited politely for Olivia to complete her deliberations.

"What do you think?" Imogen said when at last Olivia had eaten her final slice.

"Hmm, well..." Olivia began, "It certainly seems as if Mr Dermici has something to hide. I find it suspicious he tried to tell you they don't load trucks from there, because we know for a fact they do."

"You do?"

"Oh yes, you see, there has been some surveillance of his place in the past due to the fact that he was suspected of drug smuggling." Olivia took a drink of her diet coke which she had asked the waiter for saying she preferred it to mineral water.

"And was he?" Bernadette wondered.

"We couldn't prove it and we didn't have enough for a warrant. That's always the problem, getting a warrant."

"Right, so what about now?"

"Hmm, people trafficking is different, I mean, it's certainly upping the ante. Based on your report to me, I think we can attempt some initial investigations, surveillance perhaps, but for sure I'm going to try and persuade my super to let me open an investigation. I have a nose for these things, and I would put money on those people having been trafficked in from there, put on the lorry."

"We could find out, perhaps, something which might help," said Bernadette thinking aloud, "We are going to London next week to try and interview some of those girls. They might tell us something about where they were put onboard."

"Good, although I'm sure the British cops will have asked them already," said Olivia.

"Yes, but maybe they won't tell, they might be in fear of their lives," Imogen ventured.

"That might be true too. There will be members of the gang over there, so be careful."

"We intend to."

"Would you like a dessert?" Imogen asked Olivia.

"Don't mind if I do."

Tiramisu was chosen by all, along with two coffees and tea for Olivia.

"Delicious, this," Olivia said after having eaten half of hers, "Your tea is so much better though."

"Good to know." Bernadette's eyes twinkled.

"I gather congratulations are in order, from what I've seen in the press," Olivia said to Imogen.

"Yes, thanks, in fact, I'm surprised I'm not being followed around by paparazzi," said Imogen laughing.

"That certainly could become a problem. One thing I'm pleased about," Olivia continued, "I got my lunch date with you after all."

Imogen laughed.

"You win some, you lose some." Olivia shrugged. It was no secret she fancied Imogen and had done from first meeting. However, Imogen had never felt the same.

"So, what's with you and Carole?" Bernadette enquired deftly changing the subject.

"She's young, erm... new to the scene, and in a way, I'm kind of one her first, so I'm not sure she won't want to play the field a little rather than settle for the best," Olivia sighed.

"I'm sorry, I thought she'd be good for you." Bernadette took a sip of her coffee.

"Don't apologise, she's great, I love her to bits..." she paused, "Yep, there it is, the L word. I wasn't going to say it but..."

"She doesn't feel the same?" Bernadette said sympathetically.

"I don't know, and to be honest, I'm afraid to ask."

"Because you don't want to get hurt."

"Yes. I have been, you might not think it to look at me, but I'm not all the tough act people think I am. Cut me and I bleed, profusely as it goes." Olivia gave a light laugh.

"You've been hurt before," said Imogen perceptively.

"Yes, I have, badly too. You see banter is my way of concealing how I really feel."

There was a sudden seriousness in her tone, as if a layer had been peeled off for them to see. There was a hint of moistness in her eyes. There was real emotion behind those words.

"I know what it's like to be hurt," Bernadette told her.

"Well then, you know..."

"I'm sorry."

"Don't be, it's in the past. I was young, she was older. One of my seniors actually. She initiated me into, let's say bedroom activities. I fell for her hard. I thought, unwisely it turns out, she felt the same, but she didn't. One day she requested a transfer down south and, in a week, she was gone, without a note, nothing, not a fucking thing. I didn't know I could cry that much." A solitary tear tracked down Olivia's cheek.

"Fuck!" said Imogen.

"It's OK, I'm over it. Just, well, happy memories and sad ones too. That's life, isn't it? So, you see, I can see me in Carole, the young person I was then. I don't want to hurt her either."

"But I'm sure you won't do that." Imogen smiled.

"No, but will she?"

The question hung there as Olivia sipped a little more of her tea.

"I thought I could never love again," said Bernadette, "But Eve came into my life, and she has helped to heal me."

"You see that's what I need, an Eve," Olivia chuckled.

"You don't think Carole?"

"I don't know."

"Eve is younger than me by around ten years."

"Interesting," Olivia acknowledged. "You two seem happy together, and I can see she loves you."

Olivia had seen them together at Eve's opening night for her gallery show. She had brought Carole, and Bernadette had thought they seemed good together.

"You can't swim if you don't get into the water," Imogen said suddenly.

"Ah, yes, you are, of course right, I know." Olivia drained her cup. "Anyway, I've got to get back to the station, and get this show on the road as regards the bad boys down at Balik Transport. We'll see what's what. If I wanted to, say, interview your client, would you let me?"

"One or both of us would have to be present but, in principle, yes," Bernadette replied.

"Great. Well, I'll make tracks. Thanks for lunch."

Olivia got up and spontaneously both Bernadette and Imogen gave her a hug. Olivia smiled and strolled off down the street to find her car.

"Wow, I wasn't expecting *that*," said Imogen.

"Now we know a bit more about the real Olivia," said Bernadette.

"Goes to show you never can tell."

"No, no you can't. Let's hope her investigations can reveal something to help us."

"Yes, it would be good."

"I think we should focus on getting over the London early next week, don't you? See if you can set up a meeting with some of those refugees, if you can. Also, maybe it's worth meeting with the opposition to parlay perhaps?" Bernadette moved on to their case.

"Really? You think?"

"I don't know, but it might help to find out why they are going for Callum so hard. See if we can squeeze some information out of them."

"If you say so."

"Why not? Let's walk into the lion's den, are we not witches?" Bernadette laughed.

"Well, we are bitches, I know that much and lesbian bitches to boot."

"The best kind."

They both giggled.

"What about Andrew?" said Imogen, "Shall we ask him about the PA?"

"Hmm, it's Friday afternoon, he might be mellow, let's rattle his cage," Bernadette agreed.

"Sounds like fun."

✳ ✳ ✳

When they returned to the office, they decide to tackle Andrew on the subject of getting another PA. Andrew looked up when they entered his office. He was wearing a shirt with faint pinstripes and no tie. His desk was covered in files and papers and he had been typing at nineteen to the dozen.

"Ah, what's this?" he said, "A delegation?"

"Of sorts." Bernadette smiled sliding into a seat.

"I see, and to what do I owe the pleasure of two lovely barristers at once?" Andrew quipped.

"We want to ask you something," Imogen replied sitting down next to Bernadette.

"I didn't assume you had come here for an amiable chat. Chance would be a fine thing."

"Oh, come on, Andrew, you're always busy, you don't want us coming down here gossiping," Bernadette laughed.

"Well true, but occasionally it might be nice," Andrew said with a twinkle in his eye.

"We will remember that next time and remind you of it when you kick us out for disturbing you. Anyway, there's the weekly meeting for news."

The weekly meeting was held on Thursday afternoons usually and chaired by Bernadette. It was an informal affair with snacks and non-alcoholic drinks where everyone shared what they were working on.

"You know me too well," Andrew replied, "So anyway why *have* you come to disturb my peace of mind?"

"That's more like it." Bernadette smiled.

"We want to talk PA's," said Imogen.

"PA's?" Andrew looked puzzled. "What about PA's?"

"We would like to get another one to back up Alison," said Bernadette coming to the point.

"Another PA?" Andrew looked aghast. "Surely you can't be serious?"

"Oh, come, Andrew, it's not *that* strange a question, is it?" said Imogen.

"Don't mind him, darling, he always reacts like this," Bernadette chuckled.

"I do not!" said Andrew indignantly.

"And then you always deny it," she continued remorselessly.

Andrew let out a big sigh. "Alright, fine. Explain why you feel you need another PA."

"OK, well, the workload we are generating is a lot for one person. Alison has done quite a bit of overtime recently to keep up," Bernadette began.

"For which she has been paid," Andrew put in.

"Yes, but work life balance, Andrew, it's not good for staff."

"I work long hours."

"You are a business partner and it's different, you earn considerably more than she does. You have a vested interest in the firm. She has her salary albeit with overtime."

Bernadette felt strongly about not taking advantage of staff. Many firms did so and as a result, had some very unhappy individuals working for them. Bernadette's staff liked working for her, not least because she was very fair, and cared about them.

"Alright, I take your point. But even so, is there really enough work for two people?"

"Imogen is beginning to take a caseload, not the big cases. We work those together, but she's taking on minor ones and winning some of them mark you. So now Alison is doing work for me and for her. Before Imogen was taking some of the load because she was working on cases with me.

That's not what's happening now, and my plan is to ease Imogen into taking on more on a gradual basis," Bernadette explained.

"Hmm, and how do you feel about it, Imogen?"

"I agree, and I feel bad putting too much pressure on Alison, it's not fair," Imogen said sincerely.

"Right, well, I understand. I'm not opposed to it, *if* the cost is justified, and I'm all about saving money where we can."

"If that's what you want, I can suggest one way..." Bernadette began.

"No, if it's what I think you're going to say, then no!" said Andrew firmly.

Bernadette smiled. She had played her trump card, Juanita who had not justified her salary the entire time she had been working for the firm.

"It was just going to be a suggestion," she said innocently.

"Don't even start about Juanita," he said severely.

"My lips are sealed." She made a zipping motion with her finger across her lips.

"Now you are mocking me."

"I'm just teasing you, Andrew."

"That's exactly what Jessica says. You Irish women are all the same!"

"And you love us." Bernadette smiled.

"That's as it may be!"

"So," Bernadette returned to the point, "What about another PA?"

Andrew regarded her for a moment, and then like a man acknowledging the inevitable, he said, "Fine, I'll do the figures and we'll see."

"Thank you, Andrew, you are a darling as always."

"Oh, yes, flattery gets you everywhere you think!"

"Irish women?" Imogen laughed.

"Exactly, now buzz off the pair of you, I've got hundreds of things to do, and even more now you've started up with this PA farrago."

Bernadette laughed too, blew him and kiss and they breezed out of his room.

"He'll agree to it," she said confidently as they got themselves a coffee.

"Really?"

"Oh yes, that's code for him saying yes. If he was going to refuse it then he would have argued until the cows come home."

"And has he?" said Imogen as they walked up the stairs.

"He has but not very often. Something he feels strongly about he will."

They stood together on the landing.

"And did he win?"

"Oh no, are you mad? Of course, he didn't win, but it just took longer to wear him down," Bernadette laughed.

"Poor Andrew, we must be the bane of his life," Imogen said laughing.

"He loves it, never think he doesn't. But he's a man, and he doesn't like to let us think we can wrap him around our fingers."

"I'll remember that."

"Feminine wiles, work every time."

* * *

The case papers had arrived late in the day, evidently, Shane had put a rocket under whoever was responsible for not having sent them. Callum had been released and was now back at his father's home. These were all things for Monday, Bernadette reflected as she drove home. It had been a good week, and now she was about to make it even better by fulfilling her fiancée's craving for a Shibari session. These had to be done right, and Bernadette had introduced more ritual into it in the form of being very assertive to Eve. Eve would assume a submissive demeanour once their game began, but Bernadette knew she enjoyed every minute of it. There were times when the tables were turned, and Eve became the dominant one in a different game they also played. This evening, however, was all about Eve, and primarily for Eve.

When she arrived home, she kicked off her shoes as usual and hung up her jacket. This was a thing she did every day, and then later she would put them away. Eve came sashaying into the hallway. Bernadette noticed she was wearing a satin robe which left nothing to the imagination, and high see-through mules. She found this instantly arousing as Eve snaked her arms around her neck and pulled her in for a kiss. It was long and steamy. It was all Bernadette could do to stop her hands from wandering under that tantalising robe. But she did not, as the Shibari session would never, otherwise, take place.

"Mmm, hi beautiful," Bernadette said as Eve gently bit her lip.

"Hi." Eve's voice was husky, and she certainly seemed in the mood for something. "Are you hungry?"

Bernadette certainly was, although eating was starting to be the last thing on her mind. "I am a little, are you?"

"Mmm hmm, let's eat first, shall we?"

"First?"

"Before anything you might have got planned," Eve said shooting her a saucy look.

"It depends, did you behave yourself today?" Bernadette asked knowing this was expected of her.

"No," said Eve in a tone of defiance.

"In that case, I've got plenty planned for you, my girl," Bernadette told her severely.

"Oh well... shall we have dinner then?" Eve said with a happy smile.

Bernadette followed her into the dining room where the table was laid. She sat down and Eve brought her a plate of sausages, mash and peas with onion gravy. She poured Bernadette a glass of Pinot Noir, and then brought her own plate and took a seat herself.

"Delicious, one of my favourites," said Bernadette appreciatively, cutting into a sausage.

"They are from the local butcher. He doesn't put any additives in or much filler."

"They are delicious, my darling," said Bernadette having consumed a mouthful.

"So, how was the hearing, did you manage to get bail?" Eve asked, pushing some mash and peas onto her fork.

"We did, well, Imogen did..." Bernadette related the events of the day to Eve's delight, in between mouthfuls. She talked about Olivia, and also Andrew's reluctant surrender to them wanting a new PA.

"You always get your way, my darling," said Eve, finishing up her food.

"I do, but so do you, in fact, more than I do."

"Oh, you! That's not true." Eve pouted.

"You've got me completely besotted and you know it," Bernadette laughed.

"But not tonight, hmm?" Eve said in a voice now filled with expectation.

"Yes, you are right," Bernadette took her cue, "I'm very tired of your disobedience, darling, and it's time you faced some consequences for your actions. Don't you think?"

She made her voice stern because she knew Eve liked it.

"Yes." Eve nodded.

"Yes, what?" Bernadette raised an eyebrow.

"Yes, Ms Mackenna."

"Better, now go upstairs, and sit on the bed and wait for me there."

Eve didn't move, Bernadette knew this was deliberate.

"I said, now!"

"Yes, Ms Mackenna," said Eve and left her chair with alacrity. Bernadette listened to her padding upstairs with satisfaction. She promised herself to make it a good session for Eve's sake and went to get the list off the fridge.

When she arrived in the bedroom, Eve was sitting up straight on the bed with her hands folded in her lap.

"I am glad to see you did as you were told," said Bernadette.

"Yes, Ms Mackenna," said Eve meekly.

"I'm going to get ready now, so close your eyes."

"Why?"

"Because I said so!"

Eve closed her eyes, and Bernadette removed her clothing. She had recently purchased a leather corset which pushed up her breasts and formed a very satisfying cleavage. She put on a favourite pair of red stiletto mules and then stood in front of Eve holding the list.

"Open," she said quietly.

Eve did so and her eyes roved over Bernadette appreciatively.

"Now then, Ms White. Your behaviour has been exceptionally bad. You have been spending money on frivolous things, you misbehaved at my office by seducing me, you kissed D'Arcy in the most brazen fashion in front of me, and you've been naughty while I've been at work I'm sure," said Bernadette sternly.

"I have, yes." Eve nodded.

"Is that my rabbit on the floor?" Bernadette said spying the object which had strategically been left on there by Eve.

"Yes, I used it today."

"You are very bad, extremely bad, my girl. What do you think should happen to you?"

"Consequences..." Eve said quietly.

"What did you say? Speak louder!" Bernadette let loose her assertive side now, exactly as her fiancée wanted it.

"I said, consequences, Ms Mackenna."

"Good, and that's exactly what you are going to get. Now strip off that robe and lie down on the bed on your back."

Eve did so, while Bernadette retrieved the rope they used for their sessions from the cupboard. She began to tie her fiancée's arms above her head, to the railings of the headboard.

"Oh... God... oh..." Eve gasped already aroused by this activity.

"This is what you get for misbehaving," said Bernadette binding her arms intricately down towards her shoulders, and then lacing the rope around Eve's torso and around her breasts. She made sure it was tight and had become quite expert in what she was doing. She had watched many videos in order to become proficient and she had also, by now, had a lot of practice.

Eve gasped as the rope bound her more and more tightly and she felt more constricted. Once she had finished Bernadette looked down at her with satisfaction.

"Are you going... to fuck me... Ms Mackenna?" said Eve biting her lip again in an incredibly arousing fashion.

"If you ask me nicely," Bernadette said softly bending down so her lips were millimetres from Eve's.

"Are you going to fuck me? Please, Ms Mackenna."

"Do you want me to?" Bernadette whispered.

"Oh, yes, oh God, yes, please... please fuck me... please..." Eve said her voice throbbing with the emotion driven by the intensity of the sensations from her bindings.

"Yes, I am going to fuck you, Ms White."

Bernadette moved away, and put on a strap on dildo, she knew Eve loved this. Then she knelt between Eve's legs and slid it gently in.

"Oh... God... fuck... oh... my God..." Eve gasped as Bernadette began to thrust, looking into her eyes.

"Fuck... oh... please... harder... please... harder..." Eve pleaded as Bernadette picked up the pace and thrust harder, deeper, and listened with pleasure to Eve's gasps as each thrust went deeper.

"Oh... oh... fuck... oh... oh... fuck... fuck... fuck... ohh."

Bernadette knew Eve was close and suddenly she pulled out, and quickly replace the strap on with her tongue. She had barely flicked more than three times when Eve climaxed with a loud scream.

"Oh... ah... ah... my God... ah... ahh... ah... ahh." Eve cried out and her body tensed against the bonds feeding back more pleasurable sensations to her.

It took some time for the spasms of her orgasm to subside, and for Eve to relax.

"Oh," said Eve softly, "Oh, my darling, oh, my darling."

Bernadette leant down and kissed her softly, deeply. She retrieved the camera Eve used for photographing her sessions and took some pictures for Eve. Then she sat beside her and looked down lovingly at her.

"Have you learned your lesson, Ms White?" She smiled.

"I think so," said Eve smiling back.

"Only think so? Let's see if we can make that a bit more definite, shall we?" said Bernadette mendaciously, she leant down and retrieved the rabbit.

"Are you going to?" said Eve looking at it wildly, "Are you..."

"Oh yes, I am," said Bernadette turning it on.

"I don't think I can take it, please, honey... I..."

"It's not for you," said Bernadette sitting up on the bed and straddling her girlfriend, "It's for me... oh... oh... fuck... oh my God... oh... oh... oh... Jesus... ahh... ahh."

It took seconds for her to climax and as she was doing so, she moved the rabbit down to touch Eve between her legs.

"Oh God... Oh... fuck... fuck... fuck... fuck... ohh," Eve shouted as a second wave hit her, "Oh please... oh God... I can't... oh...oh... ohh."

Bernadette turned off the vibrator at last and lay down beside her fiancée.

"Was it to your liking?" she said softly.

"Yes, fuck, yes though you really are a bitch when you want to be," Eve said smiling.

"Isn't that the point?"

"Yes, very much so, darling. I loved every minute of it and now you've worn me out."

"Shall I untie you?"

"In a little while, just hold me, darling, please."

"OK." Bernadette lay on top of Eve and put her arms behind Eve's back to hold her close.

"I love you, you beautiful girl," Bernadette whispered.

"I love you too."

* * *

Later that night when the dishes were put away, and they had gone to bed, Bernadette lay in the darkness holding her love.

"That was so good, tonight, my honey," Eve murmured.

"Was it? I'm glad."

"I'm glad too, you are so understanding of my needs."

"I love you. Of course, I would be understanding."

"Everyone isn't like you."

"Aren't they?"

"No, why do you think I had to go and pay to be tied up," Eve laughed.

"I never want you to feel you have to do anything like that again. Go somewhere else, I mean."

"I won't," said Eve turned around and kissing her softly.

"I can still feel your ridges," said Bernadette, running her hand along the indentations the rope had made on Eve's skin.

Eve liked them, and said they were the marks of love. They would have faded by the morning.

"Was I assertive enough?" Bernadette asked her softly.

"Yes."

"I try my best."

"You do it very well."

"Imogen says I would make a good dominatrix," Bernadette chuckled.

"Oh, but you would."

"Would I?"

"The best."

"I'm only a dominatrix for you," Bernadette whispered, "Only you."

"*And* in the courtroom."

"That's different, it's work, and this is pleasure."

"See, I knew you liked it," Eve giggled.

"More than I realised."

"Do you like this?" Eve's fingers were teasing Bernadette's nipples.

"Yes, but I thought you said I wore you out."

"Well, now I'm all horny again."

"Is that so?"

"Mmm hmm."

"And what are you going to do about it... oh... fuck... Eve... oh... God..."

CHAPTER FIVE

The weekend began with a training session for Eve and Bernadette. Once Eve put on her personal trainer persona, she became far more assertive than Bernadette in full flow. They went for a five-kilometre run and then finished off with various aerobic exercises.

"Jesus, you are still killing me with this stuff," said Bernadette drenched in sweat and gratefully accepting the glass of water she was offered.

"It's good for you and if we don't do it then you are going to be back on a diet, honey," Eve said smiling.

"I certainly don't want that!" said Bernadette with feeling. She had not enjoyed watching her weight so much, although Eve had made sure she had very filling and nutritious meals. They had also been exercising every day to start with at that point. Now they were keeping it up for maintenance, and Eve still made her watch what she ate. Bernadette was, to be fair, more conscious of portion size and they had limited their alcohol intake which wasn't a bad thing either, she felt. Far too much wine had been consumed in the past, and now her wine cellar was more modest and lasted longer.

"No, so we have to do this at least three times a week."

"I know," Bernadette sighed.

"Let's have a shower, eat a proper breakfast, and then I guess we are going to D'Arcy's?"

"Yes, we are, because we promised and Imogen will be upset if we don't go, and so will D'Arcy."

"Oh, I want to go, we can swim, use the gym, we'll do some martial arts, and D'Arcy will give us delicious food, what's not to like."

"I'm quite looking forward to it myself, to be honest." This was quite an admission, Bernadette realised.

"You didn't use to relish going there," Eve said as they went upstairs.

"It's true, but then D'Arcy has grown on me I suppose," Bernadette sighed.

"Take your clothes off," said Eve once they were in the bathroom.

"So assertive."

"Wait until I get you under the shower."

"Mmm, is that a promise?"

"You better believe it."

They kissed lightly and then began to undress.

* * *

They arrived at D'Arcy's in time for lunch, driving in through the iron gates which opened automatically for them now they were a known quantity to the bodyguards who kept tabs on D'Arcy's security.

A high stone wall with spikes on top of it surrounded D'Arcy's property. There was a sweeping curved cobbled driveway, and to the left a well-kept lawn. On the right a low wall retained a series of terraces with ornamental conifers and low hedges, behind that were some taller evergreens.

At end of the driveway was an expanse of cobbled stones with a circular stone fountain in the centre and low box hedging. There were formal gardens to the left and right. The imposing mansion made of stone rose up in a wing shape. There was also a separate L shaped garage and cottages for the security guards and other staff.

D'Arcy who had no doubt seen them from the window ran lightly down the front path barefoot, wearing a light sunny yellow summery dress with embroidered patterns, and thin straps at the shoulders. She flung herself into Bernadette's arms like a mini dynamo.

"Oh, darling, so lovely to see you," she said breathlessly giving her a kiss on the lips.

Now she had permission from Imogen, she felt able to express herself in her inimitable fashion.

"Hello, D'Arcy, it's lovely to be here," Bernadette laughed. She was also wearing a flowery cream dress with shoestring straps and flip-flops. Eve was wearing a similar style in green and flip-flops to match.

She was given the same treatment, although perhaps the kiss might have lingered longer than needed. "God, Eve, darling, you have such soft lips," D'Arcy said appreciatively.

"She really does," Bernadette agreed, unable to be the least bit jealous of this blonde bombshell. She had found that one simply had to accept D'Arcy as she was, or not accept her at all.

They brought their bags and followed D'Arcy back to the house. Imogen had been standing watching the proceedings under the portico on the paved area. She was wearing a purple sundress which set off her flowing red hair nicely and she was also not wearing shoes. Once inside Bernadette and Eve followed suit kicking off their flipflops and following D'Arcy up the curving staircase which was part of the large and very high atrium which comprised the hallway. They dumped the bags in their room, and lunch consisting of Tuna niçoise, and buttered baguettes followed.

The conversation flowed freely over the latest case, Eve's pictures and D'Arcy's latest movie prospects. Over the course of the afternoon, they swam, used the jacuzzi, the gym, and Eve did some martial arts practice on the lawn with them. In her usual style, D'Arcy had naturally acquired *Karategi* the traditional martial arts clothes for them all but in black which she said was much more fetching. They learned some self-defence moves accompanied by great hilarity.

"Can we do some more of those martial arts thingies tomorrow?" asked D'Arcy as they lingered over a dinner of coq au vin, served with rice, and salad. Her chef had prepared the repast which they all told her was delicious. She had opened a bottle of Frascati which was one of Bernadette's favourites.

"If you like," Eve replied.

Bernadette addressed herself to the food, which she was enjoying immensely and listened to the pair of them with interest.

"And when are you going to draw me again, Eve?" D'Arcy pouted.

Eve had done several drawings of D'Arcy for her exhibition which were nudes and had sold for quite sizeable sums.

"I didn't bring my materials, D'Arcy, but next time," Eve told her.

"She's doing spanking pictures now," said Imogen.

Bernadette giggled at this, which was typical of Imogen's bluntness.

"What?" D'Arcy coloured slightly hearing this. She was no prude, but Bernadette suspected it was close to the mark in terms of her sexual tastes since she and Imogen had got together.

"They are NOT, Imogen, they are metaphors, and they have some flagellation in them but that's an analogy," Eve laughed.

"Well, OK," said Imogen in a tone which didn't quite sound as if she believed her.

"Hmm, flagellation... well... in that case..." D'Arcy said speculatively. It seemed as if she was perhaps considering the idea.

"No," said Imogen firmly.

"But you were in that picture with the whip and everything," said D'Arcy with another pout.

"That's different."

"I don't see how..."

Imogen gave her a quelling look and D'Arcy subsided. This was not lost on Bernadette nor Eve. Imogen was still the boss of this relationship, that much was clear. She may have curbed her jealousy, but she was still very assertive towards D'Arcy when she wanted to be. However, D'Arcy didn't seem to mind. In fact, according to Imogen, she liked it.

Although, Bernadette couldn't help but think it was prudent for D'Arcy not to be involved in those types of pictures, since the press would pick up on any kind of fetish style art involving D'Arcy.

"It wouldn't be good for your image, darling, don't you think?" said Bernadette coming to the rescue.

"Oh, yes I see, perhaps you are right," said D'Arcy. Her image was everything, and she had been very much pilloried in the media in the past. Her past had been thoroughly exposed to the press including the invented and exaggerated parts of it. Her agent had impressed upon her the importance of keeping her private life as private as she could. She was certainly trying harder to do so. Once bitten twice shy, and the court case had cost her dearly in terms of her state of mind.

"That's what I meant, honey," said Imogen reaching over and squeezing D'Arcy's hand.

"You're so strict," D'Arcy whispered.

"Because you want it," Imogen whispered back.

The exchange though said in undertones was heard by both Bernadette and Eve, although, they pretended they hadn't.

"So, anyway," said D'Arcy moving on from this topic, "When are you and Eve going to get married?"

This wasn't necessarily a topic Bernadette wanted to discuss, but it was no surprise D'Arcy brought it up. She loved to get involved and run other people's lives if she could.

"We haven't set a date," said Bernadette sliding a glance at Eve.

"But why? I mean, we want to get married very soon. Don't we, honey?" D'Arcy looked at Imogen.

"Yes, we do," Imogen assured her with a smile.

"And you two were first, so you should get married before us," D'Arcy continued.

Bernadette sighed inwardly, what D'Arcy said was true and she just wasn't confronting it at all. She opted for prevarication knowing full well this would probably not wash with D'Arcy at all.

"I know, we've got to think of a venue, who to invite, things like that, get a dress."

"Oh, my goodness but you could get married here," said D'Arcy immediately, clapping her hands.

"We could, I guess..." said Bernadette who had not really considered the idea.

"I think it's a good idea," Eve put in.

"You do?" Bernadette said surprised.

This was unexpected and perhaps it signalled to her Eve was keen to finish the job.

"Yes, why not, we got engaged here. Maybe it would be a good idea."

D'Arcy immediately interpreted this as assent from them both.

"Right," said D'Arcy, "That's settled now you two just think of a date and we can make all the arrangements."

There was something about the way D'Arcy said 'we' which made Bernadette feel as if all the arrangements would suddenly slip from her grasp as D'Arcy took over. She forbore the say anything at this juncture and she didn't want to upset her friend. Though, in some ways, she wanted to do the arrangements, in another way she wasn't getting on with it. Perhaps it might be a good thing, she mused.

"Yes, we'll discuss it for sure," said Eve with a smile.

"Then once you've tied the knot, Imogen and I can go next, and that will be such fun! I have such great ideas for our wedding," said D'Arcy happily.

Bernadette wondered what Imogen would think of this, and indeed whether her family had been spoken to. They would no doubt be aware now from the media attention. She resolved to quiz her about it at the next opportunity. There was a point where Imogen had not told her family she was gay. Imogen had been very reluctant to broach it with them. They hadn't talked about it again. Imogen had not mentioned it to Bernadette since, but surely, her family would know by now. In a way, she and Eve were Imogen's family now, in any case.

They finished the main course by the time the discussion about weddings was over, and there was a cheesecake to follow with coffee. Afterwards, they repaired to D'Arcy's movie room, which she had set up with a big screen and comfortable seats to watch one of her movies together. This had been Imogen's idea. She was very proud of D'Arcy and in fact, D'Arcy was a very fine actress when given the opportunity and a role to shine in. They all pronounced the movie fantastic and D'Arcy was duly gratified with their praise.

After the movie, they repaired to their respective bedrooms. D'Arcy and Imogen had a bedroom a few doors along the hallway from them. Their room was nicely appointed, and they had stayed in it before. D'Arcy was a very tasteful decorator and not too ostentatious in spite of her wealth. The room had a four-poster bed, windows facing out to the front, and comfortable chairs. They also had an en-suite bathroom with a rain shower and jacuzzi bath. The colour theme was yellows, oranges and golds. The bed had crisp white linen, and the floor, like most of those, were polished wood.

Bernadette stripped off her clothes and put on a short black satin classic nightdress with shoestring straps and advanced on Eve. Eve wore a similar styled maroon one but with a lacy front. Wordlessly Bernadette began to kiss her and was about to move the activities to the bed, when Eve pulled away.

"Listen," she whispered.

"What?" said Bernadette who was feeling exceptionally frisky and was running her hands under Eve's nightgown.

"That, can't you hear it?"

"Babe!" Bernadette protested as Eve tiptoed to the door to their room and eased it open a crack. She beckoned to Bernadette. "What?"

"Come here, listen."

Bernadette did so and as she neared the door there was the unmistakable sound of a leather paddle on bare skin, making a very audible *smack* in rhythmic repetition.

"Fuck!" said Bernadette and moved to close the door.

"Don't, I want to hear," said Eve her eyes suddenly bright with anticipation.

Bernadette listened again and through the stillness of the corridor they could make out both Imogen's and D'Arcy's voice in between the smacking noises.

"This *smack* is to teach you *smack* to behave *smack* do you understand *smack*..." Imogen was saying.

The smacks were punctuated by little gasps and squeals from D'Arcy.

"You've *smack* been asking for this *smack* all week *smack* and now you're getting *smack* a well-deserved *smack* spanking..."

"Oh... oh God... Imogen... darling... ow... yes... oh... I have... ow... ow... oh my God... ow... I'm so sorry... darling... ow... I deserve it... ow... yes I do... ow..." D'Arcy was saying.

Bernadette who had been intent on listening to this performance with a slow smile playing on her lips suddenly turned her head back to Eve. To her surprise, Eve was pressed against the wall next to the door, with her head laid back and her hand moving quickly between her legs. Her eyes were closed, and she was biting her lip listening intently to the sounds.

Wordlessly, Bernadette pressed against her, and gently removed Eve's hand replacing it with hers. If Eve was going to get off on this then she was going to be the one getting her off. They continued to listen to the now very audible spanking while Eve got closer and closer to her climax. Suddenly she squeezed legs tightly, shuddered and moaned quietly though it was clear she was suppressing the desire to turn up the volume.

"Oh... honey... honey... honey..." Eve breathed, pushing up on her toes tensing her muscles.

As she relaxed, Bernadette kissed her now fully aroused and almost rampant with desire herself. She shut the door quietly and led Eve to the bed. She lay back, opened her legs by way of invitation but Eve needed no second bidding and set to work with her silver tongue.

"Oh... fuck... my God... Eve... what you do... oh... oh my God... Eve... oh... fuck..." Bernadette cried out unable to stop herself, "Oh... oh... oh... oh... oh... oh... ohh." Lost in the sensations of her fiancée's tongue she rapidly approached her climax exceptionally noisily, until the wave broke, and she cried out her voice echoing around the room, "Oh... Eve... oh... God... Eve... ohh."

It took some time to come down from the endorphin high but finally she slid under the covers. Eve stood up and went to listen again, but Imogen had obviously finished her chastisement of D'Arcy.

"Well," said Eve, also slipping under the covers and pulling in close, wrapping her arms around Bernadette, "That was loud."

"Me or them?" Bernadette giggled.

"Both," Eve giggled too.

"I know Imogen thinks she's hard done by because I've seen her having sex twice, so maybe this will mollify her a little."

"Hmm, is that so? Then we should do it again, but we can both be thunderously loud this time," Eve said mischievously.

"Let's have a rest first, and then maybe..." Bernadette said softly.

"I love you." Eve kissed her.

"I love you too."

"I love you more."

Bernadette smiled, in the dark.

"It really turned you on, didn't it?"

"Yes, yes it did."

"You're such a naughty girl." Bernadette kissed her again.

"Do you think badly of me?"

"No, why should I?"

"I don't know," Eve sighed.

"Kiss me, darling," said Bernadette, "Just kiss me."

"I thought you wanted a rest."

"Well, maybe now I don't..."

❋ ❋ ❋

In the morning, at breakfast, they all appeared in robes or dressing gowns. Given it was Sunday Bernadette and Eve had simply lain in bed snuggling close, enjoying the intimacy of not having to do anything in particular. Bernadette thought back to the previous night and how Eve had become so aroused by the sound of Imogen spanking D'Arcy. There must be triggers there somewhere she felt, although she wasn't sure she had the courage to ask Eve, and certainly not at D'Arcy's place. She shelved it until maybe a more propitious time, perhaps the following weekend. It wasn't that she felt in any way less of Eve, but she wanted to understand, and if there were secrets, she wanted to know what they were. After all, they were to be together for life, there shouldn't be secrets between them, she reflected. She pushed the thoughts aside, if she carried on then Eve would pick them up like the witch she was.

"Hello, lovebirds," said D'Arcy with a smirk on her face. This told Bernadette their efforts to be heard had not gone unnoticed.

"I hope we didn't disturb you last night," Bernadette replied taking a seat.

"No, quite the contrary, it was very.... enlightening."

"I'm glad to hear it," Bernadette said smiling apparently unfazed by the innuendos.

Constantina came in and greeted them effusively. It had been her night off the previous night. She was the live-in housekeeper, who had also been a witness at D'Arcy's hearing. She was a feisty good-looking woman of around forty years of age.

"Ah, Bernadette, how are you, how are you, and, Eve, oh so nice for seeing you," she said as they both gave her a hug.

After a few minutes catching up, she went off to the kitchen to bring in the breakfast. It consisted of eggs, bacon, mushrooms, tomatoes, fried aubergine, homemade hash browns, toast and coffee.

"This is delicious," said Bernadette eyeing it hungrily.

"I guess a night of rampant sex does wonders for the appetite," said Imogen.

"I'm sure you would know," Bernadette shot back, "Anyway, it's nothing D'Arcy hasn't heard or seen before."

She was referring to the time D'Arcy turned up unannounced at their place one Saturday when they had just started handling her case. They were in the middle of a Shibari session and Bernadette had left D'Arcy downstairs for a few moments, so she could finish the job. D'Arcy however, found her way upstairs, and observed them in *flagrante delicto*. This was some time ago. They had been trying to be more circumspect since then, but it appeared when they went to D'Arcy's house, somehow all bets were off.

"Well, now *I've* heard it, at least," Imogen replied her eyes dancing.

"And that's as far as you are going to get," Bernadette told her firmly.

"She's no fun, is she, Eve?" Imogen said in a teasing voice.

"Well... she's a lot of fun, at least with me," Eve said teasing her back.

"Can we get off the subject of sex now?" Bernadette put in.

"You brought it up," Imogen laughed.

"I did not."

"Didn't sound like it, last night."

"Oh stop!"

"Fine, but to be honest it was better than the porn channel," Imogen giggled.

"I said stop it!"

All of them collapsed in a fit of giggles and then for the next few moments devoted themselves to eating the breakfast which was otherwise going to get cold.

"I've never thought of having aubergine, it's delicious," said Eve, "Do you like it, honey?"

"I love it," said Bernadette.

"Then I will try to get some for our breakfasts too, sometimes."

"See how she looks after me," said Bernadette to the others.

"We've certainly heard it," said Imogen at once.

"I'm not going to hear the end of this am I?"

"There's still quite a bit of mileage in it, darling, so..."

Bernadette shook her head. Neither she nor Eve mentioned the spanking noises, however. They wanted to preserve D'Arcy's modesty on the subject. Bernadette assumed D'Arcy thought they wouldn't have heard anything because they were being so loud themselves.

"So, are we doing some more martial arts?" D'Arcy wanted to know, tiring of sexual banter.

"Sure, if you like," said Eve, "And exercises, a swim."

"A bit like yesterday then," said Imogen.

"Yes, it's great to be able to relax."

"Have we sorted out the hotels and stuff for next week?" Bernadette wanted to know.

"I'll finalise it on Monday."

"Not work, not today." D'Arcy made a face.

"Sorry," said Imogen contrite.

"It's OK, my darling, I love you." D'Arcy leaned over to kiss her.

Bernadette observed this with interest. It would seem as if whatever went on in the bedroom brought them closer together. It couldn't be a bad thing.

After breakfast, they had a swim. Played croquet on the lawn out the back with a croquet set which D'Arcy had just acquired. This engendered much hilarity and good-natured arguments. Eve led them in an exercise session, and after lunch, they did martial arts again. D'Arcy in particular entered into it with great enthusiasm and said she was going to get a personal martial arts trainer for her and Imogen. They swam and had tea and then finally they had to go.

"I've had a lovely time, darling," said Bernadette hugging a tearful D'Arcy.

"Don't cry, honey, we'll see you again soon," Eve told her.

"I just love having you both around, it was so nice, just like a family, and I'll miss you when you're gone," D'Arcy sniffed.

"Well, you are part of our family now, all four of us together," Bernadette found herself saying.

"Oh, really?" said D'Arcy brightening up.

"Yes, so cheer up, buttercup, we both love you to bits and Imogen too, we will see you soon I promise."

They kissed Imogen and D'Arcy goodbye. Bernadette watched a slightly forlorn D'Arcy with her arm around Imogen waving goodbye as they pulled away.

"Do you think she'll ever grow up?" Bernadette wondered as the car picked up speed.

"Do you want her to? She wouldn't be D'Arcy if she did," said Eve.

"I suppose you're right."

"You love her to bits, admit it," Eve said smiling.

"I do, it's true, she annoyed me so much for a long time but now she's part of our sisterhood."

"Amen to that."

✳ ✳ ✳

Monday arrived all too quickly and once more the alarm, and the light sneaking around the cracks at the edge of the blinds woke Bernadette and Eve.

"Oh God, is it that time already?" Eve said sleepily.

"Yes, it is, my love." Bernadette smiled.

"You were certainly my love last night," said Eve snuggling close.

"And you mine."

They kissed lightly. They had spent the evening before not doing much at all. Eve had read a book while Bernadette lay on the sofa with her head in Eve's lap, so that Eve could stroke her hair. She liked this and also the luxury of lying there thinking about nothing much at all. She had dozed off, and then after a light supper, they had gone to bed, with inevitable consequences. The exercise and the sex had tired them both out.

"I slept like a log."

"Me too," Eve yawned, "Anyway, come on, go and have your shower, I'll sort out your clothes."

"Yes, OK."

Bernadette completed her morning ritual She had a shower, washed her hair and let Eve plait it for her. Eve did two pigtail plaits and tied them up. Then Eve did her makeup and Bernadette got dressed. Eve had laid out a light blue skirt, pale yellow blouse and a black jacket, coupled with strappy heels. When Bernadette came downstairs the usual tantalising odour of eggs and bacon assailed her.

Eve put Bernadette's plate of scrambled eggs, bacon and toast down on the breakfast bar, and a mug of coffee. She took a seat herself.

"Thank you, darling," said Bernadette digging into her eggs.

"My pleasure." Eve smiled.

"Can you, maybe get some clothes out for us, in case we go tomorrow, I think enough for us until Friday, we'll probably come back then. I'll need smart lawyer like stuff, and some casual for evenings. Please, darling, if it's not too much trouble," said Bernadette.

"Of course, and I'll sort my clothes out too, do you think we'll fly out tomorrow?"

"Yes, I think so. Imogen is arranging everything so I'm leaving it to her."

"OK, well, I'll make sure we've got our passports and stuff ready."

"Yes, good thinking. And also, just think, when we are married, you can get a new one, with your new name in, if... if you want to."

"Of course I do." Eve hesitated and put down her fork. "Are we going to get married? I mean soon."

"Yes, we should."

"OK, well then, after this week's over, let's talk about it properly."

"Yes, let's."

"Do you promise?"

"I promise."

Eve pulled her closer and held her against her half naked torso. "Because... you know, if you break that promise I'll have you standing upstairs with your hands on the wall for an hour in heels," she whispered.

"An hour!" Bernadette's eyes grew wide.

"Yes, so... don't break your promises to me lightly." Eve's eyes danced.

She was, of course, referring to a game they played during Bernadette's diet where Eve had 'punished' her by this method for eating biscuits, which Bernadette had done on purpose. It was half an hour that time followed by sex. Bernadette had found it arousing as well as extraordinarily difficult in many ways.

"You witch," Bernadette breathed, "And now you are making me so horny."

"Eat your breakfast darling," Eve told her letting her go.

"OK." Bernadette almost pouted but she sat down and finished her meal, and then her coffee. Eve did too.

"I've got to go now," said Bernadette.

"Mmm, then come here." Eve stood up, tilting up her face for a kiss.

As Bernadette kissed her, she felt Eve's hand move lightly under her skirt and then inside her knickers. Her fingers began to move relentlessly. The suddenness of it turned Bernadette on even more.

"Oh... fuck... I didn't expect... oh fuck... oh... shit... oh... fuck... ohh," she cried out climaxing very quickly. Eve had already aroused her and it didn't take long to reach the finish line.

"Is that better?" Eve smiled, removing her hand and smoothing down her fiancée's skirt.

"Oh, yes, much."

"I'm glad."

At the front door, a still flustered Bernadette was once more lost in her fiancée's kiss before opening the door and getting into her car. She drove it away almost on automatic still on a high. Eve was waving from the doorway barefoot and fancy free, just as she always did, and just as Bernadette always loved her to be. She smiled to herself and turned on the radio.

✳ ✳ ✳

Back in her office, it wasn't long before Imogen arrived with two coffees and an armful of papers. She deposited these on the coffee table by the sofas, and Bernadette took her seat beside her.

"Well?" she said taking a sip of her drink, "How was the rest of the weekend?"

"It was good, very good." Imogen smiled. "Was it good for you? Oh well, I know it was, of course in one way."

This was a way for Imogen to get one more dig in about the noise, but Bernadette let it pass. It was going to be one of their little jokes, she could tell.

"We loved it, all of it," said Bernadette.

"I'm glad, it meant so much to D'Arcy, she cried like a baby after you were gone, it took me some time to console her."

"She feels things deeply I know."

"Perhaps you can come again soon? For D'Arcy, I mean, I loved having you too, of course, I did," Imogen said softly.

Bernadette could tell from this speech, how much D'Arcy meant to her friend. This was a deep and true love for certain, and it made her very glad.

"By the way, you never mentioned it, but did you hear anything, I mean, on Saturday night?" Imogen asked suddenly.

Bernadette wondered what to say and opted to prevaricate.

"I never mentioned it no..."

"So, you did, didn't you? I can tell," Imogen said at once.

There was nothing for it but to come clean, after all.

"We were sparing D'Arcy's blushes. And you said she was shy about your, activities, so..."

"Thank you," said Imogen gratefully, "So what did you hear exactly?"

"Erm, well, the distinctive sound of D'Arcy's bare backside being paddled, and some of the things you were saying..."

"Oh," said Imogen, she thought about this for a moment and shrugged. "Well, it can't be helped, she was due a spanking and it had to be done. She wanted it anyway. I'm sure Constantina knows all about it because we know Juanita does. So, you are not the only ones."

"Indeed, but I think they've been discreet."

"I hope so," said Imogen ruefully, recalling some of the other sessions she and D'Arcy had indulged in.

"Yes. There is one thing, and I hope you won't take this amiss."

"I don't suppose I will at all, what is it?"

Bernadette explained how Eve had become aroused by the sounds of the spanking and what had ensued.

"Really? Goodness, she obviously is more into it than you know," said Imogen surprised but smiling just the same.

"Well, yes and that's what worries me."

"Why? Why be worried. She hasn't asked you to do it, has she?"

"No, she hasn't, and I don't really want to go down that route."

"Well, you don't have to. She obviously finds the vicarious pleasures enough. I mean, I can make a recording for her if you want," Imogen sniggered.

"Oh no, don't. Poor D'Arcy, it would be very wrong."

"I was only joking, darling, I would never do that to her."

"Thank goodness."

147

"Look, your fiancée is turned on by stuff, that's all you need to know. Does it really matter if it's between you?"

"I guess not, I just don't want to feel there are secrets. She should feel safe to share with me," Bernadette said sounding a little emotional.

"Has this less to do with Eve than it does to do with Rebecca? Because *that* is what it sounds like," Imogen said frankly.

"I guess," Bernadette sighed.

"If you want to ask her about it then you should. When it's a good time. But be prepared for revelations."

"What's that supposed to mean?"

"It means secrets are sometimes best kept in the past."

"Well, now you've got me really worried. Is she going out and getting spanked or something? Is that what you are saying?" Bernadette said with great concern on her face.

"No, silly," Imogen laughed, "It's just we all have a past, don't we? Sometimes we might not like the past of someone for whatever reason, I don't know? I'm just trying to say don't go there unless you really feel you must, that's all. If you must, you must."

"Oh... well, I think perhaps I must..." Bernadette replied after some thought.

"For a hard-nosed bitch lesbian lawyer, you are so sensitive, darling," said Imogen taking her hand.

"I know, I'm like a piece of fucking jelly inside," Bernadette sniffed.

"Never say so. So, look go on, ask her, I mean, what could possibly go wrong? You love each other, if it ends up somewhere difficult you will get through it."

Bernadette knew Imogen was trying to help but everything she was saying almost seemed to make it worse. However, she wasn't one to shy away from things. She knew she had to face her fears and if this was a fear, then she would need to front up. She resolved to talk to Eve, very gently on the coming weekend, and find out the truth about her past. If indeed there was a truth to be discovered. Having put the thoughts aside for the moment, she turned her attention to the case.

"We've got the papers?" she asked Imogen.

"Yes, they contain the pleading which we've seen. A sworn affidavit from Kevin Clinton accusing Callum of being involved and admitting his own involvement. It also contains a transcript of Kevin's interview with Met detectives. There are various bits of CCTV footage from the depot where Callum left the truck which proves he was driving it, so there are stills from those. There is a copy of the tachometer for the truck, border control papers and so on," Imogen told her leafing through it.

"That's it?"

"Yes, pretty much."

"So, they are relying on a single witness statement?"

"Well, yes, but the statement makes a strong case in their view, I suppose."

"Is there any mention of the sexual relationship between them?"

"No."

"That's good because we can spring it as a surprise. We need to insist their witness is brought to court for cross examination."

"OK, sounds good."

"Then we should try to establish from the refugees where they were put onboard the truck. If their testimony is good, we can maybe get them to testify or get sworn affidavits," Bernadette continued thinking it through.

"Right, but they may not have seen Callum even so."

"No, but knowing they were put on in Ireland places a different emphasis on it. We could argue if it goes against us the crime should be prosecuted in Ireland and not the UK, thus avoiding extradition either way."

"Good thinking."

"But that's a backstop. We need to somehow prove Callum wasn't involved."

"OK, but how?"

Bernadette and Imogen spent a moment drinking their coffee and pondering this point. It wasn't easy at all, since there was nothing concrete to prove he did not do it barring his word. His word against a witness. Bernadette knew the aim of the British police was to get him to the UK. They had to have the stated intention to charge and prosecute him, which they were certainly going to do. However, they would also try to break him down and gain a confession to ease the passage of prosecution. Getting a confession was all too easy sometimes if enough pressure can be applied.

"If there is a way we can establish for certain the time he picked up the truck and then establish a timeline for the illegals getting put on it, then we can argue the link is tenuous or the probability is he didn't know about it."

"They will counter argue even if he didn't help to load it, he still knew," Imogen said, playing devil's advocate.

"OK, true, but that is harder to prove, and when it comes down to their word against his, then his will more likely win. He's an Irish citizen and extraditions are not done lightly."

Bernadette liked Imogen to challenge her, this was one of the good things about having a junior. She would put Bernadette on the spot, and it was better to be made to think it through in the office than when they got to court. In court, there was not too much time to ponder. A lawyer had to think on their feet and quickly. Things often came in from left field and had to be rebutted almost off the cuff.

"We need to talk to Callum then to get more details," Imogen pointed out.

"Yes, after we get back from London, so next week."

"And do we still want to meet with Mason?"

This was a point of contention, however, the practice of lawyers meeting the opposition lawyers outside of the courtroom was very common. Bernadette was well aware many 'deals' had been made in this fashion in order to avoid the chance of a negative verdict. However, she was not a fan. She was a fan of the truth and not of making a deal. She also didn't approve of fraternising with the enemy as such. It smacked of disloyalty to her client. Her job was, however, to get the best result and sometimes talking to the opposition was prudent if nothing else it gained a better understanding of their intentions.

"Yes, know thy enemy, make it a lunch date, somewhere very posh where he will find it hard to refuse. No lawyer refuses a free lunch, particularly if it's an expensive one."

"OK," Imogen laughed, "I will remember it for future reference."

"Believe me it's true. There are certain QC's who pride themselves on their extravagance and leading a top-drawer lifestyle. They make a good deal of money and they don't hesitate to flaunt it."

"Not you though, you are far more modest."

"Yes, I am it's true, although I try to dress the part, but I don't need several pairs of Louboutin's and Gucci handbags to do so," Bernadette said earnestly.

"I wouldn't mind at least one pair though."

"I'm sure D'Arcy will buy them for you, if you mention it in passing." Bernadette grinned.

"I know," Imogen sighed, "I just don't want to take advantage. She always wants to buy me things."

"Listen to me, you are going to be married soon. So technically you will be assuming her lifestyle as her wife. Which means what's hers is technically yours too and you should try to have less scruples about enjoying her wealth with her. I mean, unless she has mentioned a prenup, of course, has she?"

"Well no," Imogen said looking worried, "Should we..."

"No!" said Bernadette firmly, "No such thing, go into it wholeheartedly or not at all. It's not as if she has a whole bunch of family. I mean, she does but she's not on terms with them. If anything, she should be protecting you. You should also help her draft a will once you are married."

"Really, gosh? Isn't that presumptuous?"

"No, it's not, out of the two of you, you are the one who should be protected and if you won't mention it to her, I will!"

Imogen could see the martial light in Bernadette's eye, and she knew Bernadette must feel very strongly about it.

Bernadette certainly did, she wanted her friend looked after in the event of something happening to D'Arcy.

"Would you? I... I would say I can, but I know I'll chicken out," Imogen said gratefully.

"You are funny. You can spank her, but you can't talk to her about making a will."

"I know, it's lame, but..."

"I'll talk to her, don't worry, I've got your back." Bernadette smiled.

"I know you have, darling and I'll always have yours."

"Except where you were going to work for Shane," Bernadette teased.

"Oh don't! You have no idea how bad I feel about it. I mean, if it's still an issue I'll gladly go over your knee and we can settle it that way..."

"No! Don't I'm teasing, don't take me so seriously. And really, Imogen, that's not the way to solve all your problems," Bernadette laughed.

"It's one way." Imogen pouted. "It works for me and D'Arcy."

"For you and D'Arcy, yes," said Bernadette with emphasis.

Imogen laughed at this. She reached out and took Bernadette's hand affectionately.

"God, I love you, so much, have I told you that?"

"Yes, many times, and I love you too, and you know that."

Bernadette squeezed her friend's hand and held on to it.

"Is there anything else we need to do while in London?" Imogen asked.

"Unless we can interview the prosecution witness or we find someone else we can talk to, then I doubt it."

"What about the investigating officer in the Met?"

"I doubt the Met are going to want to talk to us, they want a result for them. Talking to the defence counsel is not going to be in their interests."

"I suppose you are right, anyway, it's probably enough for two days to get interviews with those refugees and lunch with the lawyer."

"So, will you make the arrangements?"

"Yes, we will pick you and Eve, up tomorrow morning from your house. Leave everything to me. D'Arcy has sorted it and I've spoken to Andrew about charging the client a nominal sum for expenses on a *per diem* basis."

"Are we reimbursing D'Arcy with that?" Bernadette asked curiously.

"Well..." Imogen hesitated.

"Offer it to D'Arcy, if she chooses not to take it then." Bernadette shrugged. "Anyway, we will incur some expenses for taxis and the lunch and so on, and we need to be reimbursed for those."

"OK, sure." Imogen looked relieved.

D'Arcy wouldn't take the money, Bernadette knew, and she was past the point of trying to argue with her friend's fiancée. D'Arcy did as D'Arcy wanted. They had all learned that from close association. The only person able to reign her in, in the slightest, was Imogen. The best thing was to simply lay back and enjoy the ride, Bernadette mused philosophically. In any case she knew D'Arcy could well afford all of the extravagances she indulged in and so didn't feel bad about it.

"Are you taking your paddle?" Bernadette asked with a smile playing on her lips.

"Of course, if nothing else as a reminder for D'Arcy to behave herself."

"And what exactly constitutes behaving?"

"Oh well, anything I don't approve of, obviously. Things we've discussed she's not to do…"

"Like?"

"Like going out on lunch dates and not telling me about them, flirting outrageously with people, or sometimes just because she just wants to be spanked… stuff like that."

Bernadette laughed. "I'm actually impressed how you've been curbing your jealousy though."

"It's been very difficult, believe me. But I am learning to temper myself, more."

"Keep it up, darling."

"I'm doing my best. We actually have a good life together. We certainly have a very good sex life too," Imogen said with a smile.

"Why don't you let your house go then, or rent it out or something?"

"I've discussed it with D'Arcy and that's what we're going to do. I'm going to rent it out because it's an asset for us."

"Good, very good."

"Anyway, sweetness, I've got to get on with all these arrangements."

"Sure, you carry on, I'll catch up on some other cases meanwhile."

Imogen gathered up the papers, and the empty cups. She leaned over, gave her friend a peck on the lips and left the room.

Bernadette watched her go. Their bond had become so strong, it was now unbreakable. There had been a moment when she thought Imogen was going to leave and work for Shane Wilson, and her heart had almost broken in two. She sometimes wondered if she had not met Eve, and Imogen had not met D'Arcy whether she and Imogen would have made a couple. It was destined to be a question which was never answered. It was probably just as well, Bernadette mused, considering her friend's deeper and kinkier sexual desires. Bernadette wasn't sure she was up to getting her backside regularly tanned with a leather paddle, in fact, she was fairly sure she wouldn't be. It certainly wasn't a rabbit hole she wanted to go down. Shibari was a bridge she had crossed for Eve, but how much further she would go, was an interesting question.

CHAPTER SIX

*O*n Tuesday morning, they had to rise earlier than usual, since D'Arcy's car was calling for them at seven a.m. Bernadette usually did not leave for work until around eight or eight thirty which gave them more time in bed. Even then if Eve was extra frisky, she had been late when she didn't have court. However, they got up on time, showered and got dressed.

"I'm so excited," said Eve over breakfast, "This is like our first holiday together outside of Ireland, well really Dublin."

"A working holiday, darling." Bernadette smiled.

"I know, but still."

Eve had dressed comfortably for travelling in a pink cotton lined skirt, matching blouse with collar, and black jacket, with pink flip-flops. Bernadette was more formal with a black skirt, white blouse, black jacket and black mules. Eve had packed a selection of clothes and shoes for both of them in two medium suitcases. Bernadette smiled when she saw them, but Eve said there were clothes for work and for going out in, plus nightwear, cosmetics, and other things she said were necessary items. Bernadette did not demur. She had not had to do anything, and she was happy.

Eve had made them a cheese and mushroom omelette for breakfast, with toast and coffee. She said they needed to be set up for the day.

"You're so good, darling, I should hire you as my PA, we are going to be getting another one soon at work," Bernadette joked consuming a mouthful of her omelette with relish.

"I am already your PA, your dresser, your make-up artist, your cook, your housekeeper..." Eve said with a laugh.

"Oh God, when you put it like *that*, it sounds like I do nothing. Shit, I mean..." said Bernadette a little abashed by this list of things Eve did for them.

"Don't look so worried, I wouldn't do it if I didn't want to, I'm quite domesticated you know and I'm an artist, and you keep us very well."

"Are you sure?" Bernadette at once was chagrined feeling she had been imposing on her fiancée all this time.

"I'm teasing silly. I like to nurture and look after you. I told you from the start. It's how I love you, well... partly, you know the other parts."

"Don't think I don't appreciate everything you do. Perhaps I'm not saying it enough, I'm sorry."

"Stop it. You take things too much to heart, my darling. I do all this for us, so that when you come home I have you all to myself and it's all I want really."

"Is it?"

"Yes."

"But what about you? Things for you?"

"I've got my art, it's what I've always wanted to do, and I've got that. I can be a woman of leisure if I wish. I'm earning money too, for us. You love your work. I wouldn't have it any different. I love what I do."

"Well, good. I don't want you to think I take you for granted."

"You don't, and if you did, I would tell you, and you would be up in the bedroom with your hands on the wall in no time," Eve laughed.

Bernadette smiled and reflected that Eve, in a way, was the one who called the shots. So, she wasn't at all hard done by. She got exactly what she wanted when she wanted it, and Bernadette knew it and she loved her for it. Eve had domesticated her and tamed her. She had wrapped Bernadette around her little finger. Perhaps it was what she needed all along.

"You are a witch!" Bernadette said severely.

"And you love it, now finish your breakfast."

"Yes, miss," Bernadette giggled, addressing herself to the food.

After they finished, they loaded the dishwasher, and sat down to wait. In a short while, the doorbell rang. It was D'Arcy. She was almost jumping up and down with excitement when Bernadette opened the door.

"Oh, this is such fun," she said launching herself into Bernadette's arms and planting a big kiss on her lips.

"Hello, D'Arcy," Bernadette laughed, and watched her repeat the performance with Eve.

"Come on, girls, let's get on," said Imogen standing just outside and smiling at her fiancée's antics.

D'Arcy was wearing a short leather mini skirt, crisp white top and a white leather jacket which all look very expensive, and were probably designer labels, along with black strappy heels. Imogen had a black skirt on with a black jacket and white shirt, rather like Bernadette, and black court heels.

Eve and Bernadette grabbed the bags, set the alarm system, and locked the front door. Carragh was waiting at the car and he took their bags to stow in the boot.

Bernadette and Eve got into D'Arcy's black Hyundai Santa Fe 4WD Premium Plus which had seven seats. They sat in the rear seats. Imogen and Darcy sat in the middle ones. D'Arcy had a black Mercedes S class which she mostly used but when there were four of them there wasn't the room.

"Ready?" said Carragh from the driver's seat.

"Yes, let's go!" trilled D'Arcy.

There was a second bodyguard in the passenger seat who was going to drive the car back to D'Arcy's house. Carragh would accompany D'Arcy everywhere she went in London for personal protection.

"Are we all ready for our adventure?" said D'Arcy as the car pulled away.

"I'm looking forward to it for sure," Eve told her.

"We are going to have such fun, while these two are working."

"I hope so."

"I know so, I've got it all planned out."

D'Arcy chattered on in her usual fashion as they drove out towards Dublin airport. It was a short fifteen-minute drive and when they arrived, instead of being dropped off as Bernadette expected, the car drove through a special gate onto the tarmac.

"Aren't we going to..." Bernadette began.

"No, we're not going on a scheduled flight," said D'Arcy.

The car stopped close to the steps of a small jet.

"What?" Bernadette exclaimed.

"I hired us a private jet." D'Arcy's face was a picture of delight.

"Goodness!" Eve squealed, "How amazing!"

Bernadette looked from Eve to D'Arcy and thought again how Eve starting to sound in many ways like D'Arcy. She smiled to herself at this. A transformation was happening that was certain.

"Don't we have to go through immigration, stuff like that?" Bernadette wondered.

"No, it's taken care of as it's a flight to the UK, we don't really need the passports, but we've got them as ID," said Imogen.

"Well..."

The white Hawker 900XP jet sparkled in the sun as they boarded. The interior was surprisingly spacious with cream leather plush seating facing each other and a table in between. Along one side at the back was also a sofa style seating arrangement. There was a small galley and a toilet at the back.

"Welcome aboard," said a pretty looking young female attendant who was waiting to see them onto the plane along with her male counterpart, "Please take a seat where you'd like, and we'll serve you some refreshments shortly."

"Wow," Eve exclaimed, "I've never been on a private jet before."

"Me neither," said Bernadette as they took seats opposite each other and strapped in.

"Nor me." Imogen smiled as she took a seat herself.

"Enjoy, darlings, enjoy," D'Arcy said putting on her seatbelt.

Carragh stowed the baggage and took a seat behind them all at the back. The attendants closed the doors and the plane began to taxi down the runway.

"Welcome aboard," said the pilot, "Our flying time will be approximately one hour and twenty-five minutes. I wish you a pleasant flight and thanks for using World Jet."

The flight attendants went through the standard safety briefing while Bernadette relaxed back into her seat and smiled at her fiancée. The jet completed its taxi manoeuvres and the pilot kicked up the revs on the engines which started whine loudly. He released the brakes and the jet launched itself down the runway. Unlike the larger planes, Bernadette had flown in the G force from this was quite intense, and they took off at a steep angle. She looked out of the window and watched the city of Dublin fall away. A glance around showed her the others were doing the same. She could just pick out the Criminal Courts of Justice and a couple of other buildings before Dublin disappeared from view. The flight attendants were buckled up impassively in their seats, paying scant attention to anything, they no doubt performed this type of flight several times a week.

Shortly after take-off, the plane levelled off. The attendants unbuckled and went to the galley in order to prepare some refreshments.

"I suppose you fly like this quite often," Eve said to D'Arcy.

"Well, sometimes, darling, yes, depends on the movie company. I mean, it's better for privacy obviously and I can slip in and out without all the press. But otherwise, I fly first or business on the long hauls," said D'Arcy in matter of fact tones.

"How the other half lives," murmured Imogen.

"But, darling, you are now the other half," D'Arcy reminded her.

"Oh, yes, so I am."

The flight crew served them each with a glass of wine or a soft drink, with a prawn cocktail, a small salad, and slices of teriyaki chicken with rice. There was a chocolate mousse for afters. The meal was nicely served on china plates with proper cutlery unlike the usual plastic arrangements of scheduled airlines. Bernadette and Imogen did not take the wine, and they all pronounced the food delicious.

They whiled away the flight chatting about London, and D'Arcy said she hadn't been there for some time. D'Arcy had done quite a bit of filming there so knew it quite well. Bernadette had been a few times in her youth, Eve had predictably spent a bit of time there, and for Imogen, this was her first trip to the UK. D'Arcy was happy because she would be able to introduce Imogen to the big city.

Shortly they flew over the City of London and D'Arcy pointed out all the sights to her fiancée, then they turned south and finally landed at Biggin Hill. The airport consisted of a large two-story white building proclaiming itself as "Biggin Hill Airport", plus several other buildings for the various private aircraft companies which used it. They taxied to a standstill and the steps were let down.

To Bernadette's surprise, a stretch limo was waiting for them. The flight attendants bid them fair well and they disembarked. Carragh put the bags in the boot and sat up front with the driver.

"You pushed the boat out on this trip, D'Arcy," said Bernadette entering the Limo and looking around it with interest.

"Oh darling," D'Arcy said, "I just thought a bit of comfort would be nice."

"Very nice, the last time I was in one of these was for a very rowdy hen party." Bernadette instantly regretted the words leaving her mouth.

"Oh gosh, yes, you and Eve, you need to have a hen party," said D'Arcy at once.

"Oh, no, no, no, we don't need..."

"But you do, darling, even if it's just us four, we can get really drunk and..."

"D'Arcy, no! You know about you and drinking. That's in the past, remember," said Imogen firmly.

"But, honey, it's for Bernadette," said D'Arcy beginning to pout.

"Put your lip away!"

"Oh you, I'm not a child."

"But you behave like one sometimes," Imogen replied implacably.

D'Arcy shot her a look of defiance and reached for the bottle of champagne which was provided for their use. It had not been opened, and Imogen simply removed it gently from her grasp. She poured out a glass of diet coke, put some ice in it and wordlessly handed it to D'Arcy.

"You see how strict she is with me," D'Arcy said to no one in particular, and looked as if she was going to stamp her foot.

"I'm giving you a warning," Imogen said quietly into her ear, "You know what's going to happen if you carry on like this."

Eve and Bernadette looked from one to the other. Eve decided to come to the rescue before things escalated.

"Listen we don't have to get drunk, honey, we can have a nice hen night though, have fun, maybe watch old movies, stuff like that, at your house, hey?"

"Ooh yes, we could have a sleepover in the living room, like teenagers. I never had one of those." D'Arcy brightened up at once, forgetting her earlier petulance.

"Well then, we shall, won't we, darling," said Eve looking at Bernadette for confirmation.

"Of course," said Bernadette, "We can all wear matching pyjamas."

"And go skinny dipping in the pool," D'Arcy said, getting carried away.

"Of course," said Eve looking at Bernadette. Her fiancée shrugged. They both knew it wouldn't be the first time.

Imogen relaxed and sat back with an indulgent smile, now her fiancée seemed to have settled down. The route took approximately an hour and they drove up through Brixton, across Vauxhall Bridge. They turned right up Millbank and past the Houses of Parliament. Eve entertained Imogen with her knowledge about the London landmarks and sights, pointing things out right and left. They went up Whitehall past Horse Guards and D'Arcy informed them that one person she had never met was the Queen, although she had apparently met several dignitaries, and other members of the Royal Family in her time at premieres and parties for the hoi polloi. They drove past

Nelson's Column, up Piccadilly via Regent Street arriving finally at Portland Place and pulling up at long last outside The Langham Hotel. This was their destination although, Eve and Bernadette had been unaware they were staying somewhere quite so plush.

As they got out of the limo, they gazed up at the massive stone building in front of them, with an arched columned entranceway which went all the way up to the first floor.

"Jesus, are we staying here?" Eve exclaimed, looking at it in awe.

"Oh, yes, darling, and wait until you see where," D'Arcy told her.

"What happened to bijou and a boutique hotel?" Bernadette asked.

"I decided this was so much better and Imogen agreed," D'Arcy said to her, "It's my treat, anyway."

"Then, thank you, darling," said Bernadette realising there really was no stopping her at all. Imogen would have gone along with D'Arcy's plans because she only reigned her in when she felt strongly about something. D'Arcy did as she wanted most of the time with Imogen's full approval.

"Just wait, wait until you see what's in store," D'Arcy said again in animated tones.

When they entered the foyer, D'Arcy certainly turned a few heads being instantly recognisable, but she was treated like a VIP with great deference, and after a brief check-in they were escorted personally to the second floor. They were then shown into what proclaimed itself to be the 'Infinity Suite' and as they walked up the polished buff tiles of entrance the corridor, Eve exclaimed out loud, "Holy fuck, D'Arcy, this is amazing."

The corridor opened out into an atrium with a master bedroom to the left, and a second bedroom to the right. In front of them was a semi-circular lounge cum dining room. The décor was tasteful and muted, with blues and creams, and ceilings with moulded covings. The living area provided a view of the city.

"Do you like it?" D'Arcy asked.

"I do, very much, darling. But it must be costing you a fortune," said Bernadette with a frown.

"It's nothing really, honestly, sweetheart," said D'Arcy airily.

"Don't worry about it, darling, she can afford it I promise you, and she wanted to give us a nice treat," Imogen told Bernadette in a way which communicated that Imogen didn't want her to make a big deal about the expense.

"Well, but thank you so much for this. I mean, it's quite a surprise," Bernadette said to D'Arcy.

"A good one though?"

"A very good one, it's marvellous." Bernadette kissed her and gave her a hug, which left D'Arcy wreathed in smiles.

Carragh left the bags in their respective rooms, and then retired to his own one-bedroom suite next door. D'Arcy had an emergency walkie talkie which he provided for her so she could use to contact him at all times of the day or night. He would also make sure they were secure at night and check the suite himself regularly in case of intruders.

"Shall we have a tour?" D'Arcy said.

The master bedroom proved quite sumptuous, with a king size bed, a day bed, and a table and chairs. The furnishings were again subdued, and in a similar fashion to the hallway but expensive. There was a beautiful bathroom with a mix of mosaic tiles, large wall tiles, a walk-in shower, bath, toilet and basin. All well-appointed. The second bedroom was similarly furnished and also a good size. The bathroom was smaller with a Victorian bath, a smaller shower, basin and loo. The tiles on the walls were similar to those in the other bathroom. Each room also had a walk-in wardrobe for hanging clothes. There was also another toilet just off the hallway. The décor had a synergy and was tastefully done without being too opulent.

"I don't know what to say," Bernadette said when they had seen everything, "I've never stayed anywhere half as grand or luxurious as this, you're spoiling us, D'Arcy."

"Because I love you, both of you, so very much, and of course my Imogen. My darling, darling beautiful Imogen, I love her the most," said D'Arcy simply.

Imogen kissed her then, blushing at the compliment.

"I love you too, and you are exceptionally beautiful, my darling. Now, we should unpack, and then what about lunch? I mean, I'm kind of hungry," said Imogen.

"Oh, we've got private dining if we want and that man who escorted us is our personal butler, who will sort everything out we need."

"Great, then let's get settled in and order something up."

Imogen and Bernadette opted for the Chicken tikka pie, and cauliflower puree from The Wigmore, and Eve the braised pork belly, hispi cabbage, and smoked sausage, while D'Arcy had the plant-based vegan cheeseburger, with pickled jalapeño in their living-cum-dining room. After lunch, Bernadette and Imogen left in a taxi for the offices of an organisation handling accommodation and all other matters for asylum seekers.

The offices of the Refugee Assistance Organisation were in an area of east London. The offices were in a non-descript grey sixties style building just north of Docklands. The taxi dropped Bernadette and Imogen outside. They entered the premises through a glass double door and found themselves in a carpeted area which was quite well fitted out. Although it wasn't plush, it wasn't cheap either. The reception had posters all over the walls, leaflets, and booklets in many different languages. Sitting at the two reception desks were two women.

"Can I help you?" asked one of them looking up. She was wearing a hijab and Bernadette thought she had pretty eyes.

"Imogen Stewart and Bernadette Mackenna, we have an appointment with Damsa Adi, we are lawyers from Dublin," said Imogen handing over her card.

The woman examined it briefly and then asked them to take a seat. She picked up the phone, presumably to call Damsa.

"Nice place," said Bernadette looking around.

"Yes, it's a charity organisation, they exist on donations and they get some lottery funding," Imogen told her.

"You've done your homework."

"Just like you taught me. I can tell you who the head of this NGO is, the patrons, whatever you want."

"I'm impressed." Bernadette smiled.

At that moment Damsa Adi appeared. She had shoulder length black hair, hanging free. She was wearing a black skirt, and a blouse with a flowery pattern, and black mules.

"Hi, Imogen, Bernadette?" she said with a smile.

"Yes," said Imogen standing up.

"Come this way, please."

She led the way through another set of doors and down a corridor to what they assumed was her office. It was chock full of filing cabinets, and shelves with legal books. Her desk was a typical light-coloured wood with aluminium legs. A computer and screen sat on the desk, which had many files on it too, reminding Bernadette of Andrew's desk and office. Behind Damsa's desk was a shelf with what looked like family pictures and personal items. In one corner of the office by the window was a small round table with some chairs.

"Take a seat," Damsa said in a friendly tone indicating the meeting table. She picked up the phone and spoke to someone about coffee and then came to sit down. "Now, I've read your emails, Imogen, but just explain again why you want to see these refugees."

"We are representing a client, Callum Jenkins, a truck driver, an attempt is being made to extradite him back to the UK for trafficking these women," Imogen explained.

"Sure, I get that part but what possible help can they be to you?"

"Well, there are two things really. The first is whether they might recognise Callum, and the second is where they got on board the truck. Whether it was in Ireland or somewhere in Europe."

"Is that important?"

"Yes, because we are working with the Garda on an investigation into the depot where the truck was picked up in Ireland. If there is evidence the truck was loaded there, then it becomes an Irish based crime which helps us and helps them."

"I see."

Just then a man entered the office carrying a tray containing three coffees, milk and sugar, and a plate of digestive biscuits. Damsa distributed the cups and they helped themselves to milk and sugar. Imogen took a digestive and nibbled it.

"What I'm concerned about," said Damsa frankly, "Is how is this helping our women and our girls? They are vulnerable people, what is your client to them? Your interest is with your client and not really with people who suffered incredible hardship and a lucky escape from a life of sexual slavery."

It seemed to Bernadette that Damsa was verging on saying no to their request. Certainly, it appeared the way things were heading. She felt perhaps it might be prudent to intervene.

"Damsa," she said, "What exactly is it you do?"

"We work for refugees here, I'm sure you must know that."

"No, I mean what do you do, personally, here?"

"I'm a lawyer, qualified some time ago, I started working for this organisation because nobody was really helping these people."

"And what drives you to do that?"

Damsa looked at her as if she didn't feel this was relevant to the discussion but she answered anyway, "I was a refugee myself. I come from Iran. My family fled when things became difficult. My father was outspoken, he was a very successful businessman, but he was also good at getting into trouble. We knew perhaps one day he would end up in prison, so we left, with nothing. My father did not want me brought up there. So, we came here. In Iran we were rich, we came with just the clothes on our back."

"Then you felt somehow you had to give back to people who had suffered a worse fate than you?"

"Yes, exactly, and so I am very protective of their interests."

"Why do you think I do what I do?"

Damsa regarded her curiously. "You're a defence counsel, it's your job."

Imogen laughed at this. "I guess you haven't researched her."

"Well, no," Damsa admitted, "I was pretty chocka with work, to be honest, so..."

"You probably have a cynical view of our profession, although you are a lawyer yourself." Bernadette was equally blunt. "I can see you probably do. It is my job, but I do it because I believe in justice. I believe in making sure someone who is innocent doesn't go to prison."

"OK, and you think your client is innocent?"

"Yes, yes, I do, because otherwise, I wouldn't be representing him. I'm not one of these lawyers who tries to get guilty people off. I try to make sure justice is done for those who deserve it."

"She does more than try," Imogen added, "She succeeds most of the time."

"What makes you so sure your client isn't guilty?" Damsa asked her.

"I can't really share the evidence we have but I don't believe he is. I have a nose for these things. If I thought he was, I would not be representing him."

Damsa took a sip of her coffee.

"You know these women are afraid. The police have already interviewed them, and they told them very little. They said they don't know anything. These sexual gangs are predators, they have a long reach. We can't protect them completely. If they talk to you, then they might become targets."

Bernadette glanced at Imogen. This was a breakthrough. Damsa was leaning more now towards saying yes.

"Can't we at least try? Even if we can get one of them to speak it might help us. I promise you if they won't talk or anything then we'll walk away," Bernadette said.

"What is your ultimate goal, are you expecting them to give evidence in court?"

"If it was relevant then yes, but there may be ways we can arrange for them not to be identifiable or done via a video link, something like that. At the least, an affidavit would help us."

"OK, well, that would only work if they were willing to put themselves on the line."

"So, in principle are you saying you'll help us?"

"In principle, you've convinced me. God knows why but I believe you are sincere."

"Thank you."

"When do you want to see them?"

"Tomorrow? If we could?" Imogen asked her.

"It's a tall order, but I'll do my best. Let me talk to them, and I'll bring them to the centre here, if they will talk or perhaps at their accommodation, if they feel more comfortable there. I'll call you later or in the morning, OK?"

"Yes, thank you, we're grateful for your help," said Bernadette.

"You are welcome, I'd do the same in your position." Damsa had conceded perhaps because she felt some sort of empathy towards them. She did not owe Callum Jenkins anything, Bernadette knew that, and it was Damsa's job to protect her own charges.

Damsa sipped her coffee and so did the others. "You came all the way from Dublin just to interview my refugees, I'm impressed."

"Yes, and a couple of other things too," said Bernadette.

"You have dedication I'll give you that."

"She is totally dedicated, I've yet to meet anyone more so to her clients," Imogen put in. She was a champion for her boss and would take on anyone who might have a go at her or try to disparage her.

"I'm sure," said Damsa with a smile, holding her hands up in mock surrender, "I never meant to imply otherwise."

"So, you came here with your family?" Bernadette changed the subject.

"Yes, my father and mother. My mother is no longer with us, sadly. My father runs a business and of course, he was pleased I became a lawyer. Less so when I joined an NGO, I could have been coining it in the City but it's not what I wanted."

"And yourself, do you have your own family?"

"I have a son, but I'm divorced."

"Sorry."

"Don't be, it was just one of those things. He was, let's say, abusive and I left in the end. For a refuge, you see the pattern?" Damsa gave a sardonic laugh.

"I see you're very dedicated to your job."

"Yes, well." Damsa looked to see if they had finished their drinks. "On which note, and without meaning to be rude, is there anything else I can help you with?"

"Does this happen a lot, sexual trafficking?" Imogen asked her.

"Yes, but unfortunately quite often they don't get caught. Certainly not at first. So sometimes by the time they've come to us they have suffered a lot of irreparable harm."

"What are their chances of asylum?"

"Good usually if they can prove it was for sexual purposes, and their lives are in danger from return. Not hard to prove." Damsa shook her head, it was obviously quite sad.

"Why do you think they do it?" Bernadette wondered.

"For a better life. Many come from poor families. It's unusual to get Vietnamese because that isn't a particularly repressive regime although many are not well off. I think sometimes they want to take away the pressure from their family, and they get conned. The best thing would be to catch the people in the country who are doing this then perhaps it might stop, or at least lessen."

"Do you have any idea of who is behind the trafficking, in Europe?"

"No, we don't get involved. You can imagine it's a dangerous business best left to the police. We are just here to pick up the pieces I suppose," Damsa sighed.

Bernadette looked at Imogen, but she had nothing further to add.

"We won't take up any more of your time, you've been most helpful, thank you."

"I do my best." Damsa smiled. "Assuming you can see them, please keep all location information confidential it's a safety thing."

"We will, of course."

Damsa showed them out and told them she would be in touch by the morning.

They managed to hail a taxi after a few moments and headed back to the Langham.

"What do you think?" said Imogen as they travelled in the back of the taxi, "Will she help us?"

"I think so, yes. I hope you didn't mind me butting in, it's just I thought she was going to say no," said Bernadette looking worried.

"Of course not, we're a team remember, the lesbian lawyer bitches. I was thinking that too, so I am glad you helped to turn it around."

"What do you think the girls have been doing while we've been gone?" Bernadette wondered.

"God knows!"

"Are we all set for the lunch date with Mason Beamish?"

"Yes, that is on Thursday."

"Where are you taking us?"

"The Waldorf," said Imogen with a smile.

"Good choice, I'm sure he will be happy with that," Bernadette laughed.

"He accepted the invitation without any hesitation I can assure you."

"See, I told you, dangle a free lunch and it will get you everywhere with his kind."

"What kind is he exactly?" said Imogen with interest.

"You'll see, but he's a typical public school, Daddy has lots of money and I think I'll become a QC, type."

"Oh dear."

"Indeed."

They returned to their suite to find Eve and D'Arcy lounging around the living room in towelling robes.

"What you have been up to?" Imogen asked them.

"Oh, we've been for a swim in their beautiful pool, and we've had a body massage at the spa, it was lovely. They've got a gym too," said Eve smiling.

"Wanted to try to Chinese cupping but Eve wasn't keen," said D'Arcy.

"I should think not, doesn't it leave round circles all over your body?" Imogen said distastefully.

"Oh, does it? Oh gosh."

"What else have you got planned?" Bernadette asked them.

"I thought we could take a ride out see the sights at night, and then have something to eat?"

"Sounds good to me, can we order up some coffee in the meantime?" Bernadette sighed kicking off her shoes and sinking into one of the armchairs.

"Of course, darling, you can tell us how it went today," said D'Arcy picking up the phone.

* * *

Eve and Bernadette were alone in their bedroom after eating dinner at a nice but predictably posh restaurant which D'Arcy had picked. Carragh had hired a limousine to drive them around Central London mainly so Imogen could see the sights at night, but all of them loved it.

"Have you enjoyed yourself so far?" Bernadette asked Eve as they lay together enjoying the luxury of the bed.

"I've had a wonderful day, darling." Eve kissed her lightly.

"I'm glad."

"But I wish I could have spent it with you."

"I'm sorry, you knew this was a working holiday."

"Yes, I know, but I'd like to have a holiday soon, just for us, do you think we could?"

Bernadette realised they had never really considered doing this at all. She'd become a homebody and so was Eve, they seemed to be comfortable just being together. They did go out at the weekends for drives or stayed over at D'Arcy's place. It was time to up the ante, she realised. Couples were supposed to do things like taking a week away or even two. Work commitments always seemed to be an issue, but Bernadette now had Imogen, she ought to be able to leave her cases for a couple of weeks. Once this case was over, she resolved to do something about it.

"I do and we should, you are right, and I'm sorry. I feel as if I've been quite neglectful in that way," Bernadette whispered.

"Don't feel like that. I didn't mean to make you go and feel all bad about it. Sometimes you need to get away like this to realise what you are missing."

"We won't be able to afford something this grand," said Bernadette smiling in the darkness.

There was light creeping through the curtains from the streetlights and other buildings outside. It was never really ever dark in London, Bernadette mused.

"I don't want something grand. I want something comfortable, friendly, nice. Maybe near the sea or not far from it, or with a swimming pool. Somewhere hot, too."

"You choose, darling, we'll go wherever you want, as long as it's not a war zone. Also, somewhere which isn't anti-gay obviously."

"Thank you, and yes, it has to be lesbian friendly," Eve chuckled.

"Do you like this bed?" Bernadette whispered.

"Mmm, comfy."

"Shall we christen it?"

"Why not?"

Eve slid her arms around Bernadette and pulled her close. She kissed her with a sudden urgency. The touch of lips ignited them both immediately, coupled with the proximity of naked skin to skin.

"I love you so much," said Bernadette raking her nails lightly down Eve's back.

Eve hissed in her breath. "Oh God, I wish you could tie me up, fuck... do it again..."

"What, this?"

"Oh yes... mmm..."

"What about this?" Bernadette's fingers moved slowly but inexorably between Eve's legs.

"Oh... fuck... yes I want *that*... fuck... oh my God... fuck... yes... I do... oh... more... don't stop..." Eve moaned softly. They were both conscious of D'Arcy and Imogen across the hallway but doubtless, they were doing the same thing.

"Oh... fuck... oh... oh my God... ooh... ooh..." The wine from the meal coupled with the different setting increased Eve's arousal but things were taking a little longer than normal. Eve had perhaps had a glass or two too much.

Bernadette slowed her pace, and kissed Eve more passionately.

"Talk dirty to me," Eve begged her whispering, "You know what I like... tell me about... D'Arcy..."

"Well..." Bernadette whispered back, this seemed to be Eve's favourite topic at the moment, "I'm sure D'Arcy is going to be getting a red backside this trip, didn't you see her behaviour in the limo?"

"Oh... God... yes... yes... you're right... mmm..."

"Before long, I'm sure Imogen will be getting out that paddle, and ordering D'Arcy to strip, then she'll bend her over the end of their big bed... and..."

"Oh... fuck... yes... yes... oh... God... yes... ohh... ohh." Eve arched her back pushing hard into Bernadette's hand as the wave crashed through her. "Oh God... that was good... so good."

Bernadette smiled. "Was it OK?"

"It was more than OK, just like it always is," Eve breathed coming down from her high.

"I love you, so much, my angel." Bernadette pulled her close and held her tight.

CHAPTER SEVEN

The next morning the four of them sat down to breakfast at their dining table. They all opted for the Full English which consisted of eggs, bacon, sausages, grilled mushrooms and tomatoes. This was accompanied by toast, fruit juice and coffee. The breakfast menu was extensive but none of them wanted to succumb to the temptation to overindulge.

"Delicious," said Bernadette.

"It's nice to eat something I haven't cooked for a change," Eve agreed.

Bernadette shot her a guilty look at once.

"Not because I don't like cooking, and I love cooking for you, darling, so don't look like that!" Eve said at once.

"She's a worrier, all the time," Imogen put in, cutting into her scrambled eggs.

"Not *all* the time," Bernadette protested.

"Yes, you are," Imogen laughed.

"Not when I'm asleep," Bernadette said triumphantly.

"She does, even then," Eve chuckled.

"Oh fine."

"Poor Bernadette, you shouldn't worry so much, darling," D'Arcy said sympathetically.

"Can we move on from my unruly state of mind now," Bernadette said laughing.

"What are you doing today?" Imogen asked D'Arcy.

"Ah well, I'm taking Eve to Knightsbridge, shopping and to Harrods, we'll have lunch there I think."

"Lovely. Eve, try not to let her buy the whole shop."

"Oh, poo! I'm not that bad, I might get one or two things for me, and of course, for Eve."

"If you say so, darling," Imogen replied smiling indulgently.

"What about you two?" Eve asked Bernadette.

"We are waiting for a phone call from the refugee place and then we are going to interview the refugees hopefully, or at least one of them," said Bernadette.

"Oh, have you time for a swim?" Eve asked hopefully.

"With you?"

"Yes, of course, please?"

She looked so eager to spend some more time with Bernadette, she could not refuse.

"Yes, why not, let's go after breakfast."

"Why don't we all go?" D'Arcy said at once.

"Let them go, darling, and stay here with me, won't you?" Imogen flashed her a saucy look and ran her nail lightly down D'Arcy's bare arm.

"Oh... well... oh! Oh, I see, but we only just... oh!"

It was plain enough Imogen was trying to give Bernadette and Eve a bit of space. Bernadette mouthed 'thank you' when D'Arcy couldn't see, and Imogen winked surreptitiously.

After breakfast, Bernadette and Eve had a longish swim in the beautiful sixteen metre blue pool with subdued lighting and black slate walls. There was a sauna and steam room, they briefly used those, and after one further swim, they returned upstairs. There was still no call from Damsa. Bernadette dressed in less formal attire, a pale blue skirt, pale yellow top, and blue jacket, with some kitten heeled low mules. Imogen, did likewise, dressing down in a darker blue dress, jacket and flats. They did not want to look too formal for their meeting with the refugees as that might intimidate them.

D'Arcy and Eve left on their trip both wearing jeans, sneakers, a top and jacket. Bernadette and Imogen broke out their laptops and checked their emails.

"Do you think D'Arcy is going to spend lots of money?" Bernadette asked at length having dealt with various bits of correspondence.

"I expect so, I can't stop her anyway, it's her money. I can curb some things, but I can't really tell her what to do with her own money," Imogen sighed.

"So, you're the boss of her, but not really." Bernadette smiled.

"I can curb her behaviour, and she knows what to expect if she breaks agreements we've made. So, I can bring her into line sometimes but not in everything. She's a free spirit, I'm not trying to mould her. She can just be very tactless, sometimes thoughtless and act like a spoilt brat. Spoilt brats get spanked and she knows it, and has agreed to it," said Imogen frankly.

"I see," said Bernadette with a slight smile.

"What?"

"Nothing, you've figured it out and I take my hat off to you in a way."

"You've figured it out too."

"Not all of it."

"Are you still worried about what we talked about, with Eve?"

"Yes, and I'm going to tackle it this weekend," said Bernadette with resolve.

"OK, don't say I didn't warn you though, about Pandora's Box." Imogen smiled.

"I know, but in the pursuit of real truth between us, I have to do this."

"I understand, and if... you know, you need to talk, or anything then pick up the phone, day or night."

"Thank you."

"I'm always there for you, darling, you know that."

"Likewise."

Imogen's phone rang, it was Damsa. She gave a thumbs up to Bernadette and wrote down an address. After a very short conversation, she disconnected.

"It's on!" she said to Bernadette with a smile.

"Woohoo!"

"Yes, indeed, let's call up a taxi."

* * *

The refugees had been temporarily housed by the council on the White City Estate in the west of London. The estate which originally consisted of blocks of red brick flats four stories high had apparently since been improved by the addition of some low level terraced and semi-detached properties. The taxi dropped them off outside a brick end of terrace house with a concrete drive at the front gated off by black iron gates. To the side was the front door which contained two glass panels and a small porch roof. A wooden fence joined the property to the next tranche of terraced houses. There was a wooden gate in the fence which most likely went through to a rear garden. Assuming Damsa was already there, Bernadette and Imogen went up to the door. Bernadette knocked and shortly after the door was opened.

"Hi, Bernadette, Imogen, come in," said Damsa.

They entered into a small hallway with bare floorboards, a stairway led to the upstairs, and there was a door to the left and one straight ahead which looked as if it opened out to the kitchen.

"Come through," said Damsa, taking them to the left into an open plan living room-cum-dining room.

The room was neat though sparsely furnished and had patio doors leading out to a long narrow back garden which had some trees and was mainly laid out to grass.

Seated at the dining room table were two young women between twenty to twenty five years old, both Vietnamese. They stood up politely when the others entered.

"This is Anh, and this is Kim," said Damsa by way of introduction, she explained who Bernadette and Imogen were, although no doubt they had been told this already. She did not mention their surnames as this would preserve their privacy in the first instance.

Anh had a pretty face with brown eyes, and full lips, with long dark hair. Kim had brown eyes too and was equally beautiful as her friend, though her hair was somewhat shorter being shoulder length.

"Shall we sit down?" said Damsa.

They all took seats around the table and the two women looked at them expectantly.

"So," said Bernadette with a smile which was returned.

Anh said, "I am pleased to meet you, and my friend also. I speak English quite well, but I will have to translate for her. She understands a little but not much."

"Oh, OK."

"We can answer your questions, Damsa has explained why you have come here," Anh continued.

"First then," Bernadette began, "Can I say how honoured we are that you are willing to talk to us, we realise you've endured much to get here. We have quite a few questions, but if you don't want to answer any of them please let us know. It is, of course, your right not to answer."

"Thank you," said Anh. Kim said something in Vietnamese. "She says thank you also," Anh translated.

"If it's OK, I'd like to ask a bit about you both, what is it you did in Vietnam?"

"I was employed as a tour guide," said Anh, "I learned my English at school, studied hard. Kim was the daughter of a farmer in the country."

"Right, and if you don't mind, can you explain why you became a refugee?"

This might be a touchy subject, but it had to be asked, their motivation was of interest to understand the case better.

"I lost my job. I could not get any work. I wanted a better life. A friend told me how I could get here and put me in touch with someone."

"Why did you lose your job?"

"The boss, he was not nice. He wanted to... you know... make me do things."

"He wanted you to sleep with him?" Bernadette said bluntly.

Anh nodded and looked shamefaced. She lowered her eyes. To her, it was probably a very shameful thing.

"Don't be ashamed," said Bernadette reaching out her hand to Anh as an automatic impulse of compassion. Anh took it and held it fast still looking down. "These things happen all the time in Ireland and the UK. It's awful. We have laws against it here."

"In Vietnam too, there are labour codes and offenders can be punished. If you can prove something. But if you can't prove it then..." Anh left the rest of it unsaid.

"So, he made it difficult for you to work again?"

"Yes, if I would try to get a job with someone else, he would speak to them and say terrible things. He became obsessed with me, saying I must marry him. I didn't want him. I didn't want to be near him. I had to get away."

"Couldn't you move somewhere else in Vietnam?"

"These things are not so easy." Anh sighed deeply.

Damsa noting the women seemed quite comfortable announced she would make them some tea and left the room.

"And Kim?" asked Imogen who had been silent until now.

Another exchange ensued between Anh and Kim, and then Anh said, "She had no work, she comes from a poor province. Her father wanted her to get a husband, and she didn't want to."

"Why is that?"

Anh, paused for a moment considering if her answer might be found offensive, and then decided to take the plunge. "She does not like men."

"We understand," said Imogen, "We're both gay... so..."

This was conveyed to Kim who chattered quite excitedly for a moment.

"She says then you will know how she feels." Anh smiled.

"We do," said Bernadette. It seemed best not to labour the point. Her reluctance to obey her father's wishes was abundantly clear. It seemed plain enough what pressures had made them try to start a new life. She did not really know what the attitudes to LGBT were in Vietnam and resolved to look it up.

"How did you come here? By what route?" Imogen asked Anh.

"We travelled through Russia, Eastern Europe, and then to Ireland. It cost us a lot of money. My family helped me to get the money. They thought I would be able to earn more and send it home. Kim borrowed it from someone and now she owes a lot of money."

"So, if you go back?"

"The man will kill her, and the gang will kill me or kill us both because we know their secrets. We will be arrested by the authorities they will want names, and if we give them names then we will be killed. The police here already asked us for names, but we didn't want to talk. We are afraid," Anh said simply. It was matter of fact without rancour or embellishment. Just a statement of the consequences to them, of what they had done.

"We're interested about the part where you came to Ireland," said Bernadette, "How did you get onto that final truck in the barrels?"

"We came in another truck from Europe to a big place where there were many trucks."

"Can you describe it?"

"I will try..." Anh launched into a description of somewhere which sounded remarkably similar to Balik Transport. Apparently, they'd been kept in a large shed and then put into the barrels on the truck.

"So, you definitely changed trucks in Ireland?" Imogen asked wanting to be sure.

"Yes."

"How did you know it was Ireland?"

"I could tell by some of the accents. I asked someone where we were, and he said, in Ireland."

Damsa brought the tea, she had made it in a pot. She poured it out for each of them, and they took their own milk and sugar as they wanted. Bernadette sipped her tea before asking the next question.

"Wasn't it uncomfortable in those barrels?" she said.

"Yes," Anh laughed, "But if you had been on some of the terrible journey's we have, it was nothing. Also, we're quite small, so it was OK. They made holes in the barrels for us to breathe, but it was dark, hot. We had to hold it in if we needed the toilet."

"Ouch," Bernadette winced, "You must have wanted to come here very badly."

To her, it sounded absolutely dreadful, unthinkable. Then she knew she had led a comparably privileged life.

"Yes."

"Did you know that you were being trafficked for sex?" Imogen said bluntly. She felt perhaps they could be open with these women who had endured so much hardship.

"No, of course, we did not until the police told us. If it was for that we would never have come."

"Were you scared when the police found you?"

Kim nodded, it seemed she had understood this question. Anh said, "I was relieved, it was almost like being rescued. Once we found out what was planned for us, I was glad they had found us. I can't think how bad it would be if they had not."

"I can't imagine what you went through," said Bernadette sadly, "It sounds simply terrible and frightening."

"Wisdom comes after foolishness. But only if you learn from the mistakes. My father told me."

"And have you?" Imogen smiled.

"Perhaps we learned too late, we should have stayed in Vietnam. But Damsa has given us hope, hope we will get asylum."

"Their chances are good," Damsa put in, "I've dealt with such cases before, we've succeeded more than we failed."

"They are lucky to have you," Bernadette replied.

Damsa simply inclined her head.

"We feel very lucky," said Anh.

"If I show you a photograph, can you tell me if you recognise this man?" Bernadette said to Anh.

"Yes." Anh shrugged.

She pulled a photo of Callum from her bag and put it on the table. There was no flicker of recognition in either of the women's eyes.

"No, I haven't seen him," said Anh. A conversation between her and Kim elicited the same answer. "The men mostly wore masks so it would be hard to tell for certain, but just from the shape of his face, and his head I don't think so."

"Did they use each other's names, when talking?" Imogen wondered.

"Yes, they maybe thought we didn't know English and I pretended to only speak it a little."

"Did you hear the name Callum at all?"

"No, I don't remember that one."

"What about Omer?"

Anh thought about this, and then nodded. "It seems familiar."

Bernadette and Imogen exchanged glances. This was significant indeed.

"Tell us a bit more about your journey," said Bernadette, sipping her tea.

Anh related some of the details of their ordeal which seemed in part harrowing, but they were also not treated too badly. Perhaps the smugglers wanted them to not be alerted to the real reason they were being transported, lulling them into a false sense of security. They were promised a job, a new identity albeit fake, and a place to live. It was unfortunately believable if you were a person so desperate to leave. Even for someone as well educated as Anh, she had been incredibly naïve, Bernadette reflected. In hindsight, it seems Anh knew it but there was nothing to be done about it but to move forward. Their stoicism was what most impressed Bernadette. She had purposely got them to talk, to gain more of their trust as much as anything, in order to ask them a key question.

"I'm going to put something to you, and you can say no, but I'm asking you to consider it," she said at length.

"OK." Anh looked at her without suspicion.

"If I was to ask you, or even both of you to sign an affidavit which outlines what you've told us, would you be prepared to do so? We can arrange for anonymity in court."

There followed a fairly long conversation between Anh and Kim which sounded very much like an argument.

"Kim wants to know why you want this?"

"Damsa may have explained it to you already, but we represent a client who we believe is not guilty. The British police want to extradite him on charges of trafficking, we are fighting the extradition."

"Is this him?" Anh asked her pointing at the photo.

"Yes, that's him. We believe he's innocent, and we don't believe he knew about it."

"What will happen if you lose?"

"He will be brought to the UK and charged. He will face fourteen years in prison for a crime he didn't commit."

"How will our evidence help you?"

"It might sway the judge. Even better if you were willing to give evidence by video link, we can make that anonymous too."

"I see."

She spoke to Kim who shook her head vigorously.

"Kim doesn't want to," she told them.

"OK, and yourself?"

"I need to think, even if it is anonymous, as you say, the gang will still know it was one of us. I may be putting all of them in danger by this action."

"I understand, and it's a big ask, but I have no option but to ask you. An innocent man may go to prison, it's my job to prevent it if I can."

"I will think about it."

"We're here until Friday," said Imogen, "If you can let us know before so we can prepare the affidavit."

"I will, I just need some time."

"Thank you for considering it," Bernadette told her.

"You are welcome," said Anh.

"Is there anything else?" Damsa asked them.

"No, thank you for giving us your time."

"I'll call a taxi," said Imogen pulling out her phone.

The taxi arrived promptly, and they said goodbye to the women and Damsa who said she would be in touch.

"Do you think there's a chance?" Imogen said as the taxi headed back to their hotel.

"There's always a chance, yes. If it's a good one, I don't know," said Bernadette frankly.

"Yeah, I think you're right."

"Let's prep an affidavit when we get back, just in case."

"Good plan, the girls will be out anyway. God knows how much Eve is spending, I dread to think."

"I guess you are going to have to get used to it."

"I know."

"But otherwise things are... OK?" Bernadette wondered.

"Yes, they have been so far. I gave her a fair warning in the car, and she won't get another one," Imogen said pursing her lips.

"It sounds as if you want her to misbehave."

"Sometimes I'm just itching to give her a spanking, something drives me to it, I must be a terrible person underneath it all."

"I understand, and you're not, stop it."

"Do you?"

"The same thing which drives Eve to want Shibari." Bernadette shrugged.

"I think D'Arcy has the same drive, she pushes me when she really wants me to be firm with her, I'm sure of it, perhaps she craves it too," said Imogen pondering things a bit further.

"Well, you two are matched, otherwise it wouldn't work would it?"

"Yes, you're right."

"If you need us to get out of the way, for a bit, you know, just suggest we go for a swim," Bernadette said, thinking if Imogen and D'Arcy wanted to play their games then it would be best done in private.

"Oh, I doubt I'll need the paddle this holiday, I only brought it for a joke, to keep her in line," Imogen laughed.

* * *

They returned to the suite and as predicted, Eve and D'Arcy were not there. They ordered some lunch from the butler whose name was Jackson. He was a middle aged rather portly gentleman with grey hair, a pleasant demeanour and excellent manners, who had apparently been to Butler school to learn his trade. They both chose burgers with fries and salad.

"Oh my God," said Imogen, biting into hers, "This is just, heaven, absolute heaven."

"Yes, too right, I suppose it's alright to indulge ourselves, after all, we don't do this every day," said Bernadette feeling a little guilty.

"Of course, come on, darling, who gets to do *this* every day?"

"You're right, let's just enjoy it."

When they had finished, Imogen sat writing the affidavit for Anh. Bernadette checked up on her emails and worked on some of the other cases they had on the go. When Imogen had finished, Bernadette looked over the affidavit which was fairly simple in content. It stated how Anh had come to Ireland and what happened there, how they were put onto the truck at the depot, and that she did not recognise Callum. To Anh's knowledge, he was not one of the people involved.

"If she signs this, it will be a good thing, but it would be far better if she would be a witness on the stand," said Bernadette once she had read it.

Imogen seemed unconvinced herself, even though she had written it.

"Do you really think it will help our case? I mean, it's just her recollection of what happened. The prosecution will negate it. They'll say just because she didn't see him, doesn't mean he wasn't there. If she is on the stand then they'll push her to say she can't know for sure"

"Of course, they will, darling, but what has she got to lose by telling the truth? Far more than their own witness and we are going to crucify him."

"Will we?"

"Yes, have faith in me, my love, we are going to take him down. I am damned if Callum is going to prison for something he didn't do. For the sake of a weaselling liar."

"You don't know he's a weasel," Imogen laughed.

"I do, he is, I've met people like him and even if I haven't met... him. I know them, they are the lowest of the low, they would turn their own mother into the law if it saved their own damn skin. No fuck it, Imogen. I don't precisely know how we can win this, but we have to."

"There's another reason," Imogen said seriously.

"What?"

"He's one of us, he's gay."

Bernadette laughed in surprise. "That's true though there are gay criminals too, but Callum is no criminal."

"We should look after our own."

"You know not long ago you were questioning if you were really gay..." Bernadette said, recalling how Imogen was in two minds about her sexuality for a long while.

"Oh... I know, but it's because I had to come to terms with it myself. I had to understand why I'd been with men if I was gay."

"You may be bisexual after all?" Bernadette cocked an eyebrow.

"Yes, but I don't think so. I'm more and more attracted to women since D'Arcy, although of course, I don't want to sleep with them."

"I know, and I understand. After all, gay men have often married women or partnered with them before discovering their true sexuality. They also did it to hide it from society. It can also be the other way around."

Imogen considered this. "True, very true. Anyway, I've decided I'm gay and that's all there is to it."

This was typical of Imogen, Bernadette reflected. Once Imogen had made up her mind it was almost impossible to shift.

"Good, that's progress, and what about your family? You've proposed to D'Arcy, but I assume you haven't told them."

Normally Bernadette kept out of Imogen's family business feeling it wasn't her place to say anything, but she felt it was perhaps time to quiz her on it.

"Not directly, no," Imogen admitted, "They would have seen it in the papers and on the television."

"Did they contact you?"

"No."

"Don't you think you *should* contact them?"

"I..." Imogen paused, she looked very unhappy all of a sudden, "I don't know what to say to them. They are probably mad at me or something."

"Or they don't know what to say to you. I mean, it's none of my concern really, honey, but if you love them, why not just call?"

Imogen went silent for a while. Bernadette ordered up some coffee and let her think.

After a while, she spoke, "You are right. I do love them. I don't see them all that much, but I care about them. Also, it is your concern, you are my friend, and nothing is off limits, particularly my family."

"Then open the bidding, it can't be worse than going to court."

"Oh, it's infinitely worse. They are the worst of judges. The very worst. All my life I've been judged. Imogen your grades aren't good. Oh, I see you got a second class with honours and not a first. I mean, fuck." Imogen made a face.

"Well, you're marrying a millionairess and a famous one to boot, so you've fallen on your feet this time. They surely can't find anything to criticise. Besides they've got to meet D'Arcy sooner or later."

"I know but that's *not* why I love D'Arcy. It's nice and it's fabulous she's rich and famous but it's not why I love her."

"Why *do* you love her?" Bernadette wondered. Although she and Imogen had talked about love before, things had moved on and was intrigued to hear the answer.

"I love her because she makes my heart sing, she gives me butterflies. She makes me feel special, beautiful, and she is so... beautiful inside and out. She is everything to me, she's my life. Without her, my heart would break and my very soul would be ripped from my body." Imogen was quite emotional by the end of this. "Also, she makes me scream in the bedroom like you wouldn't believe."

Bernadette nodded and laughed lightly. "There we are then, that's true love. You've described everything about why I love Eve. I can well believe the bedroom part."

"Bitch! You know you've heard it for yourself," Imogen giggled.

"I didn't want to mention it but, yes."

"Anyway, I'll do as you suggest when we get home."

"Good, that's my girl." Bernadette reached across, took Imogen's hand and squeezed it.

"Have we anything else to do today?" Imogen took the conversation back to work.

"I don't know. What about trying to see the senior investigating officer on the case?"

"Hmm, do you think it's a good idea? We're seeing Mason tomorrow and they might complain to him if we piss them off. He would become less cooperative."

"Yes, true. Defence barristers don't usually talk to the Garda who are pursuing their clients. I just thought we might get something out of them."

Imogen shook her head. "Far be it from me to disagree but I very much doubt they would tell us anything useful."

"I tend to agree with you, it was just a thought. So, hopefully, after Mason, we'll have the affidavit signing. We could always try the investigating officer after lunch."

"Yes."

"I feel like we've come over here and not managed to do much," said Bernadette shooting her a guilty look.

"Oh, for God's sake, will you relax? If anyone should be worrying, it's me, the junior. We had to come here for that interview if nothing else. Come on, darling, ease up on yourself and me too," Imogen said crossly.

"I know, I need to," said Bernadette with a sigh, "Eve wants us to go on a proper holiday."

"And so you should, what a great idea."

"It would be, wouldn't it. I know, I've been neglectful, and I know it," Bernadette said sadly.

"Really, darling! Stop beating yourself up, you've been so wonderful to Eve. That's just silly. Anyway, anytime you want to go on holiday then I will be able to hold the fort no problem."

"Thanks, darling. We might as well have a good time while we are here then."

"My thoughts exactly, in fact, I insist on it. If not for me then for D'Arcy and for Eve. D'Arcy is so happy to be able to treat you two. You have no idea how much she loves you both. This trip means a lot to her."

"I know. Ignore me."

"You worry too much. Eve says so and she's right."

"She's too much of damn mind reader." Bernadette rolled her eyes. "I can't get anything past her, the witch that she is."

Just then Jackson appeared with their coffee and put it down on the table. It was accompanied by some biscuits and cake which he said he felt they might enjoy. They thanked him, he bowed and discreetly withdrew.

"Oh my God, I'll be back on my diet at this rate!" said Bernadette.

"It's only one week, I'm sure your metabolism can cope."

"You are right, and the cake looks rather delicious, I will just have to force myself to eat it," Bernadette said taking a slice.

* * *

D'Arcy and Eve returned from their excursion and to Imogen's surprise D'Arcy did not arrive loaded down with shopping bags. Eve put her purchases away until later, and D'Arcy pulled Imogen into the bedroom for a tête-à-tête'. Bernadette and Eve decided to leave them to it.

"D'Arcy was remarkably restrained," Eve confided while they went for a swim before dinner.

"And how did you manage that?" Bernadette asked as they rested at the side of the pool.

"I just pretended whatever it was didn't really suit her, and then she didn't buy it."

"You evil little witch," Bernadette laughed.

"I know but imagine what would have happened otherwise. In any case, she spent a large sum of money as it was."

"And did you buy anything?" Bernadette said kissing her lightly.

"D'Arcy did buy me a couple of things which I'll show you later, and I got a nice jacket and skirt for you."

"Babe, you didn't have to."

"I did though."

"Love you."

They went out for dinner at Claridge's at D'Arcy's insistence. It was a stylish modern restaurant serving a range of high-class dishes which were less expensive than Bernadette expected and far more delicious. D'Arcy kept up a constant stream of chatter and flirted outrageously with the waitress who recognised her at once. Bernadette watched Imogen carefully, but it seemed she was managing to keep herself under control. Bernadette felt it was harmless enough. They returned to the hotel seemingly without incident and retired to bed.

"Have you had a good day, my darling?" Bernadette asked Eve kissing her gently.

"Yes, I really have. I loved Harrods we had a nice lunch there. It was tiring though. I was glad to get back to the hotel."

"I was glad to see you back. I'm sorry I could not be there, but we will plan our holiday when we get back, I promise."

"Thank you, my sweetheart."

"You can thank me in other ways."

"Mmm, you mean like this?"

"Oh, yes, just like that... oh... God... Eve..."

CHAPTER EIGHT

reakfast was an enjoyable affair. They all tried the Eggs Benedict for variety.

"So, what's on the agenda today, darlings?" D'Arcy said after consuming a couple of mouthfuls.

"We've got an important lunch with the opposition barrister, as you know, and hopefully we can get the affidavit signed too," Imogen told her.

"Where are you going to lunch?"

"The Waldorf."

"Ooh, that is one of my favourites." D'Arcy gave her a sly look.

"D'Arcy, no! You are not coming there for lunch," Imogen told her firmly.

"But, angel, can't we just... I promise we'll be quiet." D'Arcy pouted.

"No! This is business and as much as I'd love you to be there, we can't have the distraction, I'm sorry, my sweetheart." Imogen softened her tone and kissed her lightly. "Listen, remember how you wanted to go for tea at the Dorchester? You've been telling me about it for days—"

"Ooh! Yes, yes, yes!" D'Arcy clapped her hands interrupting. "We will! I will make the booking this morning."

"There, is that better?"

"Much," said D'Arcy giving Imogen puppy dog eyes.

"Anyway, D'Arcy, we don't need to be rushing around this morning, we could all have another swim perhaps?" said Eve.

"Yes, let's do that after breakfast."

Following which D'Arcy was content, and the harmony of the morning meal was once more restored. Eve told them all about their trip to Harrods, and how much she had enjoyed looking around the food hall in particular. They all had a swim, used the sauna and steam room, then D'Arcy and Eve went out to find somewhere nice for lunch.

In the meantime, there was no word from Damsa much to Imogen's annoyance.

"I know they probably don't think it's important but still," she said impatiently.

"Don't fret, they might just need some time to think. I am sure she knows it's important."

"Yes, but even so!"

They were in a taxi on the way to the Waldorf where they were meeting Mason. The Waldorf stood on Aldwych just off the Strand. It was a massive stone edifice seven stories high. The ground floor was painted yellow and above that, the frontage with its large windows was punctuated by fluted Corinthian columns. The style of the hotel was Edwardian, and the two of them marvelled at the building before going in through the portico. Inside and out the building and its interior was pure Art Deco and had been carefully restored and refurbished in recent times.

They asked for directions to the Homage restaurant and were shown to their table.

"Wow!" said Imogen looking around at the high ceilings, fluted white columns with gold capitals. They were in the raised part of the restaurant, and stairs led down to the large flat area where they used to hold tea dances. The ceiling over the dance floor consisted of squares of translucent glass which gave a warm feel to the whole place.

"It's rather beautiful," Bernadette observed.

The waiter brought them the menus and they opted for sparkling water to begin with. Mason would no doubt want alcohol, so Bernadette suggested waiting until they had ordered the food.

Very shortly their guest arrived. He was wearing a sharp blue suit, black highly polished brogues, a shirt with thin pink pinstripes, and a pink tie. He was around six foot tall with a good head of black hair, blue eyes, and clean shaven. He looked the epitome of a successful barrister with expensive attire.

"Hello, it's nice to meet you a bit more informally," he said as they stood up to greet him.

"Yes," Bernadette replied.

"Ah yes." Then he said to Imogen, "You made the arrangements."

"Yes, that's right," Imogen replied with a slight smile.

They shook hands and then resumed their seats, and Mason sat down too.

"Well, this is very nice," he said looking around, "It's a while since I've eaten here, what an excellent choice."

"Thank you." Imogen smiled.

They ordered from the menu. Mason opted for the Chef's soup, followed by a T-Bone steak medium rare. Imogen chose creamy mussels followed by a three-bone rack, and Bernadette Japanese cured salmon followed by Casterbridge sirloin. They opted for a selection of vegetables and potatoes as accompaniments. Since they were all eating meat, Bernadette ordered a bottle of Bonavita Merlot, and imagined they might well need two depending upon how much Mason had to drink. She and Imogen were going to pace themselves.

"So, before we get down to business you obviously asked me here for, tell me a little bit about yourselves, you have a successful practice in Dublin I gather from what Shane told me," Mason said sampling his wine.

Bernadette noticed the flicker of a frown cross Imogen's face at the mention of Shane, but then it was gone. Imogen had evidently still some issues over Shane, which Bernadette fervently hoped were not linked to an ongoing but suppressed attraction. She resolved perhaps to ask her about it when she got a chance.

"Yes, I started it several years ago and I'm lucky enough that it's flourishing with some fee earners. Imogen here is my junior partner in crime, or rather criminal law." Bernadette laughed lightly and buttered a roll from a basket which the waiters had brought.

"Lucky you, Shane says you're quite famous in Irish law circles."

"I don't know about famous, maybe notorious." Bernadette smiled. "You and Shane are friends?"

"Oh yes, Shaney and I go a long way back to Law school. We apprenticed together but then as you do, we went our separate ways though we've always stayed in touch. I tried to talk him out of going to Ireland but for whatever reason, he insisted."

"My understanding was they made him an offer he couldn't refuse," said Bernadette lightly.

"Oh, I'm sure but he could have made far more money here for less trouble," Mason laughed.

The waiter bought the first course and they addressed themselves to eating for a few moments. Bernadette had already got Mason's measure, she felt. He was motivated by wealth just as she thought he would be.

"So you enjoy being a prosecuting QC?" she asked him after consuming most of her salmon.

He gave a short laugh. "Enjoy isn't a word I'd use. I mean, I don't enjoy, for example, sending people to prison but it's a job which sometimes has to be done and which pays exceptionally well. I try to do it as well as I can too."

"It's not a calling then?" she said quizzing him a little on his motivations.

"I wouldn't say *that*, I chose law as opposed to banking which didn't interest me. I wanted a well-paid profession to be candid. Being a silk means I don't have to do all the leg work and I still get paid. We have briefs and solicitors who do it all for us. I just have to turn up in court and do my bit. I've done my time at the other stuff, thank you."

"I see," said Bernadette laying down her cutlery.

Imogen had been listening to this conversation intently. It was plain she did not approve at all of what she was hearing. Her expression certainly revealed itself to Bernadette who knew her extremely well.

"Is that not how you see it?" he said interested, finishing up his soup.

"I do see it differently, yes. For me, it is a calling, and even a passion. I believe passionately in justice and getting justice if I can," Bernadette said frankly.

"Shane told me as much when I asked him about you."

"We also believe in doing a lot of the leg work, as you termed it, for us, it's part of the job. I actually enjoy it and I quite enjoy the challenge of being in court too."

"Yes, Shane said you were quite formidable, and not to be underestimated," he said looking at her shrewdly.

"Ah well, he flatters me there."

"No, he doesn't, she's extremely formidable and has a fearsome reputation," Imogen said suddenly.

"And you, is it why you work for her?" he said directing this at Imogen.

"Yes, we have the same passions for justice, and I've learned a huge amount from her too."

"I wouldn't doubt it."

The waiter removed the empty plates.

"That was delicious by the way," Mason added as the waiter left, "I can't wait for the mains."

"Amazing flavours, I agree," said Bernadette, "Very subtle, how were your mussels, Imogen?"

"Beautiful, loved them."

"So, then while we're waiting, perhaps you might tell why you wanted this meeting," Mason said getting to the point.

"Sure, of course."

He regarded her expectantly.

"Well," she began, "I want to know why you are pursuing my client so vigorously to the point of wanting him extradited."

"I see."

"It's a reasonable question," she said slightly nettled.

"Indeed, it is, and I'm trying to frame a reasonable answer."

"Did you think we'd come to negotiate, or perhaps look for a plea bargain?" Imogen enquired.

"The thought did cross my mind."

"She doesn't do that, it's not her style."

"Yes... so..."

"Shane told you?" she finished the sentence for him.

"Yes."

"Shane seems to have told you a lot of things."

"He err... likes to study the opposition as it were, always did, it's one of his traits I'm afraid," he said almost apologetically.

"I'm glad to have been a subject of his study then," said Imogen slightly acidly which made him look at her a little askance.

Fortunately, the waiter arrived with the main courses, and laid out dishes of cauliflower and cheese gratin, sauteed French beans with confit shallots, grilled asparagus tossed in clarified butter and *Pomme Dauphinoise*.

"Mmm, delicious," said Mason having helped himself to a liberal portion of the side dishes and cut into his steak to take a bite.

"It is rather," said Bernadette trying her own with satisfaction.

Imogen put her attention back on her food, and Bernadette hoped she might curb her belligerence a little for the sake of some détente. Halfway through his steak, Mason's phone rang. He pulled it from his pocket and looked at it.

"Damn, so sorry, I really have to take this. It's another case about to come to court, I won't be long." With a regretful glance at his half-finished steak, he left the room.

Bernadette called the waiter over and asked him to keep Mason's plate warm, then she turned to Imogen.

"Will you please lighten up for goodness sakes, darling, your animosity towards Shane isn't helping us," she said without trying to sound cross.

"I'm sorry," said Imogen at once, "I can't help it, he just makes me so angry."

"Well, we are going to have a discussion about that," said Bernadette firmly.

"We are?" Imogen suddenly looked like a naughty schoolgirl.

"Yes, you are going to tell me what the problem really is between you and Shane."

"Oh shit, can't you just put me over your knee instead?"

"No, I can't, tempting as it may be," Bernadette laughed, "But you need to come clean."

"OK, after he's gone then."

"OK, but please in the meantime, I'm trying to get some mileage out of this meal and antagonising him isn't going to help."

"Sorry, darling."

"I love you, Imogen, but just please try."

"I will, I'm sorry again."

"That's OK."

"Are you sure you don't want to spank me anyway, as a punishment?" Imogen said playfully.

"No! Now stop it."

The two of them laughed then and resumed eating. Shortly afterwards Mason returned and was grateful Bernadette had asked them to keep his food warm.

"So sorry about that, I do hate taking phone calls over meals, but it was something rather urgent."

"It's quite alright," said Bernadette. She let him eat in peace. She and Imogen had almost finished their own dishes.

He pushed his plate away at length. "That was marvellous," he said taking another drink, "Absolutely marvellous. Nothing like a decent steak to set you up for the afternoon."

"Yes, or at least a satisfying lunch."

Bernadette noticed the wine bottle was empty and asked him if he'd like her to order another.

"Oh no, not for me," he demurred, "But you go right ahead. My days of heavy lunches are over. Most of us are the same now, can't afford to get tipsy, muddles the thinking. Back in the day of course we'd be necking down a couple of bottles, but things are different now, many things."

"We're not ones for lunchtime drinking either, not in the ordinary way," Bernadette admitted.

"Ah, then I'm flattered I relaxed the rules," he laughed.

The waiter arrived and removed the plates, asked if they wanted the dessert menu. Bernadette said they may as well.

"You asked me a question," said Mason at length, "And I suppose I should answer it."

"I'd like it if you did."

"OK, well, the short answer is that we obviously think your man is guilty, and we want him to pay the price for it in the UK."

Bernadette considered this for a moment and decided to push a bit harder. "On the say so of one witness? Even I feel that's a bit thin."

He smiled. "I can see why Shane is in awe of you, you're very direct."

"It's my job."

"Then you'll know as well as I do, we want him back in the UK to prosecute him obviously. Plus we can't question him about the trafficking until he's in the UK and charged, for obvious reasons."

"You're very candid."

"You asked, I felt you deserved an honest answer," he said simply.

"Even so, I can't feel there isn't more to it. You've offered this guy a plea bargain, come on, if he rats out someone else because he'll be a useful lever into the gang."

"Well, as to that," he said slightly taken aback with her blunt manner, "I couldn't possibly comment."

"You are happy for my guy to take the fall even if he's innocent or not, because your coppers over here want to nail the gang. This is their way in." Bernadette cocked an eyebrow at him.

"Shane was definitely right about you, and of course I can't affirm or deny anything you say." He had coloured up a little and seemed disconcerted.

"It's true though isn't it?" she persisted with a smile playing around her lips.

"Is this, also, on or off the record?" he said realising he was unable to avoid her penetrating style of questioning.

"Whatever you say here is, of course, without prejudice," she replied blandly.

He thought for a moment, looking at the menu without seeing it.

"It's not always possible to do things the way you want to do them. Sometimes there are unpalatable things which are done for expediency."

"No doubt," she said drily.

He sighed. "I'm bloody glad I'm not facing you on the witness stand."

She laughed at this. "Choose a dessert if you want, we owe you one I feel."

He perused the menu and so did they. Bernadette opted for glazed lemon tart with mascarpone cream, Imogen a duo of chocolate mousse and sugar cranachan, and Mason spotted dick and custard. He confessed it was a favourite from his Harrow school days, and Bernadette was not surprised to hear he'd gone to a public school like that.

"So, Shane is in awe of me, is he?" said Bernadette picking up on what he said earlier.

"Does it surprise you?"

"Frankly, yes, I must admit he came across as an arrogant prick when I first met him."

Mason laid back his head and laughed out loud.

"Oh, he would love that, really he would. I can understand why you would think so, he's certainly got that way about him. Underneath he's quite a sweetie really."

Imogen just managed to suppress a snort at this. Mason looked at her keenly, but she pretended to cough instead.

"So far he hasn't shown his true colours then," Bernadette said wryly.

"Oh, you have to know him like I do, then you'd understand. He's a complex character."

"I'm sure."

The dessert arrived and they also ordered coffee. As they ate, they moved onto less contentious topics. Bernadette was keen to steer the conversation away from Shane because of Imogen.

"Is there anything else you want to ask me?" Mason asked once the dessert had been consumed. He flicked a glance at his watch, and Bernadette imagined he probably had somewhere else to be very shortly.

"I don't suppose you would consider simply withdrawing your case?"

"I'm afraid not." Mason shrugged. "Even if I wanted to, my hands are tied you see. We all serve a higher master."

"I don't," Bernadette replied with a smile sipping her coffee.

"Your client surely is your master, in a way, though aren't they?"

"I don't regard them that way no. I support their cause, I'm their champion."

"It's a better way of looking at it I suppose." He drained his cup. "I'm afraid I've got to go, as enjoyable as your company is, but I've another meeting."

"I appreciate you taking the time to come."

"I'm sorry I wasn't able to help. Thank you for lunch, I enjoyed it very much."

"You are welcome."

He stood up to go. Bernadette and Imogen did too.

"Thanks for your time," she said shaking his hand.

"I guess I'll see you in court."

"You will."

Imogen said goodbye, and he nodded, turned on his heel and left. They watched him go and sat down again.

"Another coffee?" said Bernadette.

"Sure, why not."

Imogen signalled the waiter who came over and took their order.

"I'm amazed the way you kept your cool with him. He struck me as a fucking pompous prick," Imogen said once the waiter had gone.

"When you are fraternising with the enemy it's essential to keep a level head."

"I'm going to have to learn how to do that."

"Your fiery temper, Imogen, you'll have to learn to curb it and you will." Bernadette smiled.

"The penalty of being a redhead."

"Indeed, but I'm sure, as D'Arcy will testify a redhead has other merits, passion, for example."

"God yes, I'm horny as fuck."

"Yes, that too."

"Do you think we accomplished anything?" Imogen wondered, it seemed to her as if they'd not really managed to achieve much.

"We did, of course. We know why they are doing it. He didn't deny it. So, we know where we stand. Callum is a scapegoat as much as anything."

"Couldn't we use it?"

Bernadette shook her head. "Not exactly as such, we can't put it to the judge, at least not in so many words. The conversation we had was strictly between us, for the most part. That's how it is, and it's why I don't really like doing them. In this case, it was necessary."

"I *do* have a lot to learn." Imogen sighed.

"Learn to be cordial and friendly in these situations, darling. It will stand you in good stead."

"I hope I can." This was said with feeling. Imogen had not quite got the hang of bridling her temper on occasions.

"You can, and you will, it comes with time and maturity."

"Are you saying I'm not mature?"

"No, darling, I mean as you get older and you have more experience, you'll deal with it better. The job of a barrister isn't always just in the courtroom, as you know."

"I know," said Imogen with a sigh, "Sometimes I think there's also so much I don't know."

"Stop, for goodness' sake, darling. You are doing so well. I've been doing this for years. I can teach you to avoid my mistakes, so you don't need to make them."

Imogen laughed. "You are so patient with me. I don't know how you manage it."

"Because I love you to bits. Now," said Bernadette, as the second lot of coffee arrived, "You are going to tell me the truth about Shane."

"Oh shit, I thought you had forgotten." Imogen shot her a stricken look.

"No, because you've obviously got something going on, darling, and I want you to tell me what it is."

"Fuck," said Imogen and took refuge in her coffee.

"Is it so bad?"

Imogen nodded.

"Have you been sleeping with him?" Bernadette said smoothly.

"What? No! Nothing like *that*! For fuck's sake, Bernadette," said Imogen nearly spitting out her drink.

"It's called the murder technique," Bernadette laughed, "You ask someone something worse than what you think they've done, and then they tell you the truth..."

"Because what they've done isn't as bad, you've told me this before," Imogen finished it for her.

"You got it, so what is it?"

"OK. I still... I still fancy him."

"OK." Bernadette raised her eyebrow.

"Don't do that to me, it makes me feel like a naughty child."

"That's not all is it, though."

"Fuck no, I fantasise about him fucking me with his great big schlong and then I see him. I get angry because it brings up those... feelings..." Imogen trailed off.

"Feelings which you want to consummate?"

"Shit you're hard, you are so fucking hard." Imogen's eyes were suddenly wet.

"I'm not, darling, but you need to face it, or you never will," Bernadette said implacably.

"Well no, I don't want to really consummate it because I love D'Arcy and it could never be. It would never work with me and Shane, even if I wanted to. I don't even love him. It's just my... fucking vagina which lets me down." Suddenly Imogen let out a big sigh, somehow admitting it to herself she felt somehow relieved.

"Better?"

"Yes." Imogen nodded. "Yes, how did you know?"

"I learned it from the best, from you." Bernadette smiled.

"Well fuck me and my big mouth," Imogen laughed.

"It wasn't so bad, was it?"

"No, but I feel bad because I feel as if I have betrayed D'Arcy even if it's in my head."

"You are silly, but I understand."

"I may have to tell her."

"Oh?" Bernadette wondered if this was wise, but she didn't say anything to her.

"So there are no secrets between us."

"It's your choice of course." Bernadette sipped her drink for a moment, "And is that everything?"

Imogen seemed to hesitate for a moment, as if considering something further.

"Yes. That's all."

Evidently, there wasn't anything else. Bernadette was quite relieved.

"OK. So, look, we all can have, let's say momentary feelings of physical attraction, but it's what we do with them which counts. If you are in a loving and committed relationship, then you don't do anything."

"Even you fancy other people?" Imogen was slightly incredulous.

"Yes, even me, I'm not a saint. But it doesn't go past that. The chemical physical thing, whatever it is, has nothing to compare to the spiritual and the physical love I have for Eve."

"It makes me feel better."

"That I might find other women attractive?"

"Yes."

"OK, well, next time I'll point them out to you. Shall I?" Bernadette's eyes twinkled.

"Oh you! You always take it to the next level."

Bernadette laughed and sipped her drink.

"I'm glad I'm not like Mason," Imogen said with feeling.

"What? A person who only cares about money?"

"Yes."

"I'm sure he cares about his job too, but it's certainly not his main motivation."

"There needs to be more for me. Much more."

"And there is so much more, my sweet, and that's why you're a partner."

"Thank you. Anyway, isn't it time for us to get going? We are due at the Dorchester soon," said Imogen changing the subject.

"Yes, of course. If you are sure there is nothing else you want to tell me?" Bernadette wanted to be doubly certain.

"Well, there is my big fantasy about you putting me over your knee and spanking me and using the very sexy assertive voice of yours but I didn't think you'd want to know about *that*..." Imogen's eyes were dancing.

"Oh stop it!" Bernadette giggled, "What are you like?"

"A girl can dream..."

"You are completely incorrigible."

"You're easy to tease."

"Yes, well." Bernadette signalled for the bill and got her credit card out to pay.

"Oh God, the food was to die for though, wasn't it?" Imogen said as the waiter brought the bill and took Bernadette's card.

"Yes, it really was."

"I would certainly come here again."

"With D'Arcy, I'm sure you'll have plenty of chances to do so."

* * *

The Dorchester sits on Park Lane and is accessed from Deanery Street. It's a seven story Art Deco building with ornate balcony railings. The Dorchester is a luxury hotel and afternoon tea is served in the Promenade. A long narrow room with marbled columns, and plush wood upholstered chairs, and benches. There are palms in dark polished wooden planters and floral arrangements of white roses in large brass urns. The curtains are greens and golds, as is the upholstery of the furniture.

Bernadette and Imogen strolled into the tea rooms. D'Arcy was waving at them and yelling, "Yoo-hoo," rather loudly. They walked along the highly polished marble floor with inlaid patterns, to a sofa and chairs on two sides of a table which was covered with a pristine white tablecloth.

"Oh, darlings, we've been waiting for ages." D'Arcy pouted. "I thought you were never coming!"

"Sorry, beautiful." Imogen gave her a kiss. "We've not long finished lunch, and then we had to get here and..."

"It's OK, I'm so happy you are finally here, what do you think?"

"It's beautiful, certainly very grand," said Imogen looking around.

"Fabulous," said Bernadette.

"Wait until you see the tea!" D'Arcy told them, "I've ordered it already and coffee for you two."

"Thanks, honey," said Bernadette, "Where's Eve?"

Eve who had not been in evidence, appeared walking towards them.

"Oh, I knew if I went to the ladies, I'd miss you," said Eve hurrying over to embrace Bernadette.

"My darling, I'm glad to see you."

"Not half as glad as I am to see you! And oh my God, you should see the ladies' room, talk about posh."

"Anyway, let's sit down, you can tell us about your morning," Bernadette said pulling her into the seat next to her.

"Well, we found this lovely little Lebanese restaurant... up the Edgeware road," Eve began.

Tea arrived on stacked white plates, and a long white dish containing finger sandwiches without any crusts garnished with flowers and greenery. There was an array of little fancy cakes, plus scones and butter with jam. Tea was served in a pot along with milk and hot water. There was a pot of coffee too.

"Wow," said Imogen, "This looks absolutely scrumptious."

"Isn't it?" said D'Arcy delighted, "Come on, dig in girls."

They consumed the sandwiches and cakes, accompanied by tea and coffee. There was plenty to go around.

"How's the food?" D'Arcy wanted to know.

"Delicious, the sandwiches and cakes are amazing," said Bernadette.

"I second that," said Eve.

"How was your lunch?" D'Arcy wanted to know once they had eaten most of the repast and were beginning to feel quite full.

"Oh, you know, he was one of those toff barristers who just care about money," said Imogen.

"Oh, how awful."

"So you didn't get anything out of him?" Eve asked Bernadette.

"We know they are using Callum to get at the gang, and they don't care if he's innocent or guilty. They are doing a deal with their witness and they need a head on a pike."

"Oh, how terrible, what is wrong with these people!" said D'Arcy crossly.

"They've got no fucking ethics," said Imogen wryly.

"Well, that's too bad of them."

"We know where they are coming from, it helps. We also know it's not so much about Callum which gives us an edge," Bernadette added.

"But you said you couldn't use it," Imogen said surprised.

"There are ways and ways, I can't use it exactly overtly, but I may be able to use it a little more subtly." Bernadette winked.

"What are you planning?"

"I'm not sure yet, but it will come to me."

"He sounds like an odious prick," said D'Arcy with feeling, "He's just the sort of arsehole I've had to deal with in the film business but worse."

Just then Imogen's phone rang, she answered it, it was Damsa. She spoke briefly and disconnected.

"Well?" said Bernadette.

"Anh says she will sign the affidavit, we will meet her at Damsa's offices in the morning."

"Great news."

"Yay, so it means I've got you for the rest of the evening," said D'Arcy happily.

"And I've got you," said Eve to Bernadette.

"What should we do? Go out and see the sights or go to a show? What do you want to do?" Bernadette said to Eve.

"Oh, I don't know. We've been out a lot already," Eve said with a sigh.

"I know but this is London, shouldn't we be going out on the town?"

"I just want to be with you, go for a swim, have a nice meal, maybe watch some TV and go to bed," Eve said catching Bernadette's hand and holding it fast.

"Then if it's what you want, that's what we will do."

She reflected Eve was quite the homebody after all. London was great but it also made one set expectations of going here there and everywhere which was also quite exhausting.

"Sounds like a great idea," said D'Arcy, "We could eat in one of the restaurants downstairs at the hotel."

"Yes, it's settled then." Imogen smiled. "I could do with an early night anyway."

Having agreed on the entertainment for the evening, they turned their attention to polishing off the remains of the tea.

CHAPTER NINE

The evening had progressed well, as intended. After a leisurely dinner at the hotel at the Palm Court restaurant, they had indeed watched a movie and gone to bed. In the morning after another full English breakfast, Bernadette and Imogen once more headed for the offices of the Refugee Assistance Organisation in a taxi to get the affidavit signed. Imogen had emailed it to Damsa the afternoon before so Damsa could print it and give Anh time to read it.

Both Imogen and Bernadette had dressed down for the day, wearing casual trousers, sandals, a blouse and jacket.

"Did you talk to D'Arcy then?" said Bernadette, hoping she hadn't, as the taxi made its way to Docklands.

"Oh, no I bottled out. Besides I didn't want to spoil things or upset her at least not while we are here. We just had great sex instead."

"Probably a good choice," Bernadette agreed thankfully.

"I might tell her at home, if the mood is right, or maybe I'll let it lie. I feel better for telling you, maybe it's enough." Imogen smiled.

"It could be a wise decision," Bernadette said diplomatically. She felt D'Arcy was quite fragile and as such might not be able to take such a revelation with equanimity. She was all for honesty but not at the detriment of Imogen's relationship. Imogen would be better learning to deal with these attractions rather than feeling driven to confess them.

"And you?" Imogen asked, "Still going to talk to Eve?"

"Yes, it's important to me, so I will." Bernadette wondered why she didn't take her own advice, but Eve's obsession seemed to go much deeper and she just felt she had to know.

"I'll be on the end of the phone if needed."

"Thanks, darling, I'm hoping it won't blow up into anything."

"OK." Imogen looked doubtful. Eve and Bernadette had had at least a couple of explosive episodes. Eve could be quite volatile in temperament, in spite of all appearances to the contrary.

"Wish me luck then."

Imogen reached over and took Bernadette's hand, she squeezed it affectionally signifying her unspoken support.

"What's next once we get back?" Imogen wondered.

"We'll need to prepare for the prehearing conference, and then get all our ducks in a row."

"Right."

The taxi pulled up at the ROA Offices, and they made their way once more to the reception. Very shortly they found themselves once more in Damsa's office where Anh was already sitting at the meeting table.

"Hi, Anh," said Bernadette, "How are you?"

"I'm fine, thank you," said Anh shaking her by the hand, and then doing the same for Imogen.

They sat down while Damsa ordered tea and coffee. Damsa was wearing a flowery style green summery dress and green flat mules. She looked at ease and Bernadette thought she was exceptionally beautiful. She almost unconsciously sized up women, she realised, and wondered whether this was a good or a bad thing. However, this wasn't the time to ponder such issues.

"Anh," she said, addressing their witness who was looking quite summery herself in a short shift and flipflops. It wasn't really summer yet, but the weather has somehow been kind in London, and it was quite warm. "You decided to sign the affidavit, Damsa tells us."

"Yes." Anh nodded.

"I am very glad you have, but can I ask what made you decide?"

Anh paused for a moment before she spoke, perhaps thinking of how to phrase it. English wasn't her first language.

"I thought very hard about this man, who you are representing. I thought for a long time about how this man may go to prison. If he truly is innocent, then this is a punishment he doesn't deserve. I thought about my own life, and how I have also felt as if I was in prison for so many years. I was afraid and lived in fear for my life, and that I would be forced to marry a man I hated."

Anh stopped, looking quite emotional, her eyes were suddenly a little brighter, moist.

"I have been given a chance for a new life, freedom, I have been lucky. But your man, he may not be so lucky. And I thought..." Anh stopped and brushed a slight tear away. "I thought... what if this man goes to prison because of me... because I did not speak out."

Bernadette glanced at Imogen they were both welling up listening to this moving speech.

"I would spend my life in freedom, but this man would not be free. Every day I knew I would think of it and hate myself for having no courage... and I cannot be that person. I decided... Anh, you must speak up, then you can never say you did not do the right thing. My father taught me I must always do the right thing and to honour my father, I must do this."

Bernadette dashed a tear from her own eye, and spontaneously got up from her chair. "Anh, may I please, please, give you a hug?"

Anh smiled, shyly and stood up. Bernadette was a little taller than Anh, but she held out her arms and embraced her.

"Thank you," said Bernadette choked up with emotion, "Thank you for being so brave."

"You are very kind," said Anh looking up at her. The two of them were crying now, as were Imogen and Damsa.

Not to be left out, Imogen insisted on embracing Anh too and thanking her.

The refreshments arrived, and it gave them time to compose themselves.

"Well," said Damsa, after sipping her coffee, "That wasn't how my meetings usually go."

"No." Bernadette laughed.

Anh laughed and drank some of her tea.

"Have you read the affidavit?" Bernadette asked her at length.

"Yes."

"Is it OK? Are you happy to sign it without any changes?"

"Yes, it's fine, I will sign it."

It was fortunate that Damsa as well as being a qualified solicitor was also a Notary Public. She was able to witness the affidavit and stamp it.

"I became a Notary Public because we do have quite a lot of these things," Damsa told them.

"It certainly makes it easier," said Bernadette.

Anh signed two copies and Damsa put a stamp on it and notarised it after taking an oath from her. She put them into a brown envelope and handed them to Imogen.

"Thank you, thank you so much, Anh, we'll ensure the court preserves your anonymity," said Bernadette.

Anh nodded and smiled prettily.

"Can I ask you one more thing?" Bernadette continued. They had come this far, she had to see if Anh would take one more step.

"I know what you want." Anh smiled. "And if it will help your man, I will testify."

"Wow, thank you, I really mean it, thank you." Bernadette smiled back at her.

"We will arrange to set up a video link and that your face won't be seen. We will maintain anonymity for you," Imogen told her.

"Thank you," said Anh.

"I am concerned for your safety. Do you think she and her friends will be OK?" Imogen asked Damsa.

"We are making arrangements to move them somewhere else which is more secure," said Damsa, "It's difficult of course, but Anh knows the risks, we've discussed them at length."

"I know I may not be safe, nor my friends, but soon I will move from them so they will be safer without me. Damsa says she will look after me."

"OK, I can't thank you enough. I wish there was more I could do for you," said Bernadette.

"We'll do our very best," said Damsa, "Don't worry."

"I will be OK. I believe my destiny brought me here, and Buddha says your destiny will find itself," Anh said.

Bernadette finished her coffee, and Imogen nodded she was ready to go.

"Thank you again, both of you, for your help. We'll be in touch with Damsa about the court appearance, it won't be for a little while in any case."

They all stood up. All the women embraced, as if they had become firm friends. Sometimes it only takes the sharing of emotion, Bernadette reflected, to bond with someone.

In the taxi on the way back to the hotel, Imogen said, "That went well."

"Yes, we certainly got more than we expected," Bernadette agreed.

"She is very courageous."

"It's a shame we can't help her more."

"What if we could?" said Imogen suddenly.

"What do you mean?"

"If she's a material witness to the case, then maybe the Garda could get her over to Ireland. They could pull some strings. She could settle in Ireland."

"Hmm, though wouldn't she be placing herself in even more danger?" Bernadette wondered.

"True, but it could be a path to citizenship."

"We can talk to Olivia. They won't be interested unless it can add something to their investigation."

"It can add the fact she was put on in Ireland. She might recognise the place they were boarded, and they want to nail those people in the yard."

"OK, we can at least try. Even if it's possible, Anh may not want to come."

"That's a different thing."

"Look at you, calling up Olivia," Bernadette said in a teasing voice.

"Stop it!" Imogen said with mock severity.

"I actually really like her. In any case, even if you had been interested, and not had D'Arcy, she probably wouldn't have been up for your games."

"You're right, that's kind of a big deal too I suppose. Finding the right person is hard."

"Then be glad you have," Bernadette said admonishing her lightly.

"I am."

"You better not be getting cold feet," said Bernadette a bit more seriously.

"Or?" Imogen's eyes were dancing.

"Don't even say it!"

Imogen contented herself with smacking the palm of one hand lightly with the other while a smile lurked around her lips.

"You are incorrigible, do you know that?"

"Yes, I do, that's why you love me so much," Imogen laughed.

"What are you like?" Bernadette shook her head and sighed.

"I'm the best ever junior counsel you've ever had, admit it."

"You are more than that and you know it. You're the best friend I ever had and I'm grateful for that," Bernadette said in a rush of emotion.

"Thank you, I'll stop teasing you... for now."

Imogen smiled and they held hands enjoying their mutual companionship.

* * *

At the hotel, Eve had packed their cases and D'Arcy announced that the limo was going to collect them after lunch. She looked a little sad, but Imogen embraced her and kissed her softly telling her how much she had enjoyed the last few days. This was roundly endorsed by Bernadette and Eve.

The flight back from Biggin Hill was uneventful, and they were soon being dropped off at home.

"Thanks so much, darling, for everything," said Bernadette giving D'Arcy a big hug.

"You have to come soon, to stay, I insist," said D'Arcy who was a little teary eyed.

"We will, we promise," said Eve, "I will teach you some more of those tricks."

"Yes, you have to, don't forget."

"We won't."

They said goodbye to Imogen and gratefully closed the door.

"I'm glad to be home, darling," said Eve.

"So am I."

"There's no place like it."

"Home is where you are," said Eve kissing Bernadette soundly.

They passed a pleasant evening enjoying each other's company, and in the morning after breakfast, Bernadette decided it was time to broach the tricky subject.

They were sitting together in the living room.

"Shall we go for a walk on the beach?" Eve said pondering their plans for the weekend.

"I'd love that, but there's something I wanted to ask you first," said Bernadette taking her courage in her hands.

"I knew it. I've known it for days."

"Oh fuck! How do you manage it?"

"Because I am a witch, and I can read your thoughts," Eve laughed.

"It's nothing bad, I promise you." Bernadette smiled.

"Go on, you've been chewing it over, whatever it is, so now you can ask me."

"If I ask you this question, can you tell me honestly? And please try not to get mad at me?" Bernadette asked her gently.

"I'm not that bad, am I?" Eve said still smiling.

"No, not *that* bad." Bernadette laughed trying to lighten her own mood as much as anything. She was approaching this with a great deal of trepidation.

"Go, on just ask me."

Bernadette took a deep breath.

"OK. Is there something you are not telling me about your past? About your sister? Because I feel as if there is."

There was a very long pause. While Eve said nothing at all and looked at Bernadette. Finally, Eve reached out her hands and took hold of her fiancée's.

"Yes, there is," she said quietly.

"Why didn't you tell me? Don't you feel I deserve to know?" Bernadette was trying not to make this sound like an accusation.

"You do, but..." Eve's voice became almost a whisper, "I'm ashamed."

"Why? You should never be ashamed. Certainly not to me," Bernadette said squeezing her hands.

"I just feel that way."

"OK, so are you going to tell me now?"

Eve let go of her hands, got up and went over to where her art desk was. She now had a cabinet to keep all her drawings in too, with wide drawers. She opened a drawer took something out, handed it to Bernadette and sat down again.

"What's this?" said Bernadette examining it, although it was perfectly clear what it was.

"It's a scene."

The picture was quite graphic in some ways. It depicted a rough looking table and a girl, perhaps sixteen or seventeen bending over it naked. There were stripes running across her buttocks. Beside her, another girl stood over her holding a cane. She recognised the girl or thought she did.

"A made-up scene or a real scene?"

Eve dropped her head. "It's real."

"Is that your sister?"

"Yes."

"Did she do this to you?"

"Yes."

Bernadette was flabbergasted and also immediately angry with her sister all over again.

"Really?"

"Yes."

"God!"

"Are you angry?"

"No, I'm upset, for you. Tell me what happened."

Eve wouldn't look her in the face and shook her head.

"Go on, please, just tell me, darling."

"It's hard."

"Well, you have to now. I only know half the story."

"Yes, but you have to turn your back to me, I can't bring myself to tell it otherwise," said Eve seriously.

Bernadette realised this must have been somehow incredibly traumatic for Eve. She did as she was bid and turned so was sitting cross legged facing away from her.

"Now can you tell me?" Bernadette said softly.

Eve began to recount the incident from her youth in halting tones.

"I was just turned seventeen, just starting to experiment with girls. I had a friend, her name was Fiona, she was pretty, so sexy, I fancied her, even maybe loved her. I found out she felt the same and we started to fool around, kissing and stuff after school and then one day, things went a bit further. It was summer, my parents were out. I thought it was just me and Fiona. We went into the garden, stripped naked, there were plenty of secluded spots. We began to get down to it when my sister caught us."

Eve paused. Bernadette did not dare turn around and could not see if she was crying. She waited until Eve continued.

"My sister was very angry. I've never seen her so angry. She told Fiona to get out and that she was the devil or something like that. Then she told me she was going to tell our parents. She said I was a dreadful sinner and they needed to know. I was scared of what they would think. I begged her not to, I pleaded with her."

Eve choked on a sob. It took all Bernadette's strength of will not to turn around and hold her in her arms.

"So, she suddenly had this cruel smile, and that's when I knew what a bitch she really was. She said she would not tell after all but then I would have to accept a punishment from her. I asked her what she meant by punishment, and she said it didn't matter, but unless I agreed she would tell my parents. If I took my punishment, then she would keep my secret. I had no idea what she was going to do, but I was desperate, so I agreed. You have to understand I was so scared of what they might think of me, so stupid of me."

Eve stopped again, and Bernadette could swear she was silently crying.

"Can I turn around now?" Bernadette said tentatively.

"No! Not yet," Eve said her voice cracking.

"OK, it's OK, I'm not turning round, I love you so much, just tell me it all."

After a few moments of silence, Eve continued.

"She told me to go to the greenhouse and wait. I asked to put my clothes on, and she said no. It was a big greenhouse, my father liked to grow plants. It was so tall too. We had a walled garden and the greenhouse was long and attached to the wall. Inside it, there was a table, a wooden table where he potted his plants. I waited in there naked, not knowing what was coming. Eventually, my sister came back, she was carrying her bible. She went to the corner where my father kept his garden canes and spent a long time before she pulled one out. A long thin one, like a metre long. I said, 'what are doing?' She replied, 'I'm going to punish you, you deserve a whipping and I'm going to give it to you. I'm going to do what our parents won't do and what you sorely need.'"

"What!" exclaimed Bernadette unable to stop herself.

"Don't speak!" said Eve almost angrily.

"Sorry... sorry..."

"I said I didn't want that, and she told me I had no choice. I had agreed to it. She said it was that or my parents. It seemed like telling my parents would be worse. So, I nodded. Then she got the bible, lectured me on homosexuality. Of course, I know now all that anti-gay stuff was put in later, but she said God knew I was a terrible sinner, the worst kind. I sort of half believed it. She told me that the bible says not to spare the rod. All this time I was standing there naked and scared out of my wits at what was going to happen."

Bernadette felt Eve move closer to her, and Eve's arms draw around her for comfort, but she kept very quiet.

"Then she put the bible down and she told me to bend over the table. She walked around in front of me, so I could see her flexing that cane. Telling me how I was going to get the whipping of my life. She relished that part, I could tell, making me scared of what it was going to feel like. She said

I deserved it for being a mortal sinner, a harlot and lesbian bitch, things like that. She said I had had it coming for a long time. I could tell she'd been planning it somehow, a way to get me into that situation. And then.... then she began..."

Eve pulled her closer now, and Bernadette could feel the wetness on her back, as Eve's tears flowed freely as did hers. Bernadette's were mixed with an indescribable anger she could hardly control. The anger of wanting to somehow physically hurt Eve's sister very badly if she only could.

"She whipped me with that cane, over and over again, but not fast, slowly. Stroke after stroke, deliberately. Each time she'd tell me I was a whore, a slut, a sinner. Then she would do it again. It fucking hurt, it stung like fire. I tried to count them, but I lost count. I cried but she didn't stop. I begged her to stop. She just told me to take it. I've no idea how many times she did it but eventually, it finished. She stood there looking at me and I could see she was so happy at what she had done."

It was all Bernadette could do to stop herself from swearing out loud in anger. Eve was still talking.

"She made me lie there for a long time before I could get up. She asked me if I had learned my lesson. I nodded though it taught me nothing but what a fucking bitch she really is. Then she let me go and get dressed. I looked in the mirror and I saw the stripes; my backside was crimson. I was ashamed, so ashamed that I had let her violate me like that. I hated her, I fucking hated her so much..."

The dam finally burst, and Eve began to sob into Bernadette's back pulling her arms so tight, while her body was wracked with sob after sob after sob. Bernadette's hands came up to clasp Eve's and she held them fast. She still did not dare turn around although every part of her being wanted to do so.

"I'm sorry, I'm so sorry, my darling," Bernadette whispered.

"She hurt me so much, Bernadette, so much and she enjoyed it, I could see it in her face, I could see how much she had loved doing that to me," Eve said through the sobs.

"I'm sorry, darling, can I hold you? Please let me hold you."

"Yes, yes, I want you to."

Almost with a sigh of relief, Bernadette turned around and took Eve into her arms. Eve sagged gratefully against her chest and put her head on Eve's shoulder. Bernadette stroked her hair softly.

"It wasn't the end of it," Eve said at length.

"No?"

Bernadette wondered what else her dreadful sister could have done, and how she was going to stop herself somehow remonstrating with her sister one way or another. If her sister was standing there right now, Bernadette would have slapped her into the middle of next week without hesitation.

"No, I thought it was over, but it wasn't. I avoided her as much as possible, while she smirked in the background. A week later she came to my room. She said that my parents were going out for the afternoon and I was to get another caning. She said once was not enough, and I was to be ready to be punished whenever and wherever she wanted. If I didn't agree she said she was going to tell my parents. She said I was a filthy sinner and she had prayed to God. God had told her she had to beat the lesbianism out of me."

Eve's voice was beginning to sound stronger, tinged with anger.

"What happened?"

"I told her to fuck off. I said no way was it happening again. I ran downstairs to my parents and I told them I was gay. I wasn't going through it again. My parents were understanding and accepting, more than I expected. My sister was livid. I think she wanted to have that power over me, and I took it away. From then on, she was against me in everything and I began to hate her. I do, hate her, I hate her so fucking much!"

"Fuck!" said Bernadette.

Eve looked at her. She was relieved, as if a weight had been lifted off her shoulders. Eve was tentative wondering how Bernadette had reacted. "Are you... angry with me?"

Bernadette was slightly incredulous., "With you? Why should I be? Fuck no, darling, I'm fuming, with your sister. I'd like to give her a taste of her own medicine. What a fucking bitch! I want to slap her so hard, I can't even begin to tell you." She softened herself a little. "But how are you? It was obviously very painful for you. Are you feeling a little better?"

"Thank you, yes, it feels better for telling you. I'm hungry now though. Would you like some lunch?"

"Sure, but shall we order a takeaway?" Bernadette didn't want her to feel obliged to cook, especially not after what Eve had just been through.

"I would like to make it, it will help me, relax me a little."

"OK, so..." Bernadette paused, she had to ask, now they were through perhaps the worst confession, "Is there more?"

They were in the zone and she felt it might as well be all out there if there was anything else. It would be good to get everything out into the open. It had all gone well so far.

"A bit, not bad like *that*, but I'll tell you afterwards." Eve smiled for the first time. "Consider this an intermission."

"OK, my darling, but can I... kiss you?"

"I want you to kiss me so badly it hurts."

They kissed. It was a full-on fireworks kiss. Bernadette felt the shivers go up her spine and wondered, not for the first time, exactly how Eve produced such a reaction in her. Eve said she felt it too, but Bernadette had never felt anything like it from anyone else.

Eve got up and went to the kitchen. Bernadette followed her and they made lunch together. They made a Vietnamese salad with zucchini and carrot noodles, other fresh veg and stir-fried pork. Eve served it up with a small portion of rice. They sat at the table very close to each other. Bernadette kept caressing Eve's arm as they consumed the food. They ate in reflective silence. Afterwards, Eve led her back to the sofa.

"So, this is round two." She smiled.

"OK, should I prepare myself?" Bernadette laughed lightly.

"My sister didn't do anything else which I haven't told you, I promise. But there was part of me which hated what my sister did," Eve began.

"And the other part?"

"I liked it, it turned me on somehow."

"Did you get off on it?" Bernadette said quietly.

"Yes, a lot. Then I would stop because I felt it was dirty. I felt I shouldn't have liked it. I never shared what happened with my friend Fiona, I kept it to myself all these years. But I've thought about it often."

"And the Shibari? Was that really part of the whole thing, an extension of it?"

"No, it's just another kink that I have," Eve giggled, "I've always fantasised about *that*."

"And this other part?"

"I tried it a bit like I told you. I tried out some spanking with my friend, and others. But it's not something I really like so much, actually doing it. But I like to hear about it, watch others doing it, the thought of it turns me on."

"OK, so you like the dirty stories, or hearing Imogen spanking D'Arcy the other night?" said Bernadette wondering where this was leading.

"Yes, and, the thing is, that I..." Eve sighed, "I watch stuff when you are at work.

This didn't sound too bad, Bernadette, and hardly unexpected from the hints Eve had given her in the past.

"I thought as much," Bernadette said not making a big deal out of it.

"I watch videos of girls on girls, you know porn and stuff and I watch videos of girls spanking other girls. I read stories about it, I've got quite a few books on my Kindle app, lesbian Femdom, books like that..." Eve trailed off again, she obviously felt bad about it somehow.

"OK," said Bernadette. She wasn't sure what else to say. It didn't bother her particularly, but it seemed it was bothering Eve.

"I'm sorry."

"Don't be sorry. I don't mind, darling, I just don't know why you wouldn't tell me. I don't mind if you watch porn or not."

Bernadette was trying to give a mild response, keep things on an even keel. There were tell-tale signs in Eve's face of tension mounting. She'd seen it before, the last thing she wanted was for this to escalate.

"I don't know why I couldn't tell you."

"It doesn't matter."

"It does matter, it matters to me. I feel as if I've let you down somehow. You must think I'm terrible." Eve seemed determined to wear a sackcloth.

Bernadette did not want her to indulge in self-castigation. Eve almost wanted her censure, and she didn't want to give it because she didn't feel Eve had done anything wrong.

"You haven't, I love you just the same whatever you've done. I don't think that at all. I just wish you felt you could have told me, darling. All this time I've been wondering about those pictures you've been drawing, and the dirty stories. I just thought there was more to it."

"You thought I was a pervert is that it?" Eve said suddenly flaring up.

"Wait, what?" Bernadette was taken aback.

"You thought I was a sick fuck who likes being spanked, is that it?" There was sudden anger in Eve's tone.

Bernadette stared at her. "I never said *that*, darling, what? No, of course not."

"You think I'm fucking slut, a whore who spends all day watching fucking porn, wasting your money, do you, do you?" Eve raised her voice.

Bernadette could see the warning signs clearly. This had happened before, she tried desperately to remain calm, to reassure her. "No. I don't, I never said it, I didn't, I don't think that, please, Eve, stop it, darling, please."

Apparently, Eve was past being able to stop herself.

"Well, I've got news for you. I don't fucking care what you fucking think, you bitch!"

"What? What did you call me?" Bernadette went white as a sheet. The wave of anger directed at her hurt her almost physically. Eve had shouted at her before, but this was different.

"I said you are a bitch, fuck you, Bernadette!"

It was almost as if she did not recognise the Eve she knew, her mind went numb.

"You don't mean that, no, no, you don't mean that, Eve, say you don't mean that, darling, please." Bernadette had no idea how they had suddenly arrived at this point and it was once again spiralling out of control.

"I know what you're thinking, don't tell me I don't know what you're thinking!"

Bernadette had no clue where this had come from, her natural instinct to hit back was subsumed by the hurt the words were inflicting on her.

"What? No, I'm not thinking anything, I'm not, really, I'm not, I promise you I don't think badly of you, I love you... I..."

Eve wasn't listening, she was lost in something, almost as if she wasn't even seeing Bernadette at all. Bernadette was wondering what to do when Eve let fly.

"This is who I am, if you don't want me like this, then fuck you... no, I mean it, honey, fuck you... just FUCK

YOU..." Eve shouted at the top of her voice, her eyes flashing blazing anger, then abruptly she stood up, turned on her heel and walked out of the room.

For a few seconds, Bernadette stood speechless. She had no idea what just happened. Things had gone from nought to sixty in less than a minute. Then she heard the front door slam. She got up almost blindly stumbling towards the living room door. A numbness which was already creeping over her triggered something inside. Something deep and hopelessly insecure. This had happened before, not with Eve. The demons rose up to engulf her. A well of despair burst inside her. She dropped to her knees and screamed, "Noooooooooo...."

It was a gut-wrenching scream, a heart-breaking scream of despair, her voice cracked.

"Eveeee... no... no... no... noooo..."

She began to sob violently, and her shoulders began to shake. The memories of Rebecca appeared in her head and all of the hurt and pain which had been walled off for so long came to the surface. She cried hysterically, until her voice was shrill, and she fell forwards onto her arms.

"Don't leave me, please don't leave me, Eve, please don't leave me, please..." she sobbed over and over again, until it became a whisper, a mantra, "Please... don't leave me..."

The past collapsed in on her. Rebecca had left her, walked away and cut her heart in two. It had happened suddenly, just like this, out of the blue. Now it was happening again. The unbearable weight and anticipation of the pain to come had been too much, it had broken her, completely.

She didn't hear the front door open again and shut so quietly, nor the soft barefoot steps padding lightly across the room. Strong arms took hold of her and lifted her up. A pair of blue eyes took in the puffed and tear streaked face, the expression of abject misery. Kneeling there on the floor, Eve took her wordlessly into an embrace and held her close, flooding her with love. Eve had unleashed her own demons and now she was full of regret and remorse.

"I'm never going to leave you, my darling, never," Eve whispered, "I'm sorry I'm so sorry for what I've done, for what I said, I'm so sorry I don't know what I was thinking, but I would never ever leave you."

Bernadette stayed silent hearing the words, but the shock of the last few moments was rendered her speechless.

"It's OK, baby, it's really OK, I promise you, darling, I promise you. I promise you I won't leave you, I won't, please, believe me, believe me, darling." Eve said softly, kissing her face, her cheeks, her eyes over and over again while Bernadette still stayed unmoving and unresponsive, almost catatonic.

Eve's eyes welled up with tears seeing what she had done. She coaxed Bernadette to her feet and took her upstairs. Eve laid her on the bed and covered her with a quilt. Bernadette's eyes were staring blankly into nothing. Eve slipped in beside her and put her arms around her fiancée.

"I'm so sorry, my darling, I love you so much, I'm so sorry," she whispered.

Time passed while Eve listened to Bernadette breathing, and soon afterwards Bernadette fell asleep.

✳ ✳ ✳

Eve left Bernadette to sleep and went downstairs to draw. Bernadette woke towards early evening and looked around the darkening room as if seeing it for the first time. She had no idea what had suddenly triggered Eve. Her head was starting to clear. She began to remember Eve had come back, picked her up. Eve had said sorry over and over again. Bernadette had been unable to respond. She had been completely numb. She was considering getting up when she heard light footsteps and Eve came into the room.

"You're awake." Eve smiled, coming to sit beside her on the bed. "How are you feeling, my darling?"

"OK," said Bernadette looking up at her.

"I... feel terrible."

"It's OK." Bernadette smiled weakly.

"It's not."

"Don't sit up there, darling, come under the covers, come in with me. Hold me, I just want you to hold me."

Bernadette wasn't someone to carry grudges and besides she was deeply irrevocably in love. Although it had hurt her deeply, her need and love for Eve overrode anything else.

Eve needed no second bidding and Bernadette turned towards her. Her arms went around Eve, and Eve sighed gratefully.

"I don't know what happened. I'm so sorry for what I did. It was unforgivable," Eve whispered.

"But I forgive you anyway," Bernadette said her lips close to Eve's.

"I called you a bitch, a fucking bitch. I screamed at you. I said such awful things."

"I know, and I still love you, and you're still here with me, and that's all that matters. Nothing else matters."

"Did you really think I was leaving you?"

"I don't know, I was so afraid. It just brought everything back about Rebecca. I froze up, I couldn't think. I just screamed..."

"I heard you." Eve gave a low chuckle. "I was just outside the door."

"Why did you walk out like that?"

"I was taking myself away because I knew I was out of control. I knew I had behaved terribly badly, and I wanted to make sure I stopped."

This was a candid confession and did much to assuage the anxiety which the outburst had engendered in Bernadette. If Eve could see what she did was wrong, that in itself was a good thing.

"Really?"

"Yes, really."

"I thought you were leaving, I really did." Bernadette became suddenly serious and it was true, she had felt exactly that. It had floored her, dropped her like a stone.

"Well," said Eve with some resolution, "Some things are going to change."

"They are?"

"Yes, for a start, I am going to control myself in future. I cannot behave like that anymore. You don't deserve it. If I start to get like that, then I'm going to go outside until I can calm myself down."

"Will you be able to?" Bernadette asked her hopefully.

"I'm going to try. If I can't then you may have to slap my face."

"I couldn't do *that*," Bernadette laughed.

"It's probably what I need," said Eve with a chuckle, though it was tinged with bitterness at her own appalling behaviour.

"I don't think I can slap you even if I wanted to, which I didn't. I was just hurt, very hurt, by what you said. I couldn't think straight."

"I know, and I'm so sorry. You have no idea how sorry I am," Eve said contritely, "When those last words left my mouth, I felt like an absolute bitch, a heel, an ingrate, unworthy of the love you've given me..."

"Stop it," Bernadette said softly, "You are never unworthy of my love, never."

"Thank you. I know you don't handle confrontation very well. I should know that by now. You should have shouted at me, given me a piece of your mind, it's what I deserved."

"I couldn't, and no I don't, not in relationships. Is it a bad thing?"

Eve laughed. "Don't look so worried. You shouldn't have to. I'm the one who needs to curb my behaviour."

"Only *that* behaviour." Bernadette smiled. "But... you said for a start..."

"Yes! Because," Eve said with determination, "The second thing, I've decided, we are getting married as soon as possible. I'm taking it out of your hands."

"What?"

This did surprise Bernadette, but Eve had a martial light in her eye.

"Hush, I'm taking charge. I'm going to make all the arrangements, and in two weeks' time we are tying the knot."

"But…"

Eve shook her head, in such a way that Bernadette knew she would brook no opposition.

"No buts, you need this, I need this. Once we are married you will know for certain I'm never going to leave you. I will have made my vows to you in public in front of our friends."

"But I haven't got a dress."

This was a weak protest because secretly Bernadette was relieved the wedding was being wrested from her grasp.

"I'm going to choose your dress, and everything else. I choose all your clothes anyway."

"So, I don't get a say in this?"

"No, you just have to turn up."

"OK." Bernadette smiled.

"OK? You're going to let me? Just like that?" Eve laughed.

"You're the boss." Bernadette shrugged.

"I'm definitely *not* the boss," Eve laughed, "You are the boss my darling, and you always will be."

She said it in such a way that Bernadette knew she meant it. Although Bernadette never really thought about who was more dominant in their relationship, perhaps it really was herself. She often felt Eve called the shots but in a much more subtle way. Bernadette always thought they should be equal partners, but perhaps Eve liked her to be the assertive one. Bernadette put it from her mind, there were too many other things to worry about.

"Well, it's nice to know," was all she said.

It didn't do to dwell on things, Bernadette knew only too well. What they had was good. They were good together. They had had these blow-ups, but they always made it up afterwards. It was hardly *that* bad, even if it seemed so at the time.

"I can be the boss sometimes, but only when you deserve it." Eve smiled.

"And what do you deserve?" Bernadette said mischievously.

"You know what I deserve and I'm sure you'll be doing it."

"You know I will, but now I want something else."

"What's that?"

"This..."

Bernadette began to kiss Eve, and the pent-up emotions now found an outlet in their passion. The kiss became white hot, and the fire spread through Bernadette's body very quickly. She had been wearing a satin robe after breakfast, when all this happened and nothing else. Bernadette quickly shrugged it off. Eve diverted herself of her own garments at the same time.

Bernadette's hands were running over Eve's skin, making Eve gasp and pull herself in tighter to feel her naked flesh against Bernadette's. Bernadette's hands paused on Eve's buttocks and she squeezed digging in her nails.

"Oh God... oh fuck... oh yes..." Eve cried as Bernadette did it again.

Her hand moved around and between Eve's legs to find her indescribably wet.

"Ah... fuck... ah... God... darling... oh... yes... don't stop... I want... oh... oh... fuck... oh... I love you... oh... I love you... oh, oh, oh, oh, ohh!" Eve screamed as she climaxed quickly under Bernadette's ministrations bucking and writhing, pushing herself hard into Bernadette's hand.

"Oh fuck, you're so good at that... oh... God... my God," Eve breathed, recovering and kissing Bernadette passionately. Eve's hand quickly found Bernadette's sweet spot so she could reciprocate.

The pent-up need in Bernadette burst almost at once. "Oh... God... fuck... oh... oh yes... oh yes... oh my God... yes... yes... yes... yes, yes, yes, yes, yes, ohh!" She orgasmed within a few seconds of being touched. "Fuck," she breathed softly, "I needed that so much, God did I need that."

Eve nuzzled her lips, a bit them gently. "I love you so much, and I'm so lucky to have you, so very lucky," she whispered.

"Are you?"

"Yes, you are so loving, so giving, so caring. You've given me your all and you've never held back."

"You've given me your all too." Bernadette smiled.

"But I did hold some things back, things I didn't tell you, important things."

"Yes, but you've told me now and it's all that matters, my sweetheart."

Eve kissed her again, and they were lost in each other, holding each other tight. A fleeting thought occurred to Bernadette that these bumps in the road only made them stronger, reinforced the bond. Then the heat of the moment claimed her once again.

✳ ✳ ✳

They spent the evening in bed, apart from a light supper which Eve prepared. There was little talking. They made love and just lay together sleeping or enjoying the presence of each other. It was perhaps a renewal of something, of even deeper feelings. It seemed as if a watershed had been reached and with it perhaps a new understanding.

On Sunday, after breakfast, Eve showed Bernadette a drawing she had made while Bernadette had been asleep after the row. It depicted Eve prostrating herself naked and Bernadette looking down at her wearing high heels and a Basque.

"Is that me?" Bernadette asked examining it, although she could certainly see the likeness immediately.

"Yes, it is and that's me."

"I thought so, and what are you doing?"

"Begging for your forgiveness," said Eve simply.

"Is it how you were feeling?"

"Yes."

"And did it help you? Drawing this?"

"Yes, it did."

To some degree, the drawings seemed to have been therapeutic to Eve. She had drawn several depicting her chastisement or persecution by her sister, although the one she had shown Bernadette on the previous day was perhaps the most straightforward and graphic.

"Do you feel forgiven?"

"Partly, yes." Eve nodded.

"What do I have to do to make you feel completely forgiven?"

Eve's eyes slid to the drawing, and she looked back at Bernadette.

"I have to make you beg me? Is that it?"

"Yes," Eve whispered.

"If it's what you want." Bernadette smiled.

Eve lowered her eyes. She was a complex character, Bernadette knew that. Eve's fascination with Shibari or her craving for it was still not explained, nor perhaps would ever be. It was a big deal to Eve, however. This desire to be somehow submissive was also perhaps not explicable either. Love meant satisfying your partner, not just sexually but on a deeper level, Bernadette mused. It meant fulfilling their needs.

"Well," Bernadette began, "I will then, but not just yet."

Eve's eyes flew up to look at hers.

"When I'm ready, you'll find a list on the fridge and then you'll know. All the things you did yesterday will be on the list, plus anything else in the meantime."

Eve smiled and took her hands.

"Is that what you wanted to hear?"

"Yes."

Eve looked almost grateful, it tugged at Bernadette's heartstrings. Perhaps others would say they were fucked up, the pair of them. Given the gamut of human frailty Bernadette had seen, she didn't think their games, the things they did, were anything much by comparison. They fulfilled each other's needs and desires. It was nobody's business but their own. She would, however, be sure to talk about it with Imogen on Monday.

"I'm not going to do it today," Bernadette continued, "Because I think you should be made to wait, don't you? A suitable amount of time to reflect on your behaviour."

"God, you are so sexy when you are assertive." A laugh burst from Eve's lips. "You have no idea how much more that makes me want you."

254

"Can you want me more than you already do?" Bernadette wondered.

"Yes, oh, yes."

They both laughed then.

"What are you like?"

"I am a very naughty witch who also needs to be taken in hand and told what to do every so often. A girl who needs to be reminded who the boss is around here when she misbehaves."

"Oh, you'll be reminded alright," Bernadette chuckled pulling her closer, "In no uncertain terms."

They kissed then, wrapping their arms around each other. Bernadette had certainly regained her mojo and was feeling so much better.

"You have to keep me in check, do you understand that now?" Eve whispered.

"I'm beginning to."

"Good."

"What shall we do today, darling, apart from the obvious?"

"Take a drive, have a long walk, do some exercises maybe."

"Sounds marvellous."

"Before we do that, I need you to take me upstairs."

"OK, then my heart, lead the way."

CHAPTER TEN

hen Monday morning came around, Bernadette found herself spooned into Eve. Eve had her arms around her holding her tight. Sunday had been a lovely day, and by comparison to Saturday, it was very far removed from the awful despair she had experienced. Bernadette reflected that as bad as it had seemed, they had become much closer. Instead of the row pushing them apart, Bernadette felt so much more love for Eve than she had ever felt before. Eve had become more loving and even more giving. Bernadette shifted around so she could kiss her fiancée. Eve would soon be her wife, and suddenly she could not wait. There was a beautiful feeling of anticipation building up inside her.

Eve opened her blue eyes and looked into Bernadette's brown ones.

"Hi, my darling." Eve smiled.

"Hi, sweetness."

"Is it time to get up?"

"Yes, yes, it is."

"Kiss me first."

Bernadette obliged her and held it just long enough before it became too steamy. She didn't want to be late for work. There were no court appearances but nevertheless, she liked to set a good example, if possible.

"Come, let's get up," she said reluctantly.

"OK." Eve sighed, yawned and stretched. She watched Bernadette slide out naked from under the covers and go to the bathroom.

By the time Bernadette returned from the shower Eve had laid out a grey dress, light blue top, grey skirt for her, coupled with a pair of pink high heel mules, with a clear band. She tied Bernadette's hair into a ponytail, did her makeup and went downstairs to make breakfast. Bernadette got dressed, admired the shoes which set her feet off nicely and then headed for the kitchen.

"Mmm, I am glad to get back to your breakfasts," said Bernadette as Eve slid a plate of poached eggs on toast with a side of bacon onto the breakfast bar. She gave Bernadette her cup of coffee and took a seat herself. "Oh, God, just so beautiful, darling, delicious." She took a mouthful of eggs and bacon.

"Better than the Langham?" Eve's eyes danced.

"No contest."

"That's the right answer!" Eve chuckled and started on her own food.

"So, what are you doing today?" Bernadette said lightly.

"I'm going to start on the wedding plans, and you are forbidden from asking me about it."

"What about other things?"

"Like drawing?" Eve teased her.

"Yes, and other things..." Bernadette left it hanging wondering if Eve would start to be more open with her. It was a kind of test.

"Oh..." Eve smiled. "Well, I might watch some porn and use the rabbit, is that what you wanted to know?" She looked mischievous.

"Yes, thank you."

"I can't help myself. You know that, don't you?" Eve returned her attention to her plate.

"I just wanted to make sure you'd tell me if I asked you," Bernadette said honestly.

"I will."

"Because if you don't." Bernadette pushed her plate away, pulled Eve towards her. "There will be consequences."

"God you are so deliciously sexy," Eve said kissing her.

"So are you."

Eve finished her breakfast, and Bernadette her coffee.

"What are you doing today?" Eve asked her, "I mean apart from telling Imogen everything which happened at the weekend."

"*That* goes without saying," Bernadette laughed. "We've got to see Callum again, and ask Olivia about her investigation, maybe tell her about Anh our witness. Then we've got to prepare for the prehearing conference which is probably going to be soon. The case is getting some attention now, in the media, and there will be political pressure going on behind the scenes."

"You sound like it's well in hand."

"Hmm." Bernadette put down her coffee cup. "I know someone else who needs to be taken in hand."

"I'm looking forward to it," said Eve with a saucy grin.

"Come on, missy, it's time for my goodbye kiss."

So, saying and on impulse, Bernadette slapped her fiancée lightly on the bum.

"Ooh, now you're getting cheeky," was all Eve would say, with a laugh.

"I'm just doing what you want, being the boss," Bernadette giggled.

"Don't let me stop you." Eve wiggled her backside temptingly, but Bernadette declined to do it again.

In the hallway, they said goodbye, with a long lingering kiss which left Bernadette a little breathless as always.

"Is it as good as it was the first time I kissed you?" Eve said smiling.

"Oh better, even better than I could imagine," Bernadette said a little flushed.

"My spells are working."

"You little witch."

"I'm *your* little witch."

"Yes, yes, you are, and I've got to go before I take you back upstairs."

Bernadette beat a hasty retreat out of the door, before her impulses got the better of her. Some days it had, and she had been very late in. On those days it was no use blaming the traffic as she only lived down the road, so she brazened it out, being the boss and made sure she stayed a little later that night. She watched Eve standing in the doorway, barefoot and fancy-free waving goodbye.

"My little witch," she said out loud smiling to herself as she pulled out of the driveway and begun her journey to work.

* * *

Bernadette logged onto her computer, knowing full well Imogen would arrive shortly with cups of coffee. She had managed to read three or four emails before her junior partner entered her office complete with the expected beverage.

"Hi, darling," said Imogen with a breezy smile, as she placed the cups on the coffee table by the sofa.

"Someone's in a good mood," Bernadette said moving to the sofa and picking up her cup.

"Ah that's what a weekend of unadulterated sex does for you," said Imogen sipping her cup.

"Just sex?" Bernadette said raising an eyebrow.

"Oh, no I gave her a damn good spanking to boot, but that just upped the ante and we both went into overdrive."

Bernadette couldn't help laughing. Imogen's sexual exploits never ceased to amaze her.

"Any particular reason for..." she enquired.

"Oh well, D'Arcy was being petulant all Saturday and acting like a little brat, so she got a little brat's punishment, and then she was as good as gold."

"I love the way you are so matter of fact about it, as if it's an everyday occurrence in your house," Bernadette said still laughing.

"Not quite every day, my darling. Perhaps once a week. Anyway, the little sojourn did wonders for our libido."

Bernadette shook her head. "But did you not... you know at the hotel?"

"Oh, we did, but we were extra quiet, even so, I'm surprised you didn't hear us."

"We were otherwise engaged, trying to keep quiet ourselves."

"Perhaps we should all have just let rip then."

They both giggled at this for a few minutes, sipping their coffee.

"OK, well, you've heard about my debauched weekend, what about yours?" Imogen asked her.

"Oh God, well... I've had a weekend and a half..." Bernadette began.

"Do tell."

Bernadette related everything which had happened in all the vivid details, accompanied by suitable noises of surprise and sympathy from Imogen.

"I did warn you," Imogen said at length, once the tale had been told.

"I know and I didn't listen."

"Oh, I wouldn't worry about it, I never listen to my own advice either."

Bernadette chuckled at this. It was all too true, Imogen was completely impetuous, at least in her personal life. She had become much more controlled in the courtroom, however, and it showed in her small successes so far.

"It's brought us closer together."

"That's a good thing, and Eve's going to organise the wedding. I mean, *that* is a result in itself."

"God yes, I'm so happy to have it taken out of my control. I was procrastinating like anything."

"I didn't like to say anything, but..." Imogen laughed.

"I've no idea what she's doing but I expect she'll be contacting you, and D'Arcy too."

"My lips will be sealed, so don't go trying to find out."

"I won't, don't worry. I'm happy for it to be a big surprise, and one I'm really looking forward to. Eve is right, it will help with my insecurities for us to get married. I try not to have them, but I do."

"I know, darling." Imogen put her hand out and took Bernadette's hand in. "This is the best thing ever for both of you."

"I know."

They smiled at each other.

Bernadette continued, "We really enjoyed the hotel, we are very grateful to D'Arcy and you, for the private jet, and the suite, all of it, it was amazing. I've never stayed in such luxurious surroundings and I'm sure Eve hasn't."

"Do you think I have? Well, apart from at D'Arcy's. I enjoyed it too, both of us did."

"Get used to it then, this is your life from now on."

"I know, I am starting to feel it's a bit more normal."

"That's a good thing."

"So back to the case, shall we try to see Callum today?" Imogen suggested.

"Yes, why not, let's see what else we can get out of him."

"OK, I will set it up."

"We should speak to Olivia too."

"I'll set it up. What about the prehearing conference?"

"Have we got a date?"

"I will chase the court up about it."

"Good thinking."

"Right, now I've given myself all this work to do, I'd better get on with it," said Imogen draining her cup.

"OK, darling, let me know when we need to go."

Imogen smiled at her and blew her a kiss as she left the room.

* * *

Olivia sat at her usual seat on the sofa with a cup of tea. They were seeing Callum in the afternoon, and Imogen had called up Olivia to come over for a chat. Olivia stirred her tea with her customary deliberation. Bernadette and Imogen sipped their coffee and waited. Olivia took a sip and then another with evident satisfaction.

"Is there something in the water here?" she wondered out loud, "Or is it just the way you make it. I mean, even my tea at home isn't this good. What is it you are doing, some kind of magic tea ritual?"

"Her fiancée is a witch, so maybe that's it," said Imogen.

"Whatever it is you've got me hooked."

"Maybe it's the tea plus the good company," Bernadette suggested with a smile.

"Now, I can't argue with that." Olivia took another sip and set the cup down. "So, apparently you had some interesting news?"

"Yes, one of the refugees is willing to testify at the hearing and we have an affidavit from her."

"Really? That is interesting. And what has she said?"

"She said they were boarded on the truck Callum drove in Ireland and put into flour barrels. They didn't recognise the name Callum, nor did they see him, but she did hear the name Omer, she thinks," Imogen told her.

"Is that a fact? Impressive work."

"All the more so since they refused to talk to the Metropolitan detectives. But our witness has a conscience at least in terms of not letting an innocent man go to prison," Imogen pressed on encouraged by the positive response from Olivia so far.

Olivia took a few more sips of her tea. "It's certainly noteworthy and I assume you are aiming to preserve anonymity. But I'm not sure why you're telling me this."

Imogen and Bernadette exchanged disappointed glances. They had hoped Olivia would bite.

"Well," Imogen said tentatively, "We thought maybe it was something you might think was useful, I mean, a witness who can confirm they were put on board over here. They might recognise the place. They said they were in a big shed sort of place which is consistent with the yard of Balik Transport."

"True, there is that. But it's not very substantial in terms of evidence. If she had eyeballed any of the people, it might be more helpful. Also, she's in the UK so I can't see how it can assist our case." Olivia shrugged.

A frown appeared briefly on Imogen's face at this, she felt Olivia was being obtuse and almost deliberately so. Bernadette noticed and decided to try a different tack.

"What if she wasn't in the UK?" she said.

"Oh well, of course, we might find it easier to interview her."

"What if you pulled some strings. If she was a material witness and was able to fast-track refugee status or more, then she might be persuaded to come here."

Olivia seemed amused as opposed to taken with this suggestion. "OK, I'm not sure what you think my superpowers are, but pulling those sorts of stunts are potentially way above my pay grade."

"Oh," said Bernadette unable to keep the disappointment out of her voice.

"I'm a Detective Sergeant, not Superwoman," Olivia laughed.

"But you could try?" Imogen suggested unwilling to give it up so easily.

"I will have a chat with my super, it so happens I'm in good odour with him at the moment. He might have some ideas. Bear in mind if she was to become part of our investigation it makes her a target and then we are probably into protective custody or putting her in a safe house, it all costs money. I have to be able to show a return in our investment."

"Her life isn't what I'd call an investment," said Bernadette with some acidity, peeved at this negative response, "She's a human being."

"I know, I'm sorry." Olivia was instantly contrite. "I didn't mean for it to come across that way. The powers that be are unfortunately not always as humanity oriented as you or I."

"Yes, well," Bernadette said a little more mollified.

"Let me think on it, that's all I can do."

"OK."

"In the meantime, we've had Balik Transport under surveillance," Olivia continued, "Some of the employees have certainly got form, and have previous connections to criminal gangs."

"Have you found out anything useful?" Imogen ventured although she was still annoyed Olivia her scheme had not found favour.

"Nothing we can move on as yet. You'll appreciate if we are going to raid the place then we can only do it once and when we think we can catch them in the act. Our other option is to put someone in undercover but it's dangerous, certainly for them and us. If they are found out it will blow our investigation wide open."

"So, in a nutshell, you haven't got much further," said Bernadette with something of an air of finality.

"It's early days," Olivia laughed, "I know you're hoping for something to help your case, but we may not get that far, I just don't know."

"Right."

"I know it's not what you want to hear, but if I find anything you can use, I'll tell you right away, I promise," said Olivia evidently trying to be conciliatory.

"OK."

"I want to help you," said Olivia earnestly, "I really do, but you have to give it some time."

"You just want our tea," Imogen shot back.

"Ouch, now that is a low blow."

"She doesn't mean it, she's just passionate about things," Bernadette put in smoothly, "You are welcome here anytime."

"Passion, now that's something I *can* get behind." Olivia laughed seemingly unfazed by Imogen's attack.

"How's Carole?" asked Bernadette feeling a change of subject was in order and noting the mulish expression on Imogen's face.

"Ah Carole, the delectable darling Carole, now she's passionate, oh yes."

"It's nice to hear."

"Things are in a good place with Carole after, shall we say, a bit of a rocky start. In fact, it's possible there might be love on the horizon if we can stick the course." Olivia smiled.

"So, it's getting serious then?"

"It might be, I'm certainly getting feelings and I think she is too. We are spending more time together, so fingers crossed."

"I'm happy for you both," Bernadette said conscious of Imogen's withdrawal from the proceedings.

"Anyway." Olivia drained her cup. "Much as I love your delicious tea, and that really is a love match for me, I've got to go. As I said, I will keep you in the loop I promise."

"OK, thanks."

"Don't get up, I'll see myself out." Olivia smiled faintly. She sauntered out the door closing it quietly behind.

"God, I'd like to give her a sound spanking!" said Imogen as soon as she had gone.

"This seems to have become your 'go to' remedy for everything lately," Bernadette observed wryly.

"Well, cheeky cow, poo pooing my idea like that!"

"She didn't exactly poo-poo it, she just didn't feel she could act on it, it's not the same."

"Well, even so, she makes me cross."

"Now who is being the brat?" Bernadette laughed.

"Oh stop! I know I need to curb my temper, I really do," Imogen sighed.

"She's actually been very helpful to us on more than one occasion and it behoves us to keep on her good side."

"You're right, I know you are. I probably need taking in hand like Eve."

"You do not!" said Bernadette emphatically, "And certainly not in the way I know you are about to suggest."

"You're no fun as a boss, do you know that?"

"You could have had *that* sort of fun with Shane, it was on offer, but you didn't want it," Bernadette pointed out.

"Don't remind me. Oh God forbid, it would have been a nightmare."

"There you are then."

"But it would be different with you," said Imogen pouting.

"Imogen! I know you are joking but..." Bernadette said, suddenly wondering if there was more to it and hoping there wasn't.

"Of course, I am silly. Well... half joking. I mean, imagine if you and me had been an item... wouldn't it have been explosive?"

"God, you're incorrigible. You know you've crossed so many professional lines lately I do not even know where to begin!" Bernadette said laughing with exasperation.

"But you love me just the same." Imogen fluttered her eyelashes.

Bernadette sighed. "Yes, yes I do. I could hardly have expected this kind of relationship with any junior counsel let alone a partner. You're more than just a friend to me now, you're like my family. I would be lost without you."

"And you let me get away with so much banter, it's great."

"I do and I will, and you know I will."

"Yes, and I adore you, darling. I practically worship the ground you walk on," said Imogen sincerely.

"Shouldn't you save that for D'Arcy?"

"Oh, now I'd let *her* walk on me in stilettoes." Imogen laughed. "Coming to think of it…"

"Tonight's game is it?"

"It might well be, though she'll have to be careful."

Bernadette laid back her head and laughed at this. "What are you like?"

"I'm the best junior partner you'll ever have."

"True and on that note, I'll treat you to lunch at Mamma Mia's."

"Sold!"

* * *

After an amiable lunch at Mamma Mia's, one of their favourite haunts, they headed for Jenkins Transport. It was situated west of Dublin near a place called Dunboyne. Rhys had bought a large sprawling estate with a manor house and then created a transport yard in the grounds, having secured a change of use. They drove into the estate via some large wrought iron gates and down a long sweeping drive with trees on either side. Apparently, there was a separate entrance to the transport yard, but they were going to see Callum who was staying at home as his bail conditions required.

They pulled up in front of a large redbrick two-story building which looked far bigger than was needed for one man and his son. Perhaps, mused Bernadette, he'd had plans for a large family. Bernadette parked her car, she and Imogen walked across the loose shingle to a set of steps leading up to the old house. The front door was opened by a man in a black suit, white shirt and tie. It was instantly recognisable as standard security garb.

"Bernadette Mackenna," she began, but was cut short.

"Yes, Mr Jenkins is expecting you, if you would just go through to that door on your right," he said.

"Thanks."

She and Imogen followed the direction in which his hand had been pointing and their heels click clacked on the highly polished wooden floor. There was a majestic staircase leading to the first floor and a landing which appeared to go all the way around on both sides. They entered a large living room which was nicely appointed with a large open fireplace at one end, sofas and chairs. Rhys and Callum, who had been sitting down by the fireplace, immediately rose to greet them. Even though it was early summer there was a fire burning in the grate which gave the place a cosy atmosphere.

"Hello, hello," said Rhys shaking their hands, "Please come in and take a seat, I'll order up some coffee."

"That would be nice, thank you," said Bernadette.

Rhys pressed a button which evidently summoned a maid in short order who was asked to provide refreshments.

"Hello, Callum, how are you doing?" Imogen asked as they sat down on one of the sofas.

"Oh, fine, I suppose, all things considered," Callum replied, "Obviously I can't go anywhere so I've been amusing myself at home best I can."

"It's good to have him home for a while," said Rhys grinning at him affectionately.

"Well, at least he's happy," Callum quipped.

"It's better than being in prison though," said Bernadette mildly.

"Yes, yes," Callum said suddenly becoming more serious, "Of course that's hanging over me no matter what I do."

"I know and I'm sorry, but we've come to update you on things, and also to ask you a few more questions, if that's OK."

"By all means."

"Is it alright if I stay?" Rhys asked tentatively.

"If it's OK with your son," Bernadette responded at once, and wondered if his father was now aware of his son's sexual orientation.

"Yes, I won't keep secrets from my Da, not anymore," said Callum.

"I know about him being gay, if that's what you are worried about," Rhys put in, "He told me the other day, but I had already guessed it to be fair."

"That is often the case," Bernadette said with a smile.

"So, there's not much you can say which I probably don't know."

"Good, good, which makes it easier, well, I'll start with where we are up to." Bernadette explained they now had a witness. She decided not to mention Balik Transport was under scrutiny but did say they had visited it and met with little success. The less people were aware of the investigation, the better.

"Do you have a strategy, for the hearing?" Rhys asked her.

"We do. We now have a witness from the women who were trafficked. They were put on, it turns out, in Ireland. She will testify to that. She also didn't recognise the photograph of Callum we showed her nor heard his name. Not that this really proves anything that can't be argued with by the prosecution."

"Then why put her on?" Rhys said at once.

"Because it adds weight to our assertion and it brings in a stronger possibility of doubt for the judge, every doubt we can put into the judge's mind is another step to dismissing the extradition request," Imogen told him.

"Oh, right, I see. Sorry, I... err... you're the professionals."

"Yes, yes we are," said Imogen assertively.

"Sorry."

"Right, well, we are planning to go on the attack with Kevin, who is their main witness. Who I am sure you know by now was Callum's lover," Bernadette continued.

"Yes, he told me."

Rhys and Callum exchanged looks. Rhys' was reassuring and Callum's seeking understanding from his father.

"We've every reason to believe he's implicating Callum because he's been offered a deal by the Crown prosecution and it's easy for him to name Callum."

"What! Fucking little toe rag!" Rhys expostulated jumping up and then taking a turnabout the room in agitation.

"Sit down, Da, come on," Callum said.

"It just pisses me off that my son has to take the rap for something he didn't do just because... because..."

"Yes, and it does us too, that's why we intend to try and shred him on the stand," said Bernadette.

"I'd like to fucking well shred him!" Rhys muttered very darkly.

"Dad!" said Cameron looking a little embarrassed.

"I'm sorry, I just get worked up." Rhys came back and resumed his seat.

"It's quite alright, we understand. We get worked up too, but we save it for court," Bernadette said in soothing tones.

Just then the maid arrived. She was pretty, Bernadette reflected watching her lay out the tea and coffee things on the coffee table. She was probably around thirty five with short blonde hair, blue eyes, and a bow mouth. The maid was dressed in a black skirt with a white top and apron, and what seemed to be excessively high heels. She recognised them as Louboutin and the outfit also looked expensive. It also looked rather anachronistic.

"Thanks, Pet," said Rhys.

She shot curtsied and left the room.

"Petra's Polish," said Rhys, "You're probably wondering why she's dressed like that. Call me old fashioned I suppose. I'm a bit of a traditionalist."

"Come on, Da, she's your Polish girlfriend for fuck's sake, she's not the fucking maid. She just dresses like that because you asked her to," said Callum bluntly.

"Hmm, yes, well..." Rhys coloured up.

"Look, my mum's dead, he's not that old and I can't blame him," Callum explained.

"Thanks for the build-up, son, now they think I'm a fucking pervert."

"We don't, I assure you and what you do in your private life isn't our concern, really," said Bernadette with a smile.

"She loves him to bits. She'd do anything for him," said Callum.

"Look I drive the trucks, or I used to, I met Petra in Poland and well, things moved on from there," Rhys added.

"Honestly, we're not judging you, Rhys," said Bernadette with a shrug.

"Aye, well."

Rhys seemed a little mollified at this and started to sort out the coffees. There was a plate of crescent shaped biscuits dusted with icing sugar and one with slices of cake which looked like a light sponge with almonds on top also dusted with icing sugar.

"She doesn't wear that all the time you know, she has got, normal clothes..." he trailed off.

"Christ, Rhys, if you are fortunate enough she indulges your fantasies a bit then good on her, and lucky you," Imogen said accepting his coffee.

Rhys grunted, and handed a coffee to Bernadette, "Help yourself, to you know... cake or whatever, it's erm Polish, Polish specialities. Petra made them."

Bernadette sipped her coffee and decided to move things along. "Our plan is to try and get Kevin to admit he's lying. I'm going to rattle him if I can. So, Callum, can you tell me anything which can help us get to him?"

"Like what?"

"Just tell us about him, if I can get him wound up a bit then he's more likely to let something slip. Tell us how you got together, that sort of thing."

"How intimate do you want me to go?"

"As far as you like. There just might be something I can use."

"OK. I met Kevin at a gay bar in London," Callum began.

"Did you go often to gay bars?" his father put in.

275

"Rhys, if you don't mind," Bernadette said shooting him a look, this was not helping.

"Oh, yes, sorry, you ask the questions, sorry."

"Thank you. You can answer that one, Callum, if you don't mind."

"Sure, I don't mind." Callum shrugged. "I used to go cruising bars, yeah, for sex. If I was in London for the night, I'd do that."

"What's your type, Callum? In men?" Imogen asked him.

"I tend to go for the macho type, a bit of leather, stuff like that, good looking muscles. I mean, I've got them too, but I like tattoos that sort of thing."

"Anything else?" Imogen raised her eyebrow.

"You mean do I like kinky bastards, is that it?"

"Do you?"

Rhys shifted uncomfortably in his seat but held his peace. He sipped his coffee. It had been his choice to stay and listen.

"No, but I like it a bit rough, if you see what I mean, dirty talk, stuff like that."

"Can you describe Kevin to us?" Bernadette asked him.

"He's about my height, got muscles too but not as well built as me. Good figure though, nice arse. He's got one of those moustaches which droops down, thick black, and a nice head of hair. Nice eyes. I loved his eyes. Square jaw, I always told him he could have been a model."

"So, he was good looking?"

"Yes, to me. I found him attractive straight away."

"You told us it was purely sexual. You weren't in love."

"No, not in love no, I loved some parts of him though," Callum sniggered.

"Oh?"

"Let's just say he was well-endowed."

"Christ!" said Rhys under his breath.

Bernadette shot him a sharp look.

"Sorry," he said at once.

"OK, you had the hots for him, I think we've established."

"Yes, I did. We met in the bar and then went back to the hotel, fucked all night. Then I found out he was a driver too working for another firm. So, it turned out we'd meet quite often, or he'd be in Dublin."

"What did you two talk about?" said Imogen.

"Sex mainly. Blokes we fancied. We were both into action films, we'd talk about which of the stars we fancied most."

"You said you did not know he was connected to a criminal gang."

"No, I didn't he never mentioned anything like that."

"Did you two communicate by text at all?" Bernadette said.

"Yeah, of course, we did."

"Were they explicit in content?"

"Not all of them, no."

"Would you be willing to let one of our team look through them?"

"What would you want to do that for?"

"There might be something we can use, and also it would establish you and he were in a sexual relationship. The only downside is we would have to submit these in evidence and lose the element of surprise. But we'd still like to look, if you don't mind. It will be very discreet I promise."

"Callum, put your scruples or perhaps embarrassment up against fourteen years in a British jail for a crime you didn't commit and then answer," said Imogen frankly.

"OK, you're right, you can if you want," Callum sighed.

"Thank you," said Bernadette, "We'll only use those we really need. I promise you."

"Go on, son, you've got to do what they say, they know what they're doing," Rhys added.

"Yes, Da." Callum smiled.

"Can you tell us anything, anything at all which might get him upset?"

This still was their best bet and they needed a line of attack.

"Yes, he's got a thing about women."

"What sort of thing?"

"He thinks they are inferior, he's a bit of a misogynist. I could easily put up with it, we used to joke about it, but he really believes women are the weaker sex."

"Is that a fact?"

"Yes, he said it's why he's glad he's gay. He can't stand women, to be honest."

"Fantastic," said Bernadette smiling.

"Fantastic?" Rhys said looking puzzled, "The guy fucking hates women and that's good?"

"Oh, it's more than good, because right off the bat he's going to hate being cross examined by a woman."

"Yes, yes I see, hmm, you're right, I see."

"Then," Imogen added, her mind racing ahead, "He probably thinks it's perfectly fine to traffic women for sex because it's all they are good for."

"Excellent thinking!" Bernadette smiled at her. "Now, the opposition won't know this, will they?"

"No, I doubt it, you'll only find out if you were in a relationship with him," said Callum.

"Which means we could let slip about your relationship with Kevin, but then our line of attack would be completely different."

"Or we could say he had a relationship with Callum and if he denies it then bring the texts into evidence," Imogen suggested.

"The prosecution could get us on it though, ask for a new hearing as they didn't have time to prepare."

"Sure, you're right, we'll have to think this through carefully."

"Anyway, Callum, did you ever have any kind of argument with him at all? Anything which we might be able to use?" said Bernadette.

"What do you mean?"

"If you'd argued, you would have given him a reason to name you to the police. It gives us an entry point, a line of attack."

"Oh, oh I see."

"So, is there?"

Callum thought for a few moments while they consumed some of the biscuits and cake. They sipped their coffee and waited.

"You know I said we weren't in love," Callum said at length.

"Yes?"

"It wasn't strictly true."

"OK, so what did you mean? Were you in love with him after all?" Bernadette asked him.

"No, I wasn't but he did have feelings for me, I think."

"You think? What made you think it?"

"He was talking like he was jealous. He started asking me what I'd been doing when I wasn't with him. Where I went, who I saw. Trying to figure out my movements."

"I see, and what did you do?"

"I got a bit annoyed, to be honest. I asked him outright if he was jealous and I told him I wasn't seeing anybody else. He denied it, of course. He said he was asking me because he was just interested in my life."

"Was this just once, or more than once?" Imogen said.

"It was several times, to be honest, but at first I said nothing, then I decided to tackle it head on."

"What happened after that?"

"He became distant, a bit more standoffish. For a while, we didn't see each other so much."

"And then?"

"He started seeing me more again. I mean, I didn't mind either way. He was a good lay, but I wasn't going to get emotionally involved with him, so I suppose I just let him walk away when he wanted to."

"Why didn't you want to get involved with him, Callum?" Bernadette asked him.

"I just didn't feel an emotional connection really, not with him. It was purely sexual. Also, I just felt something about him, something dodgy I suppose, I dunno, it was just a feeling."

"Then why did you keep sleeping with him?"

"The lure of good sex, and a fucking big dick," Callum laughed.

"Right."

"The prosecution may ask you questions like we have, just so you know," said Imogen.

"Right."

"So, it's best we've asked you first. We will try to discredit their witness and his testimony. They will, by the same token, try to discredit you and show you to be a liar. The same tactics we use, they will use. To try to needle you and wind you up. You have to try to maintain a cool head. Also try not to make smart comments like that, because they'll use them against you."

"I'll do my best."

"He's got a cooler head than me," Rhys laughed, "I'd be terrible as you've seen."

"Then it's a good job we won't need you on the stand." Bernadette smiled at him.

"You're a tough pair of nuts, I can tell," said Rhys.

"We try to be," Imogen laughed.

"I'll be honest with you, Rhys, I'm a bitch in the courtroom when I want to be, but if I need it to get results then I will," Bernadette said candidly.

"I don't doubt it," Rhys giggled, "I wouldn't like to get on the wrong side of either of you."

"Oh, you don't want to get on the wrong side of Imogen, see that red hair, she lives up to it."

"Hey!" Imogen said in mock indignation, "She's right, I've got a bad temper."

"I'm leading the defence in court, Imogen is my right-hand woman," said Bernadette with a smile.

"Do you need to ask me anything else?" Callum put in.

"So, you think if we go at Kevin on the basis he was in love with you, we might strike a nerve?"

"Yes, definitely. He was jealous I'm sure. He hadn't anything to be jealous about though, I wasn't seeing anyone else while I was with him."

"Did he ever express his jealousy at all? In words, say anything?"

"No, just the obsessive wanting to know where I'd been and what I was doing all the time."

"Before this trafficking thing blew up, were you still seeing him?" Imogen asked.

"Oh yes, in fact, I was supposed to meet up with him after the drop off. I left the truck and then went to wait at a hotel, but he never showed. So, I just went home instead. Then I found out the place had been raided."

"How did you get home?"

"I took a flight. I didn't have a return drop off like normal, so I just went to the airport and hopped on the next one I could get."

"I reckon you had a lucky escape," Bernadette observed, "They would have been out to arrest you soon enough if you were hanging around."

"Yes, I'm sure, I've thought of that, and then I'd have been truly fucked."

"So, in summary, you had a strong sexual relationship with Kevin, but you think he was in love with you. That's a pressure point we can use on the stand. We've got a two-pronged attack on him now. The pressure from the police and his own jealousy which we will assert led him to vengeful behaviour."

"Yes, I see," said Callum nodding.

"What's he like, does he have a short fuse or is he quite calm?" Imogen said.

"He's quite quick tempered. I noticed when we went out he would get quite impatient with the servers and stuff. If something wasn't to his liking, he would have a go."

A thought occurred to Bernadette.

"You said he was well built, did he do weight training, or work out?"

"Yes, he did, we sometimes went together. He had pretty good muscles on him for sure."

"Do you think he took steroids at all?"

It was a fair question. They were known to cause short tempered behaviour.

"I don't know."

"Did either of you do drugs?"

"No, I never did shit like that. I couldn't afford to, being a driver, no. If Kevin did it, wasn't when I was around."

"Ah well," said Bernadette philosophically, "It was worth a shot."

"Can I ask why you are a driver? I mean, your Dad owns this firm. How come you aren't in line to take it over?" Imogen said suddenly.

"He is," Rhys put in at once, "But I wanted him to learn it from the ground up."

"I like the driving," said Callum, "But I know I'll have to start taking the reins, if I ever get the chance now."

"We're going to do everything we can to see that you get your chance," Bernadette said quietly.

"Assuming you do get off," Rhys said to Callum, "You won't be driving anymore, I can't risk anything like that again. You're going to start helping me out and getting ready to take over."

"Thanks, Da."

"You've erm... got a nice place here," said Bernadette.

"Yes, though it's far too big. I always hoped it was going to be for the big family I was going to have." Rhys shook his head. "But then his mother died, when he was young. She died suddenly, she was hit by a car, it was an accident."

"Sorry to hear it."

"It's OK, it was me and the lad ever since."

"You never..."

"Wanted to get married again? No, it's taken me a long time to even be with someone again."

"You could still have kids, Da. I'm sure Petra would," Callum interrupted this reminiscing session.

"Now then, Callum, we've talked about this."

"No, Da, you've talked but I haven't, you've got this big house, Petra, just do the right thing, marry her and have kids, you know you want to. Stop worrying about me, I'm hardly going to provide you with a family, now am I?"

"You might," said Bernadette, "I mean, it's not unheard of."

"I don't know, I'd have to find the right bloke first and then adopt or something, it's a long process," Callum sighed.

"Anyway, we don't want to bother you with our family stuff," said Rhys conscious they were letting on more than perhaps he wanted to share with their lawyers.

"OK, well, otherwise is everything OK here, I noticed you have security?" said Bernadette not wanting to overstep the line with their client.

"Yes, I've got a firm on twenty-four seven now. I'm not taking any chances. We've got at least two who live here full time at the moment. I've got some in the yard too. We've got our main office here as well, at the back of the house, where we do all the admin and back office stuff."

"Are you expecting trouble?" Imogen wondered.

"You can't be too careful. These gangs are trouble. Big trouble. I know there are such gangs in the business, more's the pity. I'm having my boy protected at all costs."

"Seems sensible."

"I can afford it, why not."

"Right, I think we've got what need for the moment," said Bernadette.

"OK."

"We will be putting you on the stand Callum, but I'll brief you beforehand as to what to expect."

"OK, thanks."

"In the meantime, you will need to turn up to the prehearing."

"Right."

Bernadette stood up. "We'll be going then, and thank your girlfriend for the cakes."

"I'll see you out," said Callum.

They said goodbye to Rhys, and Callum accompanied them to the front door.

"Keep your chin up," said Bernadette.

"Thanks again," said Callum.

* * *

After they returned to the office, Bernadette and Imogen sat together on the sofa sipping coffee.

"Right, so we're going after Kevin on the basis of his relationship with Callum?" said Imogen.

"Yes."

"So, should we or shouldn't we reveal it beforehand, put in evidence?"

"Let's see what Micky turns up, shall we have a chat with him?"

"Yes, but what about the police pressure, the deal he's made?"

Bernadette took another sip and thought about this.

"We'll attack him on that second. So, I'm going to soften him up first with him being in a relationship which will establish when we attack him with being jealous that he's perhaps being vindictive. Then, when I've got him rattled, we will hit him with the deal he's made. Callum would be his logical target."

"Sounds like a plan," Imogen agreed.

"Of course, we don't know how he's going to respond, but hopefully if he gets angry or at least shaken up a bit he'll reveal something he doesn't want to."

"Right, I'll get Micky in here," said Imogen getting up.

"Sure."

Imogen went out of the room and reappeared a couple of minutes later with Micky in tow. Micky was a boyish young twenty-something, wearing a sharp looking grey suit, white shirt and tie. He was sporting a moustache which he'd recently started growing.

"Hi, Micky, you're looking smart," said Bernadette.

Micky took a seat and coloured up a little at the compliment.

"Thanks," he said.

"Micky, sorry we've not involved you in the latest case so far, but you've been busy with some other things, haven't you?"

"Yes, I have those investigations on the couple of cases you gave me, they've taken a fair bit of time." He smiled.

"Good, I don't want you to think I'm neglecting you," Bernadette said smiling back at him.

She was acutely conscious of the welfare of her staff and she had a soft spot for Micky. She had made him her lead investigator and she liked to keep him busy.

"I didn't think that... honestly, Bernadette, I would never think that. Besides I'm studying the legal stuff on the side like you suggested."

He was anxious to reassure her. She was his idol. He would do anything she wanted. She was acutely aware of his hero worship and was flattered. However, she didn't like to take advantage.

"Good, good and how's the martial arts training?"

This was another thing her firm was paying for since he'd been punched by someone she'd asked him to follow. She had felt exceedingly bad about this and wanted to be sure he could take of himself in future.

"Oh, great, I'm going to be a brown belt soon."

"Wow, well done, you've been working hard then."

"Yeah, I've been training hard, I want to get to black belt for sure."

"I'm sure you will, and we'll all feel a lot safer with you around."

He looked pleased when she said this.

"What's with the new moustache, Micky?" Imogen said teasing him.

"Oh that?" He touched it self-consciously. "Well, I thought I'd give it a try and Alison likes it."

"I think it looks very nice on you, very manly." Bernadette frowned at Imogen.

"She's right, I'm teasing." Imogen poked her tongue out at Bernadette.

Micky sniggered at this banter.

"How are things working out in your new office?"

Micky had agreed to relinquish his cubby hole and move to the same office as Alison Daly who was Bernadette and Imogen's PA. Imogen had originally shared the office with Alison but once Imogen got her own office, Alison had wanted some company.

"Oh, fine, Alison and I are getting on great. She's great."

They both knew Micky had a huge crush on Alison but being in an office together would seem to have calmed things down in that department.

"Glad to hear it."

"What's err... what's the craic on this case, then?" Micky obviously felt this was enough talking about his wellbeing.

"Right well, Imogen, why don't you explain it?" Bernadette smiled at her sweetly.

"Thanks," Imogen turned to Micky, "We're working on a case involving our client Callum Jenkins." She went on to give him more of the background. "So, we need you to go over there and go through his mobile phone text messages specifically for texts between Callum and Kevin his lover."

"What am I looking for?" Micky wanted to know.

"Things which show they are in a relationship, that it's more than a one-night stand. Things which show his boyfriend being jealous perhaps. Arguments, stuff like that."

"OK."

"You can snapshot some of the best ones."

"I might be able to download all of his messages depending upon the phone type," Micky suggested.

"That would be even better, we'll have to get something signed by Callum allowing us to use them if we need to," Bernadette added.

"I can draw it up," said Imogen.

"The thing is I might need a different laptop to the one I've got in order to download them though. It depends on the type of phone he has," said Micky.

"OK. Whatever you need let me know, I'll sign it off," said Bernadette airily.

"Right."

"Great, so Imogen will give you the details and you can get in touch with Callum yourself, arrange to go there as soon as you can. Don't forget to keep note of your mileage, any expenses, OK?"

"Sure, thanks."

"She just wants to look after you, Micky," said Imogen.

"I won't forget. I do appreciate it though, really."

"Is there anything you want to ask us?"

"No, it's fine, I'll get on and let you know if I need anything," said Micky.

"Keep us posted," Bernadette said.

"I will." He went stood up, nodded to them and sauntered out.

"You shouldn't tease him," Bernadette admonished her.

"I know, I just can't help it."

"Are he and Alison really getting on OK?"

"Apparently." Imogen shrugged.

"That's good, very good."

"What about the new PA, has Andrew said anything?" Imogen wondered.

"No, I'll give him a nudge. Mind you we've been busy."

"Yes, we have, so what's next?"

"We need to prep for the prehearing conference and try to get a court date for it as soon as we can."

"Good then I'll go and get onto the court now, shall I?"

"Sure."

Imogen left Bernadette's office, and Bernadette went back to her emails. She could not help thinking about the case and if they really could stop the extradition. She decided to look up the success rate of past cases to evaluate their chances. After some time, she found it to be inconclusive although perhaps Irish Courts, in general, did not favour extradition from what she had seen. Ultimately it would be for her to make the best case she could for Callum's extradition to be disallowed.

✳ ✳ ✳

Back at home, Eve greeted her with a conspiratorial air.

"What have you been up to, my darling?" said Bernadette kissing her soundly.

"Wouldn't you like to know?"

"I would but I'm sure you're not going to tell me, well, not everything."

Bernadette kicked off her shoes and followed Eve into the living room.

"Now," said Eve, "You have to promise never to look in this drawer. At least, not until I say you can."

She pointed to a drawer in her drawing cabinet.

"OK, I assume that's all the wedding stuff in there is it?" Bernadette said with some perspicacity.

"Exactly and it's off limits to you. I'm pointing it out so you can't go and open it by accident. So, promise me you won't."

"I promise," Bernadette said at once. Truthfully, she was intrigued, but she didn't want to know about it. The surprise was going to be all the greater for that.

"Very good."

Eve led her to the sofa.

"How have you been?" Bernadette asked her solicitously. She wondered if Eve was OK after their somewhat turbulent weekend.

"I've missed you," Eve whispered moving closer, so her lips were almost touching.

"I've missed you too," Bernadette admitted and meant it. Although her work took her attention, Eve was always there in the back of her mind.

"Do you want dinner now, or something hotter?" Eve's fingers were tracing a line down Bernadette's back and under her blouse. Bernadette moaned in response at her touch.

"Hotter, if you've got it."

"Oh, I've got it," Eve said kissing her, harder now passionately.

Bernadette felt a heat engulf her almost at once, and within a few moments, they were almost ripping at each other's clothes to get them off. Eve's were easier since she was simply wearing a robe and nothing more. Eve's hands feverishly unbuttoned Bernadette's blouse and then deftly pinged open her bra, exposing her breasts to her fingertips. Within a minute Bernadette's nipples stood out under Eve's ministrations, and Eve was tugging off Bernadette's skirt and knickers.

"Oh fuck..." Bernadette gasped, as Eve's fingers slipped between her legs, "You always make me so..."

"Wet?" Eve smiled.

"Yes, very... oh... oh God... fuck... oh my God... don't stop... I..." Bernadette sighed, laying back to give her fiancée better access. Eve took advantage at once and Bernadette cried out feeling the crest of the wave approaching rapidly, "Oh... Eve... oh my, Eve... oh... God... darling... oh... fuck... oh... oh... ohh!" The climax washed through her and she stiffened, her eyes closed, feeling the deliciousness of it. "Shit... oh... fuck... God... oh... fuck..."

After a few moments, it subsided and Eve was kissing her again, holding her close.

"I love you, so much, so very much," Eve said over and over, kissing her face softly.

Bernadette smiled, it was almost as if Eve had been completely untethered and this was a new Eve. An even more loving and giving Eve.

"Shall I?" Bernadette asked her, as her fingers started to slide down Eve's torso.

"It can wait," said Eve, "Let's have dinner. I just wanted to do... that."

"I love you so much, too," Bernadette whispered, "I hope you know I love you just as much as you love me."

"Silly." Eve smiled. "Of course I know."

"You seem... well, different."

"Because I'm no longer carrying secrets. This has all been my fault. I should have used what I was taught in the Ashram. The weight of your secrets will drag down your soul and anchor your feelings, until you can no longer truly feel everything. Drain the puss from the boil and the body can heal."

"Is that what you've done, drain the pus from the boil?" Bernadette couldn't help chuckling at this analogy.

"In a manner of speaking, yes, it is."

"I'm glad, it seems like it was a heavy burden on you, darling."

"I never told a soul until I told you. I felt one hundred kilos lighter," Eve told her earnestly.

"Then I'm glad to have been your confessor and to be the recipient of your unbridled love."

"I have unbridled lust now too." Eve's eyes danced.

"Didn't you always?"

"It's even more unbridled!"

"God help me then," Bernadette giggled.

"Also, none of this means I don't deserve to receive consequences," Eve told her.

"Oh, you will certainly be getting those, and no mistake."

"Good, I just wanted to make sure."

"I promise you, darling, you will be getting consequences." Bernadette kissed her.

"Something to look forward to," said Eve smiling.

"Is it?"

"Yes, of course, especially from you."

"Then I will try to make it extra special."

"Come and have dinner."

Bernadette pulled on a black satin robe Eve provided and picked up her clothes to put them in the washing basket. She followed Eve to the dining room where two places were laid.

Eve brought out a large tureen with a ladle, bread rolls, butter and a selection of cheeses.

"What have we got today?" Bernadette asked watching Eve ladle out a healthy portion into a bowl.

"It's seafood chowder, I'm trying out the recipe."

"God, it's delicious, so creamy and yum," said Bernadette taking a spoonful.

"I'm glad, help yourself to rolls and cheese." Eve took her place at the table with a bowl of her own. She proceeded to butter one of the small rolls and cut herself a few small wedges of cheese.

"Thank you, darling." Bernadette did likewise.

"How did it go today? I suppose you told Imogen all about my tantrum?" Eve said taking a mouthful of soup.

"I did, of course, and she was understanding as always."

"Did she suggest I needed a spanking?" Eve's eyes twinkled.

"No, she didn't, although, it does seem to be her usual remedy for everything these days. She said if it had been D'Arcy, then D'Arcy wouldn't be sitting comfortably for a week, but then that was nothing I didn't expect to hear. Anyway, she was hardly going to suggest something like *that* about you, not after your sister had traumatised you."

"I'm glad it's out in the open, though." Eve sighed.

"So am I frankly."

"What other news?"

"I'm sure you'll be interested in hearing she spanked D'Arcy over the weekend, and no, I don't have any details." Bernadette raised an eyebrow.

"You could make some details up to tell me later?" Eve said hopefully.

"Of course, darling, now apart from the personal stuff, we saw Olivia and Callum." Bernadette changed the subject and took a bite of cheese. She dipped her roll into her soup and bit into it. She realised she would need to buy into Eve's fantasies and if verbal stimulation was what she wanted, then she would get it.

"How did it go?"

"With Olivia, not much help so far, but Callum was interesting."

Between mouthfuls of soup, bread and cheese, Bernadette regaled Eve with the interview at Callum's and the strange relationship his father had with his Polish girlfriend.

"Oh my!" said Eve when she'd finished, "So you think you can get at this Kevin on the stand then? Rattle his cage?"

"I hope so, you never know until you try how they are going to react to questioning. If Callum is right, I can get him riled up though, then we've got a chance of him saying something in anger which will help our case."

"You're devious, I'll give you that," Eve laughed.

"Only in court, not when I'm with you."

"I know and I love you for your honesty. I don't love myself for my dishonesty." Eve pouted.

"You weren't dishonest, you were just hiding things, and you're not doing it anymore, that's different."

"You're right." Eve smiled and then an impish look crept into her face. "I could get one of those maids' outfits if you'd like it. A nice tight one, you know..." she trailed off.

"God you are so naughty," Bernadette laughed.

"So, it's a no then?"

"Well, I'm not saying that. Is it a roleplay? What would I be?"

"You'll be my strict mistress, who orders me about in that very severe voice you've got, and then, of course, because I misbehave too much, I get sent upstairs and..."

"Stop, you're making me fucking horny already, let me finish my dinner," Bernadette complained.

"So, it's a yes then?" Eve said taking another bite of her roll.

"I think I could accommodate your desires. It might make a good lead into a Shibari session, perhaps?" Bernadette's eyes were dancing.

"I'll get one this week then."

"OK."

Eve ran her bare foot up Bernadette's calf which she knew always turned Bernadette on.

"Witch," said Bernadette, "Let me eat, then we'll go upstairs."

CHAPTER ELEVEN

id-morning the following day, Bernadette was sitting in her office. There hadn't been anything further to do on the Callum case as they were awaiting a prehearing date. Micky had been put in touch with Callum and was going over for a preliminary look at his phone.

There was a soft knock at her door, and Alison came in.

Alison was tall and slim with blonde hair which she seemed to be growing longer. She wore glasses behind which a pair of pretty blue eyes peered out. Bernadette always thought she had nice lips too. Her fair complexion was sporting a few more freckles than usual no doubt as a result of the recent sunny weather. Alison was wearing black trousers, a pair of mules, and a pink blouse. Bernadette noticed her feet. Alison had an attractive pair of shapely ankles. Bernadette had a predilection for women's feet, it was often the first thing she observed. Pulling her attention back to Alison herself, she said, "Alison, hi, what's up?"

"There's a man, come to see you, he's smart looking, well dressed. I think he's some sort of politician or something."

"Oh?"

"Yes, apparently Juanita says he was insistent though he's got no appointment."

"And where is he now?"

"I put him in the meeting room."

"Right, I'll get Imogen to come in with me," said Bernadette wondering what he wanted, "Did he say anything at all?"

"He said it was a matter of great importance."

"Did he now?" Bernadette pursed her lips.

"Yes, shall I get tea and coffee?"

"That would be nice, thanks." Bernadette smiled. "And, Alison, come in a moment sit down."

"But what about?" Alison looked worried, Bernadette didn't seem too concerned about the visitor and normally she didn't like to keep them waiting.

"He can kick his heels for a bit longer, coming in here unannounced." Bernadette was already set against whoever this unnamed individual was, as it appeared, he was the pushy type.

"OK." Alison came and took a seat across the desk.

"Are you finding there's a lot of work for you these days?" Bernadette asked her.

"Well, you know... I cope with it." Alison shrugged.

"I'm not asking you that, Alison, now be honest, I know you cope but..."

"Yes, alright, Imogen has spoken to me about things. I'm having to put in more overtime than usual to get things done."

"Right, that's what I thought, and you know we are trying to get another PA in to help?"

"Yes, yes I do. Have you had any luck?"

"I'm going to chase Andrew up on it, sorry, darling, we got wrapped up in this Callum case."

"It's OK." Alison smiled.

"No, it's not, and I'm going to sort it out," said Bernadette firmly.

"Thanks."

"Have you been... growing your hair?"

"Yeah, do you like it?" Alison flicked her locks with her hand.

"Yes, it's lovely, suits you."

"Micky thinks so."

"Does he?"

"Yes, yes he does."

Bernadette wanted to ask more but she forbore to do so. Perhaps there was romance on the horizon after all.

"Right, well, I suppose I'd better see this man whoever he is."

"I'll sort out some refreshments."

Bernadette collected Imogen and the two of them entered the meeting room. Sitting on one of the chairs fiddling with his phone was, indeed, the man of around thirty five years old. He had black hair, a clean-shaven boyish face, a sharp expensive looking charcoal suit, pinstriped shirt, blue patterned tie and black highly polished shoes. As they entered, he sprung to his feet.

"Hello, hello," he said amiably as if this was his office, "I'm Oisin Kavanagh MP, I'm the Minister without portfolio."

He held out his hand and Bernadette took it. "I'm..." she began.

"Bernadette Mackenna, I know." He smiled. "And you're Imogen Stewart."

"You've done your homework," said Bernadette.

"I like to be prepared."

"Would you like to have a seat?" Bernadette indicated the sofas.

"Yes, thanks, they look very comfortable, nice." Oisin sat down.

Just then Alison brought a tray in with coffees and some biscuits.

"Thanks." Bernadette smiled at her.

Alison nodded. "You're welcome," she said before leaving the room.

"Very efficient staff you have here," Oisin remarked casually picking up his cup.

"So, you're an MP," said Bernadette picking up her own cup and taking a sip.

"Yes." He smiled but his smile didn't reach his eyes.

"What does it mean Minister without portfolio?"

"I go where I'm needed, covering briefs as I can, that sort of thing."

"What brings you here?"

"Ah, yes, straight to the point, I like that."

Bernadette did not like his manner at all, and she could feel Imogen bristling beside her.

"It's a lawyerly trait, I'm afraid."

"And you're a good lawyer, are you not? Very successful so I hear."

This was said in such a way as if to make her think she knew everything about her already.

"I gather people say I'm good, and I've won cases, for sure." She had become instantly non-committal, wary. There was something which made her think she wasn't going to like what was evidently coming.

"I think you're being modest from what I've heard you are one of the most respected lawyers in Dublin."

"If you say so," Bernadette said cordially.

His eyes narrowed, perhaps she wasn't responding as he had expected. He sipped his coffee for a moment without saying anything. It gave Bernadette time to study him. He was obviously someone who thought a lot of himself.

"We're not used to having MP's visiting us," she said bluntly, "So perhaps you can enlighten us?"

"Right," he said a little tersely, "You're representing someone, the fellah in the extradition case."

"What of it?" Bernadette said smoothly sensing at once he meant trouble.

"This case, the extradition case, you know it's quite a high-profile case, though perhaps you would not be aware."

"I wasn't particularly no, but again if you say so."

He looked peeved by her manner. "Well, it is, we in government keep a weathered eye on the justice system, and particular cases like this."

This sounded incredibly pompous and annoyed her in turn.

"I see," said Bernadette wondering if he was actually going to get to the point. However, his next statement indicated the direction in which things were heading.

"We're in some delicate negotiations at the moment with the UK Government, about things like extraditions, borders, things like that. Very crucial negotiations as it happens."

He picked up a chocolate biscuit and ate it quite daintily, then wiped his fingers carefully on a paper napkin which Alison had also provided.

"So," he continued, "If say, this fellah, whatever his name is, was to let's say gets sent to the UK after all then it would go a long way to erm... grease the wheels as it were."

He stopped and looked her straight in the eye, perhaps hoping to intimidate her. It failed.

"Could you, perhaps just run that by me again?" she said with maddening calm.

"I'm saying that the UK winning this extradition case is very important for our negotiations on very important affairs of state between us and the UK government. Does that help?" His tone was now a little belligerent.

"Right, thanks. You see because I thought I had heard you the first time, but I wanted to be sure. You are suggesting I lose the case for my client, whose name is Callum Jenkins by the way, to assist the Irish government, am I right?" Bernadette's voice had a dangerous edge which Imogen recognised only too well.

"Well," he backpedalled, "I wasn't exactly suggesting you lose the case, at least not deliberately."

"Then what are you suggesting?"

"You could perhaps withdraw from the case, say there's a conflict of interest. You could perhaps not fight as hard as you might want to." He was a little nettled.

"Withdraw from the case? We've already run up a huge amount of expenses... but—"

"If it's a matter of money, ahem... arrangements can be made," he interrupted.

"But," she carried on as if he had not spoken, "I do not withdraw from cases I've started because that would damage my reputation, as well as it going directly against my own personal ethics and those of my firm."

"You know, reputations can be made, and they can also be unmade," he replied seemingly unperturbed.

"Can they, can they indeed?" Her voice rose just slightly. Imogen could tell she was almost at the point of no return. It would not be a pretty sight.

"They can. Words had in the right quarters, can make a huge difference to a reputation in a very short space of time. On the contrary, cooperation could secure some very lucrative clients indeed, with names dropped in the right quarters."

He appeared to be incredibly smug, as if he was a man who always got his way.

"Really? Is that right?" Bernadette had reached the end of her tether.

"Yes, I can assure you..."

Bernadette lost her temper. "You can fucking well assure me of nothing. You come in here and practically try to coerce me to throw a case because of your negotiations. Then you attempt to bribe me by first offering a financial incentive and then threatening to damage my reputation and all of it in front of a witness. Well, let me give you a piece of advice, Mr Kavanaugh, nobody threatens me, and nobody stands in the way of justice on my fucking watch!"

He was taken aback, perhaps he wasn't used to being spoken to in that way.

"I would advise you to reconsider your position. I would advise you very strongly."

"And I would advise you not to try your luck much further," Bernadette shot back.

"You don't know who you are dealing with," he said also becoming angry.

"Neither do you. Nobody but nobody comes in here and tells me how to run a case, let alone throw it. That fellah, as I told you has a name, and he is innocent, and I am not going to let you or anyone else throw him to the lions. He's not going to end up serving fourteen years just because you think he's expendable."

Oisin stood up as if to intimidate her, but Bernadette wasn't having a bar of it. She stood up and faced him off. Imogen stood up too at her back.

"You haven't heard the last of this. I heard you were a good lawyer, but I also heard you were a fucking lesbian bitch and they were right about that," he growled.

"Yes, they were, and let me assure you Mr Kavanaugh that if you attempt to cross me, then you will really find out what a fucking bitch I am."

"Make that two lesbian bitches," Imogen said through her teeth.

"You think we're going to let a pair of women like you stand in the way of negotiations which are crucial to this country then you are very much mistaken."

"Oh? And who's we?" said Bernadette.

"People, people who are higher up the food chain than the two of you will ever be. You're a pair of nobodies take it from me."

This was bluster, and he knew it.

Bernadette smiled which served to enrage him further. "Have you got anything else to say?"

"If he doesn't go to England, then I will see your business goes down the fucking toilet and I'll see to it personally."

"I'll give you two pieces of advice," Bernadette replied evenly, "First don't you ever fucking well threaten me and second don't underestimate a pair of women, particularly a very angry pair of women. Now if you don't mind, get the fuck out of my office."

"You will regret this, both of you," he said before storming out of the room.

They followed him and watched him stalk down the corridor towards the front door.

"Mr Kavanaugh is leaving, Juanita," said Bernadette standing with her arms folded.

Juanita took in her tone and looked him up and down. She got the gist of what was going on.

"*Ve y vete a la mierda cara de polla*," she shouted after him.

The door slammed behind him and they all laughed.

"What did you say to him?" Imogen asked Juanita.

"Ah, I just told to him something like this to go and fuck to himself, and he's a cock face," Juanita replied.

"Excellent, well done," said Bernadette, "Only please don't do that to all the clients."

"Ah, what do you think? I knew he was a bad man from the time he comes in here!"

"That's our Juanita." Imogen smiled at her.

"Ah, it's nothing." Juanita brushed it off and picked up her magazine.

"Come on," said Bernadette to Imogen.

They got themselves a coffee and went to Bernadette's office. Bernadette who had been containing herself since he departed let fly.

"Cock head, I'll say he's a fucking cock head! How dare he! How fucking dare he. Marching in here like he fucking owns the place and then tries to fucking blackmail us into throwing the fucking case! Fuck! I'm so angry, Imogen. I'm so fucking, angry I could... well, I don't know what I could do, but whatever it is it wouldn't be good."

"Sit down, darling, have your coffee," Imogen said calmly.

"Are you not angry? Aren't you fucking angry?"

"I'm very angry, sweetheart, but you know what they say, revenge is a dish best served cold."

Bernadette let out a big sigh. "OK, you're right, this isn't helping."

She sat down on the sofa and Imogen reached out to squeezed her hand. Bernadette sipped her coffee for a few minutes as she tried to calm down.

"What the hell are we going to do?" Bernadette wondered at length.

"I don't know."

"How much clout do you think he can wield? I mean, can he give us that kind of trouble?"

"I think he was bluffing to scare us. I know his type and you know exactly what he needs," Imogen said mendaciously.

"Yes, I know your solution, I'd love to see it in his case," Bernadette laughed, "But practically speaking we need to find a way to neutralise him if we can."

"Do we know anyone in his circles who might provide us with some intelligence, something we could use?"

"Hmm, that's a thought."

Bernadette finished her coffee and set down the cup.

"I do know someone, he's not in politics but he potentially moves in these circles."

"Oh?"

"Yes, I'll give him a ring, see if we can entice him to lunch."

"We?"

"Yes, of course, you're my wing woman now. Where I go, you go."

"I like the sound of that," Imogen said with a saucy grin.

"Stop it!"

* * *

La Maison is an excellent French restaurant in the centre of Dublin with a red awning frontage. Bernadette chose a table along the long bench of padded seating. Imogen took the bench side and Bernadette a seat opposite. They ordered mineral water and waited for their guest.

Shortly, the familiar sight of DCS Jack Brogan appeared in the doorway. Bernadette waved him over. Brogan was a big bluff man nearing the end of his fifties. He had grey hair, blue eyes and a craggy face. He was wearing a blue suit, white shirt and patterned tie. Although Bernadette had only had lunch with him once before he was certainly unforgettable in manner and appearance. Irascible to his colleagues, he had a much softer social side too.

"Ah, Bernadette," he said striding up to their table, "And who's this delightful young lady?"

"That's Imogen Stewart my junior partner, Jack," said Bernadette.

"Well, it's nice to see you, and a very welcome if unexpected invitation."

"Hello, Jack," said Imogen blushing slightly from the compliment.

Brogan was old school, though by no means unaware of giving unwanted compliments. However, he and Bernadette were on good terms and he felt comfortable enough to do so.

"I remember this restaurant from last time," Brogan said, "Excellent food."

"Yes, it is," said Bernadette.

The waiter brought the menus and they applied themselves to the task of choosing for a few moments.

Bernadette and Imogen chose the *Prawn Bisque*, and Brogan the *Oven Baked Scallops* in their shells to start. For entrée, Brogan opted for the *Cote de Boeuf*, as did Bernadette, and Imogen selected the *Leg of Venison casserole*. They ordered a selection of accompanying sides, and Brogan passed on alcohol opting for diet coke.

"I'm having to cut back on drinking, Stella has been giving me fucking gyp about it, so I've confined myself to a whisky or two at night," he said gruffly.

Stella was Brogan's diminutive English wife who he adored but who ruled him with gentle admonishments and love.

"Now then, as pleased as I am to see you, and before you say anything, I did say call on me anytime. What can I do to assist you? It is assistance you need I take it?" Brogan continued.

"Do you know a politician named, Oisin Kavanaugh?" said Bernadette taking the plunge.

There was silence from Brogan on hearing this, and he took a hasty swig of diet coke. Then he called up the waiter and ordered a single malt Glenlivet. Bernadette waited patiently while this was brought and exchanged glances with Imogen. The mention of Oisin's name had apparently had a powerful effect upon Brogan. When the whisky arrived, he practically knocked it back in one go and allowed the amber liquid to slide down his throat with evident satisfaction.

"Sorry about that," he said, "It's just when you mentioned that fucking tossbag's name I had to calm my nerves otherwise I'm afraid we could have been ejected from the restaurant."

"Oh?"

Brogan drew a deep breath and it was clear he was wrestling with some sort of internal impulse to lose his temper in a spectacular fashion. However, he seemed to manage to keep calm whilst delivering a string of invective at well below the usual volume he would have employed.

"That absolute turdball is working for the justice department and I can tell you for nothing, he's a fucking pain in the fucking backside. Fucking arse bastard is what he is. I can't fucking stand him in case that wasn't clear already, and neither can the AC. Fucking tossing tossball."

Bernadette suppressed a smiled to herself on hearing this. It was music to her ears.

"I take it he's not popular with the Garda?" Imogen ventured.

"Not popular, not fucking popular! A fucking nest of vipers in fucking space suit would more popular than that scumbag tosspot," he said with suppressed fury.

"What's he done?" Bernadette asked him.

"What hasn't he fucking done? Scrutinising this, fucking well wanting us to cut that. Going through every fucking case we've had, trying to influence us to move certain cases faster than others. Throwing his fucking weight about like a fucking bowling ball on crack. We've had him up to here."

He took another sip of his diet coke and clearly was contemplating a second whisky judging by the way he fiddled with the empty whisky glass.

"He said he's a minister without portfolio."

"I'll give him minister without portfolio. I'd dearly love to give him something up his fucking portfolio and no mistake," he scoffed. "He's been seconded to the Justice Department, what a fucker. A monkey's uncle could do a better fucking job than him."

Bernadette gave Imogen a surreptitious look, they appeared to have hit pay dirt. Before Brogan could animadvert on Oisin's character any further, the first course arrived, and conversation ceased while Bernadette and Imogen consumed their soup, and Brogan his scallops.

"Delicious," he said, wiping his chin, "Best scallops I've had in ages. Absolutely first class."

"I'm glad you like them," said Bernadette.

"So, come on, what's he done?" Brogan asked her, pushing away his plate. He had clearly been brooding on the various offences Oisin had committed on his department.

"We're defending Callum Jenkins. The extradition case, I'm sure you'll have heard of it. Anyway, Kavanaugh came to our offices, and tried to persuade us to drop the case."

Brogan nodded. He would certainly be aware of a high-profile case like that one. "Did he? Did he indeed? Tell me more."

Bernadette related what had taken place, with some embellishments from Imogen. He laughed uproariously when he heard what Bernadette had said to him.

"Oh, I'd have loved to see that. I'd have loved to see that tossbag's face, it must have been a picture."

"It was," Imogen chuckled, "Then our receptionist called him a cock head in Spanish."

This was met with a fresh bout of mirth from Brogan. After which he became serious.

"So, he's been threatening you, has he? What a fucking fuckmuffin. It needs thinking about though, this. Can't have people like him interfering with the justice process. It's not right."

Whatever Brogan might be, he passionately believed in following due process. When it came to the ultimate fate of criminals, however guilty they may be or not, he relied upon the courts to give the decisions. He was a firm believer in fairness, and in the justice system itself. Interference of this nature was, to him, unthinkable.

The mains arrived, and the conversation moved on to other topics. Bernadette asked him how his star unit The Foxcatchers was doing, and he talked about some of their recent cases. He complimented the steak and said how much he had enjoyed it. Bernadette was pleased as he was a very likeable man, and he obviously liked good food.

"Well now," he said once they had all finished, "I'll see if I can take care of this little issue for you. Stop that little fucker in his tracks once and for all. Do us all a favour in fact and get him off our fucking backs."

It seemed he had been turning the problem over in the back of his mind while they had been eating and discussing other things.

"What are you going to do?" Bernadette wondered.

"Oh, nothing untoward, don't worry. But let's just say everyone slips up from time to time, especially MP's and perhaps there'll be someone there to discover it when he does. He's been a pain in the backside for months, and this is the last straw. You're doing the decent thing defending an innocent man by all accounts. I don't hold with that sort of underhanded dealing. It stinks. It's interesting to watch how hard they fall the higher they are."

He wouldn't say anymore, or exactly when, but Bernadette felt reassured he would do something. Brogan was known for being as good as his word, she knew that much.

"Well, if you *can* get him to leave us alone, it would be good, not that he was going to stop me from doing the right thing."

"I'm sure but you don't need this kind of thing hanging over you. Just leave it with me. If he bothers you in the meantime, don't worry about it."

"Thank you."

"Glad you called me and thank you for the glorious lunch. I think this was mutually beneficial all around. Not to mention your very pleasant company."

"Would you like some dessert or coffee?"

"I would love it, but I won't, thanks. I've got to watch my waistline. Plus, I've got a meeting to go to, alas. So, I'll have to love you and leave you both. Nice to meet you, Imogen."

"It's our pleasure."

They both gave him an affectionate hug, as it seemed to Bernadette they were now on those terms.

"We'll do this again," said Bernadette.

"Absolutely, just say the word."

Brogan smiled, called up his driver and left the restaurant with a cheery wave goodbye.

"He seemed nice," said Imogen as they resumed their seats.

"He's a good sort, and it's handy to have friends like him in the Garda."

"Yes, indeed, but you don't think he's going to..."

"What? Plant drugs on him or something? No, I doubt it. Jack has an impeccable record. He's not going to ruin it. However, he seems to have ways of pulling strings, and so let's not worry too much about Kavanaugh."

"No, I feel better already."

"Me too."

"Shall we have a coffee?"

"Yes." Bernadette called the waiter over. When he had gone, she said, "Eve wants to get a maid's outfit."

"Really? Do tell?"

"She wants to do roleplay. I think she might be getting one this week for our Shibari session."

"Let me know how it goes, I might get one for D'Arcy."

"The naughty maid gets spanked I suppose," Bernadette giggled.

"Variety is the spice of life." Imogen smirked.

"I'm sure, I'm surprised you haven't got one already."

"I did think about it. I'll ask Eve where she gets hers from."

"Has Eve..." Bernadette said lightly, venturing onto the forbidden ground of the wedding.

"Ask no questions, get no lies," Imogen admonished her, "Also you don't want me to tell Eve you've been prying."

"Oh, good God no, I'll be upstairs naked with my hands on the bedroom wall again. Not that I didn't enjoy it last time."

"If you want me to drop you in it then, just say," Imogen said laughing.

"No, no, not this week anyway. I don't want Eve to think I broke my promise."

"Yes, you've had enough drama for a while I'd say."

"And I'd say you're right."

They both laughed. Bernadette's relationship had been a bit of a roller coaster ride at times, but she wouldn't change it for the world or Eve.

✳ ✳ ✳

When they got back to the office, Bernadette had not been long at her desk when Imogen came in.

"You will never guess what," Imogen said brimming with news.

"Sit down, tell me!"

Bernadette moved to sit on the sofa next to Imogen and looked at her expectantly.

"We've got the prehearing date on Friday, I just heard from the court."

"What?" Bernadette was slightly flabbergasted. These types of cases were usually much longer in terms of elapsed time than that.

"I know, it's a bit strange, don't you think? I spoke to them before and they said it would be weeks. Suddenly they said, oh no, a gap opened up in the schedule and it's to be Friday."

"Hmm, I think someone is possibly interfering behind the scenes," said Bernadette with a frown.

"What, you don't think?"

"Kavanaugh, yes I do. He's obviously trying to wrong foot us now, because we won't cooperate. If he pushes the proceedings up the agenda then he thinks we won't have enough time to prepare," Bernadette said crossly.

"More fool him then, because actually, we are pretty much ready for the prehearing conference at the very least."

"Yes, it actually suits us to push this a bit harder, you're right. Although I am sure now, he'll push them to have a hearing as soon as possible."

"You don't think he'll try to influence?"

"You're thinking he'll try to get a judge who will favour the extradition, aren't you," said Bernadette pursing her lips.

"It crossed my mind, now you've said that I think it's a distinct possibility."

"Fuck! Well, I would seriously hope he can't do so, but even if he does, judges are quite a cantankerous lot and they don't take kindly to being told what to do by anyone in my experience."

"I hope you're right." Imogen looked worried.

It was true, Bernadette reflected, the choice of judge could influence a case and its outcome. No matter they were supposed to be impartial some were known to be more lenient than others, and sentences could certainly vary as could judgements.

"He is trying to load the dice against us, it's pretty clear. I'll tell you what, I will call Brogan and drop this one in his ear."

"Oh goodie, can I listen in?" said Imogen eagerly.

"Why not?"

Bernadette retrieved her phone and dialled Brogan up on speaker. He answered almost at once.

"Bernadette," he said with a smile in his voice, "To what do I owe the pleasure of this call? I mean, we only just spoke not an hour or two ago."

"I hope you don't mind, but I wanted to run something by you," she said tentatively.

"Of course, go ahead, what's up?"

"It's about Kavanaugh."

"I thought it might be but carry on."

She detected a slight note of rising tension in his voice but persevered.

"We just unexpectedly got our prehearing for the Callum cased moved up to Friday. On the pretext that an opening came up. But we're a little suspicious of it. We are wondering if perhaps Kavanaugh might be able to influence something like that, and also perhaps influence the choice of judge? What's your view? I'd be interested in your thoughts."

There was silence from the other end of the line. Bernadette looked at Imogen and wondered if Brogan was still there. They were not to know, unlike his colleagues who were used to his ways, that this was simply a precursor to an imminent explosion. It was not long in coming.

"What do I think?" he said furiously, "What do I fucking think? I'll tell you what I think. That never a more villainous fucking scum bastard walked the earth than that jumped up overpaid idle interfering fucking moron! What a fucking nerve of the man. What a tossbag flimflam piece of work. An absolute fucker of a man, a turdball of the highest fucking order and then some. Abusing his fucking privilege left right and fucking centre. It makes me so mad, I tell you, so fucking mad, I could drink an entire bottle of single malt, which I won't of course and don't tell my wife I suggested it..."

As they could tell he was blazing angry, the last part was wholly unnecessary. Since they didn't know his wife either, it was unlikely they would divulge such an intention.

"Anyway," he said in much calmer tones, "I think you're right, it's exactly what the tool moron is up to and no mistake."

Both of them were unused to Brogan's unusual turn of phrase and expressions which were unique to him and his style. Far from being intimidated, they found it quite amusing.

"So, do you think he can influence the choice of judge?"

"Oh, undoubtedly to an extent, although if I know the judges, and some of them are almighty bags of wind, I can't imagine they will take kindly to being told what to do. No indeed."

Brogan's opinion of the justices of the land was apparently not very high.

He continued, "Met more than my fair share at these fucking do's I have to go to, you know. Blasted memorials and conferences, and waste of time fucking functions. The only good part about them is the food and drink. All the fucking judges are there, fuckers that they are most of them. Pompous fucking arses. I can't see them being happy to have that jumped up shitbagging pussball pushing them around at all."

"That's good to know at least," said Bernadette smiling at Imogen who was suppressing a fit of the giggles.

"Anyway, this is all you know, under the radar, between yourselves and me, mum's the word."

"Of course, naturally."

"Good, good, well anyway, all the more reason to find something on this fucker, yes indeed," Brogan mused, as much to himself as them.

"Can I ask you something else?"

"Yes, of course."

"There's an operation going on at the moment, to investigate Balik Transport. We think that's where the Vietnamese women were put onto the truck which went into the UK. It's being run by DS Olivia Thompson. Although it doesn't seem to be getting too far as we understand it. The evidence from that might be very useful to the case, you see..."

She let this idea float to see what Brogan might do with it.

"Is there indeed? Well, I wasn't aware of this, but now I am I'll make some enquiries myself and see if I can't put a rocket under a few people."

"Thanks, much obliged if you could."

"Not to worry, as I said, happy to help. It's a mutual cause and beneficial to us both to get the tossbag out of our hair. Bear with it for the moment if you can."

"Thank you, Jack, we really appreciate it."

"My pleasure, any further developments, you let me know."

"I will."

"Bye."

He disconnected and Bernadette shot a triumphant look at Imogen.

"He's certainly a useful ally," said Imogen, "If he really can neutralise Kavanaugh."

"I wouldn't underestimate Brogan by all accounts, and maybe I should suggest inviting him and his wife to our wedding."

"Yes, why not."

"Good, well, we've got to prepare for the conference on Friday, but I think we should also go down and tackle Andrew about the PA. He's had enough time to think about it."

"Yes, let's do that. We're on a roll after all."

The two of them made their way to Andrew Bond's office. He was typing nineteen to the dozen as usual in front of his computer, with a desk strewn with paperwork, receipts and files.

"Oh, it's the gruesome twosome come to plague the life out of me again," he observed without looking up or stopping what he was doing.

"And we love you too," said Bernadette sliding into a seat.

"Oh, come on, Bernadette, you know you only come here when you want something, and now I've got it in stereo."

"If you're referring to my gorgeous and beautiful junior partner then..."

"Right, I guess you're not going to disappear, so fine!" He stopped work and turned to face them. He was wearing a blue pinstriped shirt without a tie for a change.

"You're looking remarkably casual." Bernadette smiled, knowing he took pride in his appearance.

"Well, it's nothing, I'm just busy, don't need to wear a tie when there are no clients to see," he said defensively.

"She's just teasing you, softening you up, Andrew darling," said Imogen.

"I know exactly what she's doing and don't you start on the Andrew darling business."

"Goodness somebody got out of bed the wrong side today, or perhaps Jessica gave him the cold shoulder," Bernadette quipped.

"My personal life is none of your affair," he said tartly.

"Ha! She had a go at him, I'm sure of it," Imogen giggled. He looked a little deflated at this.

"As it happens, we did have words," he admitted, "Fair ruined my day it has."

"Ah, poor Andrew, tell Aunty Bernadette what happened," Bernadette said turning on her most sympathetic voice. In truth, she had a huge soft spot for Andrew no matter how much she teased him.

"Well, it was nothing really, I mean, it's just that she had her hair done you know, yesterday, and well, I didn't notice. Then when she asked me, I couldn't see anything different. She had got a new outfit and everything."

"Oh dear."

"Anyway, she's out today buying new plates to replace the ones she smashed on the floor."

Jessica was known to have quite a temper on her. Bernadette wasn't surprised to hear this. She was very Irish in that respect and incredibly fiery and volatile.

"I suppose she hasn't forgiven you?" she said gently, seeing there was genuine chagrin in his face.

"No, and I did get the cold shoulder last night just as you said, made my own breakfast this morning, and she's not talking to me at the moment."

"But she told you about the plates?"

"Well yes, she texted me."

"Then she is talking to you and of course, she feels contrite, but you will have to make the first move," Bernadette told him sagely.

"God I'm so useless in that department, always have been," he said helplessly.

"Flowers, buy her the biggest bunch you can afford, put a sorry card in it and have it sent right away."

"Then, buy her some chocolates too," Imogen added.

"Oh, she's not fond of those."

"Lingerie then, works a treat."

"I wouldn't know where to begin."

"Well, let us take you shopping, darling," said Bernadette, "We will help you choose some."

"But... but I've got all this work to do."

"Trust me, your relationship is far more important."

He sighed. "Oh fine, OK, just give me half an hour then."

"Make sure you order those flowers," Bernadette admonished him.

"Yes, yes, of course, I will. Anyway, what did you actually come down here for?"

"Well, we're wondering about that PA, you were looking at figures, we talked about it?" Bernadette said.

"Oh that, yes fine, I looked at the numbers, Alison is clocking up far too much overtime, and another PA makes sense, so go ahead. I've got some amounts for salary ranges, and so on I will email them to you."

"Great, thanks, right well, we will leave you to it and come back in half an hour by which time you will have ordered those flowers am I right?"

"Yes, yes I will, just go away," he said smiling, "And thank you, both of you."

"It's our pleasure, you see, we do love you to bits really."

He sighed again and turned back to his computer.

"Flowers," Bernadette said as they slipped out of the door.

"Poor soul," said Imogen, "Married to a redhead."

"I'm sure D'Arcy would concur," Bernadette said wryly.

"We're not quite married yet."

"No, but you will be."

"Yes."

They reached the kitchen and got themselves some coffee.

"While we're at the lingerie I might as well pick something out for D'Arcy," said Imogen.

"I had the same idea," Bernadette laughed.

"Great minds think alike."

"Indeed, they do, darling, indeed they do."

* * *

When Bernadette got home, Eve was at the door to greet her.

"OK," said Bernadette, accepting her kiss, "Just how did you know I had got home? More of your witchery is it?"

"I wish I could say that to keep you guessing, sweetheart," Eve laughed, "By I saw it on the CCTV. I was in the living room drawing and there you were."

"Sure, of course. I might have guessed."

They had CCTV and a new entry system installed courtesy of D'Arcy when they were handling her case. Her ex-boyfriend had become threatening and dangerous, D'Arcy was concerned for their safety. She had insisted on putting in the security system.

"Anyway." Eve spied the paper bag which Bernadette was carrying. "What have you been doing?"

"Ah well, I've bought you a little something."

"For me?"

"Very much for you."

Bernadette did not shower Eve with gifts, although she certainly could have. Eve wanted her to be more circumspect. She wanted less because she said that meant more. Each gift was more special that way.

"Can I see?" Eve said eagerly.

"Come into the living room then."

Bernadette divested herself of her shoes and took Eve's hand. She led her to the sofa.

"Here you are." Bernadette handed her the bag.

Eve reached inside with smiling eyes. "Oh my God, oh fuck!" she exclaimed when she withdrew a black short net see-through nightdress with a black lacy bust and over the shoulder straps. It was gathered in at the waist. "That's so deliciously naughty!"

"Isn't it?"

"Yes, and I should try it on, shouldn't I?"

"You should, of course."

"Come on then, I'm going upstairs, come up in five minutes."

"OK."

Eve skipped off and Bernadette smiled to herself. The nightdress wasn't particularly expensive, but she had thought of Eve at once. She was happy Eve had liked it. After a few moments, she made her way up the stairs.

Eve was waiting standing in the centre of the room wearing black stiletto mules.

"Holy shit, you are so fucking beautiful," said Bernadette moving forward to take hold of her hands. "You're drop dead gorgeous and so sexy in that."

"How sexy?"

"So, so, so, so sexy, my darling."

"Show me," Eve whispered.

Bernadette gathered her up in her arms, holding her close, kissing her softly and then harder. The fire ignited almost immediately. The kiss became fuelled with passion, as her hands ran up over the material, feeling Eve's naked skin underneath.

"Oh, baby," Eve breathed, "Fuck me, darling, please fuck me now."

"I fully intend to," said Bernadette softly, leading her to the bed, and lying next to her fully clothed.

"Oh God, I want you so badly, this makes me feel so sexy," Eve gasped, as Bernadette's fingers and nails raked over her flesh. "Oh, fuck, fuck, oh."

Bernadette's hand slid between Eve's thighs and she began to use her fingers.

"Oh... darling... oh... fuck... oh... yes... oh... yes... yes." Eve's breathing became deeper. Bernadette was kissing her as her fingers kept working. Eve began to push her pelvis hard against them. "Oh... oh... oh... God... don't stop... oh God... don't stop... no... oh... yes... yes..." Eve was reaching her climax in very short order. She began to tense as she crested the wave, and her orgasm broke, "Oh... fuck... oh... oh... oh... ohh!" she cried out arching her back.

Bernadette held her as Eve's spasms subsided, and she relaxed.

"That was so good, oh that was so good," said Eve smiling, "And there I was meeting you at the door to take you to eat dinner."

Bernadette laughed, "I'm sure the dinner will keep."

"Yes, yes it will, now let me take those clothes off you, my darling."

CHAPTER TWELVE

riday morning arrived and the day of the prehearing conference. As the alarm woke Bernadette from her slumber, she found herself with her arms firmly clasped around her fiancée's body. Eve stirred and turned around to face her giving her a sleepy kiss, with closed eyes and tousled head.

"Is it that time already?"

"Yes, darling, and I've got to get up for court, my love, so…"

Eve's eyes flew open. "Of course, yes, you must. Go and have your shower. I'll get your clothes."

Shortly afterwards Bernadette, refreshed from her shower, sat contemplating Eve in the mirror, while Eve fixed her hair.

"I think a softer approach today," said Eve brushing it out and straightening it with straighteners, "Mmm *that* looks gorgeous."

"Thank you." Bernadette smiled, while Eve did her makeup, all barring her lips. That was a last-minute thing because Eve wanted her goodbye kiss. Bernadette enjoyed these ministrations, tiny acts of love, she hoped she reciprocated in her own way for all the things Eve did for her. One way was the Shibari sessions, and the next one was now overdue, but she intended to remedy this in the evening.

"Get dressed, I'll make breakfast." Eve put on the night attire which Bernadette had removed the night before and padded off downstairs.

"Sexy witch," Bernadette called after her. She chuckled whilst putting on the cream blouse, black skirt and jacket Eve had laid out. She wasn't always too formal for court, but today being important, it was probably best to look tip top professional. Cream was a little less severe than white, and she didn't want to be too forbidding.

Eve had left her some black stilettoes and although Bernadette generally preferred something strappy or mules, she accepted the choice and put them on. As she took one last look in the mirror, she reflected what a good dominatrix outfit it might make and laughed at the thought.

"Wow, you sexy fucking bitch," said Eve when Bernadette entered the kitchen.

"Do you think so?"

"I know so,." Eve came up to her and she gave her a peck before ushering her to her place and putting down a plate of scrambled eggs on toast, mushrooms and bacon in front of her. "No tomatoes in case you squirt them on your blouse."

"Am I *that* messy?"

"No, but I don't want to risk it, I ironed the blouse especially for today."

"I will be very careful then," Bernadette told her meekly.

She addressed herself to her breakfast for a few moments, savouring the creaminess of the eggs. Eve always got them just right.

"How do you think it will go today?" Eve asked her.

"Oh, alright I think, after all, it's just the prehearing."

"Is that prick faced bastard going to be there?" Eve said having heard the story about Oisin.

"Which one?" Bernadette laughed.

"Oh, the politician, you know, the one who threatened you."

"I don't know, if he does then he's showing his true colours."

"Well, he showed those already, so I think he is showing his doubly true colours."

"You're funny."

"I'll show him funny, threatening you!" Eve said fiercely.

"Was that a growl I just heard?" Bernadette giggled.

"I will certainly become a feral feline if anyone goes after you!"

"I'll tell him to watch out then."

The two of them chuckled, and Bernadette, having finished her breakfast, drank her coffee.

"You know I love you, right?" she said suddenly.

"Yes, of course."

"Just checking."

"I love you too."

"And I've got to go," Bernadette told her, "But not before I put this on the fridge."

"What?"

Bernadette pulled a piece of paper from her inside pocket and ostentatiously placed a list on the fridge door which she secured with a magnet. She had written it the night before and kept it hidden. It read, "Keeping secrets yet again; Not telling me important things; Watching porn without telling me; Swearing at me; Behaving like a brat; Throwing a temper tantrum; Making me cry."

"Oh my goodness, that's quite a list, and all of it very bad," said Eve reading it with interest.

"So... you know what's going to happen later, don't you?" said Bernadette leaning in close.

"Yes, yes I do, and I'll be thinking about it all day," Eve whispered her lips now touching Bernadette's.

"That's the whole point."

"I'm wet already."

Bernadette kissed her lightly. "Hold the thought then darling, I've got to go."

Eve accompanied her to the door, and Bernadette could see the longing in her eyes. She pondered telling Eve not to touch herself for the day but doubted Eve could comply, so she didn't.

Eve tilted her head up for a kiss, and their lips met for a passionate union just as they always did with inevitable pulse racing consequences.

"How *do* you do that?"

"I keep telling you I'm a witch, but you won't believe me."

"Oh, I believe you, I really do."

"Let me fix your lipstick, now, hold still, darling."

Bernadette let Eve finish putting on her lipstick and some gloss, picked up her bag and let herself out the door. Eve stood waving her goodbye until she was out of the gate and out of sight. Bernadette sighed, but it was a contented sigh. She shifted gears and pulled out into the main road, also mentally shifting into gear for the coming hearing.

✻ ✻ ✻

"Are we all ready?" she said to Imogen, entering her office with two coffees.

"Yes, very much so, I've got all the documents we need." Imogen patted the small wheely suitcase they used for the court.

"We've time for a coffee I think?"

"Mmm, yes please."

They sat together amicably on Imogen's sofa.

"Everything OK at home?" Imogen asked her.

"Oh yes, and it's going to be even better later."

"Oh?"

"Yes, Shibari session tonight, I just put a list on the fridge," Bernadette giggled.

"I bet Eve's looking forward to it." Imogen smiled and sipped her drink.

"Both of us are, I quite enjoy them now."

"Did you not used to?" Imogen cocked an eyebrow.

"I wasn't sure at first, but now it's kind of fun, very sexy. The real enjoyment is because Eve loves it so much, and it really turns her on."

"See, kinky can be fun."

"Yes, yes it can."

"Believe me I know," Imogen laughed.

"Yes, I know, darling, and I'm sure D'Arcy knows it too."

"Oh, she does and I'm sure she'll do something this weekend to merit chastisement."

Bernadette laughed at this and shook her head. She drained her cup and set it down.

"On that note, shall we go?" she said.

"Yes, let's."

They arrived in good time at the Central Criminal Courts of Dublin. As they mounted the steps it was evident there was quite a contingent of press who set up a clamour as soon as they saw her.

"Oh fuck," said Imogen, "They've got wind of it already."

"Yes, I see," said Bernadette, "Although maybe this time we can turn it to our advantage."

As they reached the top of the steps she slowed and turned to the reporters shouting out questions. She held up her hand.

"We are here for the prehearing conference today of the attempted extradition of our client Callum Jenkins. I can't say anything now, but if you stick around, I may have more to say later."

With that she turned on her heel and walked away, leaving an uproar behind her.

"What are you playing at?" Imogen asked her with interest.

"I'm setting up a counter movement. There's more than one way to play politicians at their own game. We can get the public onside perhaps and create a stir about this case."

"Really? It's not usually your style."

"Kavanaugh is playing dirty and so will we. I know Brogan said he was going to take him out of the game, but until then we can have some fun with it."

"You are evil to the core, a lesbian bitch lawyer of no mean order," Imogen chuckled.

"Oh, I can be when I want to be."

"I've no doubt about it."

Since the hearing was to begin shortly, they headed for the courtroom, picking Callum, and his father up on the way.

"Callum, you'll probably have to be in the dock in case the judge wants to ask you anything," said Bernadette. "In a case like this, you're not required to make a plea as such, other than perhaps to agree that you oppose your extradition if questioned on it. Otherwise leave it all to us, OK? Then afterwards come and talk to us in a meeting room, as we might be facing the press when leave. I want to brief you on that, OK?"

"Sure, OK," said Callum.

"Do exactly what she says mind, now, Callum," Rhys admonished him.

"I will, Da, don't fret so."

"OK, well, I'm just worried about you son," said Rhys a little emotionally.

"I know you are, Da, no more worried than I am, I can assure you."

"Look, nobody has to worry today, it's a prehearing and that's all you need to know, OK. Let's be calm. The real hearing is when we can all start worrying," said Bernadette trying to put a stop to what seemed to be putting Callum on edge.

"Yes, OK, sorry," said Rhys.

"Right then, here we go."

They entered the courtroom en masse and leaving Rhys on the public benches at the front, Imogen took Callum over to the dock. Once he was settled, she returned to their lawyer's station where Bernadette was setting up.

"Are we good?" said Bernadette.

"Yes." Imogen nodded.

"Great, so now we wait."

Shane Wilson and Mason Beamish arrived just at that moment and began to set up on their own bench. Shane and Mason nodded at them briefly but did not come over. Bernadette reflected this was just as well because Imogen still wasn't quite settled in her emotions as regards Shane. As it was, she noticed Imogen stole a couple of glances in his direction but otherwise studiously did not look at him. Bernadette had no doubt Mason would have filled him in on their lunch but nothing particularly untoward had been said, so she wasn't worried.

They had everything arranged and were waiting for the judge, when Imogen nudged her. Imogen flicked her eyes to the back of the court. Bernadette looked around and was annoyed to discover Oisin Kavanaugh was sitting in the rear benches which were starting to fill up with press people. He was apparently chatting to someone who might be an aide or a reporter. However, the sight of him did slightly raise her ire, and determination to do something after the hearing.

Before she could think about this any further the Tipster entered the room and called everyone to rise. A moment later the Tipster announced the entrance of Justice Colin Brannigan. The judge strode in and took a seat. He was a heavy-set man in his late fifties at least. He had grey hair, lowering bushy brows, and what would appear to be something of a scowl in his expression.

Bernadette sighed, Brannigan was very old school and known to be a real stickler in the courtroom. He had a reputation for handing out heavy sentences and believed, it seemed, in harsh punishments. He wasn't an easy judge to appear before and many lawyers considered he leaned heavily towards the prosecution. There had obviously been some tampering, and another quick look up at Oisin confirmed he was smiling to himself about the judge's appearance. She and Imogen exchanged a glance which spoke volumes about the choice of judge for the hearing.

Justice Brannigan looked around the courtroom taking in the various parties before speaking.

"Right then, we are here in the case of the DPP versus Callum Jenkins, am I right?" he said to the court in general.

"Yes, Judge," said Shane standing up.

"And you are?" Justice Brannigan enquired in a none too friendly manner.

"I'm Shane Wilson, Judge, representing the prosecution service, and I have with me today Mason Beamish QC who is not taking part in the proceedings but represents our effective clients, the Crown Prosecution Service from the United Kingdom."

"I see," said the judge in such a manner, as if he didn't see at all. However, he passed no comment on Mason's presence.

"I presume the defence counsel is yourself?" said Justice Brannigan to Bernadette, in surprisingly milder tones.

"Yes, Judge, I am Bernadette Mackenna, and this is my junior counsel, Imogen Stuart. We represent Mr Jenkins who is presently in the dock."

"Right, right, good." The judge gave her a half smile which disconcerted her even more. If the judge had been 'got to' then she expected far more antagonism in her direction which was not what was happening at all so far.

"So, this the prehearing conference as a precursor to the main hearing, as we must all be aware," said Justice Brannigan, and then he paused to once more look around the courtroom. Bernadette noticed his gaze alighting upon Oisin at the back, and all at once he inexplicably scowled with what one could only interpret as unsuppressed fury and then it was gone.

"Now then," he continued, "Before we start, I want to make a few things clear. This case is extremely high profile in the sense that all such extradition proceedings are likely to be. However, it seems this case, by the look of it has attracted particular attention today. So, with this in mind, it needs to be clearly understood by all parties, we are dealing with the attempt to extradite an Irish Citizen from his country of birth by a foreign government."

He paused to once more fix Oisin with an inscrutable glare which made the man flush slightly. Bernadette cottoning on to this realised the cause of the judge's ire was directed particularly at the errant politician without stating it.

"As such we in the justice system do not take such things lightly. Oh no, indeed. This is a very serious matter, very serious. Removing a citizen of this country without good reason or proper lawful due process is not to countenanced by anybody! And there will be due process done according to the law of this land which is Ireland. There are strict parameters for extradition that must be met and they will have to be met, that had better be understood at the start, for any such action to take place or any such judgement to be issued."

He practically barked this last sentence out, so much so that a number of people appeared to blench slightly.

"And I say this. There will be no attempt by anyone from anywhere to interfere with the process of proper justice in my courtroom on this matter. So, bear it in mind, all parties concerned."

The message was loud and clear from where Bernadette was standing. Oisin had attempted to influence the judge in some way, she was sure of it now, and he wasn't having any of it. She quietly rejoiced inside. If nothing else, they would get a fair hearing from this judge, she was certain.

"Now then, let us proceed with the business in hand," said Justice Brannigan in much more measured tones.

He picked up a list, which was evidently an aide memoir of the things he had to cover.

"So, Mr Wilson, have you served all papers and evidence on the defence?"

Shane stood up. "Yes, Judge."

"Very good, and are you likely to produce anything further?"

"Not at this time, Judge, no."

"Good." Justice Brannigan turned to Bernadette. "Have you received the said papers?"

"As far as we are aware, yes, Judge, we have," said Bernadette.

"Excellent, and I assume you will be furnishing the prosecution with any evidence you wish to bring to court?"

"Yes, Judge, in due course we shall. We are in the process of compiling any evidence and it will be served prior to the hearing."

"Good, very good," said the judge, "Because, according to what I have here, the hearing is likely to be in three weeks' time."

"Really?"

"Is it too soon?" he asked a little solicitously.

"No, Judge, I was surprised considering the court schedules are usually so full."

"Yes, indeed, I was surprised myself, but I'm not the one who sets the date so I'm not sure how it's come about."

Bernadette had a very shrewd idea of how it had come about, and looking at her junior, so did Imogen who was pursing her lips.

"Do either of you have any objection to three weeks?" Justice Brannigan continued.

"No, Judge," said Shane.

"No, Judge," said Bernadette.

"Fine, however, given the shortness of the date, all evidence must be filed two working days beforehand. Now, moving on let us talk about the witnesses for this case. I see here from the prosecution you have two, a Mr Kevin Clinton, and Senior Investigating Officer Detective Chief Inspector Harold Graham, am I right?"

"Yes, Judge, that is correct," said Shane.

"Good, and is it intended for them to appear here in person."

"Well..." Shane began.

"Judge, if I may interject." Bernadette stood up at once.

"Ms Mackenna?"

"We would ask for these witnesses to appear in court since it is their evidence which is key to the prosecution's case, and therefore we feel they should be present for a proper cross examination."

Justice Brannigan nodded at this and appeared not to demur at this request.

"Mr Wilson?"

"Obviously there is an expense to bring Mr Clinton here, not the least because he is under police protective custody."

"Judge, a man's future life is at stake with the possibility of fourteen years in prison for a crime which he strenuously denies," Bernadette shot back.

"I tend to agree with Ms Mackenna on this point," said Justice Brannigan, "Regardless of the cost element, I feel that fairness to Mr Jenkins is of paramount importance, and therefore I am ordering you to produce these witnesses in person at the hearing."

"Yes, Judge," said Shane making a face which indicated he wasn't happy about it one iota.

There was a snort of annoyance from the back of the courtroom, which Bernadette was sure was very likely to have been Oisin. The judge looked up sharply but said nothing about it.

"And your witnesses, Ms Mackenna?" asked the judge.

"Judge, we have two, as noted one of these is a vulnerable person and as such, we request anonymity as regards these court proceedings, and that they should attend by video link. The other is our client Callum Jenkins."

"What is the nature of their vulnerability?" said Justice Brannigan.

"Before I answer, Judge, I would request reporting restrictions be set about this person."

"Very well, I order reporting restrictions around this witness, who we shall call Witness A."

"Thank you, Judge, Witness A is one of the trafficked refugees who is willing to testify, we will be submitting an affidavit from this witness which we request must retain anonymity."

"Right, it seems fair to me," said the judge, "Mr Wilson, do you have any objection?"

"Judge, I don't see why this witness cannot be brought to court," said Shane in obdurate tones.

"You don't? I see, and what is your reasoning behind this?" Justice Brannigan appeared to be incredulous at this. Whatever had been conveyed to him through channels from Oisin had evidently set his back up. The move had certainly backfired and now instead of challenging the defence, he was doing it to the prosecution.

"The witness is vulnerable, as is my witness who has been required in person. Why shouldn't the same apply to Witness A?"

"I think it should be clear as to why, but I'll let Ms Mackenna make her own case."

"Judge, Witness A is subject to immigration restrictions in the United Kingdom and as such the ability of her to travel here, and have protection provided is also subject to the United Kingdom's authorities. As it is the witness has been removed to a place of safety due to her disclosures."

"So." Justice Brannigan fixed Shane with a beady eye. "Mr Wilson?"

"Well... I... err... I will have to consult with my colleagues in the United Kingdom but at this moment we accept the video link proposal."

"Right, so if you happen to want to change it then I assume you will liaise with Ms Mackenna's team and this court before the hearing."

"Yes, Judge," said Shane in resigned tones, he had realised that currently and for reasons he perhaps wasn't aware, the judge wasn't inclined to give him an inch.

"Good, very good, we've settled that question then. So, what about any technical requirements for evidence?"

"At this point, we anticipate we might require pictorial or video evidence to be shown," said Shane.

"Judge, the defence anticipates the same."

"OK, in which case please relay these requirements to the clerk of the court," said Justice Brannigan with a smile. "Now is there anything else I need to attend to at this time?"

"No, Judge," said Shane.

"No, thank you, Judge," said Bernadette.

"Splendid, I shall set all this down in memorandum and see you all here in three weeks' time," Justice Brannigan said with great affability, before gathering his notes, and getting up.

The Tipster rushed in and called the court to rise, while Justice Brannigan left the room. As he did so, there was a commotion at the back of the court where Oisin with a face as black as thunder slammed out of the courtroom.

"Things obviously didn't go his way," Imogen observed at this.

"No, it was a big surprise, to be honest," Bernadette laughed.

The press contingent was scrambling to get out of the door, in order to waylay them when they left the court.

Shane came over to their station.

"I hear you've been lunching my colleague," said Shane in a sardonic tone.

"Yes, and very nice it was too," said Bernadette amiably.

"Right, well, I'm only annoyed I didn't get the invite too." Shane smiled trying to make a joke of it.

"You weren't in London, he was." Bernadette shrugged.

Having had the wind taken out of his sails, Shane looked a little deflated. He'd perhaps wanted an argument or to engage in some banter.

"Well... hmm... I hope you got what you wanted from him then... I'll see you in court."

"Certainly, you will, see you then." Bernadette inclined her head graciously.

"Imogen." Shane nodded at her and turned on his heel. He left with Mason shortly afterwards.

"I'd like to slap him silly," said Imogen through gritted teeth.

"I thought you controlled yourself well," said Bernadette.

"I tried."

Callum and Rhys joined them, and Imogen packed up the papers.

"Let's find a room," said Bernadette as they left the court.

There was an empty one not far from the courtroom entrance, and they went inside. Once they were all seated, Bernadette said, "I don't know if you noticed a man sitting at the back of the court?"

"You mean the one who the judge kept glaring at?" Callum asked, he was evidently quite perceptive.

"Yes, that's him."

"Who is he?" Rhys wondered.

"His name is Oisin Kavanaugh, he's an MP, Minister without portfolio, who is currently working with the Justice Department. He came to our offices. He wanted us to throw the case," Bernadette said bluntly.

"What?" Rhys said incredulous.

"He is trying to do a deal with the UK authorities and Callum, if you please, is to be a gift to grease the wheels."

"Fucking hell!" Rhys coloured up and got to his feet with his fists balled up. "I'll fucking finish him, I punch his fucking lights out."

"Da, calm down, and sit down," said Callum.

Rhys subsided but still looked very angry.

"Rhys, you can't go punching MP's, you can let us deal with this and we will. What we need though is a little bit of strategy."

"How'd you mean?" Callum asked her.

"We are going to stir it, just a little with the press. Stand behind me, follow my lead. If they ask you anything, say you are innocent, nothing more. Rhys just reiterate he is innocent and say Irish Citizens should be supported by their government, and it's a travesty this has come to court. No more than that and you know nothing, I repeat, *nothing* about Oisin."

"OK," said Rhys.

"You can't ever let on you know anything about Oisin, OK, either of you. Is that understood?"

"Perfectly," said Callum.

"You are not to touch him either," Bernadette said firmly.

"By God, you sound like my old teacher at school," Rhys laughed, "I'm expecting you to get the cane out next."

"Don't be so sure I won't," Bernadette told him, then she laughed, "I'm joking. It is just sometimes things can be let slip. We cannot afford it, OK?"

"I promise you, neither me nor my Da is going to say anything. Are we, Da?" said Callum.

"Good, so I'm doing this to stir things up, it's not my usual habit to talk to the press, and I cannot jeopardise our case, but we may be able to mobilise a little bit of public opinion. It can't be a bad thing."

"Right."

"OK, well, let's go, remember only say what I've told you to say, do not answer any other questions."

"Don't worry, you've scared me shitless now," Rhys laughed.

They left the meeting room and walked out to the front of the building. The press were lined up in expectation of something good. Bernadette wasn't going to disappoint them this time. She stood in front of them, and Imogen, Callum and Rhys stood behind her. Cameras and microphones were immediately shoved into her face.

"Bernadette, Oisin Kavanaugh says justice must be properly done, and if Callum is guilty, he must face trial, what do you say to *that*?"

This was like manna from heaven, Oisin had played nicely into their hands.

"I say," she said in strident tones, as a hush fell over the reporters, "Justice must be done, that part is true. However, we mean to obtain justice for Callum who we say is not guilty of any crime whatsoever. We intend to pursue our case to the fullest extent in court. Callum is an Irish citizen and we need to stand up for our citizens. Callum Jenkins is innocent, and we maintain he should not be extradited, and we intend to prove our case in court in three weeks' time."

"Callum, what have you got to say about it?" shouted a reporter from the Irish Sun.

"I am innocent," Callum said sticking to the script.

"But are you? The prosecution says you are guilty!"

Callum said nothing more and stepped back. Rhys stepped forward.

"I am Callum's father and I say the Irish government should support its citizens. It is an absolute travesty that this has come to court!"

"Rhys, you sound angry, are you angry?" said an RTE reporter.

"That's all for now," said Bernadette, cutting off any further questions. "We'll see you back here in three weeks. Then you'll see some action I promise you."

"What do you mean by action?"

"What's the evidence, tell us that at least?"

The questions were shouted after them, but Bernadette led them all smartly away and down the stairs, smiling broadly. She hustled them away from the court as quickly as she could and towards their car.

"Where's your car?" she asked Rhys.

"We came by taxi," he said.

"Fine, I'll drive you home, get in."

She gunned the motor with Imogen sitting beside her, and the others in the back. She pulled away just as the press caught up to them to have another go. They fired off their cameras as her car sped away.

"That went fucking superbly, darling," said Imogen laughing.

"Fuck yeah, I was impressed," said Callum.

"By God you're good, I knew you were the right choice," Rhys added.

"I'm flattered, thank you," said Bernadette.

"She is simply the best," Imogen told him.

"I believe you one hundred percent."

"Let's see what that little bombshell does in the headlines tomorrow," Bernadette chuckled.

"You haven't crossed any lines though?" Imogen asked, a little worried.

"I was careful, so no I don't think so."

"I'd still like to punch that bastard's lights out," Rhys said angrily.

"Relax, we've got him a little bit on the run at the moment, and we also have friends in high places, I can't tell you more than that. Just watch this space. He'll be a pain in the arse for a while and then poof, you'll see. Have faith."

"What you're not taking out a contract on him?" said Rhys incredulous.

"No," Bernadette laughed, "Not like *that*! But perhaps he'll have a fall from grace at some point soon, we hope."

"Oh!"

"Anyway, we've got three weeks. The rush is also Kavanaugh's doing. He is trying to wrong foot us, the same as he's tried to fix the judge."

"What the fuck!" Rhys said angrily, "That's terrible, how can people like him get away with this?"

"He won't, just trust me. I wouldn't normally tell you stuff like this, but you deserve to know the truth. After it's all over then you can go for the throat, and we'll be right behind you."

"I'll fucking go for his fucking throat, and no mistake."

"Right, we'll leave it at that now. We can discuss it after the trial, if there's anything to do about it."

"Thanks, thanks anyway for being so honest."

"You're welcome."

"Do you want to come in for a cuppa when we get home?"

"Sure, why not."

* * *

On the drive back to the office, Imogen said, "That went well, don't you think?"

"The court hearing?"

"Yes, and what you said to the press. Also, Rhys, he seems like a nice man."

"His girlfriend wasn't wearing her maid's outfit today anyway," said Bernadette with a chuckle.

"And has Eve got hers?"

"I don't know, I haven't seen it so far."

"Maybe tonight's the night?"

"For Shibari anyway, with or without the maid's uniform." Bernadette smiled.

"What are you going to do?"

"Oh, I intend to be very strict, she likes it. I'll tell her off in no uncertain terms before tying her up."

"Do *you* like it?" Imogen wondered.

"I kind of do, yes. It was hard getting into the role play at first but now I kind of enjoy it."

"Hmm... so do I."

"I know that!"

The two of them laughed and Imogen returned to the case.

"What do you think are the chances of winning, really?"

"What do *you* think they are?" Bernadette liked to bounce it back to Imogen as her junior. It was part of the process of continuing to challenge her and get her ready for her step up as a senior.

"I think their case is tenuous. They are relying on the balance of doubt to fall in their favour because it's only Callum's word he wasn't part of it. He was in the right place at the right time, he did drive the truck. Now there is someone saying he knew and was part of it. If Kevin is a credible witness, then it's in their favour I guess."

"Absolutely, right," Bernadette agreed, "So our job is to introduce more doubt. Firstly by making it out to be a personal vendetta of some kind or at least some sort of act of revenge. Then we have Anh who will again help to cast some doubt, perhaps not much but it just may be enough."

"So, it hinges around how much you are able to destroy their witness."

"Yes, yes it very much does."

"I pity him then, when you go into bitch mode," Imogen said emphatically.

"I don't know, it seems to come naturally," Bernadette giggled.

"Oh, but you're so sexy when you're assertive..." Imogen began.

"Oh stop! Though that is what Eve tells me too." Bernadette was smiling.

"She's right."

"I'm going to miss you so much when you become a senior barrister," Bernadette said suddenly.

"I'll still be there. We'll still talk every day. I'll still love you to bits."

"I know but think of all the fun we have in the courtroom together."

"And out of it. Anyway, it's not for a while, so don't go getting all maudlin, darling." Imogen out her hand and touched Bernadette's arm briefly by way of reassurance.

"I know, it's just me being silly, sorry."

"Don't be, I understand and believe me I feel the same way."

"You're my best friend... after Eve."

"Stop it or you will make me cry."

"OK, let's talk of something fun."

"Sex?"

"It seems to be our favourite topic, so yeah."

* * *

When Bernadette arrived home, she had mentally prepared herself to be the bitch Eve wanted her to be. She intended to go straight into it once she walked inside. She parked, walked up to the front door and opened it. Normally Eve would come rushing up to her for a kiss, but she was nowhere to be seen. Bernadette kept her heels on, put down her bag, and hung up her jacket. She had tied her hair back into a ponytail in the car, so she looked much more severe, and refreshed her best red lipstick. She definitely felt a little bit dominant dressed up the way she was.

"Eve?" she called out tentatively.

Eve still did not appear, and she was wondering whether Eve was home, when she thought she heard footsteps upstairs. Perhaps Eve was hoping she would start off being assertive, so she summoned up her best stern voice.

"Eve, get down here now!"

There was a scurrying and Eve descended the stairs barefoot and wearing what could only be described as the skimpiest of maid's outfits. It was short, tight fitting, and black, with a white frilly bib. As outfits went, there wasn't very much of it all. Bernadette had to admit to herself she found it very sexy on her fiancée but now wasn't the time.

"Get over here," she ordered peremptorily.

Eve came and stood in front of her looking up at with a tentative half smile playing on her lips.

"You can wipe that smirk off your face for a start, missy," Bernadette told her.

Eve looked serious at once.

"What did I say to you earlier?"

"That there would be consequences, Ms Mackenna," Eve said meekly.

"Yes, exactly, and there are going to be consequences right now. You can wear that outfit for me later when you serve me dinner. But for the moment you can turn around and get back upstairs, take it off and wait for me."

"Yes, Ms Mackenna." Eve curtsied but didn't move.

"When I said now, I meant now!" said Bernadette severely.

She took a step forward, turned Eve around, and on the spur of the moment delivered a well-placed slap to Eve's buttock cheek.

"Ooh, you bitch!" said Eve running back upstairs.

"I'll show you who is a bitch very shortly, my girl." Bernadette tried not to laugh, she needed to stay in character.

When Eve had gone, Bernadette went to the kitchen and took the list she had made off the fridge. She poured herself a smidgen of wine and took a long drink to get herself a little more in the mood. Eve was playing her part perfectly, but she wasn't sure how far Eve would be prepared to go, she would find out soon enough.

She walked up the stairs, making sure Eve would hear her and went into the bedroom where her fiancée was sitting on the bed. Bernadette shut the door, it was unnecessary in an empty house, but it felt like a symbolic gesture.

"Did I say you could sit?" she demanded.

"No... erm... no, Ms Mackenna," said Eve.

"Then stand up and look at me when I'm talking to you."

Eve looked up at her with an expression which was quite defiant. Bernadette wasn't sure if she was putting it on but pressed forward with her planned role.

"You have been very bad, very bad indeed, don't you agree, Ms White?" she said.

"Yes, Ms Mackenna."

Bernadette brandished the list with a flourish. "This list says it all, doesn't it. Extremely bad misbehaviour. You didn't tell me about what your sister did. You swore at me. You've been watching pornography without telling me. You threw the biggest tantrum I have ever seen, and you made me cry. Have I left anything out?"

She strode up and down as she talked, a little like a sergeant major she felt, keeping Eve under her very stern gaze.

Eve shook her head, like a naughty girl who had been caught out misbehaving.

"No, I haven't, have I? In fact, it was probably infinitely worse." Bernadette knew she was embellishing it but was now well into her role.

Eve said nothing but bit her lip in a way which made Bernadette want to stop everything and ravish her there and then. However, with an effort, she resisted.

"You are going to be punished," Bernadette told her, "But first do you remember that picture you showed me?"

"Yes," Eve whispered. Bernadette could tell she was starting to get aroused.

"Well then, remember what you wanted to do? So, get on your knees, Eve White, who is soon to be Mackenna." Bernadette softened her tone, not know how Eve would take it.

Eve didn't immediately do it and Bernadette realised she wanted her to, perhaps, be more assertive.

"I said get on your knees! Now! Do it! Didn't you hear me?"

Eve complied, looking at her the whole time.

"Now, what do you have to do?"

"Beg you, Ms Mackenna."

"For what?"

"Forgiveness."

It was at this point Bernadette could almost not go through with it. She felt as if she was crossing lines somehow as much as Eve wanted it. She didn't want to humiliate her fiancée, although Eve seemed to want exactly that. Bernadette steeled herself and continued.

"Go on then, Ms White, beg me," she said, biting her own lip in concern.

Eve noticed and shot her a look of reassurance. Eve lowered her head.

"I'm sorry Ms Mackenna, will you forgive me, please for what I've done, I'm... I'm begging you. I'm begging you to please forgive me."

"Are you really sorry?"

"Yes, yes I am," said Eve assuming an expression of supplication. It practically melted Bernadette's heart, but she still stayed in her role. A thought occurred to her and she improvised.

She kicked off her shoes, and said, "Very well, then kiss my feet and promise me you will never do it again."

Each time Bernadette had pushed the boundaries and wondered if she had gone a little too far, but each time Eve seemed to like it, enjoy it and want it. This was a spur of the moment idea. Eve regarded her for a couple of seconds, and then leant forward and kissed each of Bernadette's toes in such a way which made them tingle, and Bernadette just wanted to take her into her arms. She stopped herself once more with an effort. She didn't want to ruin the game.

"I promise I will never do it again," Eve whispered quietly.

"Good girl," said Bernadette unable to keep a loving smile from her face, "Get on the bed, my darling, for your punishment."

Eve shot her a look, as if to say *that's not assertive enough*.

"Get on the bed, Ms White, hold onto the bed rail and don't you dare move!" Bernadette put herself back in the zone.

Eve knelt down on the bed and bent forward to grasp the rail.

Bernadette removed her own clothes, it felt sexier that way. It was time and past for putting on corsets. She retrieved the rope from the cupboard and began to expertly tie Eve up to the bed rail. She had decided to make it extra special and so the ropes went down Eve's arms, around her breasts, and even down to her legs. Eve moaned and gasped as each binding bit into her flesh. Bernadette knew she was enjoying every minute. When she had finished, she stood back and admired her handiwork.

"Is that tight enough, Ms White?" she asked her.

"Yes."

"Does it feel... good?"

"Yes, oh, yes," Eve said softly.

"Well then... I'm not sure it's really a punishment then, but still..." Bernadette looked at Eve kneeling and her naked backside was suddenly incredibly inviting. She knelt on the bed beside her fiancée and began to run her hand over the taut globes.

Eve hissed in her breath at this, and even more so when Bernadette ran her nails across the naked flesh.

"What would be a proper punishment, Ms White? Hmm?" she whispered, teasing, pitching her voice low. She could feel Eve's skin quivering a little at her touch and then without thinking she gave Eve's backside a playful slap "Is this what you want, Ms White?"

"Oh! Oh God, fuck, oh, yes."

"So, is this what you really want?" Bernadette slapped it again.

"Oh, fuck... oh!" Eve gasped, but it was a pleasurable gasp of anticipation.

Without knowing what had got into her, Bernadette peppered Eve's backside with sharp smacks saying over and over. "Is this what you want? Is it? Is it?"

Abruptly she stopped, Eve was panting, and she could tell, Eve was incredibly aroused.

"Oh my God," said Bernadette, "It really is what you wanted, wasn't it?"

Without saying anything further Bernadette moved her hand down between Eve's legs and set her fingers working.

Eve screamed, "Oh... oh... oh God... oh... oh... oh... oh... fuck... ohh!"

Eve appeared to climax almost instantaneously at being touched and her body tensed and untensed against the bonds, while she cried out over and over.

Bernadette held onto her in fascination amazed at the effect she had produced. As Eve's spasms subsided, Bernadette kissed the slightly pink cheeks all over and put the side of her own cheek against them.

"I love you," she whispered, "I love you so fucking much."

"You can take these off now, I want to fuck you so badly," Eve whispered.

"Have you learned your lesson?" Bernadette giggled.

"Yes, just take them off, please."

"Don't you want photos?"

"Please, please, I want you, I want you so badly," Eve pleaded.

"OK, OK, Ms Impatience."

Bernadette deftly removed the bonds and threw the ropes onto the bedroom floor. Eve's skin was prettily marked all over with rope impressions, but Eve did not give her time to admire them. Instead, she pushed Bernadette onto her back and her head went down between Bernadette's legs. As Bernadette felt Eve's velvet tongue begin to work its magic, she was also lost too.

"Oh... shit... Eve... fuck... oh... fuck... Eve... oh my God... don't stop... Eve... don't stop... don't... oh... I'm going... to... ohh!" Bernadette's orgasm was not long in arriving. The entire session had become incredibly arousing and by the time Eve had started on her, she was already halfway there. She pushed herself hard into Eve's mouth as wave after wave crested through her until she too was spent.

A little while later they lay together, holding each other close, their lips just touching.

"Was it OK?" Bernadette asked Eve anxiously.

"It was more than just OK. It was just how I imagined it."

"Really?" Bernadette was pleased to hear this. She was always worried in case the sessions were too much.

"It was amazing, all of it. I wasn't expecting you to smack my arse, but I liked it very much."

Bernadette gave a low chuckle. "Don't like it too much, I'm not going to be like Imogen."

Eve shook her head. "No, I don't want that. Don't think I want you to do that. It wasn't like that. It was sensual, really pleasurable, just the way you did it, not too hard and not too much. Christ, it was so arousing, I practically exploded."

"That's one way of putting it. Hmm, I will bear it in mind for the future..." she paused, thinking then asked, "And it wasn't too much? Making you beg me like that?"

"No, not at all," Eve said earnestly, "I loved it, I loved it so much, it's what I wanted, more than I wanted even. But it's definitely what I needed."

"Needed?"

"Yes, I did, don't ask me why but I felt so much better, and when you made me kiss your feet, it was so good. I loved it, so horny."

"I wanted to fuck you so much then. I was worried I had gone too far."

Eve kissed her. "No, no you didn't go too far, my darling. I know you wanted to, I could tell, but I'm glad you carried on. You did it all perfectly, I loved it."

"I did it all for you."

"But you enjoyed it too, didn't you?"

"Yes, yes I did."

"Are you sure, my honey?" Eve kissed her again, "I don't want you to do something you don't like."

"But I do like it, I like it also because you like it."

"You play the part so well," Eve chuckled.

"You do too, my darling. You're a good actress."

"How do you know it's acting?" Eve said archly.

"I love you." Bernadette kissed her again.

"Do you want some dinner? Shall I wear the maid's outfit and serve you."

"I would like you to, but not today. Save it for another day, another fantasy."

"Come on then, let's eat. We have the whole weekend for fun. Enjoy it because it's your last weekend as a single engaged female," Eve laughed.

"Are we really getting married next weekend?"

"Yes, yes we are, so get ready for it."

"How exciting."

"It will be."

CHAPTER THIRTEEN

The following week was one of great intrigue for Bernadette. Eve was brim-full of excitement all week and as tempting as it was to go and open the forbidden drawer Bernadette did not do it. She was very aware that around the office they all knew about the wedding and were very likely to be going to it. They had all commendably been sworn to secrecy, however, nobody breathed a word. She had mentioned to Eve she wanted Brogan to be invited, but she had no idea who was on the guest list. It was an incredible exercise in trust between her and Eve.

Eve in the meantime even more loving and giving than before. They seemed to have turned a corner in their relationship although Bernadette was sure there would be times when perhaps they might have a disagreement or upset. Given their relationship was almost constantly harmonious, it seemed unlikely they would have too many of those.

"Stop fretting," Imogen told her as they sat together for their morning meeting on the Wednesday of that week, "I know you are and don't deny it."

"I'm not fretting exactly," said Bernadette, "Just excited, perhaps wishing I had not agreed to keep out of it."

"It's the best decision you made, believe me. It's going to be fantastic, beautiful, everything you ever wanted. I promise you."

Bernadette sipped her coffee.

"So, you smacked Eve's arse and she liked it?" Imogen asked her.

"I've already told you this several times," Bernadette laughed.

"I know but I can hardly believe it."

"Well, I'm not planning to make it a regular thing and I'm not turning into you, as I've already said," Bernadette told her firmly.

"Don't knock it 'till you've tried it, I'm happy to lend you my paddle."

"Imogen!"

"Alright, but don't say I didn't offer."

"If I wanted a paddle, I would buy one, but I don't, and I won't be. Eve doesn't want that."

Imogen laughed.

"You are incorrigible," Bernadette said with mock severity.

"I know, so you've said, but as I keep telling you, that's why you love me."

"Yes, you're right, anyway, on other matters, has Micky managed to get anything done about these texts? We're going to run out of time soon, otherwise."

"Why don't we ask him?"

"Yes, let's do that, it's been a few days now, we should get an update."

Imogen left for a few moments and returned with Micky in tow.

"Ah, Micky," said Bernadette smiling.

"Hi, Bernadette."

"We're sorry we've been neglectful but obviously we want to know how you've been doing on Callum's texts."

"It's OK," said Micky, "I know you've both been busy with the prehearing and stuff. I've made good progress actually. I managed to download all his texts to my laptop."

"Oh goody!" Imogen clapped her hands.

"What have you got? Something interesting?" Bernadette asked him.

"I haven't been through them all, but I've got something of interest already."

Micky disappeared again and then returned with a sheaf of printouts. He handed them to Bernadette, and she passed some to Imogen.

"Holy fuck," said Imogen starting to read them. "Listen to this, I can't wait until you get to London again so I can fuck you and suck your fucking big..."

"I get the picture," Bernadette cut her off.

"I was just getting to the interesting part," Imogen laughed, "There's more like that... I want you, big boy... last night was so good... You are a sexy bastard and no mistake... I want you so bad when are you coming back... I'm going to fuck you senseless..."

"Is it just one way or both?"

"Oh, it's both and there's a lot of these," Micky said to her.

"Right so we need some from the beginning of their relationship or whenever the first lot of texts is. Then we need some from the middle and some at the end. We need to show the timeline and duration of their relationship."

"Right, I can manage that."

"Make them nice and juicy ones," Imogen added, "We can make him squirm in the witness stand."

"Yes, good point. Now are there any which show jealousy or asking Callum where he's been, stuff like that?" said Bernadette.

"Not in these," Imogen said.

Bernadette leafed through the one's she had and read a couple out.

"Where are you? I've been texting you and you didn't reply. Where have you been? Have you been out partying, I need to know! What the fuck, Cal, you didn't call me last night."

"That's good, very good, we can get him on those," said Imogen.

"We can. Micky, this is excellent work, just what we need. If you can compile what you think are the best ones and put them together for us, then we'll go over them, see if we need anything else."

"Thanks," said Micky blushing slightly.

"Are we going to put these into court, beforehand?" Imogen wondered.

"I think we have to, it's too much evidence to try to chance the judge allowing it without the prosecution seeing it. However, we'll put the affidavit in at the last minute. We'll need Callum to sign an affidavit confirming they came from his phone. We will give them no time to respond in writing or prepare for it."

"Good thinking, yes, I'll work on the affidavit, and we will finalise the texts we're going to use."

"Great, Micky, we'll meet again next week, and then we can put the affidavit together," Bernadette said.

"Sure thing, if there's nothing else?"

"No, I assume everything's OK?"

"Yes, it is, anyway I'll be off then," said Micky getting up.

"Thank you, darling," said Bernadette as Micky smiled and left the room.

"He's a good soul," Imogen said.

"He sure is."

"What else do we need to do, for the hearing?"

"File Anh's affidavit, we can do that sooner, and then Callum's right at the end."

"Great."

Usually, there should be a right to response to affidavit's but given the type of hearing this was, the affidavit's primary function was in order to question witnesses, and for the judge. There would also be submissions at the beginning and at the end by both parties.

"We'll formulate questions for their witnesses and ours."

"OK."

"How are things with you and D'Arcy? Apart from the obvious," Bernadette changed the subject.

"It's great, we are going to make wedding plans of our own once yours is done."

"A big wedding?"

"No, I don't want it. It will be intimate and then we'll do a spread for Hello magazine. It will keep the press happy and also earn us some money. Imagine that, people paying for your photos."

"That's the set you're joining."

"I know, I'm still not used to it at all and I'm determined not to allow it to change me," Imogen said firmly.

"On that note, have you introduced D'Arcy to your family?" Bernadette raised an eyebrow.

"They are coming to ours the weekend after this one," Imogen said with a sigh.

"Are you so worried about it?"

"Yes! I mean, I don't want them to be silly about it, I want them to just be normal."

"Getting married to one of the most famous actresses in this country is hardly normal," Bernadette laughed.

"Yes, well, I'm worried they'll say stupid things and embarrass me. Stuff like that!"

"I sympathise, families are sometimes that way, but you have to accept them into your fold, as they will have to accept D'Arcy into theirs."

"Oh, I'm sure they'll do that! After all who wouldn't want a famous daughter-in-law. I just hope they don't, you know, expect loads of handouts from D'Arcy. Take advantage, and things." Imogen made a face.

"Do you think they will?" Bernadette had no idea what Imogen's parents and family were like. It was true that sometimes families could be prone to expect to be taken care of if one of them came into money.

"The thing is D'Arcy will just buy them whatever, because she's like that and I don't want them sounding like a pack of money grubbers..." Imogen trailed off. "Shit, it sounds so bitchy of me."

"No, it's understandable, I mean, can't you talk to them about it?"

"Oh God no, it would make it worse. My mother would take umbrage, it would be a disaster. I'm just going to tell D'Arcy she had to run all purchases for them by me first."

"No doubt with strictures," Bernadette said wryly.

"She knows exactly what will happen if she disobeys me."

"Hmm, and is that going to be in your wedding vows?"

"Not in public, no, but we will say some in private, and yes." Imogen shot her look as if she dared Bernadette to argue.

"You will, of course, do as you both wish. What's between you is between you. As long as you both agree, darling," Bernadette said mildly.

"I've discussed it with her of course, and she wants to. She's not my slave or anything. Rather I'm hers in so many ways it's not funny. If I ever wronged her, and I did that time before, I would crawl naked on my belly and kiss her feet like Eve kissed yours, to beg her to forgive me."

"I know." Bernadette put out a hand and squeezed Imogen's hand, because she could tell Imogen was becoming emotional.

"But in the normal way of things, I will be the boss."

"You've sorted it out to your satisfaction that's the main thing." Bernadette smiled.

"I'm going to fucking well cry at your wedding you know that don't you," said Imogen bursting into tears.

"You're crying now," Bernadette observed taking her into her arms.

"I know, I'm a fucking milksop…"

"You're not, you're a beautiful, wonderful friend, and I love you."

"Don't, oh fuck, I'm going to cry even more…"

Bernadette laughed gently and stroked Imogen's hair. She mused at their friendship. She didn't know of one quite like it. Imogen was like the sister she never had, but even more than that. They had an unbreakable attachment, an enduring love, different to her love of Eve, but love just the same. Perhaps this was what it was like to have a sibling, she didn't know. Imogen was the closest she had. Imogen would have her back no matter what, and she Imogen's. It was comforting to know they would always be inseparable.

* * *

Bernadette took a day's holiday, the Friday before the wedding day. She had not told Eve, but when the alarm didn't go off and they lay holding each other in bed, Eve said, "Isn't it time for you to go to work?"

"No." Bernadette smiled.

"I'm sure it is," insisted Eve.

"I'm not going to work today."

"What?" Eve sat up in surprise.

"I took the day off, I thought you would be pleased."

"Well, I am, but you are very naughty, you didn't tell me," Eve admonished her, "I've got a lot to do today, and I will hardly be here."

"No matter, is it? I won't interfere, I promise. I just wanted to be with you the day before we got married. I mean, I'll go to work if you want me to." Bernadette pouted.

Eve looked at her and smiled down at her. She snuggled back under the bedclothes. "No, it's OK, but seeing as you are going to stay then you'll have to find ways to entertain me."

"Must I?"

"Oh yes, you really must. You can keep me entertained in between my tasks," Eve said kissing her.

"Shall I entertain you now?"

"Yes, yes please," Eve whispered as Bernadette's hand stole down her back and down her thigh. "Now that's what I'm talking about, oh... fuck... oh... yes... that is exactly what I'm... oh my God..."

A little while later, Bernadette watched Eve get up with a smirk.

"I'll have a shower first, and make us breakfast, then you relax," Eve told her.

"Are you sure I can't help?"

"No, no you can't. I absolutely forbid it and it would spoil the surprise. You can just chill out until tonight."

"What's happening tonight?" Bernadette said with interest.

"That is for me to know and for you to find out, my love, and you will, very soon. Now stay there and I'll go and shower."

"Can I join you?" Bernadette gave her a saucy grin.

"No, no you can't, not now, I've got lots to do, but later, for sure, my beautiful darling, definitely later." Eve dropped a kiss on Bernadette's lips and slid out of the bed.

For much of the day, Eve disappeared. She was picked up by Carragh in D'Arcy's Mercedes and whisked away. Bernadette was fairly certain the wedding was going to be at D'Arcy's place, but she didn't let on. The forbidden drawer also tempted her, but she didn't break her promise to Eve. She felt it wasn't fair after all of the effort Eve had gone through to keep everything from her. To spoil the surprise would be to disappoint her wife-to-be in so many ways none of which she could ever take back. She contented herself by remaining in a state of déshabillé and trying to waylay Eve whenever she returned home before going out again.

"Oh, really, darling?" Eve would say, as she arrived for the third time to find Bernadette draped enticingly against the door frame to the living room. "Again? Really?" Eve continued taking Bernadette into her arms and kissing her softly. "You'll be the death of me, and we're not even married yet. Are you going to leave some for the wedding night?"

"You've plenty in the tank, you witch, and you know it."

"Oh... fuck... what are you doing? Oh... God... I know what you're doing... oh fuck... I only just put those clothes on... Bernadette... fuck... fuck... oh my God! I love you... I love you so much!"

Eventually, dinner time came, and Eve wheeled down a suitcase. "Right then, get dressed, we're going now."

"We are? We're not eating dinner here?" Bernadette said smiling.

"You know very well we're not and I'm sure you've guessed where we're going, so come on, Carragh will be here very soon."

"OK," said Bernadette running quickly upstairs to get ready.

Shortly Carragh arrived and whisked them away to D'Arcy's house.

* * *

368

Dusk was setting in when they arrived, and the gates slid open. Carragh stopped at the end of the pathway to the house. As they got out, D'Arcy came bowling down the path to greet them. Her eyes were brim-full of news. She hugged and kissed Bernadette and Eve in turn.

"Darling, so nice to see you," she trilled to Bernadette, "Oh my God, you've got some surprises in store, but I can't say any more, Imogen will kill me, not to mention Eve. So, mum's the word."

"Come in, come in," said Imogen smiling and giving them both a hug.

"We've got dinner all ready," D'Arcy said excitedly, "Come upstairs, darlings, Carragh will see to your bags."

The main dining table was set with fine china, and crystal glasses. A large candelabra was lit with long white candles. A beautiful white and red centrepiece of roses sat in the centre of the table.

"Oh, my goodness, how fabulous," Bernadette exclaimed.

"Eve did it, she set it all out, your last dinner before you're married," Imogen said.

"Sit, sit, the food will be served shortly."

Dinner consisted of a light Vietnamese salad, followed by Boeuf bourguignon.

"Oh my God, my favourite!" said Bernadette accept the healthy portion Eve ladled out for her, with mashed potatoes and vegetables, "Mmm, that's a lot, I hope I'll fit my wedding dress."

"Of course, you will." Eve smiled, reaching out her hand and squeezing it.

"So, Imogen's family is coming over I hear?" said Bernadette changing the subject.

Imogen made a face at her, but Bernadette smiled back sweetly.

"Oh, yes I'm looking forward to meeting them of course," said D'Arcy.

"I'm sure you are."

"I'm not on good terms with my own family as you know, so it would be nice to meet a more normal family."

Imogen snorted on hearing this and D'Arcy looked at her sharply.

"Everyone thinks their family isn't normal," said Eve, "That's the way of it."

"Oh, but, darling, mine isn't at all normal as you know," D'Arcy insisted.

"Yes, I do."

"So, what about your own wedding plans, D'Arcy?" said Bernadette almost mendaciously.

Imogen shot her another look filled with daggers, but Bernadette was trying to find topics which didn't involve asking about her own wedding.

"Oh well, we're still discussing it. I suppose I want the world to know, but I think we're going to just have it much more intimate with a photoshoot for Hello instead."

"But you've surely got lots of friends," said Bernadette who was in a playful mood and knew this wasn't the case at all.

"I wouldn't call many of them friends, just people who like me because I have money. In the bad old days, they came for a wild time, I suppose, but we're not doing things like that anymore. My real friends are few, in fact, the best friends I have are around this table," D'Arcy said smiling at them all.

"Am I your best friend then?" Imogen asked her.

"You are my very best friend as well as being the love of my life, darling."

"Thank you, and likewise."

Imogen leaned across and kissed her softly.

"So, I think it will be a small wedding as I said, and I think it's best. I don't need to parade myself in front of everyone. They can read about it instead," D'Arcy continued.

"And will you have it here?" Bernadette wondered.

"Yes of course, and both of you will be bridesmaids to the two of us. We're both going to wear dresses we've decided. After all, you only get married once and I've got just the dream dress in mind."

"You had better only be getting married once, darling," Imogen said but she was smiling.

"There will never be anyone but you," D'Arcy said seriously.

"That's the right answer."

Bernadette glanced at Imogen briefly because of Shane, but Imogen looked away colouring up. Bernadette could not imagine Imogen throwing it all away for lust. She would just have to learn to deal with such impulses.

"Who's for dessert?" D'Arcy asked brightly noticing everyone had finished.

"I won't say no but I hope it's light," Bernadette replied.

"It's a cheesecake but a very light and fluffy one, my chef is a wizard."

"Then, yes please."

The plates were removed, and the cheesecake proved to be a light lemony flavour with a ginger crunch base which they all pronounced delightful.

After coffee and less contentious conversation, Eve told Bernadette it was time for bed. Bernadette meekly followed her after bidding the others goodnight.

"Are we sleeping together?" she asked, mindful of the traditions.

"Of course, I don't believe in all that stuff, do you? We start as we mean to go on."

Eve pulled her into the bedroom and shut the door, then she deftly pinned Bernadette up against the wall by dint of kissing her passionately.

"Is this starting as we mean to go on?" Bernadette whispered.

"God yes!"

Eve's hands were already engaged in disrobing her fiancée and Bernadette happily surrendered to her ministrations.

* * *

The morning of the wedding dawned bright and sunny. The sun streamed in through the windows waking them both up as they had not drawn the blinds. There was nobody to see them out here at D'Arcy's house.

"Wake up sleepyhead, we're getting married today," said Eve kissing her love.

"Oh, yes, how glorious, I can hardly believe it." Bernadette smiled and kissed her back.

"Now, remember when I made you get the marriage license sorted out over three months ago," said Eve with twinkling eyes.

"Yes, it's the only thing I've done right. Were you planning this all along?"

"Perhaps," Eve chuckled, "The row we had actually made it easier. Well, I wouldn't call it a row exactly..."

"More like a tantrum for which you were deservedly punished," Bernadette laughed.

"Mmm, I did deserve it for sure."

"You wanted me to."

"Yes, I did, and I will again." Eve kissed her. "But anyway, at the time you wanted to leave the license thingy, but you know it takes three months to get and so..."

"I know, and you were right to make me."

"See, your witch is wise as she is volatile."

"You are, my darling and I love you, I love you so much."

"I love you too, my sweetheart, but now it's time to get up, have breakfast, then in no time at all you'll be getting dressed in your wedding dress, and I will too. But you won't see me until we are ready to marry."

"Oh?"

"Yes, I don't want you to see my dress until then."

"But you've seen mine!" Bernadette pouted.

"Of course, I have silly, and that's my prerogative as the wedding arranger. I'll be waiting for you, darling. I want to watch you walk down that aisle to me. I want to watch you every step of the way and see how beautiful you are, and how you're coming just to marry me."

"Oh shit, you're going to make me cry and we haven't even started."

"You have no idea, well, I think you do, just how deeply I am in love with you. I am besotted with you. I can't get enough of you. Losing you would virtually kill me. I would be dead inside. So, if you ever think in future, I want to leave you, just remember what I've said."

"Yes, I will, and I'm sorry for doubting you."

"Don't be sorry, just believe in my love from now on, no matter how badly I might behave."

"I promise to do that, and to take you in hand if you misbehave, just like you asked me to."

"Yes, please do, now let's get up and get ready for a wonderful day, I promise you it will be wonderful."

"Can't we stay a little longer," said Bernadette her hand stealing down Eve's naked skin.

"Not today, not until later." Eve smiled, kissed her and got out of bed before things could get out of hand.

* * *

The rest of the morning passed in a whirl. After breakfast, Bernadette made a face when she was informed that she was confined to their room until further notice. But Eve promised her it would be worth the wait.

"That's what you get for letting me take charge," Eve laughed.

"It's not happening again then," Bernadette giggled.

"You're the boss, but just not for today, not until we're married."

"I'll take that," said Bernadette kissing Eve before she slipped out of Bernadette's grasp and out of the room.

Not long after, Imogen and D'Arcy arrived although they did not look as if they were dressed for a wedding, though they were dressed smartly enough.

"Come on, get dressed in some normal clothes."

"What?" said Bernadette a little shocked.

"It's OK, we're just kidnapping you for a bit and we'll explain why on the way."

Bernadette discovered Eve had packed a smart work suit, blouse and black mules. She dressed and although she complained she hadn't put on any makeup or done her hair. Imogen was adamant they had to go, or they would be late.

They headed downstairs and to Bernadette's surprise, they went out of the front door to a waiting limousine.

"Aren't we getting married here? Don't I get a proper dress after all?" Bernadette wondered out loud.

"Yes, and no, darling, stop worrying, we can't have the official ceremony here because the venue is not open to the public, so we're having a private one at registry approved venue, and then coming back here for the proper one in front of everyone," Imogen told her as they helped her into the car.

"Oh!" Bernadette said as the penny dropped.

"As a lawyer, you should know the law, silly! We tried our best to get them to approve D'Arcy's place, but they wouldn't bend the rules, so here we are. Also, it's a good job Eve got you to sort out the paperwork so we could meet the three month's timeframe. I was the one who told her to quite some time ago."

"Oh God, I've been so useless at this."

"Exactly, you have and that is why Eve and I had to take charge."

"It's almost as if you and Eve had planned it all along, and all this time you were telling me how I should get on with the wedding plans and the two of you..." Bernadette trailed off.

"The three of us!" D'Arcy put in, not wanting to be left out.

"We did, sorry." Imogen smiled. "But I couldn't tell you, and also we didn't plan for Eve to suddenly bring the time forward like this."

"You're all of you very naughty! Very, very naughty indeed!" Bernadette pursed her lips. She could not be mad, though, in fact, she found the whole thing rather exciting.

Imogen just laughed, and D'Arcy giggled. Shortly they pulled up outside a local hotel nearby and were ushered into a room which was set up for weddings. Eve was waiting wearing trousers and a blouse. She had high heeled mules on her feet. They walked up to the podium as a group, where if the solemniser showed any surprise at the attire or the informality she did not say so. Carragh remained discreetly at the back for security.

She married them in a brief ceremony which lasted only a few moments, with very short vows and without rings. Bernadette and Eve kissed, signed the register and all of them headed back to D'Arcy's in the limo.

"Well," said Bernadette, "I hope the real ceremony is a bit longer than *that*."

"Don't worry, darling, you are going to love it, I promise you," said Eve kissing her.

"Now mum's the word about all this," Imogen said, "You can tell people afterwards if you want, of course."

They arrived at D'Arcy's and Bernadette was once more banished to the bedroom.

"Well!" she said crossly as they all left.

"Patience, darling," Imogen told her, "You are going to love it, I promise you."

"Oh fine," Bernadette sat down a little more meekly on the sofa and wondered at Eve and Imogen keeping such a secret. Although she loved it really, she resolved Eve would be getting a Shibari session, nevertheless.

* * *

Coffee was soon provided by a butler who D'Arcy had hired for the day, no doubt along with many other staff to serve whatever wedding feast had been planned.

Bernadette sipped her coffee and looked out of the window which faced the front of the house. She could see some people who were no doubt in charge of parking hanging around chatting, people would probably arrive soon then. The gate was being draped with ribbons, flowers and balloons. Likewise, balloons were being put around in bunches in the car park. She did not know what the back of the house was like but assumed that was where the wedding would take place. She had not been allowed to peek, even out of the windows.

Very shortly there was a knock at the door which revealed two women with a suitcase undoubtedly full of makeup and a man dressed quite flamboyantly who announced he was her stylist.

"You are not to worry about anything," he said with a slight French accent, "Gervais is here, with Nicky and Sharon, to take care of it all for you."

"I was just wondering about my hair," she began.

He held up a hand. "No, no, no, leave this all to me. Madame Eve has given strict instructions and I promised her I would not allow you to change it."

"Oh... oh! Ooh, the little witch!" Then she laughed, "Fine, OK, go ahead do your worst."

"I assure you, Gervais does not do worst, no, he does only the best and finest styles in Ireland."

"I'm sure you do." Bernadette smiled and settled down to allow his ministrations.

As it turned out, he opted not to go overboard in the styling pronouncing her thick black locks as "utterly beautiful and ravishing." He cascaded it in waves, and slight curls, with a portion pinned back with a diamante hair ornament.

Nicky and Sharon similarly went for understated light makeup with red lips. They gave her eyebrows a pleasing clean shape and did not add false eyelashes since hers were quite long. They also painted her nails with the same shade of red. When she looked in the mirror, she said she liked it very much.

"And now," said Gervais, "In a voice filled with triumphant emotion, for the dress."

Nicky disappeared from the room and returned in short order with a white zip-up dress cover, inside of which was undoubtedly the wedding dress. With great drama, this was unzipped to reveal its contents. Bernadette's mouth formed an O of surprise.

The dress was slightly off-white cream, which she loved straight away. It was an off the shoulder, simple design, with a Bardot neckline, and short drape sleeves. She could also see there was a split in the wrap skirt part and knew Eve had done this on purpose because she admired Bernadette's shapely legs.

"Do you like it?" Gervais asked her beaming.

"Did, Eve choose it?"

"But of course, with some assistance from myself, the stylist, but yes, she said it was the perfect thing for you and she was right."

"I love it. I don't know if I would have chosen it, but I do love it," said Bernadette candidly.

"Believe me, this will show you to perfection, *absolument*, without any doubts, my darling."

Bernadette removed her robe and Nicky helped her put on a white strapless bra which Eve had also chosen. Since Bernadette was reasonable well-endowed, this was certainly needed for a dress like that. She carefully stepped into the dress and they zipped her up.

"Ah, beautiful, beautiful," said Gervais as she looked in the mirror.

"It is lovely, for sure," said Bernadette turning this way and that. She hoped Eve was going to love it as much as she thought she would. Although Bernadette personally would have probably gone for something with lace, she did not know what Eve was wearing and perhaps this was a counterpoint.

"And now for the shoes," said Gervais, as Nicky handed him a box.

He opened it and inside were a pair of clear stiletto mules with two thin see-through straps. She knew Eve would have chosen these with care, particularly because Bernadette had a great fondness for shoes.

"Oh, I love these," she said happily.

"The glass slippers for the Cinderella, the belle of the ball," said Gervais.

Once more Nicky and Sharon helped her put the shoes on and then she looked at herself once more in the mirror. She liked very much what she saw, and particularly when her leg slid out between the slit which was, she had to admit, very sexy indeed. Eve had chosen well.

"Now, we must go, but any problems today we will be around to fix it, OK?" said Gervais, "And don't sit down until after the ceremony, we don't want the creases, *n'est ce pas*?"

"I won't, I promise," Bernadette vowed and wondered how much longer it would be, and what Eve was going to be wearing. She went over for a peek into the front of the house which was now full of cars. The guests, whoever they were, must have arrived while she was getting ready.

There was nothing for it but to wait. She forbore to have more coffee in case she spilt it on her dress. She had a few surprises of her own for Eve, but those would be much later.

* * *

She did not have to wait too much longer until D'Arcy and Imogen returned.

"Oh my God, you are one sexy bitch!" Imogen said in admiring tones.

"God you look drop dead gorgeous, darling," D'Arcy agreed.

"You like?" Bernadette said giving them a twirl and showing some leg.

"It makes me hot just looking at you," said Imogen pretending to fan herself.

"Imogen, really, you are so very naughty!" D'Arcy chided her but she was laughing.

"You two aren't so bad yourselves, in fact, you scrub up very well. A pair of sexy mamas and no mistake," Bernadette told them.

D'Arcy's outfit was a satin scoop maxi dress which went to the floor, and buttoned up at the back, it had shoestring style straps and fitted her figure perfectly. The colour was ivory and complemented the cream of Bernadette's wedding gown. D'Arcy had strappy silver sandals, and her hair was partly up and hanging down in ringlets.

Imogen was wearing a satin light orchid cami maxi dress which gathered in at the waist. It had shoestring straps, and the colour went nicely with her hair. She had matching strappy mules in the same colour. Imogen had her hair braided and tied up, in a very nouveau Victorian fashion.

"Do you like them?" said D'Arcy, "We were trying to match you."

"I love it and yes they do match me very well."

"Not long now, darling," said Imogen, "But before we go down, Eve has asked me to tell you a few rules."

"Rules?" said Bernadette with a surprised laugh.

"Yes."

"Why couldn't she tell me herself?" Bernadette said lightly.

This was a new side of Eve she was only just seeing. Eve had been so efficient arranging everything. She should have guessed it, however, from the expert way Eve kept house for them.

"Well, she thought it would be best coming from us."

"OK, and what are the rules exactly?"

"Firstly, you must never ask, how much did any of this cost?"

"OK, fair enough." Eve knew her too well, because Bernadette would wonder about it for sure.

"Secondly, you must never ask, who paid for this or that?"

"Right."

Once again, Eve was on the nail. Bernadette was fairly sure D'Arcy would have had a hand in paying for some of it and she resolved to curb her natural impulse to want to cover all the cost herself. There was a time to accept help and to accept what was given with love, and that time was today.

"Thirdly, you must enjoy this beautiful day she, and well we, have created for you and understand that we've done it out of love, the sheer love we all have for you."

"Oh... oh! Shit, I'm going to cry if you carry on," said Bernadette becoming emotional at once.

"Finally, if you break the rules, you know what will happen."

"What will happen?" said D'Arcy interested.

"Nothing like you think, darling, I'll tell you later. They don't play the same games as us, now hush," said Imogen firmly.

"Oh? Oh! Oh, right, OK."

"But this day is also for Eve, I mean, isn't it?" Bernadette wondered with the focus being all on her enjoyment.

"Of course, it's also for Eve, but don't you understand how much it depends on you loving it too. She's put so much into this, we all have, believe it or not. Well, you wouldn't believe it, considering what we pulled off. And more than half of her enjoyment is that you have the time of your life, with her."

"Fuck, oh fuck it... oh..." Bernadette's eyes welled up and a tear trickled down her cheek.

"Here, tissue, let me."

Imogen patted her dry.

"It's a good job I made sure they used waterproof mascara," D'Arcy chuckled.

"Now try not to cry too much, but if you must, the girls are on hand to fix your makeup, not that you have much on you bitch *and* you look stunning," Imogen said giggling.

"You look stunning too, both of you and neither of you have *that* much makeup!" Bernadette protested.

There was a knock at the door, and D'Arcy opened it. One of the hospitality staff was holding a beautiful bouquet of red and white roses. Bernadette burst into tears.

* * *

"Right now, if you could at least hold it in until the ceremony," Imogen admonished Bernadette once Nicky and Sharon had touched up Bernadette's makeup.

"I'll try," said Bernadette.

"Well, anyway, darling, it's time."

383

They left the bedroom to Bernadette's relief, went downstairs and through to the dining room which led to the outside through a patio door.

She looked through the doors to see, a huge open sided marquee which had been set out in the garden. The pathway to the marquee was carpeted and had plinths on either side of the pathway with flowers in vases.

"Jesus," she exclaimed.

"Are you ready?" Imogen asked her.

"I think so."

"Take a deep breath, and now D'Arcy and I are going to walk you up the aisle."

"Oh God... oh!"

"Don't cry, come on, babe, hold it in now."

"Shit, shit I'm trying," said Bernadette in a choked voice.

"OK, so, shall we go?"

"Yes, yes, let's do that."

Imogen nodded to an attendant who was standing nearby with a headset on. They stepped through the door together. As they did so a string quartet struck up somewhere inside the marquee. The sounds of *Vivaldi's Spring* from the Four Seasons filtered back to them.

D'Arcy stood on Bernadette's left side, and Imogen on the right. They took hold of her hands, and like the true friends they were, began to slowly walk towards the marquee. As she approached, she could see the backs of people she recognised mainly from her work, and a few other friends. They were sat on either side of what formed the aisle. She stepped inside the marquee which was decorated with greenery and leaves, and flowers. The small select gathering all stood and turned to look at her. She recognised faces as she walked past but her eyes were only for Eve.

Up ahead where the ceremony was to take place was a raised platform, and an arbour. Eve was standing there looking utterly radiant. She was wearing a white embroidered fishtail mesh dress with a sweetheart neckline. It was strapless and carefully styled blonde curls cascaded over Eve's bare shoulders. At the back of her head, she had a partial French plait with a white floral string woven through it. She turned to look at Bernadette and her smile spoke volumes. Bernadette bit her lip at the sight of her beautiful wife to be, she wanted to burst into tears once again but managed to prevent herself with difficulty. Imogen glanced at her with concern and squeezed her hand affectionately. She knew for Bernadette this would be one of the biggest moments of her life.

Standing facing them as they approached and with Eve to his left was the celebrant. He was wearing a colourful jacket with a white shirt, black trousers and red tie. As Bernadette finally reached the podium, she did not dare look left or right as D'Arcy and Imogen helped her to step up. She leaned down and kissed them both lightly before turning away to stand and face her bride.

"My God, you are so beautiful, so, so beautiful," Bernadette whispered moving forward to take Eve's hand.

"So are you, my sweetheart, everything I anticipated when I bought you that dress, I love you, darling," Eve said smiling back.

Everyone had resumed their seats. D'Arcy and Imogen took their own seats in the front row. The audience was now full of anticipation.

"Well," began the celebrant, "I am Brian, and I'm here to help all of you celebrate the marriage between these two beautiful people Bernadette and Eve. I think you'll agree they are both looking particularly stunning today."

Eve's eyes held Bernadette's full of love and she could not look away. Her eyes were wet as the emotions rose in her breast. When she had first seen Eve standing there waiting, she wanted to cry with happiness at once.

"So, of course, I have to ask if there is anyone who knows any reason why these two lovely women should not be married, then speak now or forever hold your peace."

This stipulation was of course unnecessary in the light of their legal marriage, but Bernadette assumed he was simply following the form.

Brian waited in silence for a moment before continuing.

"It's always a relief once that's over," he quipped to a ripple of laughter, "It's all plain sailing from here."

It had at least injected a little light relief into an emotionally charged atmosphere.

"Now then, we all know marriage is a solemn moment with the exchange of vows," said Brian, "But I like to think it's something deeper, the joining of two people in love for the rest of their lives. I think we can tell that Bernadette and Eve are deeply in love. I can see it just from the way they are gazing into each other's eyes just now."

There was a collective sigh from the assembled guests and a self-conscious giggle from Bernadette and Eve. They were still holding hands, and their gaze did not waver.

"So, let's instead of being solemn discuss this as being a happy occasion where we join these two people forevermore one with the other in the bonds of matrimony. Where they will each give their vows and exchange rings symbolising their lifelong commitment to each other. I couldn't be happier or more privileged to have been asked to perform this ceremony today."

He paused and smiled at Bernadette and Eve. They broke their gaze momentarily and smiled back.

"Now, just remember, that as you say these vows, you do not do so lightly, nor frivolously, but seriously and with meaning and intent. Intent to keep your vows to each other and to stay the course you both have set. You will make your commitment in front of the assembled guests who act as collective witness to the public plighting of your troth. All of them here, I am sure, wish you happiness, and a long life filled with love together."

He paused once more before continuing.

"If you are both ready, then I shall ask you to make your commitment and say your vows."

"I'm ready," said Bernadette.

"Me too, more than ready," Eve said to accompanying laughter.

"Then first to you, Bernadette. That's right keep holding hands just as you have been doing. Now do you, Bernadette Mackenna take Eve White to be your lawful wedded wife? To have and to hold, to cherish and to love, and to keep faithfully unto her as long as you both shall live?"

"I do!" said Bernadette her voice was confident but tinged with emotion.

"Very well, you may say your vows if you have them."

"I do," said Bernadette shifting her gaze back to Eve, "Eve, my darling. I never thought I would stand here today and finally be able to call you my own. When you came into my life, I was lost, I was alone, I was adrift. You anchored me, you saved me, and you have become my safe harbour for always. I promise to love you every day, in every way I can. I promise to be faithful, to be truthful, to withhold nothing from you. I promise to keep no secrets and to always treat you with respect, and give all my love to you, unconditionally and without reservation. What is mine is yours and becomes ours forevermore. I love you, so much... so very much... you are my whole life, you are my everything and I give myself wholly to you for now and for always."

She surprised herself by not crying although her eyes were wet and so were Eve's. She had spoken clearly and in a strong voice which had come from somewhere to match the occasion. Perhaps it was her long experience at the bar, she mused.

"Very nice, very fitting, lovely in fact," said Brian, turning to Eve, "And now, Eve White, do you take Bernadette Mackenna to be your lawful wedded wife? To have and to hold, to cherish and to love, and to keep faithfully unto her as long as you both shall live?"

"I do, yes. I really, really do!" said Eve half smiling and half crying. A lone tear tracked its way down her cheek unheeded.

"You may now say your vows, Eve," said Brian.

"My darling Bernadette," Eve began and then finding it hard to continue had to stop.

"I'm the one who's supposed to be crying," Bernadette whispered, "You're the strong one."

"Not today, darling, not today," said Eve in a choked-up voice.

"Take your time," said Brian smiling benevolently on them.

Eve paused, dashed a few tears away and started again, "My darling, I told you that from the first moment I saw you I loved you, and all of this time I love you still... more and even more... every day..."

There was a muffled sob from D'Arcy and Bernadette shot a glance around to see Imogen with an arm around her shoulder handing her a tissue.

"I can't even begin to tell you how much I love you and how much you mean to me, and I don't think I ever will, because words are not enough... for that... fuck... shit... oh... sorry..." Eve choked on a sob herself.

The was a titter at the swear words, but everyone was held in the thrall of this moment of real and extreme depth of emotion.

Eve continued with difficulty, having to pause and stop between the words, to try and compose herself as best she could, rather than breaking down completely, "I... I just want you to know, that I will always take care of you... I will nurture... you. I promise you... I will never... never... ever leave you... and you must always... remember... that... you must..."

Her words were punctuated by deep breaths and attempts to prevent herself from crying. Though by now tears were running unheeded down Bernadette's cheeks.

"I will take care of you... oh, I've said that... well, I'll be doing it twice, then..." Eve laughed through her own tears. "Every day in, and in... every way... I know I've tested you sometimes... I've tested your love... perhaps... but from now until forever I am yours, in my heart... my body... and my soul. I'm yours unconditionally with all the love I have and all the love I can give."

She finished a little stronger. Bernadette mouthed, "I love you" at her.

"Beautiful words from both of you I'm sure everyone would agree," Brian said after waiting a moment for the room to settle. There was not a dry eye in the audience following Eve's very emotional and heartfelt delivery. "Now you shall both perform an exchange of rings symbolising your love in an unending circle of infinity."

Carragh, who had been standing to one side, stepped forward with the rings and handed them to Brian. D'Arcy had evidently decided it was safest to entrust them to him.

Brian held up the rings. "These, as I said, are a symbol of your love, and very lovely rings they are too."

Eve had chosen golden bands patterned with a Celtic design, and inside were inscriptions which Bernadette could not quite read.

"So this one, is Eve's I believe," said Brian, reading the inscription, "And inside it says, 'Eve in true love forevermore from Bernadette'."

There was a chorus of 'ahs' at this revelation as Brian handing the ring to Bernadette. She turned it over in her hand.

"Do you like it?" Eve whispered.

"It's perfect." Bernadette smiled.

"So, place the ring on the fourth finger of Eve's left hand, Bernadette, and say after me..."

Bernadette did so and held Eve's hand which was trembling ever so slightly in her own.

"With this ring," Brian began.

"With this ring."

"I thee wed."

"I thee wed."

"I will love and cherish you."

"I will love and cherish you."

"Until the end of our days."

"Until the end of our days."

"And let this ring be a symbol of my vows to you and my everlasting love for you."

"And let this ring be a symbol of my vows to you and my everlasting love for you."

Bernadette could not resist bringing Eve's hand up to her lips and planting a kiss in Eve's palm, then wrapping it over.

"Now, Eve, here is the ring for Bernadette, which has the same inscription, and do likewise placing it on Bernadette's ring finger."

Eve did so, and then repeated the words, just as Bernadette had done.

When this was done, Brian smiled upon them benevolently, and said, "And so by the exchanging of vows, and rings, before your wonderful friends, we have completed the ceremony and it gives me great pleasure to pronounce you both married. You may now kiss your respective bride."

Bernadette moved in almost shyly to take Eve in her arms, and their lips met with a burning fire. Somehow on this day, it felt more intense and more poignant than it ever had.

The entire audience stood up, and applauded, shouting, and hooting with pleasure. The kiss which seemed to last a long time, finally ended, and they stood hand in hand together and married at long last. Both of them had cried, and neither of them cared, because it had been a momentous occasion for them both. For some marriage was perhaps not an important thing, but for Bernadette and Eve, it was a public declaration of the love they shared, and their commitment. It was something they both had wanted, and now they had done it.

Bernadette and Eve smiled, photos were taken, and then the string quartet struck up *Eine Kleine Nachtmusik* by Mozart, and Eve said, "Shall we go?"

They stepped down together and hand in hand walked back down the aisle to the sweet strains of Mozart, everyone was cheering, clapping as they went. The two of them were smiling. Eve led her back into the dining room, and then to one of D'Arcy's living rooms where she shut the door.

"Well, Mrs Mackenna," said Bernadette with a smile lurking around her lips.

"Indeed, Mrs Mackenna," Eve said advancing on her purposefully, "I'm going to kiss you properly before they fix our makeup."

"Oh God, yes please do!"

Their lips met and time stood still. Bernadette felt nothing but the perfect sweetness of two lips meeting and the fireworks going off in her head. Although they were both burning up with desire, the wedding dresses and the occasion prevented them from taking it further. Eventually, their lips parted, and they stood holding each other.

"That was so beautiful," Bernadette told her, "Thank you, thank you for making everything so perfect."

"You liked it?"

"I loved it. I couldn't have asked for a more perfect day."

"Well, it's not over, we're having a meal shortly, and then there will be dancing. We've got an Irish band to play a mix of modern and folk music, not too loud all the time," Eve laughed.

"Wonderful."

"And you've to make a speech."

"What about you?"

"Oh well."

"You *have* to make one too," Bernadette insisted.

"Oh, you..."

"I can't believe you and Imogen having been planning this for months."

"I know, I'm sorry. It was the biggest secret ever but a good one."

"You are forgiven, completely." Bernadette kissed her. "For everything."

"Everything?" Eve's eyes grew wider.

"Well, why what else have you done?" Bernadette laughed.

"Oh, nothing, I'm just teasing you."

"Witch!"

"Your witch now, your witchy wife now."

"I know." Bernadette held up her rings to look at them. "Did Imogen help you choose these?"

"I cannot tell a lie."

"I ought to give her a good spanking," Bernadette laughed.

"Except she'd love that," Eve giggled.

"I'm glad you both did this, honestly, because without the two of you this would never have happened. I would have procrastinated forever about it."

"Exactly, see I'm not just your average naughty housewife."

"You're not a housewife," Bernadette said severely.

"Oh, but I am now, I'm Eve Mackenna, wife of the famous Bernadette Mackenna."

"Oh, you, you're an artist too, in your own right."

"Yes, but you'll always be my heroine, forevermore."

"Oh, Eve..."

They kissed again, and then Eve poured them both a glass of sparkling water from a bottle thoughtfully provided for the purpose.

"What happens now?" Bernadette asked her.

"They are getting the marquee ready for the wedding feast, and Imogen will come and get us shortly. We'll go and receive everyone's congratulations, have photos taken. People have given us some gifts which we will open later. Then we'll have the meal, and get changed, relax, and then have a dance in the evening and more food. How's that sound?"

"Exhausting," Bernadette laughed, "And you left one thing out."

"What's that?"

"The part where I get to fuck you, of course, darling."

"Oh well, *that* goes without saying. We can perhaps have a little afternoon session, don't you think?"

"Yes... please."

"I'm yours now, you don't have to say please."

"But I want to."

"OK."

They kissed once more and sat down to wait.

* * *

It was not long at all before Imogen bustled in with Nicky and Sharon in tow.

"There you are!" she exclaimed, "Now then, we need to fix your makeup and then you've got the meet and greet, have photos and we've got the wedding feast."

"You picked the right person for the job, Eve, a proper dominatrix," Bernadette quipped.

"Well, I've my whip upstairs so don't make me go and get it," Imogen laughed.

Nicky and Sharon thought this was very amusing, while they set about adjusting Bernadette and Eve's makeup.

"You think she's joking," Bernadette said sardonically.

Once their makeup was sorted, Imogen whisked them outside where a great cheer went up as they appeared. In the marquee, people were bustling around rearranging stuff into tables, and there were delicious smells emanating from behind the marquee where apparently the caterers had set up a kitchen. Bernadette firmly pushed any thoughts of cost from her mind. Her attention was soon taken up with amiably chatting to their guests standing beside Eve.

All of her staff were there, along with partners, if they had them. Bernadette's Uncle Donal was there and although she thought perhaps he would have liked to give her away, apparently Eve had discussed it beforehand and he was fine with her best friends doing it instead. Olivia had come with Carole and so had Brogan and his wife Stella. Valentino and Sophia from the gallery had been invited. One of two of Eve's friends from the gym where she had been working as a personal trainer were also present. As were, Emily O'Neal and her sister, Natasha, from a previous case, along with Oonagh Flanagan, and her mother, whom she had also represented. Eve had also asked along with D'Arcy's agent, Oscar Childe, and his assistant, Gelda. Bernadette's good friend Patrick Kelly, a psychologist with whom she attended university was also a guest. Constantina, the housekeeper, had been given the day off and was swanning around with her friend Juanita.

In short, all of these people meant something to Bernadette or Eve, friends, and also clients, whom they had at one time or another formed a bond. They came up to talk, and congratulate them on getting married, and for such a wonderful wedding. Uncle Donal gave them both a big hug and made them promise to come and spend some time with him soon.

"I was very surprised and touched to receive an invite," said Brogan when it was his turn, and having introduced his wife Stella.

"I couldn't not invite you," said Bernadette.

"Well, you are very kind, and I'm honoured," said Brogan kissing her hand in a most chivalrous fashion.

"I've told Jack he's not to overindulge in the alcohol department," Stella chimed in, "Don't want him underperforming later."

"Yes... hurumm... well... I don't think they want so many details... Stella... hurumm... my love."

"Oh hush, Jack, they seem like old friends already."

"You see what I have to put up with," Brogan said crustily.

"You two really must come to dinner soon, I'll invite you! Jack has told me so much about you, I feel as if we are practically neighbours," Stella said, and her laughter trilled across the lawn like so many musical notes.

At the end of the fairly long line were Olivia and Carole.

"Well, you two, tied the knot, good job!" said Olivia smiling.

"Yes, well done," Carole put in.

"It was a beautiful ceremony, quite lovely." Olivia smiled.

"Thank you, it's all down to Eve, and Imogen."

"Ah, Imogen, not surprised to hear she had a hand in it."

Carole squeezed Olivia's hand possessively on hearing this.

"You never know," said Eve, "It might be you one day."

"Hmm, chance would be a fine thing," Olivia laughed, "Someone would have to ask me first."

Carole coloured up at this pointed remark.

"Carole, it's lovely to see you, thanks for coming," said Bernadette trying to steer the conversation away from controversial topics.

"I wouldn't have missed it for the world," Carole averred.

Imogen arrived at their side abruptly and said, "That's enough chatting for now, you can do all the talking you want later. It's time for the photographs."

"She's the boss today, in her element, she is." Bernadette laughed as they allowed themselves to be led away into the garden for couples' photos, photos with Imogen and D'Arcy, and then all the group shots.

"You'll be pleased to know that's the last one," said Imogen satisfied once the final group photo had been taken.

She spoke to the photographer briefly, who disappeared and then the maître d called their attention by banging a gong extremely loudly.

"Ladies, and gentlemen, please taking your seats for the wedding feast," he announced in stentorian tones.

Imogen made Bernadette and Imogen stay back until all the guests were seated and then she let them walk in. She followed behind them with D'Arcy. Everyone clapped and cheered once more as they took their seat on a table which had been placed on the podium. Bernadette sat next to Eve. D'Arcy and Imogen sat on either side of them. The other circular tables were arranged around the marquee in a nice cluster, so nobody was too far apart.

The wedding feast turned out to be excellent. It was a sit-down meal with servers bustling between tables like busy bees around a hive. The starters were a choice of mixed green salad with a raspberry-infused vinaigrette, deconstructed bruschetta, Mini shrimp salad rolls and an assorted charcuterie board. Bernadette and Eve opted to share a plate of each, pronouncing it beautiful. The mains were a choice from lightly seasoned trout with parsley-caper vinaigrette, spring vegetable risotto, grilled rack of lamb with asparagus, or herb-roasted chicken and rice with fresh apricot. Bernadette opted for the lamb, and Eve for the chicken, although they ended up sharing again. Finally, the dessert offered traditional sticky toffee pudding with custard, trifle or apple crumble. There would be a cheeseboard to follow for those who had the room.

Conversation flowed freely as they ate, and the food beautifully presented and cooked was complimented by all. The meal was served with a variety of wine and soft drinks.

Bernadette moderated her intake and alternated with sparkling water in order to make sure she wasn't intoxicated. She wanted to consummate their marriage as soon as she was able, in the proper fashion and she wasn't going to be doing so drunk. She and Eve played footsie under the table and touched fingers affectionately during the meal.

When the coffee was being served, Imogen stood up and called for hush.

"Now then," she said a trifle loudly, "It's traditional, of course, at a normal wedding for the best man to give a speech. But of course, there is no best man, only me."

There were a few laughs at this.

"And this is not what you might call a normal wedding, no indeed, because it's far from normal, it's very, very special. It's special to me, and to all of you because this is the wedding of two people we love and cherish to bits, and fuck me if I carry on like this, I'm going to cry…"

There were more laughs during this and several 'ahs' too.

"I remember meeting Bernadette or rather seeing her in court a while back now, and thinking I want to work for that woman. As luck would have it I did. I mean, how could she not choose me anyway? But seriously. Bernadette has become not just a colleague but also my best friend, and now she has Eve, who is also my best friend too."

"They're my best friends too!" D'Arcy piped up not wanting to be left out.

"Yes, all four of us best friends, darling, you're right." Imogen laughed.

"But anyway, I love this woman, and also this woman, and that woman whom I'll be getting married too someday soon, and you'll probably get to hear me make another speech when I've had a bit too much to drink, like now."

She stopped for a moment to gather her thoughts while people chuckled. D'Arcy looked at her a little surprised, perhaps Imogen didn't usually imbibe quite so freely as she appeared to have been doing today.

"But anyway, what I want to say really is that I'm so happy to see Bernadette and Eve get married, and for all of us to have been privileged to be part of this wonderful celebration. Two people who are so in love deserve the best, and so join me in raising your glasses for long life, happiness, and love. Bernadette and Eve."

There was much applause at the speech, and when it died down Imogen said, "Now normally it's traditional for the father of the bride to say something, but we actually have two brides, and sadly neither of their fathers are with us. So instead I've asked Bernadette's uncle Donal to say a few words."

Uncle Donal stood up, he had a mop of grey hair, and was nevertheless a distinguished looking man wearing a rather flamboyant purple coloured suit, with a white shirt and blue tie. Her uncle was quite a character who was wealthy and had made his money in property development. He pulled out a sheaf of paper and put on a pair of reading glasses.

"I've, erm... I've known Bernadette all of her life," he began, he cleared his throat a little to get rid of the nerves and tried again, this time a little louder. "And I can tell you she always was a wonderful girl, if headstrong. She has become a wonderful and beautiful woman. It has always been me she came to for a shoulder to cry on, particularly after her parents tragically passed away." He stopped to compose himself before wiping away a tear. "It was also me in whom she confided she was gay, all those years ago, and naturally enough she did, because if you haven't figured it out yet, I'm gay too. And I'm proud of it."

"Hear, hear," shouted Oscar from another table, and several people clapped.

"Now I've helped her, I've counselled her, I watched her flourish and become the successful barrister she is. I've seen her on the stage at school, and now on a bigger stage in the courtroom. I can tell you she's quite a performer, one of the best. She's brought tears to my eyes, but in a good way, I assure you."

He stopped to take a drink from his glass, and then continued, "So it was with absolute pleasure I received the news she had found someone who has turned out to be the love of her life. That someone is Eve. What can you say about Eve? She's beautiful, she's caring, she's kind, she's loving, intelligent and in every way a match for my beautiful Bernadette. In every way. The two of them were made for each other, completely. I couldn't wish for a better partner than Eve for my Bernadette. So, without further ado, I wish them long life, and all the love in the world. Please raise your glasses to Bernadette and Eve."

Once more the toast rang out and Donal sat down as everyone applauded.

"Now," said Imogen standing up again, and slurring her words just slightly, "I believe it's only right that Bernadette should say a few words, and then Eve too, yes?"

There were shouts of "Yes" from the guests and Imogen smiled, nodded to Bernadette who stood up.

"Thank you, thank you so much, Imogen, and D'Arcy and Eve. Thank you, all of you for coming today and making it so special. If I had imagined a wedding day then this would have been it, and in fact, it has surpassed all of my expectations or wild imagination. I think I've said it all in my vows, but I'm sure you all know how much I love this woman right here. She is beyond words. I sometimes cannot find a way to articulate the depth of my feelings for her... I love her *that* much..." Bernadette paused, gathering herself, "I wasn't going to cry again, and now look at me."

There were a few laughs but the emotion in the room was once more palpable.

"Eve is my life, my everything. I honestly cannot say how I could ever live without her now, and that's the truth. I was going to say some funny stuff and make jokes, but all I can think of, Eve, is how much I love you. So, I'm going to leave it at that. And please know that every one of you here today, holds a special place for me, all of you. Thank you again for coming, thank you."

Bernadette sat down and Eve kissed her spontaneously. Bernadette wiped her eyes. "Fuck," she said, "I'm such a cry baby."

"You are my cry baby and I love you for it," Eve whispered.

Eve stood up. "I just want to say that I'm truly grateful all of you came to make this day such a wonderful one. I'm truly grateful to whatever magical forces brought me together with Bernadette. As much as she loves me, I love her, a thousand-fold, and more. She is my life, my world too, I could never live without her either. So, based on that, when we go, I guess it had better be at the same time."

There was another little ripple of laughter at this. Eve was speaking with more poise now than she had shown at the ceremony. Her voice though tinged with much emotion was steady and clear.

"But seriously, since I've been with Bernadette, I've had a charmed life, a beautiful life. I could not ask for more, and I never want for more than she gives, because she gives me so much of herself. So, thank you again for coming, and for this special day. Thank you so much to Imogen and D'Arcy, and I'd like to have a toast, to the two best friends in the world, Imogen and D'Arcy."

There was more enthusiastic applause and Imogen stood up once more. "You'll be pleased to know I'm not making another speech. The formalities are over. Stay here as long as you want, I believe there are liqueurs and a cheese board too, plus more coffee. If you want a swim, the pool is there, and we have changing facilities, towels. If you are sticking around then there will be dancing later, and more food until the early hours. So, eat, drink and be merry."

Everyone cheered, and Imogen sat back down.

"Darling, don't you think you should slow down now on the wine?" D'Arcy whispered.

"Oh, come on, it's a wedding, eat and be merry, and I'm certainly merry."

"Oh well, I just thought..."

"Don't tell me what to do, pet."

"I only wanted to make a suggestion, my love, I mean, about drinking so much..."

"Well don't!" said Imogen quite rudely and suddenly got up and stalked off.

"Oh! Oh!" said D'Arcy her eyes filling with tears, "And this has been such a lovely day... and..."

"It's OK," said Bernadette, "Don't worry, D'Arcy, I'll go and talk to her."

"Well, but she didn't need to speak to me like *that*, I was just worried and..." said D'Arcy looking terribly upset.

"It's OK," said Eve, taking D'Arcy's hand. "You go and find her, darling," she said Bernadette.

Bernadette got up leaving Eve to comfort D'Arcy and hurried out of the marquee, she went towards to house and seeing Carragh asked him, "Have you seen Imogen by any chance?"

"Oh yeah, she went inside I think, not sure where. Is everything OK?"

"Yes, yes it's fine, well, kind of." She made a face which suggested otherwise, and he nodded sympathetically. "I just need to find her, though."

Bernadette went into the house, and on the spur of the moment went back to the living room she and Eve had lately been in. There she found Imogen crying her eyes out.

"Oh my God," she said moving quickly to gather up her friend in her arms, "Whatever is wrong?"

"I'm a bitch, I've been such a rotten drunken sot of a bitch. D'Arcy's been so good, she's contributed so much to this wedding, you don't know, and I'm not supposed to tell you, and here I am getting drunk and talking to her like shit. I'm fucking awful person, a bitch from hell..."

"Stop it," said Bernadette soothingly, "You've just had a bit too much to drink, darling. We all do, and you've been so wonderful today organising it all."

"I know but what possessed me to snap at her like that? I'm stupid, perfectly horrid."

"Don't fret, darling, honestly, I will just bring her here and you can apologise."

"No!" said Imogen pulling away slightly.

"No?"

"No! I need to be punished, now! I'll go upstairs, and she can give me a damn good spanking, it's what I deserve."

"Are you mad?" said Bernadette quite shocked, "With all these people here wandering about? I mean, it's not a good idea. No really, I can't allow it."

"But it's what I need! I've been an utter brat."

"This is the drink talking," said Bernadette firmly, "And I'm not letting you do it. You are not to suggest it to her and especially not on my wedding day. Just apologise to her and it's done. If when you're sober and the guests are all gone you still feel you want her to do that, then that's between you and her, OK?"

Imogen looked at her a little teary eyed. "OK, if you think it's best."

"I do and I think you need to sober up, and don't drink anymore. Apart from anything else you'll have the worst hangover."

"I've ruined your day with my stupidity..." Imogen began.

"Stop it, unless you want *me* to take you outside and spank you in front of all the guests."

"What?"

Bernadette laughed. "Your face! Of course, I wouldn't do such a thing."

"It would be pretty horny though now I come to think of it."

"No, it would not! I just said that to snap you out of it. Now, stop it, I'm going to get D'Arcy and mind what I said."

"Yes, OK, you're the boss," Imogen said meekly.

Bernadette poured a glass of water and handed it to her. "Drink this, darling, and stay here while I get D'Arcy. You better apologise nicely."

"Shall I beg her forgiveness?"

"You can if you want but no funny business."

"OK, fine, fine!" Imogen laughed and consumed the water, holding it out for a second glass. "That's better I'm starting to sober up now."

"Good, I'm going to get D'Arcy."

Bernadette went outside, and asked Carragh to ask D'Arcy to come to the living room. D'Arcy arrived in very short order looking worried, and Bernadette ushered her inside. She stood by the door watching D'Arcy walk up to Imogen.

"Well?" said D'Arcy in hurt tones as Imogen looked up at her from the chair.

"Darling, I'm sorry, I'm so sorry, please forgive me, darling, I'm such a bitch..." Imogen began. She could see D'Arcy melting at once. "No, no you're not..." Bernadette quietly closed the door.

"Everything OK?" Eve asked her when she returned to the table.

"Oh yes, Imogen's just a little drunk." She related what had happened in an undertone, and Eve laughed her head off.

"Oh goodness, what is she like?"

"She drunk too much that's all, it's not like her."

"Oh well, I'm sure they'll be fine."

Shortly afterwards, Imogen and D'Arcy reappeared smiling and holding hands.

"Thank you," D'Arcy whispered to Bernadette when they sat down again.

"It's fine, darling, I'm glad you two are back on good terms."

"Oh, it was just a misunderstanding," D'Arcy brushed it off, "She apologised so nicely to me."

"I'm glad to hear it."

Eve and Bernadette circulated around the tables chatting to everyone they could, while cheese and biscuits were consumed along with liqueurs and more coffee. Bernadette kept a weather eye on Imogen and D'Arcy, but they were circulating too. All seemed to be OK between them. Soon people began to peel off, and go for a swim, or just to rest. D'Arcy had made some rooms available for the purpose. Those who might want to stay were easily accommodated in her very large house.

The evening event wasn't due to begin for an hour or two. So, after a quick word with Imogen who assured Bernadette everything was really fine and promised she wasn't going to get drunk again, she took Eve's hand and led her upstairs to their bedroom locking the door behind them once they were inside.

✳ ✳ ✳

"What happens now?" Eve asked her with a saucy smile.

"We both get naked, and then..."

407

"And then?"

"You will find out."

"Help me off with this dress," said Eve turning around.

Bernadette unzipped Eve's dress, and Eve stepped out of it, she hung it up in the wardrobe. She was naked underneath apart from her knickers which she deftly removed.

"You can keep the shoes on," said Bernadette, "Now help me with my dress."

Once Bernadette was also naked, apart from her shoes, and had her dress also hanging up, she said, "Now close your eyes, and don't open them until I say."

"OK, but what are you doing?"

Bernadette said nothing and instead retrieved a white lace bustier from her suitcase and put it on. Then she removed some very soft silk light white rope, just a short length, enough to tie Eve's arms.

"You can open them now, my darling."

Eve gasped when she saw what Bernadette was wearing. "Oh fuck... fuck you sexy fucking bitch."

"I bought these, especially for today. Lie on the bed." Bernadette smiled.

Eve did so and Bernadette made her put her hands above her head.

"You missed a few things out of your vows," Bernadette whispered softly, her lips close to Eve's.

"Did I?"

"Yes, so... do you promise to obey me when I want you to?" Bernadette's lips brushed her wife's tantalising her.

"Yes, yes I do, of course, I do, I want that," Eve breathed closing her eyes.

"Do you promise to take your consequences when you've asked for them? And do you promise to let me tie you up and fuck you when you deserve it?"

"Oh God, yes, I do, I want that too, so much, yes I do."

Bernadette kissed her softly, lovingly and then pulled away, she began to bind Eve's wrists.

"Like this?"

"Yes, oh yes, and more, so much more."

"OK."

Eve opened her eyes. "Oh shit... fuck... you're making me so very, very wet..."

"See, you're not the only one with surprises." Bernadette lay down beside her and began to run her fingers over Eve's naked skin.

Eve hissed in her breath in response to the touch.

"Oh... oh shit."

"Now then, you didn't think I'd let you get away with keeping secrets did you, Mrs Mackenna?"

"No... no I didn't, Mrs Mackenna. I know you wouldn't... I was hoping you wouldn't... oh... my... oh fuck."

"That's right," said Bernadette, teasing Eve's nipples lightly, "Because you're mine now, you belong to me."

"Yes... I am... oh... oh... oh darling."

"And this is how I show you..."

"Oh... yes... I love it... I... ohh..."

Bernadette's fingers had found their way to Eve's sweet spot, Eve gasped and pushed hard against her fingers. Moving her pelvis against them.

"Oh... fuck... now... don't stop... oh... fuck... I love you... so much... oh... don't..."

"You're a naughty girl, Mrs Mackenna," said Bernadette softly, "So very naughty, perhaps I should do what I did the other day... should I... perhaps... turn you over and... hmm..."

She knew this kind of talk would take Eve to the edge very quickly without fail, and it did.

"Oh... yes... oh fuck... yes... oh... oh... ohh... ohh... I'm going to... ohh... oh... oh...ohh," Eve cried out arching her back, tensing and bucking, as she climaxed.

"God I just love it when you do that," said Bernadette watching her face and smiling.

Eve finally relaxed and smiled. "Thank you, darling."

"It's my pleasure, honey, but I'm not quite finished," said Bernadette softly, straddling her wife, moving slowly upwards to the right position. "I think you know what to do."

Eve's tongue went to work, needing no second bidding. Bernadette knew Eve would like the feeling of being submissive.

"Oh... oh my... oh God... Eve... oh my God... fuck... yes... oh yes... oh my God... yes..." Bernadette felt her orgasm building as she moved her pelvis against Eve's mouth, harder faster until she could not hold it back. "Oh... Eve... Eve... I love you... Eve... oh... oh... ohh!" Bernadette suppressed a scream.

As the spasms subsided, she undid Eve's bonds and held her close.

"Did you like it?" she asked, "It was part of my special present to you."

"Part? And yes, I did, I loved it so much. I loved it when you sat on my face, you should do it more often."

"I just wanted you to know your place," Bernadette giggled, then seeing Eve's eyes widen slightly, "I'm joking. Playing with you, darling, you know it. You are on a pedestal forever as far as I'm concerned."

"Well, I loved it, I really did, and I want you to do it again," said Eve smiling, "So what's the other part?"

"Later..."

"OK." Eve made a mock pout.

"I love you and I've been wanting you all day."

"And now you've had me."

"And I will again."

"And again, and again, and again..." Eve kissed her passionately becoming aroused once more.

* * *

Having made love again and they had dozed off. Not long afterwards they were woken by a knock at the door. Bernadette got up, put on a robe and went to open it. It was Imogen.

"That's where you got to, I thought as much," she said coming into the room.

"And where did *you* get to?" Bernadette enquired closing the door behind her.

"Oh well, you know, we circulated for a while and then I made it up to D'Arcy in the bedroom, not for long though being the hosts. I assumed you two were consummating your marriage."

"You're not wrong," Bernadette said with a naughty grin.

"Is everything OK between you two now?" Eve said sitting up in bed.

Imogen sighed. "Yes, it's fine, I grovelled, much against my better nature, I took a leaf out of your book Eve and kissed her feet. She liked it. She forgave me."

"You're learning," Bernadette said smiling.

"Learning to be humble sometimes, yes. Learning not to be a bitch."

"Good girl." Bernadette kissed her lightly on the cheek.

"I know, it's a good job she loves me as much as she does."

"And you love her!"

"I do. Anyway, how did you like your wedding so far?"

"The best thing ever," said Bernadette earnestly.

"Well, it's not over. You need to get dressed in your evening attire, there's going to be a band, cutting the cake, dancing and more food. D'Arcy is downstairs organising and I have to get back, so hurry up and don't be long. No more consummating until later."

"We won't, honeybunch," said Bernadette affectionately.

"Good, then I'll leave you to it."

Imogen slipped out the door, and Bernadette locked it.

"Shall we have a wash and get dressed?"

"Of course."

"What are we wearing?"

"I've got us something nice," said Eve.

They showered, and then Eve did Bernadette's hair putting it into a French Plait. Eve left her own hair loose. She did Bernadette's makeup, and then Bernadette did hers.

Reaching into the wardrobe, Eve pulled out a dress. It was a red satin material, flounced with a Bardot neckline, thigh split and a wrap tie at the waist.

"Oh, God, that's lovely," said Bernadette, when she saw it, "And it's like my wedding dress but shorter."

"Put it on, I'm dying to see you in it," said Eve.

Bernadette did so and looked this way and that, in the mirror. "You've got a thing about thigh splits, haven't you."

"You've got such sexy legs, I like looking at them," Eve said in matter of fact tones.

"I can't argue with that," Bernadette laughed.

Eve handed her a shoebox.

"More shoes?"

"Mmm-hmm."

"Ooh." They were red stilettoes, with a see-through band, and a red ribbon which secured them around the ankle. "They are lovely, thank you, and they go so well with the dress," said Bernadette putting them on, and admiring the way her feet looked in them.

"Yes, darling, your feet are beautiful," Eve giggled.

She had, in the meantime attired herself in a silver dress with a leg split too, and a Bardot neckline with a flame sequin pattern. She was wearing crisscross strap silver stiletto mules.

"Oh!" said Bernadette, "That's stunning, where did you get it?"

"My favourite shop," Eve said being coy.

"You have a favourite shop now, this from the girl who never shopped."

"I've changed, just a little, I like shopping," said Eve sidling up for a kiss.

"I love the shoes too."

"Well, you can wear them sometimes, we share remember?"

"Yes, yes I do, and I'd like to, and I will I'm sure, but they look very sexy on you."

"Kiss me and let me fix your lipstick."

They went downstairs together and out onto the back lawn, where the sounds of the band tuning up could be heard. There were lanterns and coloured lights festooning the garden and, in the marquee, too. As soon as she saw them D'Arcy came rushing up to them.

"Oh, darlings, you two are breathtaking, absolutely beautiful. I knew the dress would suit you, Bernadette."

"So, you've been shopping too, why am I not surprised," said Bernadette with a wry smile.

"Yes, I went with Eve, we had a little day out in the last couple of weeks to choose them, and the wedding dresses too."

"Well, you've both got impeccable taste."

D'Arcy was wearing a very short and figure hugging ruched pink dress with ruffle lacy sleeves, and a strapless sweetheart neckline. She had very high pink strappy stilettoes on her feet. Bernadette could not help a few sidelong glances, as D'Arcy had the most gorgeously pretty feet.

"Oh my God, that's so you," said Eve taking in the dress.

"Do you like it?" D'Arcy did a twirl.

"Love it."

"Love the shoes," Bernadette said.

"Oh yes, I knew *you'd* love the shoes," said D'Arcy slyly turning one foot this way and that so Bernadette could have a better view.

Imogen joined them, in a midi crochet lace style blue dress with a silver underdress. She was wearing silver mules and Bernadette mused her red flaming hair looked amazing in contrast.

"You look stunning, sweetness," she said to Imogen.

"Doesn't she!" D'Arcy added possessively.

"She does," Eve agreed.

"Well, you two are drop dead gorgeous," Imogen replied, "As are you, my darling, so beautiful."

This last to D'Arcy who could never be left out of a round of compliments, as Imogen knew very well.

"Anyway, go and talk to your guests, and soon we'll cut the cake. Then there will be a buffet and dancing," Imogen said.

"Yes, let's go."

Hand in hand, Eve and Bernadette went into the tent. Circulating around and chatting amiably with everyone while taking compliments. All her staff had stayed and were all very smartly done up. She made sure to admire everyone's attire and even spent some time talking to Juanita who predictably was wearing the shortest figure hugging outfit she could and high platform heels which Eve mendaciously referred to as 'stripper heels' when they were out of earshot. One or two people had gone but the majority were still in attendance, and many were staying the night.

Eventually, they cut the cake, which was quite a simple three-tiered design with white icing and decorated in white and red icing sugar roses. On the top was a pair of figurines which had apparently been specially made to look like Eve and Bernadette for them to keep as a souvenir. They cut the cake, which was duly distributed to the guests to accompany the extensive buffet of cold cuts and salads.

After the meal, and a suitable rest, the band struck up, and Bernadette led Eve onto the dancefloor for a slow passionate first dance. Everyone cheered and clapped particularly when they kissed. Then the dancing began in earnest, and the women kicked off their shoes dancing with their partners and each other. There was a mix of modern and folk style music, the atmosphere was heady, and the wine flowed freely. Nothing more occurred to mar the joyous occasion, and late into the night, Bernadette and Eve found themselves walking alone in D'Arcy's garden barefoot and holding hands.

"This has been one of the best days of my life," Bernadette said at length, "Of all the ways I could have imagined having a wedding this was perfect, so perfect."

"I feel the same way." Eve smiled. "And it's perfect because of you, and because I'm married to you."

"Are you happy?"

"I'm ecstatic, gloriously so, and you?"

"I'm so happy, my heart is so full."

"Was it so important then, to get married?" Eve asked her seriously, pulling her close into an embrace.

"It turns out somehow it was. I wanted to somehow bind you to me forever."

"I was already bound to you, but I wanted this too, for both of us. You and me against the world."

"You make it sound so dramatic," Bernadette laughed.

"Kiss me, my darling wife."

"I will..."

Nothing more was said for quite some time.

* * *

After a late start in the morning, and breakfast with all those who had stayed, people began to drift away until at last, it was just the four friends, Bernadette, Eve, Imogen and D'Arcy.

"God I'm worn out," said D'Arcy as they flopped in her living room.

"We've got some gifts to open yet," Eve told Bernadette who was similarly laying back at ease on one of the sofas.

"Oh goodness, yes, we should have done it while everyone was here," she said at once contrite.

"We will write them pretty thank you notes," said Eve practically, "But we should open them just the same."

"They're in a living room downstairs," said D'Arcy, "I had them brought in last night."

They all repaired to the aforementioned room, where the gifts were laid out on a table at the side. There were several envelopes too. Eve and Bernadette spent a happy few minutes opening the cards and reading them out, and then all of the gifts. These were very tasteful and not too ostentatious. It seemed people had been asked to give something personal rather than practical, and they had done so. It was not as if they were setting up home, and they had all the usual things couples need already. There were ornaments, pictures and other mementoes which would mean something to them both.

"How lovely, these all are," said Bernadette as they got to the end.

"There's erm, actually one more," said Imogen, handing them a rather thick envelope, "It's from D'Arcy and me."

"Oh God!" Bernadette exclaimed, "But you've done so much already."

"*You've* done so much, darling, over the years, you have no idea. All of this time being our friend, both of you. This is something you deserve, and you *will* accept it. It's something you both need and I know you won't do it otherwise."

With this cryptic utterance, Eve urged Bernadette to open the envelope. When she did so, Bernadette burst into tears. It was a fully paid holiday to Phuket including first class return flights.

"Oh God..." she sobbed, "It's so nice of you... oh... oh goodness... I can't believe it... I... but this must have..."

"Hush," said Eve putting a finger on Bernadette's lips, "Remember the rules."

"Yes, you're right, sorry," Bernadette said as Eve wiped away her tears, "I'm so grateful, we both are."

"It's gay friendly," said Imogen smiling, "We checked, and honestly we felt it was the best present we could give you."

"It's more than just the best, it's, well, it's just... I'm over the moon... so thoughtful and so generous... thank you..."

On impulse, Bernadette jumped up, she hugged and kissed Imogen, and then D'Arcy who was beaming at their pleasure.

"Imogen let me indulge myself on this one," said D'Arcy, "And believe me I have, wait until you see the hotel."

"Thank you again, so much!"

Eve embraced them both too kissing them both soundly.

"You can go right after this court case," said Imogen, "In fact, I'm ordering you to."

Bernadette laughed. "OK."

"See, she does everything I tell her," Imogen quipped.

Eventually, the day came to an end, and their things were packed away in D'Arcy's car so that Carragh could drive them home. Teams of people had also been packing up the contents of the marquee in the meantime, and D'Arcy said they would be taking it away on Monday morning.

They had spent the rest of the day talking, relaxing, reminiscing and swimming. When it all came to a close D'Arcy was in floods of tears as they said goodbye.

"Oh, D'Arcy, I'm the one who should be crying," said Bernadette giving her a hug.

"I know but well, it was so lovely, and I hate it when things come to an end."

"But we'll see you soon."

"You can take me to lunch," Eve told her hugging too and giving her a kiss, "This week."

"Oh yes!" D'Arcy brightened up, "I know just the place."

Their last view was D'Arcy and Imogen hugging each other and waving goodbye.

"I'm sorry it's over too, in a way," said Bernadette a little sadly as the limo pulled out of the driveway and into the road.

"We've got our whole lives ahead of us, together, and a wonderful holiday to look forward to," Eve said relaxing back into the cushions.

"I know, I didn't know what to say when I opened the envelope, it was so generous, beyond generous."

"Love isn't counted in Euros, darling, but in the actions and gestures which give another pleasure no matter the cost," Eve pronounced sagely.

"You always know the right thing to say."

"I try."

Bernadette's hand stole across to take Eve's in hers and hold it fast. She closed her eyes and let all the happiness of the last two days seep through her like a balm to her oft troubled soul.

CHAPTER FOURTEEN

With the wedding behind them, Bernadette turned her attention to the court case. The hearing date was looming ever closer, and they needed to prepare the submissions and filing of any evidence. The next two weeks would be crucial in gathering what they need and getting it into the court on time.

On the Monday after the wedding, Imogen was drinking coffee with Bernadette in her office.

"Have you recovered?" Imogen asked, taking a sip of her drink.

"Yes, kind of, it was a lovely day, one of the best days of my life to be honest. I never thought I'd say so but it's true," Bernadette replied with a smile.

"Do you feel… different?" Imogen cocked an eyebrow at her.

"It's funny but I do, and so does Eve. I feel somehow more connected and it's as if a weight was lifted off my shoulders."

"The worry she was going to leave you?"

Imogen was nothing if not perspicacious.

"Yes, exactly."

"You know it was all in your head though, right?"

"Yes, I do, but because we said those things, our vows, and we made that commitment, it just feels, I don't know, more secure, if it makes sense?" Bernadette sighed.

"It does and I'm not trying to rain on your parade, I was just trying to go over it in my own head, considering I'm going to go through the same thing in a few months."

"Don't tell me you are getting cold feet, because I'm going to be very cross with you," Bernadette said at once.

"No, not cold feet, just wondering if it makes that much difference. It's why I wanted to know from you."

"Well, it does. You know it does legally for a start. For you, that is a huge issue considering D'Arcy's position. I don't mean to be mercenary, but you are my friend and I want you to be protected, I'm sure D'Arcy does too."

"I know *that*! But I wanted to understand the emotional part of it better."

"Emotionally I just feel more settled, secure. I feel as if we've solemnised our commitment which we have. It doesn't change my feelings, but it has strengthened our bond. I got to say the things which I needed to say formally, officially and in front of everyone, and so did Eve."

"What you did and said was truly wonderful," Imogen agreed, "I cried, D'Arcy cried, we all did. There is no doubt it was a fabulous day all round. I wouldn't have missed it for the world."

"You were very much part of it, and I'm so grateful to you, both of you."

"It's nothing, believe me. If you're thinking of the financial stuff which you should not be, then forget it. Don't ever give Eve a hard time about it either, promise me that. If you ever do find out, and you probably will, who paid for what, then you need to let it go. I need you to promise me this one thing."

Imogen sounded so sincere, that as much as Bernadette was curious, she never wanted to upset her friends. They had undoubtedly covered a lot of the costs of the wedding. She didn't know how she could repay their kindness but knew somehow, she needed to for the sake of her own peace of mind. If not financially, then some other way, of which she wasn't certain.

"I know exactly what you're thinking," said Imogen cutting into Bernadette's musings, "And let me remind you that without you, D'Arcy would not have won her libel case, and without you, I wouldn't have been with D'Arcy and found the love of my life. Those are just two things I've thought of, and I'm sure there are many more. You don't owe me or D'Arcy anything, we are your friends, we love you, so much, you and Eve too."

"I know, I can't help worry and I'm sorry, I know I should not." Tears sprang to Bernadette's eyes.

"You know you are a very rare thing, a jewel. We all know it, darling, and we cherish you. Without you there would be no law firm, none of us would have jobs, Eve wouldn't have launched her art career. I would never have found you and been your friend. I've never talked like this before, but you need to be told for your own sake."

"Where did I find a friend like you?" Bernadette said wiping her hand across her eyes.

"Come here, come to Imogen." She took Bernadette in her arms, as she had many times before, and Bernadette cried softly into Imogen's shoulder.

"Let it all out, darling, you're tired, you've had an emotional weekend," Imogen said softly stroking her hair.

Bernadette nodded clinging to her friend. It was cathartic and after a while, she felt better and sat up.

"OK?" Imogen said gently.

"Yes. Thank you. I do feel better. God, I'm forever crying on your shoulder."

"That's what friends are for. Now, do you promise to let this go about the money?"

"Yes, yes I do." Bernadette nodded.

"Good." Imogen smiled. "And if you don't, I'm going to tell Eve, then you'll be in trouble."

Bernadette laughed. "Oh don't, I'll be up in the bedroom for an hour with my hands on the wall."

Imogen laughed too. "How awful, I'm not sure I could do it either."

"Are things OK, with you and D'Arcy?" Bernadette asked, changing the subject.

"Yes, I acted like a bitch as you know. She accepted my apology. I offered her the paddle, but she declined to use it, thank goodness. She said she would only consider it if I did something really bad."

"Oh my God, what's really bad?"

"I don't know. And I don't want to find out either."

They laughed at this and Bernadette felt better, lighter. She had to let things go, she knew it, and she determined not to worry about the cost of the wedding again or who had paid for any of it. The universe would set the balance right if needed, Eve had always told her this, and she had to trust her wife's innate wisdom.

"So, turning back to work," said Imogen with a sigh, "What's the plan?"

"We need to finalise what we're going to do about Callum's affidavit. I think we have to go ahead with texts, as we said, and put it in at the last minute. It won't give them time to marshal their defences too much."

These were standard lawyer games. Going at the last minute was a trick many used to prevent the opposition from reacting to it. Bernadette wasn't above these types of strategies when it was warranted.

"OK, and we'll file Anh's affidavit?"

"Yes, we can do that, give them something to chew on, we need to make the arrangements for her to video conference for the hearing."

"I'll talk to Damsa."

"Then there's Olivia, maybe Brogan will have given them some help to move things forward."

"Yes. Let's hope. See if she gets in contact."

"We need to prep up the questions for cross examination."

"OK, it all seems straightforward now."

"I think we'll be in good shape for the hearing. There's not much else we can do but go in guns blazing."

Imogen laughed at this analogy. "I guess if you put it that way."

"It's the only way, darling. We have to destroy their witness and their case, if we can."

"I'll get onto Micky and we can sort out the texts, maybe we should go through them ourselves."

"Perhaps we should, if they are on the server."

"I'll talk to Micky."

"OK, darling, well, we'd better get on with it I suppose."
"Yes, indeed."

Imogen got up from the sofa, took the coffee cups and left the office. Bernadette reached for her phone, she wanted to send her wife a text. The thought of it sent chills down her spine. Eve was *her* wife, *hers*... for always. She smiled and composed a sexy but loving message.

* * *

By Friday, most of the preparation had been completed for the hearing, although they had not heard anything from Olivia. On her drive home, Bernadette wondered if this operation was going to be a write off as far as the hearing was concerned, in spite of Brogan's avowed intention to help it along. He wasn't a miracle worker, however, and in any case, the investigation may not assist them at all. She also wondered about Oisin but again, he had probably exerted as much influence over it as he could. The judge for the hearing was definitely annoyed by his interference and this had worked in favour of the defence.

One excellent outcome was the emergence of a campaign in the press supporting Callum and questioning why the UK was trying to extradite one of their citizens on flimsy evidence. A Facebook *Free Callum* page has been started up which was garnering much support. There was little to worry about justice wise since this was not a jury trial. Public opinion would be unlikely to influence the judge, but it was raising the stakes against Oisin's undercover shenanigans, and she hoped it might help to neutralise his efforts.

With that in mind, she pulled up at home, and went inside looking forward to seeing Eve. She wasn't disappointed and had just put her bag down when Eve bowled into the hallway almost knocking her off her feet.

"Oof," said Bernadette, "I'm glad you're pleased to see me."

She was silenced by her wife's eager kiss for several moments.

"Hello, my darling wife," said Eve smiling once their lips had parted.

"Hello back, my beautiful wife."

"I never get tired of saying that." Eve led her by the hand into the living room.

She gave Bernadette a glass of wine and sat down next to her on the sofa.

"So, how was your day?"

"Oh, nothing special, just prepping up for court and we're pretty much done. Not anything exciting, what about yours, darling?" Bernadette sipped her drink gratefully.

"Well, I," Eve announced, brimming with news, "Had lunch with D'Arcy."

"Oh? Somewhere nice?"

"Just her favourite, you know. Chapter One, downstairs in the basement. Private."

"And was it good?"

"Oh yes." Eve smiled a knowing smile. "Very good, we're best of friends now."

"Weren't you before?"

"But not like this," said Eve in conspiratorial tones.

"And I thought I was your best friend, especially now we're married," said Bernadette with a mock pout and a sotto voice.

"Oh, silly, next to you, of course. You're my very bestest of friends, my lover, my life, my everything..."

"I know, and I love it, I was joking," Bernadette laughed, "But what about Imogen, she's your best friend too, isn't she?"

"And Imogen, of course! Stop it! Darling, I'm trying to tell you something interesting," Eve said giggling.

"Sorry, I'll be quiet, go on." Bernadette pretended to put on a straight face and tried not to laugh.

"Well, anyway... she confided in me," said Eve with a secret smile.

"Oh? What about?" Bernadette was now interested and took another sip of wine.

"All about the *spanking*," Eve said dramatically.

"Oh... really?" Bernadette raised an eyebrow.

"Yes, yes, she had been wanting to tell someone."

"What did she say? Doesn't she like it or something?"

"Oh no, she loves it. I mean, not totally while it's happening, but she assured me she really does like it."

"Oh, oh I see." Bernadette was doubtful hearing this but waited for Eve to tell her some more.

"Yes, she told me how it all started, you know after she kissed me in the courtroom. Imogen was very angry with her, she said. She was scared Imogen would leave her but instead, well, you know what happened."

"That was really the first time?"

"Yes, and she said how it felt almost cathartic. You know she's oblivious sometimes to other people's feelings, and she said Imogen had taught her to become more attentive, caring, paying more attention to how Imogen feels."

"And all this across Imogen's knee?"

"She said so." Eve shrugged.

"She found it helpful?"

Eve chuckled. "Well, in a manner of speaking, but she said it also makes her as horny as fuck."

"There we are then, that's a payoff, I guess it's a win-win."

"Yes."

"And presumably you told her about us in reciprocation?"

"Of course, how could I not? You tell Imogen everything. She knew about the Shibari anyway, she's seen us having sex while I was tied up." Eve's tone was a little challenging.

"I know, and it's OK. Don't look at me like *that*. This was bound to come out in the end. We are all good friends after all. It couldn't remain a secret forever."

"Yes, sorry. I didn't mean to be defensive."

"Don't be silly. It was probably a big deal to D'Arcy to confide in you."

"Yes. It was, I think she feels the need of a friend, you know, not just Imogen."

"You're right, and it's your right to have a friend to talk to apart from me, and I accept that."

"As long as you're not... jealous," Eve said tentatively.

"No, no I'm not, silly."

"Thank you."

Eve put out her hand and took Bernadette's in hers.

"So, you'll be doing lunch with her a bit more often?"

"I think so, yes, and shopping sometimes."

"That's great, I think it's a good thing. And can I tell Imogen that you know about their secret?"

"I guess so. I mean, I'm sure D'Arcy knows I'll tell you because I tell you everything... well, most of the time, but from now on, you know what I mean." Eve coloured up.

"Put it in the past, we said no more secrets and we meant it."

"Yes." Eve nodded.

"So, what should we do now?"

"Dinner?"

"Mmm, and let's have a relaxing weekend, just you and me. Especially after the one we've had."

"We will, I've made you Stroganoff."

"Oh God, sex on a plate..."

"Followed by sex off the plate."

Bernadette laughed and allowed Eve to pull her up and take her to the dining room.

* * *

The weekend passed in a lazy fashion. They went out for a run, and then a walk on the beach had lunch at a country pub. Eve spent time drawing, and Bernadette watched her lazily from the sofa. She didn't really feel like doing anything much except enjoying Eve's company. She had also recently rekindled a taste for romance novels and was making her way through Jane Austen. It was perhaps the wedding which had precipitated this mood.

On Monday, she was back in the office with Imogen, for their morning chat.

"How was the weekend with the family?" Bernadette asked sipping her coffee as usual.

"Oh, God, don't... just don't," Imogen said dramatically with her hand across her brow, "It was fucking exhausting."

"Was it so bad?" Bernadette cocked an eye.

"It was better than I expected but they just kept on asking so many questions about us, how did we meet, when did I find out I was gay, on and on and on like a fucking bunch of Torquemadas or something," Imogen said crossly.

"Oh dear." Bernadette was sympathetic, she knew Imogen had been dreading it.

"It's my fault really." Imogen sipped her coffee. "I hadn't told them anything, so they would be curious at the very least, I just didn't expect then to be *that* fucking curious."

"How did D'Arcy get on with them?"

"Oh, they *love* D'Arcy. D'Arcy the wonder woman entertained them for hours with stories about her life in the movies. They watched two of her films in the theatre. Swam in the pool, all that stuff."

"So really it wasn't *that* bad."

"No, D'Arcy likes them. She thought my mum was very sweet, and my dad too. My sister and my brother were there, asking all manner of awkward questions."

"You know I've never met your family," Bernadette said suddenly, "What a terrible friend I must be."

"No, you're not," Imogen protested, "Why should you? I don't really like them all that much if I'm honest. I never made a big deal of it."

"Why? Were they mean to you or something?"

"No, nothing like that, it's just I suppose nothing was ever good enough for them." There was a bitter note to Imogen's voice.

"Oh."

"I don't feel they ever supported me. My mother and father really wanted me to get married I think, not become a barrister."

"What about your siblings?"

Imogen sighed. "Oh well, they're both a lot older than me, I was an afterthought. My sister is ten years older and my brother twelve years older. They weren't even at home for that many years. Just when I was growing up and then they were gone. I felt like an only child. Just me. A mum and dad who never really wanted me. Accidental Imogen they called me. Their little accident."

"Oh, Imogen, I'm so sorry."

Imogen shook her head. "Oh no, I'm over it. Fuck that. It made me stronger and more determined to do well and show those fuckers what I am made of."

"Well, you certainly showed them now!"

"Oh, they were impressed alright by all the finery, of course. The money, it talks their language."

"Were they... did they?" Bernadette didn't know how to say it.

Imogen filled in the blanks, "Embarrassing? Vulgar? No, thank God. They were quite circumspect really. Though I'll no doubt become the favourite child or sister when they want something."

Bernadette laughed. "Give them nice presents at Christmas, that will keep them happy."

"Oh fuck, Christmas, what am I going to do then? They'll want me to invite them, oh God."

"You don't have to, of course, why not have them the weekend before," Bernadette said reasonably.

"I want you and Eve to come for Christmas. The four of us to spend it together. I don't want anybody else. I mean, I know it's a long time away, and it's not fair of me asking you and..."

"We'd love to come," Bernadette exclaimed at once, "I'm sure Eve will agree."

"Oh, fantastic, wait until I tell D'Arcy. How exciting. Oh, it's going to be so lovely. D'Arcy is going to be so happy."

Bernadette smiled.

"There you go. Oh, and there's something I should tell you," Bernadette began.

Imogen cut her short, "D'Arcy told Eve about our games, yes I know. D'Arcy told me."

Bernadette let out a sigh of relief.

"Well, I hope you don't mind."

Imogen shrugged. "Why should I? it's not a secret now so that's quite good really. I can be more open, all of us can."

"As long as you're OK with it."

"It had to come from D'Arcy, and it has."

"So, we're all good?"

"Yes, we are."

Bernadette smiled, reached out and squeezed Imogen's hand affectionately. She wondered what being more open entailed but did not like to ask. She felt quite strongly some things were best kept behind closed doors.

Just then Alison put her head around the door.

"That detective, Olivia, the one who likes the tea, she's here to see you, I've put her in the meeting room complete with... tea."

"Oh, you're a gem, darling, an absolute gem," said Bernadette.

"I guess we'd better go and say hello, see what she wants." Imogen stood.

Bernadette paused for a moment. "Alison, I've been meaning to say we've got the go ahead to get another PA, so we need to prep up some adverts, you know. Sorry with everything that's been going on, I just didn't..."

"Oh, good, it's fine, honestly," Alison said, "I'll liaise with Andrew, put something together, run it by you."

"Great."

"I'll get you two some coffees," said Alison as they went to the meeting room.

Olivia was sitting at her usual place on the sofa stirring her tea. She was looking very pretty, Bernadette thought, wearing a black suit, court shoes and a light pink blouse.

"Ah," she said, looking up at them, "Good to see you again after such a wonderful occasion at the weekend."

"I'm glad you enjoyed it," said Bernadette as they took a seat.

"I'm glad *you* enjoyed it, both of you. A stunning pair and beautiful ceremony, well, all of it really."

Olivia nonchalantly sipped her tea. Alison came in briefly to hand them their coffees.

"So, anyway, I didn't come here to talk about your wedding, as pleasant as it was," said Oliva when Alison had gone.

"OK." Bernadette sipped her coffee and waited for Olivia to come to the point.

"Your case, well, my case really. Balik Transport."

"Yes," said Bernadette sitting up a little.

"It seems some important people suddenly took a great interest in them." Olivia sipped her tea and delicately took a biscuit from the plate thoughtfully provided by Alison.

"Oh?" Bernadette said innocently, while Imogen could not resist a slight smirk.

"Yes, they did, all of a sudden, out of the blue. You wouldn't happen to know about it would you?" Olivia shot Bernadette a questioning glance.

"I... err..." Bernadette demurred and hid her face behind her coffee mug.

"A certain DCS Jack Brogan seems to have become personally involved, so I'm told. The same Jack Brogan who was at your wedding, I believe."

"She's not a detective for nothing, the game's up, darling," Imogen giggled.

"Fine, fine, you got me, yes I spoke to Brogan, not just about *that* though," Bernadette laughed.

"Oh?"

"Yes, erm... there's a politician who..."

"Oisin Kavanaugh, been running riot all over the Garda, and wants to make sure Callum Jenkins goes to the UK," Olivia interrupted her.

"She's good, so very good," said Imogen.

"I make it my business to keep my eyes and ears open. That's how you survive in the Garda."

"I guess it's your job."

"Anyway, as I was saying, the transport thing suddenly went right up the priority list. Surveillance orders got signed, the lot," Olivia continued, taking some more tea.

"Well, it was a good thing surely?" Bernadette said with a smile.

"I'm not complaining, no. In fact, I'm pretty happy about it, as it goes."

"That's good."

"I did not know you had friends in such high places."

Bernadette said in a slightly apologetic tone, "I got to know Jack through another case, he's a really nice man."

"I don't blame you for using your contacts. He has a top unit, doesn't he? The Foxcatchers?"

"Yes, I believe he does."

"So, you know, if it ever comes up in conversation, and he says he's looking for new detectives... well..." Olivia tailed off, but the meaning was clear enough.

"I'll bear it in mind, if it does."

Now Bernadette understood perfectly where Olivia was coming from. The Foxcatchers was a different style of unit by all accounts, run by DI Gallway who was known to be an excellent leader. Many detectives would have liked to work on his team if they could. Bernadette was well aware Olivia wasn't a big fan of her current boss and would welcome a change.

Olivia inclined her head, drained her cup and came to the point. "The thing is, and it can't go beyond this room, we're about to raid them, Balik Trading. This week. I can't say more, but naturally, something may eventuate which may assist you. That's all I'm saying, and I shouldn't be telling you anything at all... but you've done me a favour, well, more than one, so..."

"If I need you to testify, will you?" Bernadette asked her at once.

"Yes, of course."

"Will the judge..." Imogen said.

"Allow it? If we insist there is relevant testimony then, yes, I think so," Bernadette replied.

"The hearing is next Monday," Imogen said practically.

"Look if there is anything, anything at all you can use, I will contact you right away," said Olivia.

"Thanks."

"Anyway, that's all I came to say, thanks for the tea, and thanks again for the invite to the wedding."

"Maybe one day we'll come to yours?" Imogen ventured.

"Chance would be a fine thing," Olivia snorted.

"Well, anyway, D'Arcy and I will be getting married and I would like you to come."

"That's kind of you. And I accept in advance of course."

"I'm not sure when it will be, but anyway."

"I'm going anywhere." Olivia laughed getting up. "I can see myself out. I'll be in touch."

After she left, Bernadette turned to Imogen.

"You're really inviting her to your wedding?"

"Yes, why not?"

"I thought you weren't her biggest fan, to be honest," Bernadette said candidly.

"Oh well, I think it's time I buried the hatchet, and I did that weeks ago after we took her to lunch. She's not trying to surreptitiously hit on me anymore." Imogen shrugged.

437

"I don't think she really was trying to hit on you, darling."

"She wanted to."

"Yes, that's true. But then who wouldn't?" Bernadette raised an eyebrow.

"I agree, I mean, I'm quite a catch. D'Arcy thinks so." Imogen pretended to preen herself like a particularly fine bird.

"Well, you are, of course."

"Do you think this raid will help us with the case?" Imogen changed the subject.

"Hard to say, one can only hope."

"No matter, we've got this," Imogen said firmly.

"I'm glad one of us thinks so," Bernadette laughed.

"Come on, darling, lesbian bitch lawyers remember."

"You're right, we're going to do this."

"Love you."

"Love you too."

CHAPTER FIFTEEN

The week and the weekend passed by quickly, or so it seemed to Bernadette. It was the first day of the hearing. The alarm went off early, as she did not like to rush.

"Mmm," said Eve stretching in the bed and giving her a lazy kiss.

"Court today," said Bernadette.

"I know, you get up and have your shower, I'll put out your clothes."

"Thank you, my darling." Bernadette smiled and slid out of the bed.

She padded out of the bathroom and sat patiently while Eve straightened her hair. She always let Eve do what she wanted with her hair.

"We'll just make it straight, darling," said Eve, "Very lawyer like."

"Thank you, babe."

"Now, let me do your makeup."

Eve was very deft and quick with Bernadette's makeup. Eve said Bernadette didn't need much on and kept it quite natural. Once this was done, she left Bernadette to dress and went down to make breakfast.

Eve had laid out a black suit with a skirt, and a soft cream blouse. She put out a pair of black strappy sandals. On the first day, Eve liked to make sure Bernadette was formal until they knew how the case was going. There might be a need to be softer on occasion and dress appropriately.

After checking herself in the mirror, she went downstairs where Eve was just placing a plate of scrambled eggs, mushrooms, and bacon with toast on the breakfast bar. She sat down to eat, and Eve put a cup of coffee next to the plate. Eve took a seat beside her with her own breakfast.

"So, darling, are you OK? Not nervous?" Eve asked her.

"Not especially though this is my first extradition case."

"I'm sure it will go OK, honey."

"Yes, of course, it will. It's just the first day you know, I always dread them." Bernadette sliced into her eggs on toast.

"Aw, darling, you never said."

"I didn't want to worry you. It's just all in my head, you know." Bernadette took a mouthful of her breakfast.

"I'm your wife now, we tell each other everything, remember?" Eve chided her.

"I know. It's just the first day. It's like having a first day at school over and over again," Bernadette laughed.

"I'm sure it will go well, just like it always does," Eve said putting a hand on Bernadette's arm in reassurance.

"Yes, I'm sure. And you? Are you working today? Or going out with D'Arcy?"

"Oh, I've got plenty of drawing to do and you know we've got to get on with our gym, and the conservatory. I'm going to do some costings, get some quotes."

"You're so efficient, my love, I'm impressed. I mean, after the wedding you arranged, I'm sure you could anything."

"I've got some hidden talents." Eve smiled at the compliment.

"OK, well, I'm going to have to leave you to it." Bernadette drained her coffee and pushed away her plate.

Eve accompanied her to the door. They kissed goodbye, and Eve waved her off from the front door. Once she pulled out from the driveway, Bernadette's mind was on the hearing. She was mentally rehearsing and preparing for what was to come.

* * *

Bernadette picked up Imogen from the office, and they drove to the Criminal Courts of Justice. Callum and Rhys were to meet them inside the main court building. As they mounted the steps, there was a large contingent of press and down on the pavement quite a number of people waving placards demanding Callum's release.

"Well, looks like what you said worked," Imogen observed.

They had been watching their build up on Facebook. There were support groups on social media and lots of press about the forthcoming hearing. Oisin had featured somewhat prominently in the press urging that justice is seen to be done. It was clear from his stance that everyone knew he wanted the extradition to go ahead. However, some opposition MPs were also speaking out against it which was good. Reporters starting shouting questions as soon they neared the throng.

"Bernadette, what's your prediction for today?"

"Are you confident you can win?"

"Oisin Kavanaugh wants Callum to go to the UK, what do you say to that?"

Bernadette wasn't going to say anything, but this goaded her. She stopped briefly and spoke, "What I say is that justice needs to be done, and we are here to see that it is. Callum Jenkins is not involved in this crime and we intend to show that in court. Nobody should presume upon the courts and the justice system of Ireland. We want fairness, and we intend to get it. Thank you!"

She turned away ignoring the shouted queries and walked swiftly into the building with Imogen.

"Was that wise?" Imogen asked her once they were inside.

"Probably not," Bernadette laughed, "But I was provoked."

"Don't let them, that's what you always tell me."

"I know," Bernadette sighed, "But it was just some fighting words. Nothing too bad."

"No, darling, but you know, take care."

"Yes, mum."

Imogen laughed and they headed for the courtroom. Callum and Rhys were waiting outside for them.

"Any questions, before we go in?" Bernadette asked them.

"No, I think we're fine," Rhys said, and Callum nodded in agreement.

They had been to see them both for a final briefing the week before, so there was no real need to go to a meeting room.

"Right then." Bernadette smiled. "Let battle commence."

The courtroom was already filling up with press and public when they entered. Imogen made sure Rhys got a seat near the front, and then took Callum to stand in the dock. There was a court official to sit beside him during the hearing.

Imogen re-joined Bernadette who was getting out their papers and the court bundle containing all of the evidence on numbered pages. The judge would also have a copy of this and there would also be one in the witness box.

While they were preparing, Shane and Mason arrived and began to set up their station. They nodded in Bernadette and Imogen's direction. Bernadette accorded them a brief smile.

Very shortly after this, Imogen nudged Bernadette. She looked back and there was Oisin, having turned up like a bad penny. Bernadette pursed her lips, but his presence was only to be expected.

A few more moments went by and the Tipster entered the room. He called the court to order and they rose for the judge. Justice Brannigan entered the room and took his seat. Another glance at Oisin, Bernadette noted he was looking daggers. She had half expected to see another judge due to Oisin's interference but apparently, his influence did not quite extend that far.

After surveying the courtroom with what appeared to be his natural scowl he spoke, "Ah, so we are here for the hearing of the DDP versus Callum Jenkins, a matter of extradition to the United Kingdom."

He paused for a moment before continuing, "Now, I just want to address one small issue since it has come to my attention that there was apparently some discussion about me recusing myself from this hearing. I want to scotch any such rumours and state, I have no personal connection with any parties in this matter. I do not know Mr Callum Jenkins nor his father. This trial will be carried out with the proper and full impartiality expected by the justice system."

He fairly thundered out this statement all the while looking fixedly at Oisin. Bernadette had not heard any recusal rumours but the fact the judge felt he had to say it, meant there must have been yet a further attempt to replace him with someone more favourable to the outcome. Oisin Kavanagh did not look pleased.

"Now then. I recognise the parties before me today from the prehearing, am I right?"

"Yes, Judge," said Bernadette.

"Yes, Judge," said Shane.

"Excellent, so no need for further introductions, I have all your names here. Mr Jenkins, I see over there in the dock. Good. Now I remind the parties of the form of proceeding. This is not a jury trial, and the decision whether or not to extradite Mr Jenkins will be made by me. The prosecution and defence will make their initial submissions. We will then have witnesses from both sides and hear evidence as per usual. After which, there will be a further opportunity to make final submissions. I shall then deliver a judgement on the matter. Are we quite clear?"

He looked expectantly at the two sets of lawyers who both signified their agreement.

"Good, very good. We will take suitable breaks of course, and also have a lunch break."

He sighed, almost as if he wished they could have a lunch break already.

"Right, so if there are no questions, we can take the first submission from Mr Wilson."

Shane stood up, shuffled his papers on the mini podium in front of him. Took a quick look around the courtroom and began, "Judge, it is our submission that this case is as plain as it is simple. nineteen Vietnamese women were put onto a truck and concealed in flour barrels. This truck was driven by Mr Callum Jenkins whom you see over there in the dock."

The judge glared at him slightly, not impressed with the implication he was incapable of already knowing this. However, he forbore saying anything.

"We know he drove the truck, and in addition, we can bring forensic evidence to prove he did drive it."

"Has he denied driving it?" Justice Brannigan wanted to know.

"Well, no, but..."

"Right, carry on."

"As I was saying, *should* Mr Jenkins attempt to deny it, we have evidence that he did drive it. He brought it from a transport yard in Dublin across the channel to a depot in London where he left it. The Metropolitan Human Trafficking Squad subsequently raided the premises, along with immigration officers and apprehended the nineteen women who we understand were intended to be trafficked for sexual purposes which is, as I'm sure you know, illegal in the United Kingdom and also in this country. It carries a sentence of up to fourteen years in prison, and as such meets the conditions for extradition. In addition to being trafficked, they illegally entered the United Kingdom, and of course Ireland, plus many other countries on the way. This in itself is an offence of aiding and abetting illegal immigration."

He paused, to see how the submission was being received. However, the judge did not appear to be particularly moved by his speech so far.

"We also arrested an accomplice of Mr Jenkins, one Kevin Clinton, who has named Mr Jenkins as having been implicated in the trafficking, saying that he had full knowledge and is complicit in the crime. Mr Clinton will testify under oath to that effect. Based upon this testimony, we request that the extradition order is granted. Mr Jenkins will be charged with the offences mentioned by the police in London, and a prosecution brought against him. We contend natural justice should prevail in this matter, and the police in the United Kingdom should be free to pursue their prosecution of Mr Jenkins."

Shane coughed slightly as the judge fixed him with an unnerving stare. "We submit that the extradition order should be allowed, and Mr Jenkins be extradited to the United Kingdom."

He stopped abruptly. Bernadette reflected, when laid out like that in open court, it didn't sound as convincing as perhaps the prosecution thought it was.

"You understand our justice system has a presumption of innocence?" Justice Brannigan asked him in a deceptively mild tone.

"Yes, of course, Judge."

"Yet, your case seems to imply a presumption of guilt, wouldn't you say?"

Shane wasn't perhaps expecting the judge to be quite so direct. "Well..." he said, "Well... we want Mr Jenkins to be given the chance to prove his innocence in court as is only right and proper, if indeed he is. Unless the passage of justice is allowed to run its course, then how can we say if he's innocent or not?"

"Thus, assuming he's guilty," said the judge implacably.

"The police and prosecution service believe there is a strong case that he is involved in this crime, Judge, as we will seek to show during this hearing," Shane said sounding rattled.

"We will hear your arguments in due course, no doubt," said Justice Brannigan a little sardonically.

"Yes, Judge, this completes our opening submission." Shane sat down looking a little flustered.

"Mrs Mackenna?" Justice Brannigan said turning his attention to Bernadette.

"Yes, Judge." She stood up and waited.

"I hear you are to be congratulated, am I right? You were recently married, I believe?" He smiled.

"Yes, Judge, I was, thank you."

"We the judges are up on current affairs, contrary perhaps to certain popular opinion." The judge shot a sharp look in the direction of Oisin who glared back.

There were murmurs in the press throng as they seemed to cotton on something was going on behind the scenes of the hearing, although they didn't really know what.

"In any case," Justice Brannigan continued, "Let's hear the submission from the defence."

"Certainly, Judge," said Bernadette smiling, she glanced down at her papers. This wasn't a major opening speech, and so she dispensed with her usual court ritual. There was no jury and only the judge to appeal to. It would be a simpler affair altogether however she could not forbear to forgo Shakespeare entirely and hoped the judge would not decry it.

"Judge," she said, "The case for the defence rests upon our presumption and, indeed, assertion of the innocence of our client. The prosecution, other than on the say so of a witness who claims Mr Jenkins was involved in the crime of trafficking, has brought nothing concrete to prove their case."

She stopped noting the judge was attentive to her words.

"The great bard himself wrote this and I quote: 'Since what I am to say must be but that which contradicts my accusation and the testimony on my part no other but what comes from myself, it shall scarce boot me, to say 'not guilty', mine integrity being counted falsehood, shall, as I express it, be so received. But thus: if powers divine behold our human actions, as they do, I doubt not then but innocence shall make false accusation blush and tyranny tremble at patience.'"

The judge looked a little askance at this reference but continued to listen carefully.

"What I'm trying to say, Judge, is that Mr Jenkins does profess his innocence. It is his word against the prosecution's witness. From the prosecution standpoint, they are in fact saying that my client is a liar. But we, the defence, place our reliance on you, to judge, as the effective power divine in this courtroom, whether or not it is the case, and we believe you will judge our client to be truthful. Moreover, surely the case to extradite Mr Jenkins must be proven beyond reasonable doubt. We say that there is reasonable doubt. Our own witness will cast the shadow of doubt even further upon this case. We intend to show through cross examination that the testimony of the prosecution's main witness is flawed, and that he is the one who is lying, and not Mr Jenkins."

She paused, glancing at Imogen who gave her an encouraging smile.

"The prosecution is not working from a presumption of innocence at all. They want to get our client to the United Kingdom to charge and begin a prosecution against him. However, we suggest that they also want to interrogate him and build a stronger case against him than they currently have. Mr Jenkins is an Irish citizen. A citizen of this country and he has rights. We contend that an Irish court should not extradite one of our citizens unless there is undeniable proof he has committed or is implicated in the offence they want to charge him with. They do not have that proof and we submit that the extradition order should be refused."

"A laudable speech, Mrs Mackenna," said the judge, "You are right to indicate there is a burden of proof, and let's see if it exists. Your reference to Shakespeare is apt, although I am not appointed here by divine intervention, however, we will let that pass as poetic license."

He chuckled a little at his own joke, and Shane Wilson looked annoyed. It did not seem to Bernadette that the judge was overstepping his impartiality, however.

449

"Thank you, Judge," she said sitting down, well satisfied with the result.

It had not been a long speech, but there was no need in this case for too many words. Her opening speeches were usually more dramatic and telling, but the case rested on the testimony of the witnesses and what she could do to damage the prosecution's case.

"I think we have time to begin the witnesses before morning break," said the judge, "Mr Wilson, call your first witness."

"I call Detective Chief Inspector Harold Graham," said Shane.

The clerk of the court repeated the call, and shortly DCI Harold Graham entered the court. He was around forty years of age, with grey thinning hair. He was a slim man with a blue suit and black shoes, a white shirt and blue tie. He looked every inch a professional police officer. He took the stand, swore the usual oath and stated his name and rank in the Metropolitan Police Force.

"DCI Graham," said Shane, "You are the Senior Investigating Officer on the trafficking case, is that correct?"

"Yes, it is," said Graham, he had a slightly northern twang which probably meant he started out in a force in the Midlands in the UK.

"Can you give us a rundown of the operation from your perspective?"

"Yes, we have had the yard under surveillance for some time with undercover officers in place. We received intelligence that there was a consignment of people coming in to be trafficked. We knew they were destined to end up in criminalised illegal brothels."

"Just a moment, did you say consignment? Is that what you said?" Justice Brannigan interrupted.

"Yes, Judge, I did." Graham wasn't fazed by the question.

"These are people aren't they, and yet you're referring to them as if they were merely goods or chattels."

This was a pointed question and the judge looked somewhat put out to hear such seemingly callous language.

"Yes, Judge, of course, they are, and it's just jargon."

"Somewhat demeaning jargon, wouldn't you say, Detective Chief Inspector?" said the judge in slightly acidic tones.

"Judge, I do apologise, we certainly don't regard it that way, we take a very serious view of this type of crime and are very sympathetic to the women concerned." Graham was very smooth in his delivery, Bernadette mused, he had obviously been in court on many occasions.

"Very well, carry on, Mr Wilson," said Justice Brannigan sounding slightly mollified by the explanation.

"So, you apprehended these women, did you?" said Shane.

"We took them into protective custody, and they are now being handled as refugees," said Graham.

"And, you're going to use them as witnesses, in the case?"

"It's a potential idea but unlikely since they are understandably reluctant to talk to the police. They still have families in Vietnam and are afraid of retribution," Graham replied somewhat offhandedly.

"Right, in any case, having discovered the refugees, did you also make other arrests?"

"Yes, we did."

"How did you come by those people?"

"They were either present during the raid, or we arrested them afterwards. Most of them were released either on bail or because they had nothing to do with the crime," Graham said in matter of fact tones.

"You did not arrest Callum Jenkins, however?" Shane injected a note of surprise in his tone, although in reality, he knew this was the case.

"No, we didn't at the time."

"Why was that?"

"The raid was carried out after he had dropped off the transport. By the time we tried to locate him, he had left the country."

"I see, and the timing of the raid was because?"

Shane was leading him through it without seeming to do so, in the manner that was required when questioning your own witnesses on the stand.

"We had to be sure that the cargo, sorry, Judge, the refugees, were safely in the depot. They had remained in the truck for some time and we wanted to catch them unloading it which we did."

Graham corrected himself as soon as he saw the sharp look from the judge when he said 'cargo.' Bernadette wondered how much they really did care about the refugees but kept the thoughts to herself.

"And the unloading was some time after the drop off, to be clear?"

"Yes, yes it was."

"So, Mr Jenkins had already left the country."

"Yes."

It was important for Shane to establish a desire the arrest Callum and a clear reason why they hadn't, rather than make them appear incompetent.

"Can you explain why you want to arrest him and question him?"

"I can indeed. We arrested a Mr Kevin Clinton who is known to the police. He has previous convictions for petty crime, and we know he is connected to or at least does work for a syndicate. After his arrest, he agreed to become a prosecution witness in return for a possible reduced sentence or witness protection."

"He agreed to give evidence against some of his associates, am I right?"

"Yes, he did."

"One of whom is Mr Jenkins?"

"We believe so, yes."

"And why do you believe that?"

"Mr Clinton made a statement to that effect, giving us times and dates he had met him. We confirmed these from phone records. We also have forensic evidence proving Mr Jenkins did drive the truck. We obtained fingerprints from the Garda when he was arrested here, and we've since matched them to those taken from the truck."

"Indeed," said Shane glossing lightly over this since the judge had already taken a dim view of using this as evidence.

It occurred to Bernadette they surely must therefore have seen the content of Callum's texts and noted they were in a relationship. She suspected they would attempt to play this down, and also it indicated why the phone records had not been provided in evidence. She decided to play that card.

"Objection, Judge, the phone records mentioned by the witness were not provided in evidence," she said jumping up.

"Mr Wilson?" Justice Brannigan raised an eyebrow.

"Judge, if I could confer with my colleague?" said Shane looking flustered.

The judge shrugged and gave him a slight smile.

There was a whispered conversation between Shane and Mason, before Shane stood up.

"Judge, the records were simply used to show that there was a connection between the two, and not considered material evidence in the case for extradition," he said.

This was a bluff, and he knew it. Bernadette was sure by rights they should have provided them.

"But they were meant to support your assertions about the connection and so I would suggest they are material evidence."

"Yes, Judge," said Shane unhappily.

"Very well, however in order not to delay things, I leave it to the defence counsel to let me know if they wish these records to be provided. Mrs Mackenna, what say you?"

"We will let you know, Judge, at this point I'm uncertain and need to consider it."

This gave her the opportunity to change her mind, should she need to do so. In reality, she felt they were unnecessary, but she wanted to embarrass the opposition, and she had succeeded in that aim.

"Right, then I leave it to you, but raise it in good time if needed," said the judge, "Mr Wilson, you may continue."

Shane inclined his head and was no doubt happy at the lucky escape. He resumed his questioning of Graham.

"Do you have any other reason to suspect Mr Jenkins is involved?"

"There is CCTV footage of him driving the truck in and handing it over obviously."

"So, you feel he would have known the contents of his cargo?"

This was pure supposition, Bernadette knew it. Simply presenting events in such a way that the explanation seemed plausible.

"We certainly believe so, yes. It would be common practice for drivers to be aware of what they are carrying in case they are questioned at customs."

"Why do you think Mr Clinton is, in fact, telling the truth?"

"Because he has no reason to lie, we've already caught him, and he knows we could prosecute him for the crime. He's got nothing to lose by naming other names."

"I see."

Shane thought for a moment, and then evidently decided he had asked enough. In his view, he would feel he had established his case.

"No further questions, Judge," he said.

"Thank you, Mr Wilson," said Justice Brannigan, looking at his watch, "Ms Mackenna, do you have many questions? And if so, perhaps we'll take a short break."

"I have a few, Judge," said Bernadette unable to know exactly how long her cross examination might take.

"In that case, we'll have a break," said the judge, summoning the Tipster.

* * *

455

In a meeting room, Bernadette and Imogen were sipping coffee. They had a brief word with Rhys and Callum, and told them to sit tight, since it was early days. So far there wasn't anything unexpected at all.

"What do you reckon?" Imogen ventured after a moment.

"So far so good, I guess. I've got a chance now to try and go on the attack with the good inspector."

"Yes, he didn't present a compelling argument."

"Their case is not compelling," said Bernadette, "And yet here we are. Uncontested he would be on his way to London for sure. His denial alone isn't enough to sway the judge. After all, what they have is circumstantial but not conclusive evidence he was involved or might have been."

Bernadette took another sip of her coffee.

"They already know about the gay relationship don't they," Imogen said acidly.

"Oh yes, and they wouldn't want it brought up in court, but now they know we're going to."

"We should have thought about the phone records."

"Yes, but they should have put them into evidence, they did not want to for the very reason it undermines their case."

"Fuckers," said Imogen crossly.

"That's why we are here, to ensure Shane plays fair."

"I'd give him something to play fair about," Imogen growled.

"Are you still, you know?" Bernadette cocked an eyebrow.

"Oh, no. I've buried those fantasies, in fact, prolonged contact with him is working like an antidote," Imogen laughed.

"That's good."

"Yes, he's just a fucking arrogant prick and one who doesn't really respect women either."

"Do you think so? I mean, the not respecting part?"

"He didn't respect me."

"In what way?" said Bernadette looking concerned.

"Oh, not like that, he didn't do anything without my consent, if that's what you're thinking. But I don't think he cared for me either, as a woman."

"More as a chattel?" Bernadette smiled sardonically.

"Yes, a bit like that. He fancies himself as a bit of a Christian Gray and not just the S and M part, but I think the big powerful 'I am' who lords it over his subjects or something." Imogen gave a scornful laugh.

"Yes, perhaps you're right. Anyway, so far, the judge is not impressed. I'd say."

"No." Imogen glanced at her watch. "It's nearly time, I need the loo first."

"I'll join you," said Bernadette getting up.

* * *

Court resumed with the Tipster announcing Justice Brannigan, who came in looking a little more relaxed and less forbidding than before. Perhaps tea was a restorative for the judge, Bernadette mused. Besides the hearing was now in progress and whatever interference Oisin could attempt would now be minimal. She glanced around the courtroom, but he wasn't in evidence. She shrugged thinking perhaps he had become fed up with the way things were panning out.

"Now then, Mrs Mackenna, I believe it's your turn with the DCI, is it not?" the judge said amiably.

"Yes, that's right." Bernadette stood up and studied her notes for a moment before commencing. "DCI Graham, did you at any time previous to the raid in question suspect Mr Jenkins of being involved in human trafficking?"

"No, no we didn't," Graham replied.

"I see. So, it was only after the raid, that you formed the opinion that he was involved, am I right?"

"It was more than just an opinion," Graham countered.

"Was it? How was it more than an opinion?"

"For the reasons I've previously stated when we questioned Mr Clinton, he named Mr Jenkins as a key suspect, and we know Mr Jenkins drove the truck."

"Yes, so you said. Although without concrete evidence of Mr Jenkin's involvement, it could be said that it is only an opinion, couldn't it?"

"No, I don't agree, that's not how we work. We don't arrest people just on opinions," said Graham sounding a little annoyed.

She left the topic since there was no real mileage in the line of questioning, it was more an attempt to sound him out, see how he would respond. However, it had served to soften him up a little, and perhaps unnerve him.

"Now you also said that forensic evidence, CCTV and so on, showed he drove the truck, am I right?"

"Yes, yes that's right."

"But, that evidence, in fact, any evidence you have or really, you don't have, doesn't show Mr Jenkins was directly involved in the trafficking apart from one statement from a source who is himself a convicted criminal. Isn't that true?" She was starting to zero in on him, and he knew it.

"I don't feel it's quite true. His presence and the evidence he was there, is a pointer to his involvement."

"A pointer? I don't think so, that's an assumption, not a pointer surely, don't you agree?"

"No, I don't," Graham shot back.

"But the reality is that none of those things, other than the statement of your witness, directly connect Mr Jenkins to the crime, yes or no?"

"Well..." Graham hesitated.

"Yes or no, DCI Graham?" she said it more forcefully this time.

He paused thinking it over. She had trapped him, however, since there was only one answer.

"Not directly, no," he said at length.

"Thank you," said Bernadette smiling at him rather like a panther might smile at a young deer in its sights. "Now, you claimed, did you not? That there was no reason for Mr Clinton to lie. You said he wouldn't lie because he had nothing to lose, is that correct?"

"Yes, that's correct."

Bernadette settled herself in to go for the throat. She began quite gently.

"But surely there is every reason for him to lie. If he can implicate someone else in the crime then he would get himself off the hook, wouldn't he? So, he could very well be lying to save his own skin. Couldn't he?"

"That's not how it works." Graham said this rather emphatically as if he felt he was on solid ground.

However, Bernadette was rather laying another trap into which she hoped he would fall.

"Oh? Is it not? Then please enlighten us as to how it *does* work." This was tinged with slight sarcasm but not too much, since the judge might object.

"If he lied and Mr Jenkins was innocent then we would still prosecute Mr Clinton and he knows it. So, unless he gives us a genuine suspect then his own safety is by no means guaranteed," Graham said triumphantly.

"But your whole case hinges around Mr Clinton's testimony does it not?" She floated this question like a lure, hoping he would bite.

"At the moment but we believe that is sufficient. However, when Mr Jenkins is properly questioned then we believe more evidence will be forthcoming and will simply endorse what we know already. In any case, we intend to charge him and prosecute him regardless. However, he will have an opportunity to make things easier on himself." Graham was too certain, a little too clever for his own good. Bernadette knew it and was about to exploit it.

"So, at the moment you can't be sure, can you?"

"Well, I think we can."

This was what she had been waiting for and like the panther sidling up to its prey, she pounced.

"I put it to you that you can't, and your assumption of guilt is just *that*, an assumption based upon the word of a man who by your own testimony is known to the police and is a convicted criminal."

"I believe he is involved nevertheless," said Graham flustered.

"But in summary, you cannot be sure. Can you?" She pushed him now, harder.

"Well..." Graham hesitated knowing she had got him.

However, Bernadette in full flow was relentless. She punched out the question again.

"Can you? Yes or no? You cannot be certain he is involved, yes or no?"

Graham swallowed and like so many who had faced Bernadette while on the stand, he had to admit defeat.

"Not one hundred percent certain, no. We will, however, charge him and then it is up to the courts and the case we present," Graham conceded looking annoyed.

It was a modified concession, but he had conceded it, nevertheless. This was the admission Bernadette wanted because it was an admission of doubt, as slight as it was. It was a good point to stop.

"No further questions, Judge," she said with a faint smile playing on her lips.

As she sat down, Imogen winked at her in acknowledgement of her scoring a hit.

"Mr Wilson, do you have any more questions?"

Shane stood, up, perhaps hopeful in salvaging his witness somehow.

"Yes, Judge, just one or two."

"Fine, carry on."

"DCI Graham, you have served many years on the force I take it, as a detective?"

"Yes, I have, twenty or so, mostly in CID and other units," said Graham.

"So, you've dealt with many cases, I'm sure very professionally and so on."

"Mr Wilson, I'm sure the DCI's credentials are all well and good, so what is your point?" said Justice Brannigan a little testily at this line of questioning.

"I'm merely trying to establish that DCI Graham with all his experience would not make decisions about suspects lightly and therefore if he feels—"

He wasn't allowed to continue. "Yes, yes, yes. So, you are trying to claim that because he's an experienced police officer then his suspicion of Mr Jenkin's involvement is justified. Well, of course, he thinks it's justified, that's his job," said Justice Brannigan acerbically, "And nobody, least of all, Mrs Mackenna, is saying otherwise. What she has brought out in his testimony is the fact that he, nor you can have any certainty Mr Jenkins was involved in the crime. That's what we are here to determine is it not? There's no jury here, Mr Wilson, we're all fully aware that policemen are supposed to know what they are doing without making a meal of it."

"Yes, Judge," said Shane, faintly. He evidently wasn't used to such directness from a judge. However, the nature of the hearing probably allowed the judge to make these kinds of remarks, Bernadette mused, and it was all to the good. It also showed her gambit had paid off.

"Now then, do you have any other questions for this witness, that do not involve showcasing his career in the police?" said Justice Brannigan with heavy sarcasm.

"No, Judge," said Shane realising perhaps that discretion was the better part of valour.

"Thank you, and I assume, Mrs Mackenna, you have no further questions either?"

"No, Judge," said Bernadette.

"In which case, DCI Graham, you may stand down."

Graham left the stand looking a little subdued. Defence counsel were never a favourite with policemen and Bernadette was pretty sure she would not be on his Christmas card list.

"So, we will have a lunch break shortly," said the judge, "But you may as well get your next witness underway, Mr Wilson."

"Yes, Judge," said Shane, and called Kevin Clinton to the stand.

Kevin Clinton arrived under heavy guard, with a Metropolitan Police officer on either side of him and wearing handcuffs. There were armed Gardai in place at the entrance to the court.

Kevin was around the same height as Callum, and although he was wearing a suit for his appearance, looked as if he was well-muscled underneath it. His face sported a square jaw and a thick black drooping moustache. He had a thick head of hair, blue piercing eyes, which were quite arresting in appearance. Callum was right, Bernadette mused, Kevin could have been a model.

He sat down in the witness stand and the police officers remained at an easy distance from him. Shane asked him to take an oath, state his name and occupation, as were the usual formalities.

Once this was accomplished, he started his questions.

"Mr Clinton, you are or rather you were a truck driver, am I right?"

"You could say that, yeah," said Kevin who spoke with a distinct London accent.

"What else do you do, other than driving trucks?"

"I've been involved in some crime, you know, done time for dealing, nicking cars, stuff like that."

"So, is it fair to say you're a petty criminal?" Shane asked him.

"Well, I wouldn't say petty, no not petty, no," said Kevin, who seemed to take exception to the idea that his criminal exploits might be diminished in this way.

"So, you're a criminal and you have criminal connections, is that correct?" said Shane correcting himself.

"Yeah, that's more like it, yeah."

"Do you admit to being involved in the trafficking of nineteen Vietnamese women?"

"Yeah, that's right, yeah, I was. Not proud of it though, you know, it's a job right, innit."

The offhand way in which Kevin had said this was clearly repellent even to Shane and Bernadette could read it in his expression.

"Right, so you knew about the trafficking and you were involved in it?"

"Yeah, right, that's what I just said, yeah."

"OK, so we've established that. Now, Mr Clinton, is there anyone in this courtroom you recognise?" Shane began.

"Yeah, that geezer, over there, that's Callum, my mate," said Kevin.

"Could you point him out please?"

Kevin pointed his finger at Callum, and said, "That's him."

"How did you know Callum?"

"Well, we're mates right, we met in a pub, and we were in the same line of work, so we got on."

"I see, so you became friends, is that correct?"

"Yes, yes, it is."

Bernadette noticed he did not mention anything about a relationship, and this was all to the good. Perhaps Shane thought they could get away without saying anything, but he must surely know she would bring it up. In his position, she would have pre-empted it.

"Was Mr Jenkins involved in the trafficking of these women?" Shane asked him directly.

"Yeah, yeah he was."

"So, how did it come about that he was involved?"

"Well, we were talking, you know in the pub, as you do. I asked him if he fancied making a bit more money, like, a bit extra."

"And when was this?"

"A few weeks before the job, I can't remember exactly."

This was vague and to Bernadette smacked of fabrication.

"OK, and then what happened?"

"He said he might be, and I told him about the goods, you know coming in, and if he was to drive the truck take the risk like, then there'd be something in it for him."

"And what did he say?"

"What did he say? He said yes, I'm in, I'll do it."

"What did doing it involve exactly?"

"He had to make sure he was on the roster for the truck. Then he'd be involved in the loading of the girls, you know in Dublin, and then drive the truck over and leave it."

"Why did he have to know they were in it? Why not just use him as, you know, a mule, as it were?"

"Because if he knew then he would be more careful, and he had a vested interest in making sure the cargo got through, plus if he did that job then that's another driver for us. We might want to bring in other stuff next time, we need reliable drivers. He needed to be in on it, that's how it works."

"Who is we, exactly?"

"The people I was working for, before I, well, got arrested an' all that."

Shane looked happy with the answers so far. It was pretty straightforward from his point of view.

"So, you have taken an oath and you are willing to swear that Mr Jenkins knew about the trafficking and he was actively involved in it. You are prepared to testify in court to that effect when Mr Jenkins is brought to trial in the United Kingdom."

"Absolutely I am, yes. That's what I am doing, yes."

Kevin nodded as if this was an easy ride so far. It had been for him, but Bernadette would be a far different matter.

"No further questions, Judge," said Shane.

"Good, good, so we'll break for lunch, and resume afterwards," said Justice Brannigan who didn't seem inclined to push the boat out past any kind of discomfort regarding breaks.

The Tipster bade the court rise and the judge left the court.

* * *

There were plenty of rustles and whispered conversations from the press, as Bernadette, Imogen, Rhys and Callum walked out of the court. Bernadette found a meeting room while Imogen disappeared to pick up their sandwich order from the lobby.

"Is it going alright?" Rhys asked Bernadette as they sat down together.

"As well as one might expect," she said, "Their case isn't watertight by any means, and we are down to getting the judge to accept there is enough doubt to disallow the extradition."

"Do you think we can get it?"

"I'm quietly confident at the moment."

Imogen returned with coffee and sandwiches, which she duly distributed.

"You were right about Kevin, he could have been a model," said Imogen, biting into a beef roll.

"Yes, I suppose. I thought he was very handsome but seeing him up there now, lying about me. That pissed me right off," said Callum with feeling.

"You were expecting it surely?" Bernadette asked him reaching for a sandwich herself.

"I know but it hits home when you've shared moments. He was so offhand. Just a total wanker."

"I'd like to punch his fucking lights out," said Rhys angrily.

"I'm sure you do," Imogen laughed, "But it's not going to help us if you attempt it."

"I know, I know," Rhys sighed. "I just hate the way he doesn't care about implicating my son, who is totally innocent."

"That's how criminals are," said Bernadette wryly, putting down her roll, "They don't care, and that's why I don't represent criminals."

"Good job." Rhys smiled. "I admire your integrity."

"In the end integrity is all we have. In this profession anyway."

"Are you going after him, after lunch?"

"Oh, yes, I'm certainly going to do that, I intend to fully rattle his cage and then some."

"I'm looking forward to it, if what you did with that policeman is anything to go by."

"You haven't seen anything yet," Imogen laughed.

✳ ✳ ✳

They resumed for the afternoon session and Kevin was once again escorted in under guard. When he was in place, Justice Brannigan said, "Mrs Mackenna, would you like to question this witness?"

"Indeed, I would, Judge," said Bernadette standing up.

Kevin looked her over a little contemptuously, and she bore in mind that Callum had said he was a misogynist. She smiled at him benignly and he looked away.

"Mr Clinton, you said you were friends with Mr Jenkins, am I right? Friends that's what you said?"

"Yeah, that's right, we were mates for sure." He said in an easy manner, as if she presented no threat to him at all.

"Is that what friends do, rat on each other? Is it?"

She was playing with him, just a little before going in for the kill.

"Well, you know, we weren't that close, I mean..." he let it slide.

"Not that close, is that what you said?" she posed the question lightly, lulling him into a false sense of security.

"Yes, yeah I did."

"Because you see, Mr Clinton, I don't believe you. When you say you were not that close, in fact, I'd say it was the opposite, wouldn't you?"

"What? No." He said a little disconcerted, but Bernadette couldn't believe he hadn't been briefed. If not, it would be very remiss of them and a mistake. One which may work in her favour.

"You were very close because you and Mr Jenkins were lovers, isn't that right?"

"No, come on, you're having a laugh," Kevin threw it back at her.

"You and Mr Jenkins were lovers, and you met him in a gay bar, that's the actual truth, is it not?" she said implacably.

"I'm not fucking gay!"

This was a mistake and Bernadette did not know how he felt he could deny it under oath.

"Please turn to page two seven nine in the book of evidence in front of you," said Bernadette, waiting for him to do so. "What do you see there?" she asked him at length.

"It looks like some texts."

"What do the texts say on that page? Can you read them out to the court please?"

Kevin licked his lips, and Shane shifted uncomfortably in his chair. "I err..."

"Could you please read the texts aloud to the court?"

Kevin coughed, hesitated and then realising he could not get out of it, started reading, "I can't wait until I can get to suck your fucking big cock, you horny bitch, I want it in me, right in me, and want you to fuck me until I scream... Yeah, I'm looking forward to it too, you big sexy hunk of muscle with your cool moustache... I want you, so much, I can hardly wait... Not long now lover boy..."

There was silence in the courtroom. There was some frantic scribbling from the reporters, however, at this revelation. The judge, who would no doubt have heard this and worse, didn't bat an eyelid.

"Who are the texts between?" Bernadette asked him.

"Callum..."

"And?"

"Myself."

She smiled he had no way of getting out of it.

"Right. And are those the texts which people who are just mates write to each other?"

He shook his head.

"No."

"Are they texts between lovers?"

He couldn't look at her now and looked down at the floor.

"Yes."

"So, I'm going to ask you again, were you and Mr Jenkins lovers?"

"Yes."

"That puts a little different perspective on it doesn't it?"

"No... not really..." Kevin began, looking up again.

"I put it to you that it does," she cut him off, "You wanted more from him and he wouldn't give it to you, would he? So, you decided to concoct a story to get back at him, yes?"

"Nah, that's not right, we weren't lovers for that long, I wasn't that bothered."

"Really? Please turn to page two six five."

Kevin did so.

"What is the date of the texts on that page?"

Kevin told her.

"Now please move forward through the pages to the last set of texts."

When he had done so, Bernadette said, "The date of those texts, how long after the date you told me before was it?"

"It's seven months," said Kevin.

"Seven months?"

"Yes."

"Of intimate contact, am I right?"

"Yes," said Kevin though it seemed reluctantly.

"So, this wasn't some casual fling was it?"

"I guess not, no."

"Seven months is not a casual fling, Mr Clinton, not when we can show, as you've seen in the evidence, just a selection of very intimate texts. Isn't that right?"

"Well, I err..." It was clear he didn't want to acknowledge this but had no way of getting out of it.

"Would you like to read out some more texts to confirm what I'm saying?"

"No, no it's fine, I accept it was not a casual relationship."

This wasn't good enough for Bernadette and she went at him again.

471

"I'm not asking you to accept it, I'm asking you to admit it. Do you admit you were in an intimate and long-term relationship with Mr Jenkins or not?"

There was a long pause, while Kevin considered his response. Shane was looking irritated at this turn of events, but there wasn't anything he could do about it.

"Mr Clinton?" Bernadette said eventually. "Were you or were you not in a long-term relationship with Mr Jenkins?"

Kevin sighed. "Yes, yes I was."

"Thank you."

Having got this far, she was by no means finished.

"Is it not also true that you were jealous of Mr Jenkins, you began to question him about his movements?"

"I..."

She wasn't having it and was determined to show him that prevarication wasn't going to work.

"Page two eight four, Mr Clinton."

"Yes."

He turned the pages albeit reluctantly until he found the right place.

"Read the first text on that page if you please?"

"Where are you? I've been texting you and you didn't reply. Where have you been? Have you been out partying, I need to know! What the fuck, Cal, you didn't call me last night," Kevin said reading the text.

"And the next text?"

"I am fucked off with you, Cal, have you been fucking cheating on me? What the fuck were you doing?"

"And the next one?"

"Calm down, sweetie, I haven't been screwing around on you, I've been driving, what's wrong with you?"

"And the next one."

"Fuck you, Cal, just text me next time, don't be such a c—
"

"That's enough, thank you," said Bernadette stopping him.

Kevin looked red in the face with embarrassment.

"So, were you jealous of Mr Jenkins?"

"Yes," said Kevin realising there wasn't any point in denying this either.

"So, you were jealous, and you wanted to get back at him, isn't that right?"

"I was jealous of him, yes," Kevin admitted.

"And you wanted to get back at him, isn't that correct?"

"No, it's not."

"We'll come back to this, shortly," Bernadette said, deciding to take another tack. She looked through her papers pausing for a moment. "The police arrested you for the trafficking after the raid, am I right?"

"Yes, yes they did." His voice was a little more confident now she had moved away from his relationship with Callum.

"What have the police offered you for being a witness?"

"I can't say."

"You are under oath. They have offered you a plea bargain or immunity from prosecution, is that or is that not correct?"

Kevin sighed, she had cornered him well and truly.

"OK, yes."

"In exchange for naming other members of the gang?" She raised an eyebrow.

"*If* I could name *any* other person involved in the trafficking," he corrected her.

473

"So, you could have named anyone, couldn't you, but it was easier to target your lover, is that not so?"

"I wasn't targeting him."

"You named him as an accomplice. He was your lover, we've established that. You were intimate we've established that. So, I put it to you that rather than dig up the name of a person who was actually responsible you targeted him knowing he would not endanger your life, isn't that right?"

"No! He was involved, he knew about it."

"Do you have any evidence that the discussion about the trafficking you say took place, actually took place?" Bernadette said pursuing this.

"Well, no but, neither does he showing it doesn't." Kevin also thought this was clever, but Bernadette was onto it.

"If it didn't take place there wouldn't be any evidence would there, because there wouldn't have a been a discussion would there?"

"Well, I..." he hesitated.

"Would there?"

"Well, no, obviously if it hadn't taken place then no."

"Were there any witnesses to this alleged conversation or any other conversations afterwards?" Bernadette said pushing her argument home.

"No," said Kevin looking peeved.

"Were there any texts?"

"No." He shook his head.

"So, in fact, there is nothing to corroborate your statement about any of it, am I correct?"

"He drove the truck..." Kevin began.

"There is nothing to directly corroborate your statement that Mr Clinton either knew about the trafficking or was involved in it, yes or no?"

He was squirming under this scrutiny and her unwavering gaze. When she wanted to, Bernadette could be relentless, and she was being relentless today.

"I..."

"Yes or no, Mr Clinton?"

"Jesus fucking Christ, you're a fucking hard bitch, aren't you?" he suddenly exclaimed in frustration.

"Mr Clinton, please confine yourself to answering the questions, no matter what your personal opinion might be of the barristers," said the judge somewhat dryly, though he looked slightly amused knowing how much Bernadette had pressed him.

"Yes, Judge, sorry... I..."

"Yes or no, Mr Clinton?" said Bernadette ignoring this remark.

"No, I don't have any fucking records, I don't have any texts, I don't have a fucking video, but I say he was there and we did discuss it and that's the story I am sticking to," Kevin said defiantly. He was certainly fired up and had primed himself for Bernadette to goad him further.

"Is it true you think women are inferior?" she said suddenly.

"What?" said Kevin a little startled by the question.

"Do you think that women are inferior? Is it or isn't it a true statement?" she said mildly.

"And what if I do?" he shot back belligerently.

"Well, if you do then in reality you probably think that sex trafficking serves them right, yes?"

475

Shane was on his feet at once. "Objection, Judge, what can this possibly have to do with the evidence?"

"I want to understand what he thinks about it," said Bernadette sweetly, though she knew it was a contentious statement, "After all, his attitude to the crime is material to the evidence."

"My witness is not the one on trial here," Shane said a little forcefully.

"But he is making assertions about my client and as such, Judge, I should be allowed to understand the underlying attitudes which led to it, as should the court." Bernadette was speaking in reasonable tones contrasting with the irritation Shane was evidently feeling.

"I strongly submit this line of questioning should not be allowed," Shane continued.

"But he was involved. Apparently, he's a prosecution witness and so then perhaps he disagrees with the trafficking or perhaps he doesn't, I want to know his motivation and I submit it *is* relevant."

Justice Brannigan who had been listening to this exchange, held up his hand for silence while he considered it.

"I'll allow it, Mrs Mackenna, but try not to cross any lines if you would," he said finally.

"Thank you, Judge," said Bernadette, while Shane made a face and sat down. "I will rephrase my question, Mr Clinton, do you or do you not agree with sex trafficking?"

It was a milder form of the question with a less accusatory tone.

Kevin shrugged. "It was just a job."

"It was just a job, women who have their lives stolen from them, abused or worse but you think it was just a job? That's a callous attitude, don't you agree?"

"I guess, I never thought about it," he said in an offhand way.

"So, you didn't really care about them, they were just cargo, a consignment, less than human really, is that what you're saying?"

"I wasn't saying that, I just don't think about it that way," he said defensively.

"So, if I understand you rightly, you don't really care what happens to them one way or another, am I right?"

"No, I guess not, no," he admitted at length.

"Rather like you don't really care what happens to Mr Jenkins, if say he goes to prison for a crime he didn't commit, am I right?" her voice had softened a little.

"I do care, but he was involved and that's that," he said with an air of finality.

"I'm asking you in all honestly, since you seem to value human life quite cheaply, if it makes any difference to you whether he was innocent or not, because I put it to you that it doesn't, and I say to you once more that he was an easy target without any consequences to you. The police get their man in prison and your life remains safe, is that not how it is?"

"He did know about it."

It seemed as if he had now taken refuge in simply repeating himself and digging in his heels. She was pondering whether to stop at this point, when Justice Brannigan came to her rescue.

"I think this a good time for the afternoon break. If you have any further questions for this witness, Mrs Mackenna, you may continue them afterwards."

"Thank you, Judge," said Bernadette furnishing him with one of her best smiles.

The Tipster called for the court to rise and Justice Brannigan left presumably for another cup of tea.

Before they could leave the courtroom, Mason came up to them.

"You said it was with without prejudice, what we discussed, in other words, you wouldn't use it," he said to Bernadette.

"Yes, but I did not say I wouldn't ask your witness, that's a different thing," she replied smoothly.

He gave a short laugh. "Oh, you're good, you are very good, I'll give you that."

He turned on his heel and left. Bernadette headed for a meeting room and Imogen to get some coffees. She spoke briefly to Rhys to say it was all going well so far, and they'd debrief at the end of the day, particularly before facing the press.

* * *

Imogen appeared shortly afterwards with two coffees. She handed one to Bernadette.

"So, what do you think? Shall we leave it there?" Bernadette said taking the cup from her.

"I'm not sure what else you can ask him," Imogen said honestly, sipping her coffee.

"He's starting to dig his heels in and everything I say will get the same answer now, which perhaps isn't helpful to us."

"No, you're probably right."

"I might just try to summarise where we are at, give it one more shot, see if I can't get him to let something slip." Bernadette was reluctant to let things go without pushing harder on the element of doubt.

"If anyone can do it, you can. You certainly had him on the ropes for a while."

"Yes, but he's not going to change his story, more's the pity."

Bernadette took another sip of her coffee.

"Well, you were pretty much on fire in there, it was quite a turn on really." Imogen smirked.

"Oh stop! I'm a married woman now," Bernadette laughed.

"So, you're off limits to my imagination?" Imogen teased.

"You are such a minx."

"I know, I can't help it. Don't worry, I'm going to fuck D'Arcy's brains out when I get home."

"Good, because I'm going to do the same to Eve," Bernadette giggled.

"So, courtroom action is now an aphrodisiac, who knew?"

"Incorrigible is what you are, my darling, and no mistake."

"That's why..."

"I love you, I know, and I do... always..."

They squeezed hands affectionately before getting on and finishing their coffee.

* * *

Court resumed after the break, and the Tipster having once more announced the arrival of the judge, the final session of the day began.

"Mrs Mackenna," said Justice Brannigan, "Do you have any further questions for this witness?"

"Yes, Judge," said Bernadette having decided to give it one further go.

"Very well," said the judge, "You may continue."

"Mr Clinton," said Bernadette, "I asked you a question before the break and you did not really answer it. So, let me break it down for you. You agreed that you don't value life particularly highly, am I right?"

"I didn't exactly put it that way," Kevin replied.

"How would you put it?"

"Like I said, it was a job, I wasn't thinking about their lives particularly or what would happen to them. I was being paid for my assistance in the process."

"And what was your assistance in the process?"

"Objection, is this really relevant?" Shane was up at once.

"Mrs Mackenna?" said the judge.

"Judge, Mr Clinton has accused my client of a serious crime. I want to understand what his involvement in the crime was, in order to more fully understand how he is so certain my client was part of it."

"You may continue, Mrs Mackenna," the judge said slightly wearily, Shane's objections were perhaps beginning to irritate him.

The object of his annoyance sat down heavily once more.

"Mr Clinton, what was your part in the process?" Bernadette repeated.

"It was my job to transport the women to their, erm... well, a holding warehouse until they were taken to various other places," he said.

"To illicit brothels, I presume you mean," said Bernadette in acidic tones.

"Yes, that is what I meant."

"So, Mr Jenkins was an easy target am I right? A target without fear of retaliation? Rather than your criminal colleagues. A sacrificial lamb to keep everyone happy. Yes or no?"

"No."

"I think you're lying, I put it to you that you have fabricated your testimony and without any shred of tangible evidence against Mr Clinton. Isn't that the case?" Bernadette was upping the ante now fishing for a reaction as much as anything else.

"I'm not lying," Kevin shot back angrily.

"You said you cared about him, but if you did then why would you name him as an accomplice?" she said picking up on something he had said earlier.

"I don't know," Kevin said discomposed trying to push back at her without giving an answer. He was visibly annoyed and a little pink about the gills.

"Because you don't really care about him, isn't that right, or you wanted revenge because he didn't care about you? Which is it?" she said still digging at him, chipping away at his armour.

Kevin seemed to control himself with an effort, but he declined to respond to the question. Bernadette wasn't having it.

"So, which is it, Mr Clinton? Did you care about him or didn't you?" she asked him again more forcefully this time.

At that moment Kevin who had been looking across at Callum appeared to finally lose his cool.

"Yeah well, he didn't fucking well care about me, little fucking tossing wanker, fucking arsehole, so I don't fucking care, the bastard. He can fucking rot in the prison for all the fucks I give about it." He stood up and pointed at Callum angrily. "He can get what he fucking deserves and take that, you fucking bastard, fuck you, Cal, just fuck you, you fucking little bitch, fucking wanking fucking..."

"Order," said Justice Brannigan bringing this tirade to a halt and unusually banging his gavel, "Order! Mr Clinton, please be seated and control yourself!"

Kevin, subsided, realising he had possibly screwed up, and sat down morosely. Bernadette suppressed a smile at this outburst. She had been angling for something like it, but this had been far better than she'd hoped for.

"Mr Clinton, I don't want any further disruption to these proceedings from you, is that understood?" said the judge.

"Yes, Judge, sorry," said Kevin.

"Good, well, see that it doesn't happen again. Continue, Mrs Mackenna," said the judge.

Shane was sitting silently shaking his head at the breakdown of his key witness. Mason rolled his eyes and looked up at the ceiling in annoyance.

Bernadette inclined her head to the judge and addressed herself to Kevin once more, "Mr Clinton, how much risk to you personally is there from naming Mr Jenkins?"

"Not too much, I guess," he conceded in a calmer voice.

"Exactly as I thought, not too much. So, it would be easier to implicate him than someone else with more risk to you, hypothetically, is that not the case?"

"Objection," said Shane, "The witness has already answered this question more than once."

"Mrs Mackenna, you probably *are* labouring the point, don't you think?" Justice Brannigan said with a slightly ironic smile.

"I withdraw the question, Judge," she said. She had made the point in any case, clearly enough for anyone to understand it. A glance at Imogen told her she probably had done enough, and she said to Justice Brannigan, "In fact, I've no further questions."

"Good, good, and Mr Wilson, how about you?"

Shane shook his head. Bernadette reflected he was probably more than happy to get Kevin off the stand. Kevin had already done enough damage for one day, as far as Shane and Mason were concerned.

"You may stand down, Mr Clinton," said Justice Barry.

When Kevin had been escorted out, the judge said, "I think we can adjourn for today, start afresh with your witnesses Mrs Mackenna, what say you?"

"Certainly, Judge."

"Excellent, then court is adjourned."

After the Tipster had seen the judge out of the courtroom, the press scrambled for the door wanting to be sure to catch anyone they could coming out. Bernadette and

Imogen waited, with Rhys and Callum for the media to disperse. Shane and Mason left almost immediately too.

"Let's find a meeting room," said Bernadette.

* * *

"That went well, didn't it?" asked Callum once they were all sitting together in the meeting room.

"It was fucking brilliant," Rhys chuckled, "You took him apart on the stand, I'm gobsmacked, you're amazing, in fact, you're much better than they even said you were."

"She's the business, the fucking business," said Imogen smiling at her.

"Thanks for all your confidence. Yes, it did go well, better than I expected to be fair. However, it's only half the battle. We've got to get through our witnesses intact and then we've got a fighting chance of winning it."

"You're far too modest, girl," said Rhys affectionately.

"She is, she really is," Imogen agreed.

"Right now, let's move on and talk about the press. They are going to want to ask questions, and I think we should give them something," said Bernadette.

"What are we allowed to say?" Rhys asked her.

"Follow my lead. Stick to the facts, as in yes, you were his lover. No, you were not involved. He's an Irish Citizen and Ireland needs to stand by him."

"OK," said Rhys.

"Then let's go, tomorrow we'll have a quick briefing session before you go on the stand, Callum."

"Yes, right," Callum agreed.

They walked together out of the court building and onto the steps. The press saw them and surged forward at once. Behind them, there was a very large crowd banging drums and holding up banners. New banners had now appeared with slogans like "Kevin is a liar," and "Kevin F'off back to England and leave Callum alone." There was a lot of chanting and shouting.

Bernadette held up her hand indicating she was about to speak.

"What do you think of it so far? Are you winning?" shouted one eager reporter.

"Today simply proved we are on the side of justice. I told you we were here for justice and I'm telling you again. Callum is innocent and we intend to ensure he stays in Ireland."

"Is Kevin Clinton a liar?" shouted another.

"I cannot possibly comment," said Bernadette, "You can draw your own conclusions."

"Rhys, what do you think?"

"My son is innocent, nothing he said about Callum's involvement was true. My son is an Irish citizen and the Irish government should stand by an innocent man!" said Rhys angrily.

"Callum, what was Kevin like? Was he good in bed?" shouted a man from the Irish Sun.

"No comment," said Callum dutifully.

"We'll pay you, pay you for an exclusive!" the reporter shouted.

"Come on," said Bernadette," That's enough."

She led the way from the shouting media mob and down the steps hurrying them to the car. She bundled them in and drove away.

"Jesus, they are like fucking animals," said Rhys.

"Oh worse, much worse," Imogen laughed.

"I'll drop you home again," said Bernadette.

"You don't have to do that," Rhys objected.

"Yes, yes I do."

"She's the boss," Imogen turned and winked at Rhys, "Best do what she says."

"Oh, a right tartar, is she?" Rhys chuckled.

"Absolutely."

"Stop it the lot of you, or you'll be on the naughty step!" Bernadette giggled.

✳ ✳ ✳

Before she drove home, Bernadette had sent Eve a text.

'Better be ready when I get home, my darling wife, because I am going to fuck you senseless. Your wife xxxx'

'Your wife can't wait, love you darling xxxx' came the rapid response.

Thus primed, Bernadette had made her way home quickly but safely. She opened the front door and dropped her bag. Eve walked into the hallway completely naked.

"Fuck," said Bernadette kicking off her shoes and divesting herself of her jacket.

"You said..." Eve ran her tongue slowly around her lips and bit her bottom lip in a way that made Bernadette go weak at the knees. "So I thought..."

"You thought what?" Bernadette held her close her lips touching Eve's.

"I thought I'd better be accessible."

"God you're so sexy, so fucking sexy." Bernadette's lips met Eve's and they kissed, hard passionately. Bernadette's hands and nails raked down Eve's naked back and squeezed her buttock cheeks. Eve gasped, "Oh, God, I love that... ooh."

Bernadette kissed her again pushing her hard against the wall in the hallway, her hand snaking down between Eve's legs, and to her immense satisfaction found her very wet. Her fingers began to work.

"Oh... fuck... oh my God... fuck... oh... oh... ahh... yes... please... more... please... oh..."

Eve's head was laid back, and her eyes closed. Bernadette was kissing her neck and making her squirm under the ministrations of her fingers.

"Oh... fuck... yes... yes... don't... stop... oh... darling... yes... oh..."

Bernadette could feel her getting closer as she bit into her shoulder, gently but hard enough for her to feel it, and then again.

"Oh... shit... fuck... fuck... fuck... oh... I'm going to... ohh!" Eve shouted as her climax hit her, and tensed arching her back, screaming out loud.

Bernadette held her watching her smiling, enjoying the pleasure she had given her beautiful wife. Eventually, Eve subsided and kissed her softly.

"Is it my turn now?" she said softly.

"Later, darling. I'm going to sit on your face."

"Oh shit... you're making me horny all over again."

"Put on that maid's outfit and you can serve me dinner."
Bernadette smiled.

"Oh, God... you are such a bitch, a horny bitch, I love it..."
Eve said hurrying away to get dressed up.

CHAPTER SIXTEEN

"What brought that on last night?" Eve whispered in the early hours of the morning. There was still an hour or before the alarm was due to go off, but they were both awake.

"I don't know, I got a bit horny from my cross examination, I was being a bit of a bitch, it kind of turned me on," Bernadette laughed softly.

"Oh, you are turning into a dominant little bitch, now aren't you?" Eve whispered moving closer.

"Not like that, and you wish," Bernadette chuckled.

"Hmm, I do wish it sometimes, for sure."

"And I give it to you sometimes."

"Yes, yes you do, and I love you for it and everything you do."

They kissed again gently. They fell asleep in each other's arms without making love. They were both still tired from the previous night, as Eve had worn her maids' outfit at dinner and served Bernadette in an extremely provocative manner. Both of them had become so horny they had gone upstairs right after dinner and made love.

The alarm sounded soon enough, and Bernadette crawled out of bed for her shower. By the time she returned,

Eve was waiting with her clothes laid out. She tied Bernadette's hair in a French Plait which suited her very well. After doing Bernadette's makeup, Eve went downstairs to make breakfast.

Bernadette put on the grey skirt suit, soft lilac blouse and grey mules, which Eve had put out for her. She wanted a softer image for her own witnesses, and this suited her well. She went to the kitchen, when Eve was just placing a plate of her usual scrambled eggs, toast, and mushrooms on the breakfast bar. Bernadette sat down and accepted the cup of coffee. She took a sip and then started to slice into her eggs and toast.

"So, it's Callum today, and then the Vietnamese girl?" Eve asked her.

"Yes."

"But haven't you really scotched the opposition's chances yesterday?"

"We gave it a good shot, but our witnesses still have to undergo cross examination and survive that," said Bernadette taking a mouthful of scrambled eggs.

"Callum is innocent though, isn't he?"

"Yes, I'm pretty sure of it," said Bernadette.

"Then it shouldn't be an issue should it?"

"No, but I always worry until the judgement or the verdict is in."

"Oh, darling, it's going to be fine." Eve smiled at her provocatively.

"And how can you be so sure?"

"Because I'm your witchy wife, remember?"

"How I could I forget," said Bernadette, as she finished off her breakfast. She took a sip of her coffee and smiled.

Eve ate her own breakfast and smiled too while Bernadette ran her fingers lightly down her arm.

"Come on," said Bernadette once Eve had finished, "Come and kiss me goodbye."

Eve followed her to the hallway and kissed her softly and with the passion they always felt.

"I'll see you later."

"Yes," Bernadette whispered.

"Shall I be naked?"

"Surprise me."

She pulled out of the driveway, watching Eve wave to her and once more counting the blessings which had brought them together.

* * *

Bernadette and Imogen arrived at the courts for their second and probably last day. Avoiding the reporters on the steps and the huge shouting crowd, they headed inside and located Callum, and Rhys. In a meeting room replete with coffee, Bernadette spoke to Callum.

"You've got to keep your cool today, OK?" said Bernadette.

"Yes, I will."

"Shane is going to try, if he can, to pull a number on you. He's going to test you and accuse you of lying. You just need to stand firm on what's true."

"Yes." Callum nodded.

"Do not, I repeat, do not do what Kevin did yesterday."

"Listen to the boss lady," Rhys joked.

"Da!" Callum protested.

"He's going to be OK, don't worry," said Rhys, "I know my son."

"Yes, I'm sure, but cross examination is tough, and once he's on the stand I can't talk to him again until he's finished," said Bernadette.

"I promise, I'll be OK," said Callum.

"Great, well, we should be done today, I think, and then we'll get a judgement soon after."

"Will we get one today?" Rhys asked her.

"It's likely the judge will want some time to think about the legal arguments, and so on, and then he'll give it. It could be a few days."

"Oh." Rhys looked disappointed. "Oh well."

"The wheels of justice I'm afraid, but he's got to make a decision that's hard to appeal, otherwise we're just going to go through this again. He has to make sure he's applied the law correctly according to the evidence presented."

"Look at it this way, it's few more days," said Imogen.

"It could be my last few days of freedom," Callum mused.

"No, don't think like that, be positive."

"Yes, yes indeed," said Rhys, "None of that negative Nancy stuff now!"

"Oh, Da."

"I think it's time to go in, and then you'll be on," said Bernadette.

✻ ✻ ✻

They took their places and waited. The Tipster arrived, announced the judge and Justice Brannigan entered. He took his seat and had a quick look around the courtroom before addressing Shane.

"Mr Wilson, do you have any other witnesses, I don't believe so, but I just want to check."

"No, Judge, that's all, thank you," said Shane standing briefly.

"Right then, Mrs Mackenna, I believe it's time for your witnesses in which case."

"Thank you, Judge," said Bernadette, "I call Callum Jenkins to the stand."

Callum left the dock and took his place on the witness stand. He took an oath of affirmation and confirmed his name and occupation.

"Mr Jenkins, or may I call you Callum?" Bernadette asked him.

"Callum is fine."

"You are, as stated, a driver for your father's haulage firm, Jenkins Haulage, am I right?" Bernadette said.

"Yes, that's right."

"And your sexual orientation is homosexual, is that correct?"

She wasn't usually quite so blunt, but this had to be out there right away to avoid any ambiguity. She also wanted to tackle the relationship issues first before tackling the crime.

"Yes, it is."

"Thank you, and you were in a relationship with Kevin Clinton, is *that* right?"

"A casual relationship, yes."

She wanted to establish exactly how the relationship was from his point of view. The fact he was very open about it was significant. It would contrast to Kevin's reluctance to admit to the relationship at all.

"Can you elaborate what you mean by a casual relationship?"

"We had sex, a lot. In fact, that was pretty much the raison d'être of our relationship."

Bernadette was glad for Callum's frankness. She pushed it further.

"So, when you said casual, you meant predominantly sexual, am I right?"

"Yes."

"You weren't in love with Mr Clinton?"

"No, I wasn't."

"Did he have feelings for you?"

"I don't know, I suspected he did."

"And why was that?"

"Because he got possessive and jealous. He was constantly asking me where I was going, who I was seeing, stuff like that. He used to get angry and think I was seeing other people."

The texts had backed this assertion up and she had already played that card, so she didn't labour it further.

"Were you seeing other people?"

"No, I wasn't, only him."

"So, to clarify, it was an exclusive sexual relationship?"

"Yes, that's right."

Bernadette was happy she had covered this quite succinctly and now moved on to the nub of the hearing.

"Were you aware of Mr Clinton's criminal activities or indeed, his criminal connections?"

"No, I wasn't aware of them."

"You spent a lot of time together did you not? Did you talk at all, find out what he did, meet his friends?"

She had to ask this because Shane would attack him on it. It was pre-emptive questioning to discourage him from going there.

"We had sex, it's what we did. We didn't talk about work. We went to gay bars and spent time together. I never met his friends and I never asked him or wanted to know about his work."

"Why was that?"

"I wasn't in love with him. I liked him and he was good to spend time with. I didn't want to meet his friends. You meet friends when you start to care emotionally about someone, and I didn't."

"You didn't care about him?" She wanted to be sure.

"No, not in that way, I didn't."

"What did you talk about?"

"Movies, books, being gay, stuff like that," Callum laughed.

"Right, and did Mr Clinton ever mention, even once, the idea of you becoming involved in sex trafficking?"

"No, he didn't, and I had no idea about it."

"He never asked you to become involved?"

"No, he didn't."

It was obviously his word against Kevin's, it would depend on who the judge believed in the end.

"When did you become aware of the sex trafficking?"

"I read it in the paper I think, and thought isn't that the depot I left the truck at? Then it, sort of clicked, and shortly afterwards I was arrested by the Garda."

Bernadette continued into the final part of her questions, which was to go through the timeline.

"Can you take us through from the time you picked up the truck, which we now know contained illegal immigrants destined for human sex trafficking, to the time you dropped it off?"

"Yes, I went to Balik Transport where the truck was parked. I picked up the keys from the office."

"Can you turn to page five nine eight please, in the evidence book in front of you?"

"Yes."

"That is your affidavit, am I correct?"

"Yes, it is."

"Is that the time and date you picked up the truck in paragraph five?"

"Yes, it is."

"And over the page, on paragraph nine, is that the time you dropped it off?"

"Yes."

"OK, thank you. So, returning to what you said, you picked up the keys from the office?"

"Yes, I signed for the truck. I went to the truck checked it over for tyre damage, made sure it was secure and the customs seal was intact."

"Was it?"

"Yes."

"What did you do then?"

"I got into the truck, fired it up, checked it for fuel. As I remember it was full, and I filled in the start time on my timesheet. I drove the truck out to the ferry depot and waited to board. I put the truck on board. During the ferry trip, I was up on the observation deck and then I had something to eat, a snooze. We got to the other end, I drove through the immigration and customs check. They did a cursory check of the truck and then I drove it to the London depot. I parked it, handed the keys over. I signed and filled in my timesheet. I left the depot and headed back to Dublin."

"That was it?"

"Yes."

It sounded straight forward, and she wondered what Shane would go for. Time would tell very shortly, as Bernadette was almost finished.

"You had no idea there were illegal immigrants onboard?"

"No, none at all."

"When you did your pre-inspection did you notice anything unusual, hear any noises, anything like that?"

"No."

"So, you were completely unaware of the truck carrying anything other than the expected load?"

"Yes, that's right."

"Did you know what the load was?"

"It was flour barrels, it said so on the manifesto."

"Is it normal for the driver to see the actual load?"

"No, it's not, unless it's an open load and then you have to be sure it's tied down properly. If it's sealed, then you don't touch it at all. You assume it's been loaded correctly according to the manifest."

"Where did you think the truck had been loaded?"

"In Spain, as far as I know."

"Thank you."

Bernadette decided she'd been through his testimony as far as she could and now had to let Shane do his worst. He undoubtedly would attempt it. She knew Shane's style and had a shrewd idea what line he would take.

"No further questions, Judge," she said.

"Jolly good," said Justice Brannigan, "Mr Wilson, I think you can start your cross examination before we have a morning break."

"Thank you, Judge," said Shane standing up.

He gave Callum a hard stare. Callum looked back coolly at him and quite dispassionately. He wasn't in the least intimidated by Shane.

"Mr Jenkins, or perhaps I could also call you Callum?" said Shane. He was using the age-old trick of first names, to appear friendly at least at first. Formality could also be intimidating. The use of first names was designed to lull the witness into a false sense of security.

"If you want." Callum shrugged, it did not change his demeanour towards Shane.

"Well, Callum, you stated you were in a sexual relationship with Kevin, yes?"

"Yes, he didn't deny it either," said Callum who had heard Kevin's testimony.

"No, agreed, but sexual intimacy presages some other kinds of intimacy in terms of knowing things about each other, wouldn't you say?"

"Not necessarily, and not in this case," said Callum somewhat obdurately.

Shane decided to go for a more direct line of attack.

"So, you're asking the court to believe, you were intimate, but you didn't talk about his job or his work?"

"Yes, I am because that's how it was," Callum shot back, he was immediately irritated by Shane's attitude and it showed.

Bernadette secretly hoped he would calm down. She glanced at Imogen who pursed her lips, indicating she thought the same.

"You met up a few times a month, is that true?"

"Yes, quite a few, and some weekends if I stayed over."

"So, you spent a lot of time together and in all that time it was just about sex?"

"Yeah, I don't know what your sex life is like but mine was pretty intense, that's how I am," Callum said frankly.

Shane looked slightly disconcerted and there were sniggers from the public benches. However, he opted to ignore this and press on. He had been quite mild over the last couple of questions, but he now became a little more belligerent and obnoxious. Bernadette knew this was deliberate in order to try and get a rise out of Callum.

"You had no idea, none at all he was involved in crime?" Shane sounded incredulous, sarcastic.

"No, I've already said so."

"But you would say that, wouldn't you?"

"What do you mean?" Callum scowled.

"I mean you would say *that*. You are maintaining your innocence and yet he says you knew all about it. You're not going to admit to it, even if it is the truth, am I right?" This was sneering, just a little, pushing a little harder now.

"Well, he's lying and that's what I'm saying, what he said didn't happen."

Callum neatly sidestepped the yes or no answer Shane was angling for. If he had said yes, then he was admitting to the possibility he was just saying it for the court. So far, he was just about keeping his cool, but Bernadette could see signs in his face this might not last.

"It's just stretching credibility too far, to expect the court to believe you had no inkling whatsoever of his criminal activities, that he didn't discuss it with you at all, don't you agree?" Shane came straight back at him, in a way calculated to annoy him.

"No, I don't, and I didn't," Callum retorted a little heatedly.

"Why would Kevin say you did know? Why would he say that, do you think?"

"I don't know."

"I put it to you he said it because it's true."

"Well, it's not!"

There was a little too much pushback in Callum's response, it would tell Shane he was starting to get to him. Bernadette knew Shane would capitalise on this and simply come back harder. Which is exactly what he did, punching out his next question.

"And what if I say you're the one who is lying, you knew what was in the truck, you probably even helped to load it and now you've been caught out and you are trying to evade the course of justice, that's really what happened isn't it?"

Callum hesitated for a moment. The direct forceful attack took him by surprise. The hesitation, however, Bernadette knew, could make the judge think perhaps there was some truth to what Shane was saying. Callum was controlling himself with an effort, she could see it.

"No," said Callum evenly, visibly annoyed now, "Not it's not."

"You're also telling the court you had no idea what was in the truck? You had no clue at all there were illegal immigrants inside it?"

"I didn't the truck was sealed. I had no reason to open it and so I didn't know they were in there. I wouldn't have driven the truck away if I had discovered it. I would have called in the Garda!" Callum had raised his voice. Shane's tactics were working.

"Let's cut to the chase, shall we," Shane said pursuing him harder still, "I put it to you again that you are lying. You knew all about the trafficking, you were going to get a cut from the proceeds, and you drove the truck knowing full well it contained illegal immigrants, isn't that right?"

"No, it's not right, it's not fucking well right at all!" Callum had lost his cool, and this was exactly what Shane wanted.

"Really? Not right? I think you know it is, why don't you just save us all a good deal of time and trouble but admitting it now, and suffer the rightful consequences of your egregious actions?" Shane said trying to drive home his advantage with a little too much enthusiasm.

"Mr Wilson!" said Justice Brannigan.

Shane had perhaps overstepped things a little by bringing his opinion into it and using somewhat inflammatory language and he knew it. It had been worth a shot, however, because the effect of it had been to make Callum go red in the face. Bernadette was worried Callum was going to blow, contrary to everything she had told him beforehand.

"I apologise, Judge," Shane said at once, "I will rephrase the question."

"Thank you," said the judge.

"Callum. Let me put it to you more simply. Why not admit the truth? The truth that you drove the truck knowing full well there were illegal immigrants inside. Admit you were part of this crime and face the consequences squarely, just like your lover Kevin has done. Why not do that and be fair to everyone here, what do you say?" Shane had dropped his tone, and sounded almost like a friend, confiding, trying to help.

Callum regarded him steadily but with a fulminating eye, Shane had goaded him unreasonably and the condescending manner of the last question didn't help. He'd had enough of Shane, and he exploded.

"Because I didn't do it! You keep saying I did it and I fucking well didn't, don't you get it? I didn't bloody do it! Kevin is a fucking liar!" Callum shouted exasperated.

Bernadette sighed. This wasn't how she wanted it to play out. Callum's manner had not helped him at all. He sounded like a guilty man. At the very least he sounded no better than Kevin who had also lost his temper. Now the two of them were back on a level playing field, one person's word against the other.

Shane had relied on goading Callum and it had worked. He really did not have anything to get leverage on Callum or any way to substantiate he was lying. This was the problem with having come to court with only one witness and no concrete evidence. The case was flimsy and so Shane had opted to attack Callum directly and make him react thus weakening the idea that Callum sounded truthful. For this case was all about how the judge perceived the responses in the end. If he didn't believe Callum was telling the truth, then Callum would be sent to the UK and that was that. It was a possibility Bernadette now felt she might be facing.

"No further questions, Judge," said Shane well satisfied with what he had managed to do.

"Mrs Mackenna, do you want to ask your witness anything else?" said the judge.

"No, Judge, thank you," said Bernadette. The damage was already done, and she hoped she might recoup something with Anh. There seemed little else to tip the balance in Callum's favour.

"You may step down, Mr Jenkins," said Justice Brannigan.

Callum left the stand, and the judge said, "I think we will take our morning break now, and then we can have your video witness, am I right?"

"Yes, Judge."

"Excellent!"

The Tipster entered the courtroom to adjourn the court.

✳ ✳ ✳

In a meeting room with Callum, Rhys and Imogen, they were sipping coffee. Imogen was on the phone to Damsa making sure everything was set up for the Anh.

"How did I do?" Callum was asking.

Bernadette sighed. "I'm not going to lie to you, losing your temper like that wasn't helpful."

This was the mildest way she could put it, in real terms she felt it was a complete disaster.

Rhys shook his head. "He's like me, hot headed, aren't you son?"

"Sorry, Bernadette, he wound me up something rotten."

"It can't be helped." She shrugged.

"How much damage has that done, to our case?" Rhys said bluntly with a sideways admonishing glance at his son.

"I can't say but because Callum and Kevin both lost your cool, it makes Callum look the same as him. I wanted Callum to contrast with him, sounding the more plausible, and now I can't guarantee the judge will view it that way."

"Oh fuck!" said Rhys.

"Sorry, Da." Callum looked contrite.

"It's OK, son, you've done it now, I just hope this amazing lady here can still save us."

"It's me she's saving, Da."

"No, son, not just you, because I will have to bear the pain of fourteen years without you and I can hardly even think of it without wanting to weep my fucking guts out," Rhys said, his voice hoarse and eyes suddenly moist.

"Let's calm down, shall we," said Bernadette, "All is not lost yet. Just regard this as a setback and I'll be doing everything I can to make sure it goes our way. What's the saying, it's not over until the final whistle?"

"Yes, you're right," said Rhys, "Although I wish the Welsh Rugby team would think that way."

Bernadette gave him a tight smile. "I'm sure."

"You probably don't follow rugby, it's a passion of mine, I'm afraid."

"Da, she doesn't want to hear about your sporting interests now," said Callum intervening.

"Yes, sorry," said Rhys.

"It's fine and Shane can be intimidating for sure, so I understand," said Bernadette trying to persuade herself as much as anything.

"Oh, I'm not afraid of his sort, he pissed me off, but he didn't intimidate me," said Callum.

Bernadette picked up on this at once.

"What do you mean his sort?"

"Oh, gay pricks like him, ten a penny in the clubs."

Bernadette stared at him in surprise.

"But Shane isn't... gay..."

"Oh, he's gay as fuck, trust me, my gaydar is well tuned, maybe it's why I got so annoyed. I felt like he was... eyeing me up or something," Callum laughed relieving the tension they all felt.

Bernadette was half listening and still absorbing the first revelation.

"Wait... Shane is... gay?" She started to laugh too.

"Is that funny?" Rhys wondered.

"I can't tell you why, but it is, not because he's gay but just because we know a fair old bit about him," Bernadette told him.

Imogen got off the phone. "It's all arranged, no problem at all... wait, what are you all talking about, and what are you laughing about?" She looked from one to the other.

"Callum says... wait for it... Shane is gay," Bernadette told her.

"What?"

"He's gay, trust me, gay as they come," Callum said.

"Oh my fucking God!" Imogen said.

Rhys shook his head. "I'm not sure what's happening here at all, this is all over my head."

"Look, I can't say more, but Shane and I have history," Imogen told him.

"Oh... oh!"

"You wouldn't be the first," said Callum.

"The first to what?"

"Sleep with a gay guy."

"Maybe he doesn't know," Bernadette ventured.

"Oh, he knows believe me, whether he's admitting it or not, is another matter."

"Right, well, I think..."

They didn't find out what she thought because the meeting room door opened, and Olivia appeared.

"There you are, I've been looking all over for you," she said to Bernadette.

"What's up?"

"I need to talk to you both urgently."

Imogen looked at her watch. "We've not got much time."

"Come on, Callum, that's our cue," said Rhys getting up.

"Sure," said Callum following him out of the room.

"So, what's going on?" said Bernadette to Olivia once they had gone.

"We raided Balik Transport, and guess what?"

"What? Sorry to hurry you, it's just we're due back in court," said Bernadette.

"We've got evidence the illegals were put onboard there. We've actually got CCTV footage of it. The idiots didn't erase their own fucking evidence. There is no sign of Callum, but what there is, is the CCTV of him inspecting the truck and driving it off. Also, we found a customs seal maker, and other equipment."

"That's brilliant, are you able to stick around, I'd like to get you in front of the judge."

"Sure, I can do that for you."

"Great, well, we've got to get back into court."

"I'll come and sit in the courtroom, then if you need me," Olivia said.

"I could certainly give you a hug, you're a superstar," said Bernadette getting up. This was just the tonic she needed after Callum's debacle with Shane.

"Don't let me stop you," Olivia laughed.

✳ ✳ ✳

Court resumed, and with Justice Brannigan once more in his place, Bernadette waited expectantly.

"Mrs Mackenna, is everything ready for your video witness?"

"Yes, Judge." She stood up. "But before we do so, I would like to make a request."

"Which is?"

"Some evidence has just come to light, Judge. I have been informed that a raid was carried this week on Balik Trading by the Garda. This is the depot where the truck in question was loaded, and now the Garda has video evidence among other things, which we believe can absolve our client. We'd like the opportunity to call the SIO to give evidence."

"Objection." Shane was on his feet at once. "This evidence has not been submitted to the court under the agreed guidelines, and we won't have any time to examine the ramifications of it."

"I appreciate your concern, Mr Wilson," said Justice Brannigan dryly, "However, you would have the opportunity to cross examine the witness, so I can't see how this puts you at a disadvantage. After all, Mrs Mackenna has said the evidence has only come to light."

"Well, Judge, but..."

"I think I'm duty bound to admit the evidence, Mr Wilson, both counsels will have sufficient time to ask all the questions they want."

Shane sat down, looking unhappy.

"Thank you, Judge," said Bernadette, "I'll call the new witness after our video witness."

"Very well, but it's likely to be after lunch," said the judge.

"I understand."

"Then, let us continue," said Justice Brannigan.

"We are connecting with our witness, and from now we will refer to her as Witness A," said Bernadette.

Imogen nodded to the Clerk of the Court, and the court video screens came on. Anh could be seen on the video monitors in the courtroom, but her face was in shadow.

"Witness A," said Bernadette, "Are you able to hear us?"

"Yes," said Anh.

"Excellent, so I want to ask you please, can you tell us in your own words how you came to be trafficked to the United Kingdom."

Anh spent some time describing her journey, with some prompting from Bernadette and a few questions. It was exactly as she had told Imogen and Bernadette when they interviewed her. There was a hush in the courtroom while she was speaking. The story was harrowing and also very sobering.

When she finished, Justice Brannigan said quietly, "Well, now that was a very sad story, very sad indeed. Do you have any further questions for Witness A, Mrs Mackenna?"

"Yes, I do," she said.

"Witness A, I want you to take a good look at my client." She beckoned to Callum who came to stand next to her so that he was in view of the camera.

"Yes," said Anh.

"Have you seen this man before?"

Anh shook her head.

"No."

"Thank you." Bernadette indicated to Callum to sit down. "Now, you said, you were loaded onto the truck in Dublin, is that correct?"

"Yes, yes, it is, well, I didn't know it was Dublin, but I knew it was Ireland, someone told me that," said Anh.

"And are you sure you did not see the man I just showed you during the loading process?"

"No, he wasn't there, I didn't see him."

"Does the name, Callum, mean anything to you?"

"No."

"You've never heard that name before?"

"No."

"You did not hear that name at the truck depot?"

"No."

"Thank you, no further questions, Judge."

The evidence was tenuous, and Bernadette was sure Shane would be able to point out the flaws in it during his cross examination. However, the purpose of Anh's testimony was to cast doubt upon the case rather than provide Callum with an iron-clad defence.

"Thank you, Mrs Mackenna," said Justice Brannigan, "Mr Wilson, do you have any questions for Witness A?"

"Yes, Judge," said Shane standing up.

"Given the nature of this witness, and what she has endured, could I ask you to bear that in mind while questioning her?" said the judge mildly.

"I will be as circumspect as possible, Judge," said Shane.

"Thank you, please carry on."

Shane looked up at the screen. "Witness A, you said you had never seen the man known as Callum before and you hadn't heard his name, am I right?"

"Yes."

"But it doesn't mean he wasn't there, does it, just because you didn't see him?"

"I don't believe he was there," said Anh.

"Yes, but surely you could not have seen everyone who was there. You would not have. So, it's possible would you not agree he could have been there?"

"I don't know, I suppose so, but I don't think he was."

This wasn't equivocal enough for Shane, so he tried again.

"Yes, so you've said. Can you also tell me, were some of the men wearing masks?"

"Yes."

"So, you couldn't have seen their faces properly, then could you? It's perfectly possible Callum might have been there wearing a mask. Is it not so?"

"That's possible but I don't think so."

"But it might be possible, yes, or no?"

"Yes, it might be possible."

This was the answer he wanted. To throw shade onto her testimony. They were two lawyers playing with degrees of doubt and hoping the judge would lean more towards their version than the other.

"Thank you, no further questions, Judge." Shane sat down.

It wasn't possible or certainly politic for him to press Anh, and he knew it. So, he opted instead for a much milder line of attack which simply tried to discredit the plausibility of what she had said.

"Mrs Mackenna?" Justice Brannigan said, in case she had any more questions.

"I do have something I'd like to ask her, yes." Bernadette stood up.

"Continue."

Bernadette beckoned Callum over.

"Witness A, I'm going to ask Callum to speak and I want you to listen carefully, OK?"

"Yes," said Anh.

"Callum, could you just say your name, and a few words about yourself?" Bernadette asked him.

"Sure, I'm Callum Jenkins, I'm a truck driver. I drive trucks for a living and my father is the man who owns the haulage business. I'm his son and I work for him."

"Thank you, Callum. Witness A, did you hear Callum's voice clearly?"

"Yes," said Anh.

"Have you ever heard his voice before?"

"No, I have never heard it before."

"You're sure about that?"

"Yes, I'm very good with voices, I listen carefully, I was a tour guide, I'm used to listening carefully to accents, and I've never heard it before," Anh said emphatically.

This was gold, for Bernadette. Anh had come across as very articulate in English and so her testimony couldn't be attacked from that point of view. The only issue was, as Shane had pointed out, whether she really could be sure Callum was there or not. What Bernadette had managed to do was negate to some degree Shane's line of questioning. It would still be for the judge to decide whether or not Callum was likely to have been there. Anh's testimony did tip the balance a little more in their favour.

"No further questions, Judge," said Bernadette with a smile.

"Mr Wilson?"

"No, Judge," said Shane. Bernadette had outsmarted him on this witness, although he would certainly not be defeated as yet.

"Witness A, thank you for your time, we are going to disconnect the video now," said the judge.

The video went off and he addressed the court, "Right then. We'll take an early lunch, and then hear from your new witness, Mrs Mackenna, and hopefully, we can get your final submissions in before the end of the day, yes?"

"Yes, Judge," said Bernadette.

"Yes, Judge," said Shane.

The Tipster called for the court to rise, and the morning session ended with Justice Brannigan leaving the courtroom.

* * *

Over lunch, Bernadette and Imogen were joined by Olivia. Callum and Rhys had opted to go for a walk to cool off, but Bernadette warned them to steer clear of talking to the press or anyone else. Rhys said he'd seen a café near the courtroom and fancied a fry up. Imogen had ordered in sandwiches and coffee for the three of them.

"Well, what do you think?" Olivia said accepting a chicken and salad roll from Imogen.

"About?" Bernadette took a sip of her coffee.

"Your chances?"

"Improved hopefully with your testimony." Bernadette reached for a beef baguette with salad.

"We can't give you any footage you realise that, it's all on my say so."

"I know and at the very least it should enter some doubt, we sure as hell need it after Callum's little performance out there."

"Oh?"

"He lost his rag with Shane," Imogen laughed, taking a bite out of her own ham, egg and salad bap.

"Not hard to do from what I've seen," Olivia chuckled.

"Oh, he's good at winding up the witnesses, unfortunately, Callum took the bait. It just made him seem as bad as their witness Kevin who had already lost his cool in spectacular fashion," Bernadette added.

"Is it that harmful to your case?"

"It depends, I wanted a clear contrast between the two of them and it's not going to be that anymore."

"Ah well, let's see if I can't give you a helping hand." Olivia smiled.

"How's the investigation going?" Imogen asked her.

"Very well, I think we might get a major score on this one. Drugs, weapons, the lot, as well as the people smuggling."

"Sounds good."

"We might want to bring your witness over here after all," said Olivia.

"It will be good for her, but she'll need some assurances about being able to attain refugee status," Bernadette said.

"Perhaps your friend Jack can pull some strings for us, hmm?" Olivia cocked an eye.

"Why don't you ask him, you are the SIO?"

"I might just do that."

The three of them addressed themselves to the food for a few moments, and once she had finished her sandwich, Bernadette said, "How are things with Carole?"

"Very nice, thanks, still ticking along."

"I'm glad to hear it, she seems like a nice girl."

"Oh, she's nice, naughty but nice." Olivia smiled.

The rest of lunch was taken up by discussion of the afternoon session and what Bernadette planned to ask Olivia. No mention was made about the possibility of Shane being gay although Bernadette was sure Imogen was dying to talk about it. She was sure it would be a topic of conversation later.

✳ ✳ ✳

They took a loo break and then returned to the courtroom. Bernadette was happy to see Callum and Rhys already there.

"Everything OK?" she asked Rhys as she passed him.

"Yes, the reporters tried to collar us, but we didn't say anything."

"Good. We will say something at the end of this afternoon session."

"OK, we'll be guided by you."

Bernadette patted his shoulder affectionately and returned to their station.

The Tipster announced Justice Brannigan who came in and sat down looking quite perky. He was no doubt anticipating the end of the hearing, Bernadette mused.

"Now then, you have a new witness for us, Mrs Mackenna?" said the judge.

"Yes, Judge."

"Then let's get on."

"I call DS Olivia Thompson to the stand," said Bernadette.

Olivia was sworn in, confirmed her name and profession, and Bernadette began her questions.

"You are Senior Investigating Officer on an investigation which has relevance to this case, am I right?"

"Yes, I am," said Olivia.

"Can you tell us about it?"

"We have been undertaking an investigation into Balik Trading which is the depot from which the truck was driven carrying the Vietnamese women who were being trafficked for sexual purposes. We also now know it was loaded at the site, and that is where the women were put on board. We also found equipment to make the customs seals for other countries, so that the seals can be broken, and then reinstated with forgeries."

"So, you have evidence confirming this?" It was important to establish this part.

"We do. We have preliminary statements which indicate this to be the case. We made a number of arrests and these people are in the process of being charged. We have internal CCTV footage which also bears this out. However, at present, we cannot release any of this as it is being used for cases against the perpetrators."

"Quite. But as you are under oath, can we take your word on this matter for the moment, that what you say is correct?"

"Yes, I've seen the footage myself, and of course I know what was said in interviews with suspects and made in statements."

"Thank you. Do you see our client Callum Jenkins standing over in the dock?" Bernadette pointed at Callum.

"Yes, I do."

"Can you tell the court if he has appeared in any of the CCTV footage you have seen, or whether his name has been mentioned?"

"No, it hasn't appeared in any internal footage. His name has not come up so far during questioning."

"Do you think it's likely he was involved?"

"Objection," said Shane jumping to his feet at once, "The DS cannot possibly know for sure, and it is purely conjecture when their investigation is not complete."

"I'm simply asking her professional opinion, Judge, surely it's allowable?" Bernadette shot back.

Justice Brannigan thought for a moment, and then said, "I think perhaps I will accept the objection. It's really for me to decide, based on what I've heard, what the balance of probabilities are."

"Thank you, Judge," said Shane shooting a look of triumph at Bernadette.

"I withdraw the question, Judge," said Bernadette ignoring this. "DS Thompson, can you tell us if there was any video footage of Callum Jenkins?"

"Yes, there was, footage of the outside when he collected the truck."

"And what did it show?"

"It showed him walking around inspecting the truck, then getting in and driving it away."

"Did he open the back of the truck?"

"No."

"And this is footage which you personally saw?"

"Yes."

"Objection," said Shane jumping to his feet again, "Judge, this is all very well but since we cannot have the video footage in this courtroom then we are taking the word of this officer, which although I'm sure is truthful, it's also technically hearsay since the evidence cannot be directly viewed. I am submitting that what was on that video should not be admissible, unless we can view it."

"Judge, DS Thompson is a serving officer in the Garda, surely her testimony should be sufficient?" Bernadette wasn't letting this go without a fight.

"I'm minded to allow it," said Justice Brannigan, "But I can't give it the same weight as I would if I had been able to see it, and I take the point on board."

"Thank you, Judge," said Bernadette accepting the concession, "I've no further questions for this witness."

"Mr Wilson?" Justice Brannigan asked.

"Yes, I do," said Shane getting back on his feet.

"Carry on."

"DS Thompson, you claim you have no evidence so far of Mr Jenkins being involved, but you can't rule out there might be some revealed, yes or no?"

Bernadette rolled her eyes this was almost the opposite of what she had asked and was disallowed. However, she held her peace.

"No, I can't rule it out, but I can say..."

"That's all I need, a yes or no answer, thank you," said Shane cutting her off.

Olivia pursed her lips. She wasn't happy at this cavalier treatment.

"And with the video, you mentioned. Although it shows Mr Jenkins didn't look in the truck at the depot, he could have done so later on, out of sight somewhere on the road, yes or no?"

"Well, that's a big assumption..." Olivia began.

"Yes or no, DS Thompson," said Shane interrupting.

"Yes, he could have." She looked as if she would say more but realised the game he was playing.

"Thank you, that's all I have, Judge," said Shane well satisfied with himself.

"Do you have anything more, Mrs Mackenna?" said Justice Brannigan.

"No, thank you, Judge."

"Very well, DS Thompson thank you for your time coming here today, you may step down, your work is done."

Justice Brannigan was almost jovial as this was the last witness. Bernadette got the impression the judge was going to be more than happy to put the hearing to bed. She could hardly blame him. It was difficult and also not at all cut and dried. A lot of pressure rested on the judge making the right decision since it was a matter of sending an Irish citizen to trial in another country, and possibly prison. This wasn't something to be taken lightly.

Olivia got down from the stand and went to sit back in her seat. There was an expectant buzz from the assembled press on the benches.

"Now, do either of you need any time, say half an hour to prepare your final submissions or can we get on with them?" Justice Brannigan asked the two counsel.

"A few moments might be nice, Judge, in the light of the recent evidence," said Shane.

"Very well, we'll adjourn for thirty minutes after which you can deliver your final submissions."

The Tipster was already halfway into the courtroom on hearing those words.

* * *

"We've had more fucking breaks than any other hearing I've been at," said Imogen as they drank another coffee.

Olivia had not joined them because she said there were phone calls to be made, but she wanted to stay until the end. Callum and Rhys were spending the break together and so it was just Bernadette and Imogen in the meeting room nearby.

"I don't think it is really," Bernadette laughed, "It just feels that way."

"I'm pretty sure the judge doesn't want to be here," Imogen replied sipping her drink.

"Yes, me too, but overall, he's been quite fair."

"Let's see if he is when he makes his judgement."

"How do you think it's going to go?" Bernadette asked Imogen, wondering what her opinion on it might be.

"I don't know, personally I think he shouldn't send Callum to the UK, but then I'm biased."

"OK, but what do you *think*?" Bernadette sometimes pressed her, a little, it was part of her passage to being a senior barrister.

"Oh fine." Imogen considered it for a moment. "I think our case is still stronger. They have only got the testimony of a witness and we've exposed the weakness in that. Even though Callum lost his temper, Shane couldn't get him to admit to anything. We've brought more doubt in with Anh and also Olivia which supported what Anh was saying. So overall I think the balance of probabilities should fall in our favour."

"I think so too, but you can never be sure until the judgement is in."

"Yes, very much so."

"Let's discuss the summary."

"Sure, but by the way, D'Arcy texted me to ask when we might be finished. I'm not sure if she's coming here to surprise me or something."

"Who's a lucky girl then."

* * *

The discussion about their final submission took up the rest of the break, and Bernadette returned to the court in good spirits. Once they were in place, the judge breezed in hot on the heels of the Tipster. He sat down, gave the courtroom a cursory glance before speaking.

"Mr Wilson, would you like to give your final submission, if you please?"

"Yes, Judge." Shane stood up and rustled his papers for a moment. "Judge, the position of the prosecution remains adamant. Mr Jenkins should be extradited to the United Kingdom."

Having made this bold statement, he paused for effect.

"We stand by the testimony of our witness. Whilst we accept, he had a sexual relationship with Mr Jenkins, other than his denial, nothing concrete has been presented which categorically rules him out from knowing about the trafficking. We have his own denial without any concrete evidence. We have Witness A who said she had not seen or heard him, or his name. However, that doesn't mean he wasn't there. The evidence of DS Thompson doesn't absolve Mr Jenkins. He could still have known about it."

He stopped and took a drink of water.

"Therefore, we don't believe the police and the prosecution service in the United Kingdom should be denied the opportunity to pursue a legitimate prosecution of Mr Jenkins. It is intended to charge him, as I mentioned at the beginning of this hearing and then prosecute him under United Kingdom law. We don't believe there is sufficient reasonable doubt not to allow the extradition to go ahead. In conclusion, our submission is that we ask the court to give permission for the extradition of Mr Jenkins to be allowed."

"Thank you, Mr Wilson," said Justice Brannigan who had been listening carefully to what Shane had said. "Mrs Mackenna, you may give your submission now, if you please."

"Thank you, Judge," said Bernadette standing up.

"More Shakespeare for us, Mrs Mackenna?" said Justice Brannigan smiling.

"Well, Judge, I could naturally say 'Truth is truth to the end of reckoning' but I'm sure you already believe that, being a judge," she quipped.

"Indeed, Mrs Mackenna, anyway, please carry on."

Bernadette nodded and composed herself briefly. "Judge, you asked about Shakespeare and I would quote from Macbeth, when he says, 'What, can the devil speak true?' Bringing that quote into context, can the devil, a criminal, speak true? Can Mr Clinton, a known criminal, speak the truth? Should the court believe him? We are talking of a man who by his own admission is a career criminal, lies are surely his stock in trade. Why should he be believed now? Other than it suits the Metropolitan Police of United Kingdom to do so, because it fits their narrative, it fits their desire to find someone, anyone to nail with this crime."

She paused. It was a hard-hitting speech. She wasn't pulling any punches.

"Enter, stage left, our client Callum Jenkins. A man caught up by circumstances and the misfortune to have entered into a relationship with Kevin Clinton. Evidence shows, Mr Clinton was jealous, possessive, and by his own testimony on the stand, he was angry Mr Jenkins did not share the same feelings as he did. How did that anger manifest itself? By fabricating a story under pressure from the police to implicate Mr Clinton. In other words, if Mr Clinton dobs someone else in, to use the vernacular, then he will get off far more lightly. And who better than his blameless lover. No comeback from his criminal friends, he doesn't put his own life in too much danger, and he throws an innocent man to the wolves."

Bernadette took a breath, flicked a glance at Imogen who gave her a smile of encouragement.

"We have a witness, who is one of the women actually trafficked. A harrowing tale but she risks her own life to stand testimony that she had not seen, heard of, or heard Mr Jenkins. We have DS Thompson, who gave testimony that a raid on the premises of Balik Transport did not reveal anything about Mr Jenkins being involved in the trafficking. A video albeit unseen by the court corroborates his version of events that he checked his truck and drove it to away from the depot."

She was winding up for the finish.

"In summary, we submit this case hinges around reasonable doubt. Is there reasonable doubt that Mr Jenkins was involved in the trafficking? We submit based upon the evidence presented to this court that there is. The case to extradite him is not beyond reasonable doubt, instead, there is sufficient doubt to mean that he should not be sent to the United Kingdom. Mr Jenkins, a citizen of Ireland, is entitled surely to the same yardstick as anyone brought to court accused of the crime. We ask the court to deny the extradition on that basis, there is insufficient evidence and reasonable doubt of his involvement in the crime. Thank you."

She stopped and waited for the judge to speak.

Justice Brannigan did so at length. "Thank you, Mrs Mackenna. Thank you both for your professional conduct in this case. Indeed, the evidence and your submissions provide much food for thought. This is a weighty case, for certain. The extradition of a citizen of this country can never be taken lightly. Therefore, I reserve judgement for a period of two days, after which I should be in a position to give you my decision. Bail conditions stand as previously set. You will be notified of the date and time for the judgement to be delivered, and I will see you all then."

The Tipster came in and adjourned the court. Justice Brannigan left the room. There was a big scramble by the press to get out of the door. Callum came up to them wreathed in smiles.

"Is that it?"

"Yes, but it's not over yet, of course," said Bernadette.

"No, but your speech was incredible, amazing."

"Thank you, I did my best."

"It was brilliant, quite brilliant," said Rhys who had also arrived.

"Thanks, honestly, I can't tell you if it's been enough, but I hope so."

"You've done everything I hoped and more," said Rhys sincerely, "And I want you to know, whatever happens, I'm truly grateful to you."

"You are welcome, I'm glad to have represented you, Callum, I hope for all our sakes we can get a result."

"Are we going to say anything to the press?" Imogen cut in.

"Yes, yes, we are, follow my lead as always."

"We will."

Olivia who had been standing at the side while this conversation was going on, came closer.

"Well done, great speech," she said to Bernadette.

"Thanks, lovely, and thanks for your timely intervention."

"No problem, I'll let you know if anything interesting arises, but anyway I've got to dash. Most enlightening, I'll try and make it for the judgement." She hurried away out of the court.

The court was now empty, and the other barristers appeared to have gone.

"Shall we go?" said Imogen.

"Yes."

They walked out of the courtroom in a body and were about to head for the exit when Shane Wilson appeared. They stopped as he was standing in the way, looking a little agitated.

"Imogen," he said, ignoring the others as if they weren't there, "Could I have a word... please?"

Imogen looked at him doubtfully.

"Look, I've been wanting to say something to you, and well, if you wouldn't mind?"

She looked at Bernadette who shrugged, and then back at Shane.

"Fine," Imogen said to him and then to Bernadette, "I won't be long."

Bernadette watched her walk away around the corner, and then on impulse, she said to Callum and Rhys, "Wait here a moment, would you?"

She followed the other two and on rounding a corner could see Imogen standing with her back to the wall and Shane almost standing over her.

"Come on, Imogen, you've been avoiding me all this time. Can't we just be friends?" he was saying.

"I don't want to be your friend," said Imogen.

"We had a good thing going, but you had to go and fucking spoil it. Going with your fancy woman? You're not a lesbian really, Imogen, don't be so fucking daft."

"Shane, can you stop, please? You and me, are well and truly over."

"It's not fucking over, you bitch, admit it, admit that you fancy me, you want me don't you, admit it..."

Bernadette was about to move in on them, when D'Arcy and Eve came running up to her.

"Bernadette, where's my Imogen, where is she?" she said concerned.

Bernadette pointed to where Shane had an arm on either side of Imogen trapping her against the wall.

"Oh my God!" shrieked D'Arcy, "Imogen, I'm coming!"

Before Bernadette could do anything sensible, D'Arcy bounded over to Shane and Imogen.

"Get off my fiancée, you bastard!" she shrieked, grabbing one of his arms, and stepping inside his leg, she threw him beautifully and he landed flat on his back. "How dare you! How dare you, touch her! I'll..."

"It's OK, D'Arcy," said Imogen putting her arm around her fiancée, "It's OK."

Bernadette and Eve had now arrived and stood looking down at Shane.

"What the fuck are you playing at?" Bernadette demanded as he tried to sit up.

"I... err... I..." He seemed lost for words and got unsteadily to his feet.

"You what? You've breached ethics, what you've done is tantamount to sexual harassment and in front of witnesses. What the fuck is wrong with you?"

"I don't know, I don't know what came over me. I'm truly sorry, Imogen, really. Sorry," he said looking shamefaced.

"My junior is within her rights to lay a complaint against you with the bar association at the very least."

"I know, and I've no right to ask you, but I'd really hope you won't do that. I'm an idiot, I just don't know what I was doing."

"You listen to me," said Imogen recovering herself, "Stay the fuck away from me in future, other than if we have to meet in court. If you ever, ever do anything like that again, I will take you to the fucking cleaners."

"No, I won't, I... I promise you that..." said Shane turning to go.

"Stay away from my fiancée!" D'Arcy said fiercely.

"You're a very lucky man, you won't be so lucky next time," said Bernadette.

Mason appeared and grabbed onto Shane's arm. "Shane, what the fuck are you doing? Have you lost your fucking marbles?" He turned to the others. "Look, I'm very sorry, very sorry. It was completely unprofessional of him. I was about to intervene when your fiancée did such an excellent job, and serves him right, bloody idiot. You will have a written apology from him tomorrow. Thank you for your understanding."

He grabbed Shane's arm and pulled him away quickly. "What the hell, mate, you were bang out of order. That's your career nearly gone down the toilet, you complete fucking fool!"

After they had gone, Bernadette said to Imogen, "Are you OK, darling?"

"Yes, just a bit shaken up."

"I should think so."

"I'm glad I came along when I did," said D'Arcy still angry.

"That was a pretty impressive move," Eve observed.

"I learned it from you, darling," D'Arcy said smiling.

"Well done."

"We can discuss this tomorrow, Imogen, if you want to take it further, I'll support you," said Bernadette.

"I think this calls for dinner at my favourite restaurant," said D'Arcy.

"We have to speak to the press on the way out," said Bernadette.

"OK, but after that, join us?"

"Yes, we will," Eve said.

"Let's go, Callum and Rhys will be wondering what's going on."

They returned to the courtroom where Rhys and Callum were patiently outside of waiting with their suitcase completely oblivious to the drama which had recently unfolded. They headed once more for the entrance to the main building.

The press was lying in wait, just as Bernadette expected. She stopped in front of the crush. Further down the steps were yet more people with "Free Callum" banners chanting and shouting. Bernadette stopped and held up her hand.

"The hearing is over, as you know I'm sure. We are hoping that the strong case we have made will prevail. We came for justice and now we are hoping to get it, for Callum's sake."

"Do you think you'll win?" shouted a reporter.

"I can't say, obviously, we are very hopeful. We put forward a good case, I think we've got a good chance."

"Would you put a bet on it?" said a wag from the Irish Sun.

"Would you?" she shot back.

There was general laughter.

"Is that your wife?" shouted someone else.

"Yes, this is she, Eve Mackenna." Bernadette smiled and put her arm affectionately around Eve's waist.

"Give us a kiss then!"

"Kiss her!"

"Not today," said Bernadette, "But if we win, I'll give you a kiss to remember."

"Callum, what have you got to say, do you think you're going to win?"

"Come on," said Bernadette, "That's all folks, the show's over."

They started to walk away with people shouting questions at D'Arcy and Imogen, as well as Callum and Rhys.

Once they got to Bernadette's car, they called a taxi for Rhys and Callum. Having seen them off, Bernadette and Eve drove to Chapter One in Parnell Square, and parked. Then they met up with D'Arcy and Imogen in her usual private dining cubby hole.

*   *   *

"Are you feeling a little better, darling?" said D'Arcy after they had ordered their meal.

"Yes, quite a bit," Imogen replied, sipping a glass of wine, "It was quite a shock."

"I'm sure," said D'Arcy planting a kiss on Imogen's lips.

"You arrived just at the right time," Bernadette said smiling, she sipped her sparkling water, as she was driving and didn't want to drink.

"You were amazing," said Eve tucking herself in close to Bernadette.

"Thank you, you have to come and teach us some more moves though," said D'Arcy.

"Yes, of course, I will."

"You should have seen his face though," Bernadette laughed, "When you took him down, that was funny."

"He didn't know what had hit him," said Eve.

"No, that he didn't," said Imogen.

"I just can't understand why he was doing that to you though, Imogen," said D'Arcy who had now had time to think about it.

Bernadette and Eve exchanged glances. Imogen had obviously not told her about Shane.

Imogen took a long drink of wine, and said, "Darling, I have to tell you something about Shane, and I hope you're not going to be very angry with me."

"Angry, why should I be angry?" said D'Arcy puzzled.

"Because I haven't told you everything about my past, not everything."

"I see."

Bernadette coughed discreetly. "Eve and I can, erm... take a walk... erm..."

"No," said Imogen, "Stay, we're all friends here, so you should stay."

"Yes, stay," said D'Arcy, "Please, it's OK."

"I erm... I was Shane's lover briefly," Imogen said to D'Arcy.

"Oh! Well... I see but..."

"That's not all, and I need to tell you the whole."

Imogen told D'Arcy the truth about Shane. The introduction to Fifty Shades style of relationship, and how she had had a few very torrid dates with him where he had introduced her to domination and submission, sex and spanking. The whole of it including his offer to her to become his full time submissive and junior counsel. How she had slapped his face in the restaurant. Then finally with tears running down her face, how she had experienced sexual attraction for him not long ago.

"I'm sorry, so sorry," Imogen said choking on her words, "I should have told you, told it all."

D'Arcy was silent, for a long while but she held Imogen's hands tightly, looking at her with pursed lips.

"Say something, D'Arcy, please..." said Imogen on the verge of sobbing her heart out.

"You should have told me, all of this," said D'Arcy, "I told you everything about me."

"I know, I'm sorry, darling."

"I'm disappointed in you, Imogen, very disappointed that you didn't tell me."

"Oh... shit... does that mean you're going to dump me now?" said Imogen bursting into floods of tears.

Bernadette and Eve could hardly bear this, and Bernadette was longing to take Imogen into her arms, when D'Arcy took Imogen into an embrace.

"Of course, I'm not going to dump you, sweetheart, of course not, don't be silly," said D'Arcy stroking her hair.

"I'm a bitch, I'm a fucking bitch," said Imogen sobbing into her shoulder.

Bernadette nudged Eve, and they discreetly left the booth. The waiter was just appearing with the starters and Bernadette told him to take them away just for a few minutes. They went out of the front door and up the stairs onto the pavement.

"Oh God, poor Imogen," said Eve, "I really felt for her then."

"Yes, but they'll get over it, just like we have," Bernadette replied.

"We did, didn't we." Eve paused. "Kiss me. I've missed you."

Bernadette did so, oblivious of passers-by, and then they walked for a bit hand in hand, while Bernadette told her about the day's events, and about Callum's assertion, Shane was gay. They had a chuckle about that and mused as to his obsession with Imogen. When they felt it was politic, they returned to the restaurant and back to D'Arcy and Imogen. Bernadette was pleased to see the two of them were smiling and seemed in better spirits.

"D'Arcy has forgiven me," said Imogen.

"Of course, I forgive you, how could I not forgive you? I love you, you're everything to me, even if you upset me by not telling me about Shane. I'm your fiancée don't forget!"

"But no more secrets. Like you and Eve, we're going to be the same with each other. We are going to be completely open and honest from now on," said Imogen.

"Yes, yes we are," said D'Arcy, "But what did we also agree, Imogen?"

It seemed she wanted them to be in on everything from here on. Bernadette wasn't so sure she wanted to know about the additional revelation and could certainly take a guess at it. She wasn't wrong.

"When we get home, I'm going to get a spanking, from D'Arcy, for keeping secrets," said Imogen quietly.

"Really?" Bernadette raised an eyebrow.

"What's sauce for the goose, and don't tell me you don't deserve it, darling," said D'Arcy slyly.

"Something to look forward to then," said Eve with a giggle.

"I'm not so sure about *that*," Imogen said with feeling.

"Oh, come on, darling, how many times have you..." D'Arcy laughed lightly.

"I know, and you're right, I deserve it."

"Yes, yes you do, and you are going to find out how much when we get home," D'Arcy said with some relish warming to her new reversal of roles.

"Yes, well, I'm glad you've sorted it all out satisfactorily," said Bernadette happy to move on, "I'll tell the waiter to bring the starters now, I put him off, poor man."

"Oh, yes, I'm starving, I wondered where it was," said D'Arcy instantly diverted.

Soon enough, harmony was restored, and the four of them ate and talked until it was quite late, and it was time to go home. They bid an affectionate goodbye to D'Arcy and Imogen. Then drove home themselves.

"Well, that was a turnup for the books," said Eve, once they were in the car.

"Wasn't it?"

"You know I'm going to want a story later."

"I know." Bernadette smiled, and slipped her hand into her wife's.

"I love you," said Eve.

"I love you too."

CHAPTER SEVENTEEN

he morning after court Bernadette and Imogen had their usual coffee in her office, and Imogen sat down gingerly on the sofa.

"Oh, darling," Bernadette said with concern.

"I'm a bit sore," said Imogen wiggling her behind in an effort to get comfortable.

"I take it D'Arcy meted out your consequences last night," said Bernadette sympathetically.

"And then some, fuck, it was worse than Shane once she got that paddle in her hand."

"Sounds like she was making up for all the times you've done it to her." Bernadette sipped her coffee.

"She's not getting too many chances at it, I can tell you, my arse was bright red at the end, redder than my hair. I was close to screaming point a couple of times," said Imogen ruefully.

"Well, you started it, darling, so..."

"I know, and I should have told D'Arcy about Shane, I'm happy I got it off my chest."

"What happened after your chastisement?"

"Oh well, we fucked each other's brains out, it was so fucking hot. I'm fairly worn out, to be honest."

"I'm glad, for you. I mean sorry about your backside though."

"Oh, it'll be fine, I'll be fine. Don't worry about me, it will remind me never to keep such secrets from D'Arcy again."

"I do worry though, darling."

"Well, I'm OK."

"What about Shane though? Callum says he's gay."

"God, I don't know what to think, he must be bisexual perhaps because I can tell you he certainly enjoyed fucking me... so..."

"You're not still thinking about that, are you?" Bernadette said with concern.

"No, oh no. That incident left me cold, scared even, I didn't know what he was going to do."

"D'Arcy showed him."

"She certainly did," Imogen laughed.

It was a topic to return to at some point, Bernadette felt but for now, she changed the subject.

"So, we're almost done with Callum's case."

"Yes."

"We'll need another big case."

"No, what you need is your honeymoon, so we don't need another big case to make you not want to go, darling," Imogen said firmly.

"Yes, you're right."

"You and Eve need to go, and soon. I can hold the fort, there is nothing pressing."

"No, gosh, you're right, we have to."

"Exactly, so I'm going to liaise with Eve about this, as you're hopeless, darling, and arrange it all."

"Honestly, you two... so bossy," said Bernadette, squeezing her hand affectionately.

"But you love it, and you need it, because you are all about work, and if we don't make you take the holiday you won't do it."

"Thank you, I love you."

"I love you too, and so does, Eve."

* * *

The morning of the court judgement arrived. Bernadette showered and Eve put her hair into a ponytail. She had laid out a charcoal skirt suit with a pink blouse for Bernadette, and a pair of black wedge mules. Bernadette went downstairs for breakfast. Eve was dressed in a crème knit midi dress which she would top with a blue cotton jacket. She was wearing white thong mules with kitten heels.

She slid a plate of poached eggs on toast, bacon and mushroom, with a hollandaise sauce.

"Yummy," said Bernadette picking up her cutlery.

"Something different for today." Eve passed her a cup of coffee, and sat down with her own plate.

"Thank you for coming with me."

"I wouldn't miss it for the world, darling, and plus you promised the media a kiss, and kiss they shall have."

"You're the best wife."

"No, you are."

They laughed, and Bernadette went back to eating her breakfast.

"Do you think you are going to win, today? Because I think you are," said Eve after a few moments.

"Have you worked your magic, you witch, is that what you're saying?"

"Wait and see." Eve's eyes twinkled.

"I love you so much."

"I'm looking forward to our holiday. Our honeymoon."

"Me too."

"Let's go," said Bernadette draining her coffee, while Eve put the empty plates in the dishwasher.

"Not until you kiss me, goodbye."

"But you're coming with me," Bernadette protested, but it was only half hearted.

"And?"

"Come here then, witch."

* * *

Bernadette, Eve and Imogen arrived at the court in good time. On the steps were more press than ever, and a massive demonstration of "Free Callum" supporters blowing whistles, banging drums, shouting and yelling slogans. The Garda were out in force keeping them on the pavement. Bernadette was heartened by all of this support, perhaps it was a good omen after all.

They pushed past the throng and into the court. Callum and Rhys were waiting, and the four of them headed to the courtroom.

"Well," said Callum, before they walked in, "This is either my last hour of freedom or my first hour free of worry."

"Have faith, chin up," said Bernadette putting a hand on his arm.

"I'll try."

"I don't know what I'll do if he's sent to England," said Rhys tearing up.

"Come on, now," said Imogen, "It's not over until it's over."

"You're right," said Rhys pulling himself together with a visible effort.

"Ready then, let's go." Bernadette led them in, and Eve went to sit with Rhys on the front benches. Bernadette and Imogen took their places, and Callum went to the dock. Shortly afterwards Shane and Mason walked into the courtroom. Shane did not look in their direction, but Mason nodded at them affably enough. It wasn't his neck on the line after all. Shane had sent a written apology to Imogen as promised, and they now had this on file. They wrote back with a strongly worded letter warning him if it ever happened again, they would take action against him.

As far as Bernadette and Imogen were concerned, this was an end to it. Imogen had also put the whole fancying Shane thing behind her. Bernadette reflected sometimes it needed a dramatic happening to change things.

She laid these reflections aside, as the Tipster came into the courtroom to announce the arrival of the judge. Justice Brannigan sat down at his bench and swept his gaze around the courtroom.

"Ah, so we're all here? Excellent. Now, this is going to be the judgement in the case of the DDP versus Callum Jenkins. Thank you all for bearing with me, there were a number of matters to consider and I have done so, I've now reached a conclusion which I shall deliver."

He paused to look at his notes and then continued.

"A case of extradition is obviously complex and difficult at times. The offence must be punishable by imprisonment in Ireland and by a sentence of at least a year. There must be intention to charge and pursue a prosecution, not merely to investigate. It must not be a political offense and cannot carry the death penalty."

Justice Brannigan took a sip of water and perused his notes again.

"In the case of the DPP versus Callum Jenkins, the offence with which he will be charged carries a sentence of fourteen years in the UK and is similarly an offence in Ireland. The offence of trafficking for sexual purposes is not a political offense and the death penalty is not involved. Therefore, as regards the law, this extradition request meets the conditions of Irish law. However, and here is the nub, we don't simply release our citizens to the United Kingdom, or anywhere for that matter, just upon their say so. The court must be convinced there are reasonable grounds on which to charge the person in question. We can only view those potential charges were they to be laid in Ireland. Our laws or similar and so the comparison is not, if you'll pardon the pun, out of court."

He stopped again, chuckled at his own joke and glanced around the room. Everyone was very attentive.

"Whilst this is not a trial, as such, it is a hearing to examine the evidence which has been brought before it. The prosecution alleges Mr Jenkins has committed the offence with which the Crown Prosecution in the United Kingdom intend to charge him, and this is mainly based upon the evidence of a Mr Clinton who as we have been made aware has confessed to being involved in the crime himself. The prosecution's assertion is that Mr Clinton's testimony must be valid since he wouldn't name Mr Jenkins unless there was some truth to it, for fear of losing his own advantage by turning Queen's evidence. The court accepts there is some validity to this argument."

Shane looked pleased on hearing this, Bernadette noticed, but the judge was carrying on.

"I said, *some* validity. However, the burden of proof is on the prosecution as it always is in this country, and therefore to gain a conviction the court must be satisfied that their case is proven beyond reasonable doubt. It is the same with this hearing even though, as I said, it is not a trial. With this particular case, we firstly have Mr Jenkins, who is adamant he is innocent and knew nothing about the crime. He drove the truck, and nobody is denying that including Mr Jenkins himself. He was in a sexual relationship with Mr Clinton and neither of them is denying that either. However, that circumstance does not amount to proof Mr Jenkins knew about the offences being committed. Any idea that he would know, simply because he was in a relationship, is an assumption and not a fact. In addition, we heard from two defence witnesses who brought evidence to say Mr Jenkins was not known to be present within the bounds of their knowledge when the Vietnamese women were loaded onto the truck before being taken to the United Kingdom."

Shane was now down in the mouth, and Bernadette began to be reasonably hopeful of a good resolution.

"In any case, one could obviously say that even though these witnesses vouched for Mr Jenkins not being present, he could still be aware of the crime. However, no evidence has been thus far presented which indicate this to be true. Again, it could be an assumption, but an assumption without evidence is still... an assumption. So, based upon the evidence which has been presented and heard in court, the decision has to be made upon whether or not it is beyond reasonable doubt Mr Jenkins was involved. That is, in the end, all it can be based on. No assumptions, or what might or might not be, but simply the evidence as we have seen it and as we have heard it."

He paused once more. This last had been delivered with much authoritative weight. Bernadette was impressed by the way Justice Brannigan had laid it all out. There was an air of anticipation now, as the judge seemed to be winding up.

"My view, having heard the evidence, and all submissions from both parties, is that there is more than just reasonable doubt about this offence, the doubt is very clear. On the balance of probabilities, it is my view Mr Jenkins was not aware of the crime being committed. Therefore, it is my decision that the extradition request be dismissed. I cancel the bail conditions. Mr Jenkins, you are free to go. Case dismissed."

Justice Brannigan stood up without further ado, and the Tipster rushed in to call everyone to rise. With a brief nod to the court in general, he left the room. There was an immediate uproar and massive stampede for the door, in order to get whatever statements could be obtained from the participants.

Shane stalked out of the courtroom as soon as the judgement had been given. Leaving Mason to wander over and proffer his hand to Bernadette.

"Well played," he said, "Great defence, you're everything they say you are and more."

"Thank you," said Bernadette, "That's magnanimous of you."

"I'm just telling it like it is. I can recognise talent when I see it. You certainly have it. As far it as goes for us, you win some, you lose some. We won't appeal this, there's no point. Mr Clinton is going to find he's going down for a lot more than he expected after all."

This didn't bode well for their witness who would now feel the hammer of the British justice system fully on his shoulders.

"Thanks." Bernadette smiled.

"I'm sorry about Shane. I gather he wrote to you, and I can only apologise again."

"It's not your fault," said Imogen.

"He's my friend, but I've no idea what got into him. Anyway, thanks for not ruining his career."

"I'm not vindictive," said Imogen, "But he can't do it again."

"He won't, believe me, in fact, I may have convinced him to return to the UK, made him an offer he can't refuse."

"It's probably for the best, if so. We won't say anything, but word gets around, you know how it is," said Bernadette.

"Indeed, I certainly do. Anyway, nice meeting you and thanks again for the lunch."

With that, he strode away. Their attention was claimed by Callum and Rhys who were jubilant at the result and insisted on hugging them both. Then Eve came to give them a hug too. Olivia arrived and the process was repeated again to much laughter.

"Well done," said Olivia, "You got the right result."

"Thanks," said Bernadette.

"I didn't see Oisin in court today or the other days," Imogen observed suddenly remembering.

"Oh, haven't you heard?" Olivia said smiling.

"Heard what?"

"It was on the news this morning, Oisin Kavanaugh was arrested for involvement in sex trafficking. Yes, we uncovered evidence during our investigation which led us right back to him. He ran for cover, but we tracked him down and nailed him."

"Well, I'll be," said Bernadette, "No wonder he wanted to bury it."

"It comes home to roost," Olivia laughed, "Your friend DCS Brogan is over the moon."

"I must give him a ring."

"Not now," said Eve, "We've got to give the press what they are waiting for."

"Yes, let's go and do this thing."

Outside the court, a huge cheer arose when Bernadette appeared with Callum and the others. Bernadette, as usual, held up her hand for hush.

"I am pleased to say justice was done today. An innocent man was prevented from being extradited on what was a flimsy case. However flimsy it was, though, it had to fought and it had to be opposed. We cannot allow our citizens to be taken to another country and prosecuted for offences they did not commit. What happened today was the right judgement and a sound one. That is what we came for and we got the result for Callum. I couldn't be more pleased for him and his father. If we do not stand for justice, if we do not protect the innocent then who will? Thank you."

Another cheer went up, and the reporters yelled out, "What about the kiss, you promised us a kiss."

"I always keep my promises," said Bernadette with a smile gathering Eve up into her arms and kissing her soundly while the cameras were popping off nineteen to the dozen. To make it even more spectacular Bernadette leaned Eve back in the classic movie pose and the reporters all shouted their approval. They finished kissing at length and the next thing the media wanted was to interview Callum and Rhys.

"Go for it," said Bernadette, "And go and talk to your fans."

The "Free Callum" movement were going wild with jubilation down below now they had heard the judgement.

"You must come over for tea again, soon," said Rhys as they said goodbye on the steps.

Bernadette, Imogen and Eve hurried away leaving the press with Callum and Rhys, who would no doubt be busy for some time to come. It would very likely help his business too, Bernadette mused, as they reached the car. Imogen jumped in the back, and Eve in the front. Bernadette gunned the engine and pulled away heading for the office.

"So, now that's over, you are going on holiday," Imogen announced.

"I am?"

"Yes, it's all arranged."

"Isn't it exciting, our first real holiday together?" said Eve.

"God yes, I'm looking forward to it."

Bernadette reached over and Eve took her hand, just they always did. Bernadette smiled. It had certainly been an excellent day and it was set to get even better.

* * *

A week later, Bernadette laid back in her first-class seat on a Cathay Pacific flight to Hong Kong where they would transfer to a flight for Phuket. It had been a tearful departure at Dublin airport where D'Arcy and Imogen had dropped them off.

"You have the best time," said D'Arcy, "Though I'm going to miss you both so much."

"I'll miss you too," said Imogen, "Our morning chats."

"Will you be OK? We've been over everything, haven't we?" said Bernadette with a worried expression.

"One hundred times," Imogen laughed, "Now go, and see you in two weeks."

"Email me if there's a problem."

"I won't... now, please... darling, get on the damn plane."

"Come on, sweetheart!" said Eve laughing.

They embraced and kissed their friends and walked through to the departure gate. From then on it had been a different world. The First-Class lounge and then onto the plane. They both enjoyed the luxury of it all, and the service. Eve was just across the aisle in her own seat. However, she did not remain there for long. After the evening meal had been served, she slid across to snuggle up with Bernadette.

"Did you miss me, over there?" Bernadette smiled.

"Yes, and don't think you're sleeping on your own, because you're not," Eve told her.

"Oh good, because I'd miss you too much," Bernadette sighed, "I've never been on anything like this, it's amazing."

"How the other half live," Eve giggled.

"Yes, rather nice though, I could get used to it."

"It was very kind of D'Arcy and Imogen to treat us to such a generous gift."

"You're right, we must take them back something nice. A nice present."

"D'Arcy told me the best present was making us happy."

"She said *that*?"

"Yes, she's a generous soul and you know it."

"I do," said Bernadette with a sigh, "She's grown on me for sure. I love them both so much."

"I do too, but I love you more."

"I love you and the best present of all is going on holiday with you, my darling."

"Our first ever as wife and wife."

"Yes, and it's the most wonderful feeling in the world."

"You are my world," said Eve tilting up her head for a kiss. Bernadette obliged her and as the heady sensations of Eve's sweet lips took over, it seemed just for a little while that her worries melted away. Ahead of them was sun, sea, sand and sex. Bernadette was looking forward to it all, and particularly the sex.

"What are you thinking?" Eve asked her when their lips parted.

"About sex."

"So was I," Eve giggled.

547

"What's new, you little witch?"
"And you love it…"
"Yes, yes, I do."

ACKNOWLEGEMENTS

In many countries of the world today, people can still not publicly reveal their sexuality, their differences from what others may consider the norm. Thankfully, after many long and hard-fought years, LGBTQ is recognised in so many nations, with more to follow. For what is love but simply an expression of human emotion, regardless of sexual identity, race, creed, colour among other things. Discrimination is unacceptable, in any form and should be fought hard whenever and wherever it occurs. We are all human and we have inalienable rights. These apply to all of us without exception.

With this, the fourth book in the Mackenna series, Bernadette endures as one of my most favourite characters, along with her partner Eve, her friend Imogen and D'Arcy. I make no pardon for the steamy nature or perhaps their kinks which is all part of the modern idiom in which we now live. I like contrasts and that's perhaps why I contrast their private and public life in this way. Who doesn't want to know what goes on behind closed doors? Witness the plethora of reality shows. I think they are larger than life but also, I feel they could be real. That's how I like to portray them. I can imagine them having the conversations they have and doing the things they do.

The series is dedicated to love and courtroom drama. It's not trying to change the world. It's just written out of love. Love is love, and that's all that matters. It comes in all forms, and I've simply tried to portray some of these. Bernadette Mackenna being gay is simply part of her story, it's part of who she is. I hope you enjoy the romance, and the spice, and everything else, and the other characters. I hope you can love Bernadette too, and the other characters with it.

I would like to mention and acknowledge my good friend Kaitlyn who is a fellow writer and whom I met through Twitter. She is, in fact, a very talented writer and an all-round beautiful soul who is incredibly supportive of her friends. We've had some interesting chats about writing, and I hope one day she'll get to this book and read this little piece which is to thank her very much for her friendship and support. We all have our own story, and life can break us, or we can move on and prosper. She chose the latter, I'm full of admiration for her ability to do that and try to see the good in everyone if she can.

If you would like to keep up to date with all the Bernadette Mackenna news, then please subscribe to my newsletter here. There will be news, insider knowledge, be the first to know about upcoming releases, special offers and much more. Join up as a subscriber and you can always write to me too if you like.

https://www.subscribepage.com/DIGallwaySubscriber

ABOUT THE AUTHOR

D.R. Bailey was raised in a family of bibliophiles. From an early age he developed eclectic tastes in fiction including; SciFi, Romance, Crime, and the Classics. Some of his favourite authors remain Gerald Durrell, Jane Austen, Peter James, Ellis Peters, and Isaac Asimov.

At the age of eleven he wrote his first fictional story about his toy teddy bear clan. Since then he has gone on to have some of his non-fiction article published in magazines and also a fictional crime series.

He has engaged in several different careers and says that these life experiences have all contributed greatly to his penchant for storytelling. Bailey has now penned his debut full length crime novel, which is a genre he is particularly fond of.

Printed in Great Britain
by Amazon